THE *Complete*
COUNTING SERIES

KELLY JENSEN

Contents

Counting
FENCE POSTS

*T*here are over two hundred thousand fence posts between Syracuse and Boston. Henry Auttenberg likes numbers—it's his job—but he isn't going to count them all, even if the view outside the rental car is less confounding than the driver, his attractive but oh so obnoxious colleague, Marcus Winnamore. It's Christmas Eve, and Henry would much rather be home with his family. When the blizzard that grounded their flight forces them off the road, however, he's stuck with Marc until the storm passes—or a plow digs them out.

As the temperature outside plummets, the atmosphere inside the car slowly heats up. Henry learns the true reason for Marc's chilly distance—he's not exactly straight... maybe... and he's been fantasizing about Henry's mouth, among other things. Confession laid out, Marc is all for sharing body heat... and more. Henry isn't interested in being an experiment, but as the night and cold deepen, he could be convinced to balance certain risk against uncertain reward.

Chapter
ONE

*F*ields of snow slid past the passenger-side window, the monotony of white broken only by fence posts. Henry had been counting the posts for a while. He had one tally for posts leaning at odd angles, another for missing railings, a third for gates. In approximately twenty-five miles, there had only been two gates.

How many fence posts would mark the miles from Syracuse to Boston?

Henry fiddled with the vent on his side of the dash, directing the feeble draft of heat more toward his knees, and snuck a quick look across the driver's side of the rental car. He meant to check the other side of the road for fence posts, but found Marc's profile too distracting. Snowy banks and posts blurred behind the angle of Marc's strong nose, his lips, chin, and jaw. When Marc's brow wrinkled, Henry knew it was time to turn away, lest he get caught staring.

Lusting after straight guys wasn't healthy. Nope. Been there, done that, not doing it again. Counting fence posts was better for his sanity and his heart. Returning his attention to his own window, Henry added the posts he'd missed to his tally and looked toward the next gate. He wondered if all the snow-covered fields on his side of the road belonged to the same property. Somewhere, perhaps beyond the distant line of trees bordering the far edge of the fields, there might be a house. Inside, a family would be cozied up together in the soft glow of a lit Christmas tree, while Henry was stuck in a rental car with Marcus Winnamore.

"Signal lost," the GPS announced in a bored tone.

Marc smacked the dash-mounted unit. "You've got to be kidding me."

"It's probably just a pocket." Henry gestured vaguely toward the windshield. The blizzard that had diverted their flight from Boston to Syracuse loomed on the horizon; a long, ruminating cloud, stretching endlessly north and south. "Or it could be the storm."

"We're still two hundred miles from Boston," Marc said, smacking the GPS again. "We won't hit weather for at least another hour." And from there, they'd plow through, because Marc had never met an obstacle he couldn't defeat. Over, under, around, or through. He probably had that tattooed somewhere on his body.

Henry lost a moment imagining just where that ink might be and how it might flex across Marc's pleasantly muscled frame.

He'd been excited by the opportunity to travel with Marc. They weren't the only Boston University graduates at Beck and Meyer, but they were often mentioned in the same breath because of their interview scores—which were supposed to be private, yet never were. Henry had beaten Marc by one point. He'd known the minute he met Marc that it would be the last time he topped him in anything, however.

They were both tall, both had brown hair. Both had graduated with honors and a position with one of the most prestigious financial consultancy firms in the Northeast. There the similarities ended. Marc was four years older and seemed a decade wiser. He carried his height with confidence and had a set of broad shoulders illustrating he didn't spend all his hours behind a desk. When Marc smiled, everyone else smiled. When he scowled, cowards looked for cover. The brave were rewarded with hearty backslaps and invitations to Mulligan's on Thursday afternoons. It was easy to believe he'd charmed his way through college, but he hadn't. Marc had earned his position at Beck and Meyer, and he'd already advanced to Senior Acquisitions Analyst by the time Henry joined the firm.

This was the first time they'd worked together. At the airport, they'd done the brief introduction thing, even though they had been employed by the same company for over two years. "Call me Marc," Marc had invited over a firm handshake. Then he pulled out a slim laptop, flipped it open, and proceeded to work until boarding and all through the flight. In Chicago, he'd only spoken to Henry to deliver instructions, and they retired to separate hotel rooms without sharing dinner.

The second day on-site had passed in much the same way. Henry had learned a lot by watching Marc—from the way he handled clients to the precision with which he approached each aspect of the deal. He'd hoped for a little more one-on-one time, though, and not just because he had secretly fantasized about his colleague for, well, two and a half years. Marc would make an excellent contact within the firm. If Henry could permanently partner with him, he'd go places.

After three days in his company, Henry just wanted to go home.

"Earth to Auttenberg."

"Huh?"

Marc pointed at the glove compartment. "See if we have a map."

Henry eyed the compartment with some trepidation before opening it. Used condoms were the least disgusting things he'd found in the nooks and crannies of rental cars.

Marc was stabbing a finger through the air again. "Do you need directions? It's right there."

Sighing, Henry flipped open the compartment and braced for untold horrors. Fence posts slid by uncounted as he waited for something to crawl out of the murky depths and bite him. Nothing stirred but a badly folded map. He grabbed the nearest corner and pulled it out.

"We could just head back up to 90." Henry sorted through the folds until he found Miami. "This is a map of Florida, by the way."

"Fuck."

The hair along the back of Henry's neck bristled. He'd never heard Marc swear. Ever. Guy defined the word irascible, but he usually kept a civil tongue.

"Continue on highlighted route," the GPS chimed in.

"GPS is back up."

"So I noticed," Marc said, kindly not appending *doofus* to the end of his statement.

"We must be past the hold up on the interstate by now."

Marc shook his head. "I don't want to backtrack. I think 20 will take us all the way to 88."

"I thought we were on 13."

"And that's why I'm the organ-grinder and you're the monkey."

Cheeks heating, Henry turned his attention back to the map. He opened it all the way out and looked for the original creases before carefully refolding it. When he was done, he had a neat packet with a beach scene across the front. The blue of the sky had faded a little, but the sun looked bright. Glancing up from his slice of paradise, he counted fence posts for a little while, starting a separate tally. Beneath the monotony of the count, he calculated how many posts there were in a mile, then plotted the course between Syracuse and Boston in posts. Over two hundred thousand. Thinking about counting them all made him tired. He wished he was back in Boston already, sprawled across the love-worn furniture at his parents' house. His sister would be there too with her husband and kids. Would they wait for him before following the Christmas Eve tradition of opening one present each?

"How long have you been with Beck and Meyer now?"

Starting, Henry turned away from wishes and snowy fields. "Uh, two and a half years?"

"You're not sure?" Marc glanced over, one dark brow quirked

over an equally dark eye. He had those brown eyes that could be black. Henry tried not to meet his gaze too often because he feared he'd get lost searching for the line between iris and pupil—and that would mean he'd been staring.

Staring at straight guys like a lost puppy was a good way to get his ass kicked.

"Um, yeah. I mean, sure I'm sure. I started in 2012. August."

"Right out of BU?'

Henry cleared his throat. "Right."

"You should watch those tics in your speech, and never turn a statement into a question. Makes you sound unsure."

"Um, okay."

"See, that right there is what I'm talking about. Don't say 'um,' ever. Pause if you need a second to put your words together."

Turning away, Henry leaned toward the passenger-side window, hoping the crisp outside air might magically leach through the glass and cool his cheeks.

"Not talking is only half a solution," Marc went on. "Knowing when to be quiet and observe is a definite skill, but to make an impression, you have to open your mouth."

Inhaling quickly, Henry banished all thoughts of opening his mouth in the vicinity of Marc's... *anything*. Then he paused, letting an "um" fall by the wayside. "Thanks for the advice."

Marc gave him a sideways look. Apparently deciding Henry had been sincere, he turned his attention back to the road. "You're a smart guy. Everyone knows it. Your analysis of the financials for Chicago was really insightful. You caught trends most would miss. That's why I asked you along this trip." Marc had asked for him specifically? "But if we're going to continue to work together, you need to find your tongue."

Henry loosened his collar. His blush had spread down his neck and across his shoulders. The curse of pale skin often meant that particularly intense emotions lent a flush to approximately 80 percent of his body.

He searched for his tongue and found it. "Is this a performance review?"

"No, I'm just making conversation."

"We've had three days to make conversation. Why now?"

"You don't want to talk?"

"I appreciate the advice, really. Ah—" Cutting himself off, Henry leaped to the next word "I'm just wondering why you want to talk now, when you basically ignored me for the whole trip."

Marc glanced over again, dark eyes sparkling over a dangerous smile. "Your panties in a bunch, Auttenberg?"

"My name is Henry, and I don't wear panties."

That black gaze dropped to Henry's lap. "Going commando under your suit pants? Isn't the wool itchy? You don't want to end up with a rash."

"It's a good thing I've got a couple days to recover, then."

"You're not taking off the week between Christmas and New Year's?"

"Are you?"

"No, but all our client offices will be closed. It's going to be pretty quiet."

Relieved to have moved the conversation away from underwear choices, Henry said, "I figured it would be a good time to start checking the data on Hiddenger."

Marc's brows shot up. "Hiddenger is going to be my client."

"I know."

A smile eased across Marc's mouth. "Still waters run deep."

"Is dropping clichés part of your prescription for being more talkative and memorable?"

Rather than take offense, Marc chuckled. Then he cast another significant glance at Henry's crotch. "Tell me you're not really going pants-less."

"Why are you so interested in my underwear?"

Interestingly enough, Marc blushed. At least, Henry thought he did. His darker complexion hid most of it. "Just making conversation," he muttered.

Henry let a few more fence posts pass by uncounted before adding a batch load to his tally. Then he said, "Boxers."

"Huh?"

"I'm wearing boxers under my suit pants."

Marc tipped a nod toward the steering wheel, and the next mile rolled by in something like companionable silence—Henry quietly satisfied with his end of the conversation, weird as it had been. He'd almost held his own—or had at least shown himself to be less of a doormat than Marc might have assumed.

"Signal lost," the GPS reported.

Remembering he still held the map, Henry shoved it back into the open glove compartment and sealed the hatch. Then he pulled out his phone. "No bars."

Marc shifted in his seat and reached into a pocket. He produced a phone and handed it across to Henry. "See if you can get anything with mine."

The device was warm, and cradling it in his palm, Henry allowed his thoughts to wander toward the hip it had been nestled against. He checked the network status. No signal. "Nothing."

"Dammit." Marc tapped the GPS again.

Flakes of snow drifting toward the windshield distracted Henry from a pointless daydream involving Marc's long, tanned fingers. "It's snowing."

Despite the white fields and brooding clouds covering the horizon, those first few flakes embodied a moment of wonder. Even at the age of twenty-four, he marveled at the quiet efficiency of snow. He appreciated the way a fresh blanket covered murk and slush, washing the world with soft brilliance.

"Let's hope it doesn't amount to much. The storm should be moving away from us."

It should be, but as the swirl of snow across the windshield increased, the horizon became less distinct. Then the fence posts lining the side of the rural highway began to disappear.

Chapter
TWO

*T*he windshield wipers groaned beneath the weight of the snow. Marc twiddled the control, and the wipers shuddered toward the middle of the windshield, catching against a streak of ice.

"Can you see anything?" Henry asked. He'd been sitting on the question for a while, but being a passenger in a sightless vehicle was taking its toll on his nerves. Counting the swipes of the struggling wipers only made him more anxious.

"No." Marc fiddled with the control again, and one of the wipers froze in place. The other retreated downward and failed to rise again. Snow quickly covered the small arc of clear glass. Marc kept driving for a full sixty seconds—each counted beneath Henry's breath—before nudging the vehicle toward the unseen side of the invisible road. "Going to pull over for a few."

Henry searched for something to mark where the road ended and the fields began, but as the car coasted to a halt, he saw nothing but white. Heard nothing but the crunch of snow wedging up beneath the wheel arches. The car groaned and shuddered.

"I think you went too far off the side," he said.

Marc gripped the wheel and looked straight ahead, as if he sought solace in the snow piling up over the windshield. He let go of the wheel and gripped his thighs instead. "Yeah." Glancing over at

Henry, he offered a half smile, the slant of his lips somewhat self-deprecatory. "Sorry."

Wow, that was new. And that smile. Where had that coy little smile come from?

"We'll just have to wait for a plow," Henry said.

"Once this front passes, we'll dig out, plow or no plow."

Now that was more like the Marc he knew and... *knew*. Henry leaned forward to peer through the accumulating gloom. "If it passes."

"The storm is still a hundred miles away. This is just a leading edge or something."

"It's looking pretty set." Henry wasn't an argumentative guy, but he'd lived in the Northeast long enough to know that fat, heavy flakes blowing sideways with the intent of burying everything in sight was more than a passing thing.

"Signal lost," the GPS added.

"Of course it is." Marc smacked the steering wheel.

The engine hiccupped and stalled. Instantly the temperature of the air blowing from the vents dropped by ten degrees. Henry counted off another minute. Snow nearly obscured all the windows by the time he'd breathed his last Mississippi, and if anything, the wind had picked up, pushing against the car in an uneven rhythm. They wouldn't be digging out anytime soon.

Rather than say that, he chose another tack and spoke quietly, wary of inciting another attack on the steering wheel, or the GPS. "If you've got warmer clothes in your suitcase, we should probably get it now, before the snow gets too deep." They both had overcoats in the backseat, but they were more a part of their corporate wardrobe than practical cold weather gear.

"It's going to blow over," Marc said.

"But just in case it doesn't...." Henry unfastened his seat belt and pulled at the door handle. Discovering the door was locked, he located the latch and thumbed it.

Marc was looking at him, dark eyes intense in the muted light. "You seriously want to get your stuff."

"Yeah, can you pop the trunk?"

"You're wasting your time. It's not like we're stranded in Siberia. A plow will be along soon."

Swallowing rising frustration, Henry tried for a reasonable tone. "We're on, what, a secondary or tertiary road?" *Because you didn't want to backtrack.* "A plow might be right behind us, or it could be ahead of us. Or it could be halfway to the nearest urban center because already this winter is the worst on record and everyone is scrambling to keep ahead of the snow. I'm not interested in freezing to death while we wait to find out."

Henry pushed his door open and wet snow blew inside the car, stinging his cheeks and bringing tears to his eyes. The door stopped halfway, caught on a low drift. He angled his way through the gap, thankful (for once) for his lean build. Fat flakes stole down the back of his shirt collar and inside his ears. Hunching his shoulders against the cold, he climbed through ankle-deep powder to the back of the car. The wind pushed and pulled at him, apparently undecided on a direction. He slid once, catching himself on a buried fence post. By the time he got up to the road, snow stuck to every inch of him, head to toe. His jaw already ached from clenching against the cold.

Marc hadn't opened the trunk. Henry banged on it a few times before he felt the click of the release. He levered the lid up, spilling the snow already piled across the top, and reached inside for his carry-on. If they were going to be trapped inside the car for hours, or possibly the night—God no—he wanted the whole case.

Marc appeared beside him and reached in for his case. Leaving him to it, Henry made his way back around the side of the car to his open door, wind pulling at every part of him, snow stinging and burning his exposed face. He leaned in to scoop snow off his seat, then piled in with his case on his lap and pulled the door closed. Marc scrambled back into the driver's side a few seconds later, shutting his door with a slam. The following silence wedged into Henry's ears like a pair of thumbs. He existed in the moment for a while, grateful to be out of the wind and driving snow. Then his ass informed him it was cold, and possibly wet. Henry unzipped his case and sorted through the couple of folded stacks until he found his sweatpants and a hoodie.

"Are you going to get changed right there?" Marc was giving him an odd look.

"No, I'm just going to put this over top. Like layers."

"You're going to look ridiculous."

Henry shrugged. "At this point, nothing we do is going to detract from the fact we're stranded on the side of a country highway, where we ended up in defiance of a travel advisory. I don't think me being stuffed into two or three layers of clothing is going to make a difference."

"It's Christmas Eve. Like anyone was going to stay put. And Boston is only—"

"Two hundred miles away. I know." Henry kneaded the space between his brows before glancing sideways at Marc. "Are you always this stubborn?"

Marc's jaw set, his chin lifting slightly, and a muscle flickered somewhere toward his ear. He looked mad, bad, and dangerous to know—and despite being half-numb, Henry's cock twitched in interest. *Dammit.*

"You're pretty stubborn yourself, Auttenberg. And I prefer *determined.*"

"I prefer Henry."

Huffing out a sigh, Marc turned his attention back to the carry-on wedged between his torso and the steering wheel. Henry watched him peripherally and laid odds on when Marc'd give in and open the case. He had nothing to count but the agitated beat of his heart, so weighing the statistics gave him a spot of calm.

Henry pushed his sweats down beside his seat and zipped his

case closed. By the time he'd leaned around to put it on the backseat, Marc had both hands on the lid of his case, thumbs pressed against the line of the zip. Henry was facing away when he heard the zip open. He indulged in a quick smile, exchanging it for a more sober expression before turning back to the front of the vehicle to begin the process of pulling on his second layer. He paused to brush off as much snow as he could first. The exertion warmed him a little, but he'd cool off quick enough.

He didn't look at Marc while he pulled on his extra clothes, but he glanced over when he was done. Marc had donned workout gear, same as him. They now wore matching BU sweatshirts. Marc met his gaze with a crooked eyebrow.

Henry allowed another smile. "Warmer?"

"If we keep fucking around like this, I'm not exactly going to freeze."

Ducking his head, Henry pretended interest in the Coke bottle stuck in the center console until the urge to blush passed. Despite an odd interest in Henry's underwear choices, Marc was still straight. Right? Henry reached for the radio. "Maybe we can get some news on the storm."

Marc made no answer.

Henry skipped through static, fuzz, and holiday music until he found a voice.

"According to you, the world was supposed to end in August last year."

"We've been in the end times for three years already, Larry. August last year was simply the beginning of the flood."

"Wackos," Marc muttered.

"If we're getting this slammed in December, there's going to be a hell of a flood come spring." Henry skipped to the next station.

Over the low drawl of a DJ reading his backlist, Marc said, "The storm wasn't meant to extend this far west."

"Tell that to the blizzard out there."

Marc glanced over. "You sound like my uncle Bob."

"Yeah, well, the GPS sounds like my aunt Debbie."

Debbie chose that moment to chime in with, "Signal lost."

"No shit, Debbie," Marc said, reaching over to cancel the navigation program.

Henry found a news report and leaned back in his seat to listen to the list of closures and cancellations. The steady voice of the reporter lulled him for a while, as did the warmth creeping across previously numbed skin. Outside, the storm continued to buffet the car, rocking it gently. So much snow had piled across the windshield, the lights of the dash reflected back, showing ghostly images of the pair of them reclining in their seats. By the time the report cycled around to the weather again, Henry had closed his eyes in contemplation of a nap.

"With the storm taking a bizarre left turn and tracking inward, away from the Eastern Seaboard, we're looking at a wider path. Accumulation estimations have already been surpassed from Long Island to Albany, with much of the Northeast rapidly disappearing under feet of snow."

Opening his eyes, Henry peered through the rime creeping toward the center of the passenger-side window. It was four in the afternoon, but it seemed much later. The sky had disappeared. When the wind paused for breath, Henry thought he could see a single fence post poking out of the drift at the side of the road. The snow wasn't that deep yet, but the heavy gusts were piling it up against anything that stood in its way. Even if they only got a couple feet, the car could end up buried.

The snow would insulate the vehicle, right? Like an igloo?

Pity he wasn't stuck with someone more inclined toward sharing body heat. Not that he'd mind cuddling up with Marc. The object of his fantasies probably thought differently, though. Hell, if previous experience had taught Henry anything, it was that he sucked at guessing another guy's thoughts.

"I'm starting to think we might be here until the snow passes," Marc said. He'd picked up his phone and was fiddling with the screen. "Do you remember when we last passed a house?"

"I don't remember seeing any houses. Besides, we should stay with the car."

"Says who?" Marc stabbed at his phone, then shook it, as if he could bully the device into catching a stray signal.

"Experts."

"I wonder how many of these so-called experts have ever been stuck inside a car during a blizzard."

Henry noted the fact Marc had upgraded the leading edge to an actual blizzard. "Some of them. I read this book last year about how to survive all kinds of stuff. Kidnapping, plane crash, train derailing, flood, forest fire—"

"Why would you read something like that?" Marc was staring at him, mouth slightly open.

"To be prepared."

"For a kidnapping."

"We work in the financial industry, and we're party to sensitive data. It could happen."

"Or the plane could just crash, taking you and your precious data with it."

"Mock all you want." Henry pointed over his shoulder using his thumb. "Did you know we can take apart the backseat covers to use as blankets if it gets really cold?"

Marc had another strange look in his eyes. Turning away, he massaged his brow with the heel of one palm and stared disconsolately at his phone. Then he reached for the door handle. "I'm going to walk down the road a bit and see what I can see."

"Snow. You'll see snow."

"Maybe I can flag someone down."

"No one is going to be driving in this. The plows probably can't even keep going."

Marc had the door cracked open and the wind pushed inside the car in a frozen swirl. "I'm just going to walk a little way."

Grinding his teeth together, Henry pushed open his door.

"What are you doing?" Marc said.

"Coming with you." Kindly, Henry did not append the *moron* to his statement.

"I'm not going far."

"It's best if we stay together."

"Is that another of your survival tips?"

"No. Maybe. I don't know. I just don't like the idea of sitting here while you get lost."

"I'm not going to get lost."

"Can't you just stay inside the car?"

"I'm not the sort of guy who just lets life pass him by."

Henry knew if he answered that comment, he'd start babbling, yelling, and possibly cursing. He pushed open his door and climbed back out into the storm.

Chapter
THREE

"Marc!"

This was utterly stupid. The bitter wind stung his cheeks and blew right through his layers. Henry pulled his hood up and shivered as snow kissed the back of his neck. Angling his head down, he trudged back around the side of the car and fell, face-first and flailing, into a soft drift. Cold fingers crept under his clothes, stinging his skin. He clambered up to the side of the road and stood a moment, brushing himself off. When he realized new snow covered him as quickly as he dispensed with the old snow, he gave up and looked for Marc.

He saw nothing but angled streaks of white over gray. Or… what was that?

Cupping his mouth, he called out again. "Marc, stop!"

As he pushed through the snow, Henry decided there was something seriously wrong with Marc. The guy might call himself determined, but his take-charge attitude must hide a chink in his armor of charm—not that he'd been all that charming over the last three days. Not toward Henry, anyway. But any man who felt compelled to push down every barrier must be looking for something.

What was Marc looking for? And where in this frozen hell was he?

Henry pushed on, gasping as the wind tugged his hood back down. He reached for it and stumbled, arms windmilling. One foot slipped in the snow and down he went—only to have his fall arrested by a firm grip around his elbow.

"Where the fuck do you think you're going?" Marc growled. Might have growled. The wind snatched at his words and tone.

Henry tried to wrench his arm free and succeeded only in pulling Marc down with him so they both fell in an undignified sprawl across the road. If their luck held, the plow would come now, scoop them up and push them over the embankment with their car.

Marc's arms banded about his shoulders as they slid to a stop. "Stop moving. Jesus. You're like a bag of cats. Take a breath."

"I would if you'd let me up. Where were you?"

"Chasing you down the road."

Henry spat out a mouthful of snow. "But I was chasing you!"

"Yeah, well, I decided you were right at just about the same time you decided to run back to Syracuse."

"But…." Henry spluttered for a moment, then pushed Marc away from him. "Can we finish this in the car?"

Marc got to his feet and held out a hand. Ignoring it, Henry struggled upright and turned a quick circle, looking through the gray gloom for the rental.

"It's back this way," Marc said, indicating a direction.

Putting his head into the wind, Henry trudged back up the road.

The car looked abandoned and pathetic, angled halfway off the shoulder with the front end buried in a snowbank. Henry was just glad they'd found it. On the short walk back, he'd entertained visions of wandering lost in the frozen tundra of upstate New York until rescue found their solid corpses. Brushing snow from his clothing again proved a mostly futile exercise. Henry yanked the door open and thrust himself into the tepid warmth of the car. Marc joined him a moment later, having obviously tried and failed to shake snow off his clothing.

A distinctly uncomfortable quiet swelled around them. A relative quiet. The storm still blew outside the car, and the news report had been replaced by holiday advertising. No one would be going out for last-minute gifts in this weather.

Beside him, Marc breathed heavily.

"That was stupid," Henry said.

Marc turned to look at him. "No kidding."

"So you... what? Just waited by the door while I ran off down the road?"

"Pretty much. Then I figured I should come get you before you got lost."

"I wouldn't have even been out there if it wasn't for you." Wouldn't be shivering, either, or so cold his hands and feet burned.

"I'm flattered." One corner of Marc's mouth twitched toward a smile. Then he breathed in deeply and pushed out a sigh. "Listen, I'm sorry. I... I got out there and realized you were right. I couldn't see a thing. I mean, I figured there must be a house back there somewhere. The side of the road has been fenced for miles."

With 742 posts.

"Any houses could be a mile or more back from the road," Henry muttered.

"Yeah, I know. I just felt like I needed to do something."

"You can't stop a storm."

Snow clung to Marc's dark hair in great clumps. He'd forgotten to pull up his hood. He reached up to dislodge some and grunted as it slid down his face and caught in the collar of his sweatshirt.

He looked so dejected and unsure, sympathy bloomed warm in Henry's chest. "Look, I want to get home as much as you do."

"What makes you think I want to get home?"

"Isn't that what that was all about?"

Mouth forming a hard, flat line, Marc turned away. A muscle ticked halfway along his jaw. "I just hate sitting around."

A stronger gust of wind rocked the car. The windshield cleared briefly, then more snow slid diagonally across the glass, clinging in streaks and clumps.

Marc's voice, when he spoke again, floated like a whisper over the noise of the storm. "What's waiting for you at home?" he asked.

Henry felt his forehead wrinkle into a frown. "Is that a trick question?"

Melted snow trickled down the inside of his sweatshirt. Shifting in his seat, he pulled it over his head, catching his dress shirt and taking that with it. He needed some new layers. Some dry clothing. Tossing both shirts into the foot well where they might do some good soaking up the snow dripping from his pants and shoes, he turned toward the middle of the car, intending to reach between the seats to get something else from his carry-on.

Marc's face held yet another unaccustomed expression. Interest and... desire? *How's that for wishful thinking?* But there was little question about the direction of Marc's gaze as it roamed Henry's bare torso, shoulders to hips, before flicking away. Henry shivered as the heat left his skin. Marc turned back toward the windshield, scrubbed his brows with his palms, and pushed his hands through his wet hair. "No, it's not a trick question. Do you have family in Boston?"

"Yeah. You didn't think I picked up this accent in college, did you?"

Marc obviously wasn't from Boston, though he'd lived there long enough to have flattened his vowels a little.

Henry flipped open his case and surveyed the remaining clothing. Two more dress shirts, undershirts, boxers, and socks. He never bothered with pajamas when he traveled; he'd had the idea packing tartan plaid would make him seem less professional. Now he wished for the warmth and coziness of flannel. Sighing, he grabbed a handful of cloth and turned back around.

"Where is your family?" he asked.

Marc's brows rose. "Maryland."

Henry grinned. "Well, no wonder you don't have any snow sense. That's technically the South, you know."

Ignoring the jibe, Marc said, "We get snow in Maryland. Six inches brings DC to a grinding halt." His mouth curved into a rueful smile. "But I've been up here for eight years. You'd think I'd be used to it by now."

"I've lived here all my life and I'm not used to it. Besides, this much snow is unnatural. It's like we're living in North Dakota or something."

Marc's smile widened. "Yeah."

"You know, you're a lot less intimidating when you smile." Kind of. Not really? Sexier, and therefore less approachable, in one sense. Dizzying in another. And… had he just said that out loud? That odd glint had returned to Marc's eyes.

Wrenching his gaze away, Henry asked, "How come you're not heading to Maryland for the holidays?"

When Marc made no immediate answer, Henry glanced back up. All traces of humor had fled Marc's expression, and he seemed occupied by brushing the rest of the snow from his sweatshirt. Then, obviously drawing the same conclusion Henry had, he pulled it over his head, removing his shirt along with it.

It wasn't an invitation, but it was. Henry stared.

Marc's chest was beautifully carved, the cut of his muscles obvious, even in the dim light. In fact, the shadows only enhanced his build, showing off square-shaped pecs, six definite abs and a tapered V pointing directly to heaven. Henry tried to look away before the line of dark hair from Marc's navel led him to the folds of material over his crotch. Tried and failed. When he did manage to look up, Marc's eyes were hooded and focused directly on his.

Henry felt the blush before it claimed his skin—an itchy tingle starting at his neck before spreading up and down, flushing his cheeks and chest in the same instant. He shivered. His nipples tightened under the prickle of goose bumps. Below his waist, his cock couldn't decide whether to harden or retreat. The heat of Marc's gaze hinted he fought a similar struggle.

For a moment it seemed as if they'd both lean in, drawn together by an invisible string. Henry's breath shortened. Warmth flowed toward his frozen fingertips and toes. His ears burned.

Is he not quite *straight? Or does he just* want?

Henry remembered that struggle all too well. He also remembered the price of asking those same questions out loud.

Marc broke the spell, inhaling sharply and looking away. He bundled up his shirts and pushed them aside, then leaned toward Henry with a more innocent intent, angling his shoulder between the seats to rummage in his case. The scent of his skin tickled Henry's nostrils. Masculine and clean. When Marc pulled back with a handful of shirts, Henry looked down. Tucked between the dress shirts was a flash of striped flannel. A pajama top.

Henry tried not to laugh, but a small sound escaped him.

"What's so funny?" Marc asked, shaking out his new shirts.

Shaking his head, Henry lifted an undershirt and resisted the urge to sniff the fabric. He already knew it would smell like day-old sweat. That it wouldn't smell like Marc. He shook it out and tugged it over his head. He did the same with a second undershirt and reached for a dress shirt. Warmth quickly caressed his skin, but it wouldn't be long before the cold crept in again. Their breath was starting to fog.

Beside him, Marc pulled on his collection of shirts, leaving the pj top until last. As he stuck an arm into the striped flannel, Henry gestured toward it.

"I was laughing at your pajamas, but not for the reason you think."

"What reason is that?"

Henry waved a hand. "It's just that I never take pajamas with me when I travel. Well, I did the first time, but it felt weird wearing them in a hotel room. Like I was a boy playing grown-up or something."

"So you're laughing at me because I look stupid?"

"No, I'm laughing because I feel stupid."

"I really don't get you, Auttenberg." Marc's eyes narrowed. "You're like a snake or something. All quiet until someone steps on you. Is the shy thing just an act?"

"The shy thing?"

"You're quiet and reserved. Aloof, even. You never come to Mulligan's on Thursdays."

"You've never invited me."

Marc's brows drew together. "It's a public place."

Henry hitched his shoulders into a shrug. "I figured...." He clamped his mouth shut.

"You figured what?"

"I thought it was like a group thing. I didn't realize anyone could just show up."

"Like I said, it's a public—"

Henry held up a hand. "A public place, I know. But do you make a habit of going where you don't feel welcome? No, don't answer that—of course you do. You're Marcus Winnamore. There is no wall high enough, wide enough, or dug deep enough to keep you at bay."

"That's who you think I am?"

"You've been at the firm for four years, and you're already a senior analyst. You've only lost one acquisition, not even to a competitor. The CEO of the company died, and you managed to close the deal with his son three months after the funeral."

"Technically, that's not a loss."

"See? That's what I mean. Hell, trap you in a car during a blizzard, and you think you can get out and walk to Boston."

"You're the one who ran off down the road."

Henry raised his hands. "All part of the strategy, no doubt."

"Do you have a problem with me?"

Not in the way you think.

"No, I don't. I want to *be* you. Everyone does. You're the shining standard held up to every new hire. I knew all about you before I even went for my first interview, and I've only got eighteen months left to get to where you are."

A dark brow quirked. "By then I could be on the partnership track."

Squeezing his eyes shut, Henry let out a frustrated growl.

"You...." Marc's tone held none of the wry amusement of before. "You've really, um, been following my career path?"

Henry cracked open one eye. "You need to watch those verbal tics, Winnamore."

Marc's quick laugh was as much a surprise as the delight lighting up his entire face, and it was damned infectious. Henry fought the curve of his lips for only a second before giving in. They chuckled for about a minute before falling silent, then it took only one stray glance to set them off again. Another minute of quiet passed, with both of them smoothing snow from their pants and plucking at their layers of clothing. Then they were laughing again, only their humor had a slightly hysterical edge, as if they needed to find something to laugh about, while outside the storm slowly buried them alive.

Chapter
FOUR

The storm swallowed the remains of the day. Gray became dark gray, then full black. The only light inside the car came from the radio, and if not for the steadily increasing chill, it would be cozy inside their snow-packed shell.

Henry's jaw ached from clenching against an intermittent chatter. His phone lay cold against his palm. Depressing a button on the side, he woke the screen and checked the time. 6:23. They'd been stranded for more than two hours.

"We should run the engine for a little while, otherwise we might drain the battery," Henry said.

"Is this another of your survival tips?" Marc's asked, his tone more amused than annoyed as he turned the key and started the engine.

Cold air immediately hissed through the vents, making Henry regret giving any advice. Ten minutes later Marc killed the engine, and the heavy quiet of the falling snow descended once more. Henry was tempted to play with his phone—a game, or flip through his album, maybe even read one of the books he'd carelessly downloaded over the past couple of months. A little activity would warm the battery. But the incessant cold dulled the urge to do anything beyond exist. He'd even stopped looking for things to count.

Beside him, Marc had given into temptation. The reflected light of his phone threw his face into stark relief, accentuating the furrow between his brows as he concentrated on a sudoku puzzle.

Henry leaned over to check his progress and Marc gave him a quick half smile.

"Hey, no stealing phone heat."

Henry flexed his ankles. "I want to tuck a phone in each shoe. My feet are frozen solid."

"Mine too." Marc put his phone down. "Why is it neither of us traveled with a proper coat? The wind in Chicago was brutal."

Henry jerked his head toward the backseat. "Give up fashion for function? Are you mad? Then there's always the matter of where to put a bulky jacket. Showing up at the client office with a carry-on and carefully folded overcoat is bad enough. Always makes me feel like a traveling salesman."

Marc appeared to contemplate that for a moment. "We're actually one rung lower. Salesmen get offered coffee. Mergers and acquisitions consultants get suspicious looks. They always think we're there to break the company into pieces after laying off every employee over the age of thirty-five."

"Isn't that what we do?"

"If you need to ask that, you're in the wrong business." Marc's dark eyes weren't as compelling in the low light, but Henry felt the weight of his attention regardless. "Are you a team player, Auttenberg?"

"What does that mean?"

"What's your life plan? Partner at Beck and Meyer? You know they're never going to add any more names to the marquee."

They had nine partners, seven uncredited. Henry shrugged. "I haven't thought that far ahead, to be honest."

"No chart? No absolute plan, in triplicate?"

"I have goals." He cocked his head. "Maybe my plan is to ride your coattails to the top."

"You're assuming I'm aiming for the top."

"You're not?"

"The top is just another wall." Marc might have winked. It was hard to tell in the dark.

Henry let his head drop back against the headrest. "My ass is numb, and I think I'm going to lose at least six toes to frostbite."

"So take your shoes off. You've got extra socks, right? In fact…." Marc began shuffling. A couple of seconds later, he leaned through the familiar path between the seats. Light flashed as he aimed his phone at his case. "Aha! I have four pairs. I'll trade you one for your prelim on Hiddenger."

This was nice, this actual chatting. Marc's focus remained evident, but his edges seemed to have been softened, either by the storm or their shared laughter. Henry didn't dare hope it had been their intense, shirtless moment.

"I always bring extra socks." He waited for Marc to sit back down before pushing through the gap to rummage through his case. "I have four pairs too. So no deal." He pulled the rolled socks into a bundle and started digging under the case. "I think it's hat and glove time too." He had both tucked into pockets of his overcoat, but wasn't having much luck locating either in the dark.

"Losing your fingers to frostbite would suck, particularly in our profession."

Giving up the search for his hat and gloves—he could save them for when he was really, really cold—Henry turned around and flopped back into his seat. "I can type with two fingers if I have to. There is also the typing pool on the fifth floor."

"You mean the shark pool. A man is lucky to get out of there with his bachelorhood intact."

Henry grinned. "I might have heard a rumor about you and Gabrielle Steiner."

"One date, and the firm has us married." Marc cast a sideways glance in Henry's direction. "She's not my type, anyway."

Henry's pulse kicked up a notch. After shucking off his shoes, he kicked them aside and pulled one foot up to his lap, tugging off the sock as he did so. He gasped as he wrapped his comparatively warm fingers around his ice-cold toes. "So...." He waited a beat, killing a verbal tic or two, and continued. "Who is your type?"

He'd heard no rumors questioning Marc's sexuality but knew a few circulated regarding his. Considering Henry was quietly "out" at the office, he assumed any gossip about him speculated on his wild sexual habits. Everyone knew gay men were kinky, right? The fact he presented as a studious and fairly straightlaced guy (ha!) probably did little to dissuade everyone from their presumptions.

"Let's talk about your type," Marc countered.

Let's not.

Actually, Henry didn't really have a type. He'd been so focused on his career he hadn't pursued a relationship in years. Sadly, he'd had more sex with his hand than an actual flesh-and-blood partner for about two of those years, and any fantasies regarding Marc Winnamore were strictly off-limits.

Concentrating on massaging the numbness from his toes, he said, "I think you know all about my type." A quick look to the left showed Marc's reaction, and it was perfect. Henry wished he could capture it with a camera. The combination of surprise and curiosity suited the defined lines of Marc's face. Softened them again. Henry returned his attention to his feet, busying himself with replacing his cold and maybe wet socks, then adding a second and third layer.

Halfway through the process, he became aware of Marc doing the same—only his motions seemed jerkier, less sure, as if his mind were elsewhere. When they had both relaxed back into their seats, Marc turned to him. "I'm...." His mouth twisted into a grimace.

"Lemme guess. You're *not* gay, right?"

It was a blunt statement, and the moment it passed his lips, Henry wished he could take it back. But he felt as if he knew Marc's type. The overachiever, the go-getter, the guy who slapped backs and produced hearty guffaws on command. Marc was so *not* gay. Yet every time he'd looked at Henry over the past two hours, he'd been unable to hide his interest. *Was* it just curiosity, or something more?

Thinking back over the Chicago trip, Henry began to wonder if it was something more, something unacknowledged. An inclination Marc's family didn't approve of. Maryland wasn't that far away—why else would he avoid them at Christmas?

If that were the case, then Henry had just done something near unforgiveable.

"Hey, listen." Henry waited until he had Marc's attention before continuing. "I'm sorry. I mean.… Crap. That was really rude, and I'm sorry, and I should know better. As a gay man, I should freaking well know better. If you're just curious, that's fine. I'm not going to judge. I'd never… I'm messing this up more, aren't I?"

Marc reached forward to grip the steering wheel. Henry didn't need light to imagine the whitening of his knuckles. "What do you mean by *curious*?" Marc whispered toward the windshield.

This less-sure Marc was new, or maybe a version Henry had only caught glimpses of before. He couldn't decide if he preferred the arrogant, confident model or not.

"Um… have you heard the term *bicurious*?" Henry kept his tone as neutral as he could, which was hard, no pun intended.

"I'm not bisexual."

Right, just like you're not gay. Henry hauled in a breath and held it until every stinging retort tumbled back into the well. Marc didn't come across as homophobic, not really, and while he'd never made any truly friendly overtures, he'd never publicly snubbed Henry either. Not really. Until this trip, he'd seemed like a genial guy—still did when he wasn't being acerbic.

Then there was this scene right here.

Henry bit his lips. Licked them. "We can change the subject if you want."

Marc had let go of the steering wheel, but his fingers still curved as if forming fists. He clutched his fists to his chest and let out a short, sharp laugh. "This is like a bad reality show." He deepened his voice. "Trap two guys in a car during a blizzard and see what happens in *The Freezer*."

"Technically, you're the one who started this conversation."

Marc looked at him. "I know. I also know how I come off. Everyone's best friend until I'm not. Arrogance and charm. A lot of that is me. But it's also who I need to be. I guess I figured you might understand. I'm smart, Auttenberg. I know you know that, because you're smart too. You know how to play the game, and you've been doing a phenomenal job at it over the past couple of years. Maybe even better than I have. But here's the thing. Neither of us is who the other guy thought we were, are we?"

Swallowing over a suddenly dry throat, Henry nodded.

Marc issued another harsh chuckle. "Forget TV, this should be the new team-building exercise. Lock two schlubs in a car for a couple hours and see what happens. Maybe they should have us driving everywhere in teams instead of flying."

"You'd have made me drive so you could work."

Another chuckle, this one softer. "Probably." Marc glanced over again. His lips worked a moment, then he pushed out a short sigh. "I don't know what I am, okay? I'm not curious. I'm confused."

Again, Henry's mouth raced ahead of sense. "You, confused?"

"Hilarious, isn't it?"

"What are you confused about?"

In the near dark, Marc's stare got a whole lot more intense. "You."

Chapter
FIVE

*H*enry counted the pounding beats of his heart until he succumbed to the need for breath. Blood swished behind his ears, and the air he sucked into his lungs seemed to bounce and echo inside him. His feet were suddenly warm, and his teeth had stopped clattering together.

"Me?" And his voice had acquired a squeak.

Marc leaned forward. Instinctively, Henry flinched back. Thankfully, Marc didn't notice. He'd pushed through the gap again, the stripes on his flannel shirt rippling as he dug around in the backseat. When he reemerged, he had two suit coats with him. He passed Henry's over.

"Thanks."

"Sure." Marc glanced down. "I think I'm going to change my pants too. My ass is numb."

"Way to dodge the subject."

Marc waved a hand. "We've got all night. We'll get back to my confusion soon enough."

Okay, Marc needed a break. That was fair. It had been a whopper of a confession. Some guys might go their whole life without even admitting that much. But Henry wanted, no… needed the answer to a single question. "Why me?"

"You're not going to tell me you don't think you're good-looking, or worthwhile, are you?" Marc shook his head. "Half the women I've taken out have needled me about their appearance and career, as if they need my approval to exist, let alone count on a second date. I don't get it."

"I'm not a woman, in case you hadn't noticed." Not super self-conscious either. Just tragically aware of the futility of being attracted to straight guys. Seemingly straight guys. "And you know how 'the game,' as you call it, is played."

"Want to hear about my date with Gabrielle?"

"Not really."

"You live in North End, right?"

The interior of the rental car rivaled the square footage of Henry's apartment in North End, and the mortgage cost him almost a third of his take-home pay. But he loved the neighborhood. He felt as if he'd made it every time he stepped onto the street and rubbed shoulders with all the other young professionals with their shiny new suits and shiny new dreams.

"Yeah, I do."

"So does Gabby. I saw you when I went to pick her up."

"You went to pick her up?"

"What can I say, I'm a gentleman."

Henry felt his brow scrunch. "Where did you see me?"

"Jogging past Copp's Hill cemetery."

That *was* his route....

"I barely heard a thing Gabby said all night. She accused me of being an asshole, and I told her some lie about family worries." Marc cupped the back of his neck. "Which wasn't much of a lie, really, because I was wondering how my mom would react to me bringing home a guy instead of the wife and two-point-five she keeps hassling me about."

So that was the issue with the family. Might be more complicated, but Henry sensed Marc wouldn't want to dig deeper right now. He reached for humor. "Getting a bit ahead of yourself, aren't you? We haven't even gone out on a date yet." God, a date with Marc. Henry's heart rate increased, giving him a flushed shell of confidence that might harden and crack at any moment. "That must have been six months ago."

"About a week before I planned to take you down to DC. The Ackerman and Styles reorg."

"Planned?" Henry's stomach clenched.

"I didn't think I could sit on a plane with you, be in a hotel with you, and not do something I might regret."

"And now?"

"I have spent three days trying not to look at your mouth."

That… explained a lot.

Still, despite the urge to lean in and offer up his mouth, Henry found himself leaning away instead. He didn't want to. His flushed and heated skin itched for the cool touch of Marc's fingers, and all of his fantasies were slipping out of their respective corners and presenting themselves for closer inspection. But… he'd been here before. Not exactly *here*, but close enough.

"Don't take this the wrong way, but I'm not interested in being an experiment."

Shock flittered across Marc's face. "A what?"

"We work together. A night of awkward sex is going to make that harder than this"—he gestured vaguely toward the dissipating mist of breath between them—"already has."

"What makes you think the sex would be awkward?"

"Do you even know how to have sex with a guy?"

"I've watched a lot of gay porn."

Oh my God. He really didn't need to know that. Not *now*.

Henry forced a laugh. "Do you watch het porn?"

"Sure."

"And how often have you had sex like that? Like porn-star sex."

Marc didn't answer right away. Instead he fought his way into his suit coat. When he spoke again, his breath formed a thick cloud between them. Despite the heat incited by their conversation, the temperature kept dropping. "Point taken." Another moment of silence, then Marc settled back in his seat. "I shouldn't have said anything, should I?"

Henry began his own battle with his suit jacket, catching his arm on the dash and wrenching his wrist backward before he got it on. The quake of his limbs wasn't all due to the cold, but the added layer of fabric provided a little more warmth, and that helped calm him. The jacket wasn't cut to sit over four shirts, though, leaving his shoulders in a permanent pinch.

Similarly, he found himself caught between the proverbial rock and hard place. As a gay man, he wanted to offer support to someone who was obviously struggling with his identity. That it was Marc having the struggle shouldn't make a difference. But it did. Henry had told the truth about looking up to Marc, wanting to be like him. Sensibly, he'd held back the rest of it—that he'd dreamed about more. Friendship turning into a partnership, of being in a relationship built upon mutual respect and want. Not what he'd had before, and not a short bet.

Hey, daydreams were supposed to be unrealistic, right?

What he had never figured out, though, was if his secret life was any more or less wishful than anyone else's. He knew what it was like to be rejected by someone who couldn't handle the idea of being with someone of the same sex. God, he knew that pain. But still, he lusted. Stupidly, silently, while trying to maintain a professional distance.

Was that why he came across as shy?

Life made so much more sense when he had something to count.

"We passed more than seven-hundred fence posts before the storm drove us off the road."

Marc turned toward him. "What?"

"I counted them. I figured out how many we might pass if we followed this road all the way to Boston."

"Why would you do that?"

"So I wouldn't think about you."

Marc's inhale echoed through a sudden and deep quiet.

Henry reached again for some humor. "We could say it's carbon-monoxide poisoning or something. We've been sitting here for nearly three hours now."

"With the engine mostly off."

"Listen." Henry raised his hands, fingers spread. "We can hit the Rewind button if you want—"

"There's only one direction, Auttenberg, and that's forward." Of course Marc would say that. "Isn't every first date an experiment of a sort?"

"You'd really have asked me out on a date?"

"I was thinking about it."

Henry took a turn at illustrating shock, then instantly felt bad. This was a guy who'd trekked to North End to pick up a woman he hadn't even been interested in taking out. "Let's get back to the jogging thing."

Marc's groan was comical. "When you're at the office, you always have a look of intense concentration on your face. It's kind of off-putting. Part of your reserved, aloof thing. As if you're too busy to mix with the rest of us." Well, damn. "When you're running, you look different. Peaceful, somehow. And you move with a lot more grace than I would have expected. And...." Marc bit his lip.

"And?"

"You looked approachable."

"I... what? What do you mean?"

"You just have no idea, do you?"

"You're the intimidating one," Henry said. "We've covered that. Guy everyone looks up to, right? We're all following your career trajectory."

"One guy in particular with a focus so intense, I can't tell what he wants, or what he's even thinking."

"This is so weird."

"Yeah, it is." Marc took a breath and held it. His exhalation whistled between them, full of unspoken words, the loudest being a noncommittal but probing "so." A moment later he murmured, "What are you thinking?"

A lot of things, and none of them useful. Most of all, though, Henry was thinking he'd never forget the lines of Marc's face as revealed by the dim light of the car radio. The peak of his nose, the dark valleys of his eyes. The way his lips thrust forward when he thought and parted when he smiled. The flash of white teeth, the smudge of stubble along his jaw.

"I'm thinking this is a really bad idea," Henry said before leaning forward to kiss him.

Chapter
SIX

Marc's lips were dry and unexpectedly soft. Henry had imagined he might be more resistant or tense, that he might draw away. Instead Marc leaned into the kiss—to what amounted to little more than the touching of two mouths together until Marc licked his lips, tongue tip swiping and tickling. Moistening.

Henry groaned.

Bad idea or not, he suddenly needed this kiss. Because he'd wanted it, because it was obvious Marc had wanted it, and because, dammit, he now had something to prove. That maybe this wasn't an experiment. Not another mistake. Maybe Marc just hadn't known what he'd been missing—that he'd been born to kiss men—and it was Henry's responsibility to rectify the wrongs of the past twenty-eight years.

With barely a pause for breath, Henry pressed forward again, reaching up to capture Marc's jaw, scratching his thumb over the rough texture of his skin. He kissed the seam of Marc's lips, then just the fuller bottom lip, intending to tease his mouth open. Obviously no stranger to the art of kissing, Marc tilted his head so their mouths slid together more conveniently, and invited him in.

Henry fell into the experience of tasting someone new. The tease of Marc's tongue was so like him—arrogant, self-assured, but also a little coy. He wrapped his warm hand around the back of Henry's neck, setting off idle thoughts of where Marc might have found some heat. Not that Henry felt cold right now. Not really. The soft sounds Marc made were unexpected. Over the wet click and slide of lips, teeth, and tongues, his breath hitched and moaned.

Needing more than a sip of air, Henry pulled back, and Marc dipped his chin down, taking his mouth out of reach. Henry could give chase, and he half suspected Marc hoped he would. That was part of the game too. Henry rubbed his cheek alongside Marc's, showing him how it felt to have another man's skin against his, and withdrew. Just a couple inches.

Quiet breaths filled the pause. Henry licked the taste of Marc from his lips and hummed. Marc inhaled sharply. Pulling his hand from the back of Henry's neck, he leaned all the way back into his seat.

In the near dark, Henry studied the wrinkles across his palm and began counting them. Christmas carols whispered softly into the chill, and every exhalation fogged the air.

They really should start the engine again soon.

He gestured toward the key. In one of those rare moments of unspoken accord, Marc started the car. The quiet rumble of the engine competed with the carol spewing metaphorical tinsel from the dash.

His sister liked this one, didn't she?

Why was Marc so quiet?

He should let Marc speak first, right? Marc needed to be the one to decide if the kiss had been a mistake.

"Okay," Marc finally said, his voice just louder than a chorus of "The First Noel." He glanced over. "So…." He pressed his palms to his eyes again, then pushed his hands through his hair. Henry recognized a pattern when he saw one. This was Marc's "I don't know what the hell I'm doing" gesture. Marc looked at him again, intently, obviously wanting to catch his gaze. When Henry complied, he asked, "Why aren't you saying anything?"

"Because I'm the one who kissed *you*." If he said anything more than that, Henry would incriminate himself, and the sentence passed would hurt.

However Marc chose to reject him, it would hurt.

Why had he kissed Marc? God, he really should have known better.

"It wasn't how I imagined it," Marc said.

Henry drew in an audible breath.

Marc continued. "I thought it would be really different, and it was, but it wasn't."

"Kissing is kissing."

"You don't taste like a woman."

"Glad to hear it."

"And you smell all wrong, but it's not wrong. I...."

Henry waited out the pause.

"I liked it. You smelled, you felt.... Fuck." Hands to the eyes again. "I think I'm more confused than ever."

You and me both, and that could be my fault.

"Want to know what I think?" Henry asked. When Marc didn't say no, he pressed on. "I think you've just figured out that it feels more natural than you expected." Speaking of wishful thinking.... "It's only different because of what's in your head. Kissing is kissing. My skin is rougher, and I smell like a guy. Guess what? I am a guy. I'm not delicate, and my mouth won't always be soft. I won't bruise if you kiss me hard and fast. I'm not going to apologize if I bite you or leave a stubble rash across your mouth." Marc's quick breath stirred Henry's already half-hard cock into something not quite comfortable, given the number of layers over his crotch. "But the mechanics," he managed, "are the same."

Despite the panic fluttering somewhere in the vicinity of his heart, it was oddly liberating to be this frank, this forthcoming.

Henry hadn't imagined himself in the position of aggressor, or educator, with Marc. It didn't diminish his lust, nor did it make him feel superior. He simply wanted with an increased urgency. Because if Marc *was* open to discovery, then this *was* different.

This kiss hadn't ended with a fist to the jaw, a shocking flash of pain, and a hurt that had little to do with either. This might not be a mistake. Marc's looks, his words…. He'd kissed *back*, and his fists were still tucked behind his head.

But not for long. Marc pulled them out and examined them. "It's not the same." He might be counting the wrinkles on his palms, but that would be too much of a coincidence. He was probably wondering if he needed to make another attempt at blotting out reality.

Then, suddenly, too quickly, he was across the center console, hands raised. Henry had seconds to grab at air, ready himself for a yell, but the punch never landed. Instead Marc caught Henry's face between his hands and claimed his mouth in the type of kiss he'd been promised: hard, fast, and bruising. Henry's head spun, thoughts scattering toward a happy place as he rolled forward and lifted his chin. Marc growled, nipped his lips, and kissed him again. Harder.

God, take me now.

Henry searched beneath Marc's layered clothing until he found skin. Marc was warm, despite the chill, alive and sensual against Henry's palm. Henry caressed and scratched the flesh under his fingertips, reveling in the quake and rumble of Marc's breath, pulse, and hitched moans.

They rocked back, Henry's head colliding with the window behind him. Harsh exhalations muffled the thump. Henry wanted to slide his hand up, over Marc's ribs. Find a nipple. What sounds would Marc make when he tweaked that tiny nub? The multiple shirts hampered access to Marc's chest, so he reversed direction, going for the waistband of his sweats, then under, to his suit pants, and down to what he hoped to find—the firm ridge of an erection pushing at the zipper.

Marc was so hard.

He wasn't alone.

Marc's assault on his mouth continued, though at a less frenzied pace. He'd found a rhythm, one as natural as fucking—his tongue flicking and thrusting, his lips closing the deal. His hips bucked into Henry's palm, and a deep groan pushed into Henry's mouth. Marc sent one of his hands south to pluck at Henry's layers before wedging it between them. So *not* shy. As Marc took Henry's constrained erection in a firm grip, Henry thrust his elbow back onto the armrest on the door behind him, needing to ground himself.

Winter punched into the car, bringing snow and ice and bitter cold. He must have hit the window button. Almost stunned by the chill intrusion, Henry pushed Marc off him and tried to sit up. He scrabbled behind himself, hampered by the fact every movement pulled fabric across his very hard cock. His face felt numb; his brain had switched off.

"Here, I got it," Marc said, reaching around him to depress the stupidly small button.

The window shuddered upward and sealed. Marc leaned back and turned off the engine. The resulting quiet felt absolute, and Henry's ears rang. Panted breath coalesced into a dense cloud between them. Snow scattered in the icy dark. A hard shiver pinched Henry's shoulders. Reaching down, he adjusted himself so he could sit and lean away from the door. The back of his seat wasn't any warmer. He could hear Marc's teeth chattering.

The quiet wasn't comfortable. It was cold and awkward.

Henry turned up the volume on the radio, hoping for news the storm might be wearing itself out, or nearly done with New York state. "Rudolph the Red-Nosed Reindeer" pranced into the car instead.

"It's looking pretty bad out there." Marc had cleared a circle on the driver's side window.

"Yeah."

Marc glanced over at him. "We really are going to be stuck here all night, aren't we?" He actually looked as if he only just realized that fact. Or acknowledged it.

"I think so, yeah."

Then Marc grinned, his rakish expression brightening the half dark. Henry reeled from his first intended dose of Winnamore charm. Of course, a good portion of his blood had defected south of his belt.

Marc reached down to adjust himself. "You know, there's more room in the backseat."

A chuckle bubbled up out of Henry's throat. "Not feeling so confused?"

"I'm feeling very fucking horny."

"I'm flattered."

Marc's expression gentled. "You should be."

"Marc...." Doubt bubbled up, surfacing with the shivers now catching every muscle in Henry's back. Damn, it was cold in the car. Stupidly cold. "Maybe this isn't such a good idea."

"What do you mean? You're as hard as I am."

"You know what I'm talking about. We have to work together. I want to work with you. I've been trying to get assigned to your team for two years. This is... this is going to make things all kinds of awkward."

Marc shrugged one shoulder. "It doesn't have to."

"How can it not?"

"Is this how you want to spend your last night on Earth? Arguing over whether you want to get off or not? Seize the moment, Auttenberg. Live in the now."

"Jesus. We are not going to freeze to death," Henry ground out through chattering teeth.

"And we don't have to let this interfere with our work. You know as well as I do our firm takes a liberal view. They don't care who we sleep with, so long as we keep it in the bedroom. Or the copy room."

"Not helping." The fact Marc thought this thing, this whatever they were doing, might extend beyond the car had Henry's head spinning too fast.

"Then what's the issue?"

"Let's just slow down for a sec. If we weren't working together, I'd be all over you right now. You're saying we can do this and it's not going to affect our...." Henry stumbled over the next word.

"Partnership," Marc provided. "Are you always this analytical?"

"Yes. No. Dammit, we work together."

"So you keep saying. Why is that such a sticking point for you?"

"You can't really be that naïve."

Wrapping his arms around himself, Marc huddled a moment, obviously giving the situation the consideration Henry felt it warranted. Either that or he was cooking up his next argument for sex—which wasn't happening in a freezing-cold car. Henry might wonder where Marc's confusion had gone, but this charge-ahead behavior was so typical, he didn't have to. Marc had sampled something he liked and now he wanted more, operative word being *now*.

"Look, I know you think I'm not thinking straight." Marc gave a short laugh. "I'm definitely not thinking *straight*, and I haven't for a while. This is more than me just wanting to get off, though. It's.... You know when you get a sense of how something is supposed to play out? A feeling that it's the right deal, or the wrong approach? This"—he gestured between them—"feels good. It makes sense. When I kiss you, my head goes quiet. I stop thinking and wondering. As for the office thing...." Marc breathed out. "We're both adults."

"Who should know better?"

"Better than what? To act on a feeling? You know as well as I do that no risk means no reward." When Henry made no immediate answer, Marc said, "I've seen you checking me out. You're damned careful, but I know you've thought about more than just being on my team."

Henry's cheeks were suddenly the warmest part of him.

"There's more at stake here than our working relationship," he pointed out.

"Me figuring out what I want, you mean."

"I've been here before, Marc. Right here. Only last time, the guy decided it was a mistake and nearly dislocated my jaw."

Surprise registered in Marc's dark gaze. "Oh. So, that's what you meant about not wanting to be an experiment."

"I don't think you're going to punch me when you figure out this isn't want you want. But it's still going to hurt."

Marc opened his mouth, then closed it. Making a small sound in his throat, he tendered a nod and slumped back into his seat. The holiday music injected false cheer into the otherwise awkward pause, and Henry struggled between the urge to kill the radio or leave it be. It was their only connection to reality, to the storm that had trapped them in this icy confessional.

When Marc spoke again, he did so quietly. "I was going to ask you out, remember? I hadn't figured out how to do it yet. Me asking what you were doing over the holidays? I've been thinking about just that all day, trying to work out a casual way to get it into conversation."

"Actually talking to me would have helped."

"Yeah." Marc blew out a sigh.

Henry scrubbed at his forehead, noting the fact his skin had cooled considerably. "You were really thinking of asking me out?"

"You don't think all this is improvisation, do you? I'm good, but I'm not that good."

"It could just be a 'trapped in a snowstorm' thing. Holy shit, I don't want to die without checking this particular box."

"I don't think many people have 'see if I'm gay' on their bucket list."

"You might be surprised," Henry murmured. He tried for another breath, the previous one not having been all that clarifying or refreshing, and let it go with a hum.

"What?"

"In the last three"—four?—"hours, you've taken just about everything I thought I knew about Marcus Winnamore and turned it upside down. On top of that, I don't think I've ever had such a personal conversation with someone I'm…." He didn't know how to define what they were doing.

"Involved with?"

He'd been going to say *working with*. Henry met Marc's gaze. "Is that what you want?"

"Have you been listening to me?"

Yeah, he had. But except for that one painful mistake, he'd managed to confine his wants to an organized list. That's what counting was, after all. Making a list and ticking it off in the same motion. Nothing satisfied him more. This thing with Marc, though, all the wanting, the apparently not covert looks—he'd known this man could unhinge him. Even before *this*, he'd known Marc was dangerous.

"I think it's my turn to be confused," Henry said.

Marc didn't take offense. In fact, he chuckled. "I think I know something that can help with that." He leaned in, his breath warm. Lips grazed Henry's cheek, then the corner of his mouth. "What say we move to the backseat and talk about it some more."

Henry's breath caught. "You don't want to talk."

"I do want to use my lips, though."

"That is just about the worst line I ever heard."

"But you're thinking about my mouth, aren't you?"

The one moving right beside his? Every word a warm breeze across his lips? Hell yes, he was. And, really, what was so wrong with that?

In answer, Henry kissed him. Again. His rational brain cells yelled in protest. The rest, those caught up by all that was Marc Winnamore, rounded them up and sat on them.

Chapter
SEVEN

*D*ecamping to the backseat proved a complicated exercise. Henry needed the time to think, though, a space between those two amazing kisses and whatever Marc wanted to try next. He still felt he should warn Marc that sex wasn't really on the menu tonight. Not with an ambient temperature of too-freaking-cold and a lack of essentials, like slick and condoms. But as Marc was fond of pointing out, he was a smart guy. He probably knew the limits.

Marc climbed through first, and Henry moved over to the driver's seat. They then wrestled one of the suitcases through the gap to the front passenger seat. Before moving the second case, they each searched for anything that could be used to make them warmer.

Marc held up Henry's toilet kit. "No condoms?"

"From kissing to condoms. Are you sure you haven't been with a guy before?"

Laughing, Marc tossed the bag aside. "Sure I'm sure. Why the hell else do you think I'm so eager?"

Henry couldn't help grinning in response as he climbed through the gap. The burst of activity had warmed him up a little, but he had to take his jacket back off to navigate the space between the seats. Marc had found his hat and pulled it on. His coat was bundled up behind him. Henry sat with his overcoat draped across his legs. He'd found his gloves, but they weren't doing much for his fingers. His hands felt like blocks of ice. His toes fared little better, and his cock had decided to retreat for safety.

He looked over at Marc, who seemed very close in the confined space of the backseat. "Not sure we're any better off back here."

"That's because we're sitting next to each other like two teenagers on their first date."

Henry's short laugh produced a small cloud of breath. "Except we're slowly freezing to death." Another shiver crawled across the back of his shoulders.

Marc shuffled back a bit and reclined sideways on the seat. He moved one leg up and left the other dangling. "Get between my legs."

"I don't think now is the time."

"I'm not asking for a blow job. Just move so I can extend my leg."

Henry moved to the edge of the seat. Marc straightened his leg and scooted down a little more, then held up his arms. "C'mon, lie on me. Put your coat over the both of us like a blanket."

"Yeah, that might work."

Henry arranged himself so he lay over Marc. It was oddly intimate, as if they were settling in for something other than survival. *Were* they settling in for something more? Marc moved his other leg up, and Henry pulled his coat over the top of them both. Marc's coat remained tucked behind him like a pillow. When a cramp moved up the back of Henry's neck, he lowered his head into the crook of Marc's shoulder and neck. Marc slipped his arms around his back. They shivered together.

Henry pressed his nose into Marc's skin. He grinned when he heard a hiss.

"Your nose is cold." With a little more shuffling, Marc managed to turn his head. Cold lips touched the end of Henry's nose.

"Your lips are cold," Henry said.

"Why don't you warm them up, then?"

"Why aren't you freaking out over this?"

"Why do you need to keep examining it? I'm not a fence post, Auttenberg. I'm a person. I only need to be counted once."

"That...." Made sense, dammit.

Marc's lips ghosted across his. "I've had nearly six months to think this through. Now I've tasted you and I'm ready for more. That's it. Doesn't need to be any more complicated than that." He paused, breathing in, then said, "Unless you're waiting for me to apologize for being an ass in Chicago."

"No." He wasn't. "I get it. But you being done with your thinking doesn't change the fact we're barely clinging to this seat, and that it's too freaking cold to try for much more."

"Damn you and your logic." Marc lifted his hips, or tried to. He grunted and shifted beneath Henry. "Maybe you're right."

"We'll have plenty of time to experiment when we get back to Boston." Henry bit his lips together—his cold, nearly numb lips— and wondered if he'd presumed too much, despite Marc's insistence this might be something. Then Marc captured his mouth in a kiss so sweet, it warmed him from the inside out. The intimacy of their position reasserted itself as Henry moved into the kiss, shifting so he could return equal measures of warmth and need. Marc's mouth was already familiar—the shape of his lips, the tease of his tongue. His taste, the way he paused for breath almost regularly, as if they were swimming.

Regular sips of oxygen weren't the same as a proper, deep breath, though, and eventually Henry had to lift his head. He peered down at Marc, seeing nothing but shadows. The backseat was a lot darker than the front.

Marc pulled him in for another round and Henry lost himself. He couldn't remember the last time he'd spent so long just kissing. He licked and pecked, explored every corner of Marc's mouth. Marc did the same. Henry nosed Marc's ear and rubbed his sensitive lips along Marc's jaw. Nuzzled his hair, nipped his neck. Beneath him, Marc writhed and groaned. Tried to lift his hips. The evidence of his growing arousal pressed into Henry's groin, where it met a like-minded soul. They were both hard again and filled with want.

Henry shuffled backward.

Marc caught his shoulder. "Where are you going?"

Henry reached down to pull at Marc's sweatpants. "Lift your hips."

"I can wait, or we can just get off in our clothes."

"You really want to freeze to death in sticky shorts?"

"When you put it like that…." Marc gasped as Henry unzipped his suit pants and pushed down his underpants, freeing his erection, which straightened with careless glee—heedless of the cold.

After pulling off a glove with his teeth, Henry wrapped a hand around the firm shaft.

"Holy shit, your hand is cold!"

Chuckling, Henry withdrew his hand and blew on his fingers. He grabbed Marc's dick a second time.

"Not much warmer, but… mmm, that feels good."

Henry took a moment to appreciate Marc's size and shape, to familiarize himself with his lover's cock, get a feel for it. "Very good," he confirmed.

Marc nudged his hips upward. "Glad I meet your approval."

Henry bent forward and breathed what he hoped was warm air across the crown. Marc moaned. Flicking out his tongue, Henry teased what he could barely see, finding Marc's slit—and a taste of him.

"Oh God."

Closing his lips around the head, Henry hummed.

"Don't stop."

Marc shuddered. His hips thrust upward, but he managed to restrain them… just. Henry lifted his mouth away and said, "I'm not delicate, remember? You can fuck my mouth."

Marc made a strangled sound before reaching down to caress the side of Henry's face. "Want you so bad."

Taking the hint, Henry put his lips to the head of Marc's cock again and sucked downward. He heard Marc cry out, felt the jerk of his hips. Marc wrapped a hand around the side of his head—not gloved, fingers almost warm. Henry braced for the pull against his hair, his ear, but it never came. Marc caressed his neck instead.

There, with his mouth around Marc's dick, Henry once again reevaluated the man he'd looked up to—his potential rival, mentor, partner... friend? Now more. That touch at his ear, the gentle kisses—this was no experiment. Marc *had* been thinking about this, and he wanted it as much as Henry did.

Henry showed his want with his mouth, sucking up and down, adding pressure with his tongue. He grunted softly as Marc nudged his throat, and he squeezed the base of Marc's cock before tugging lightly, encouraging him. He used every trick he'd learned in college—not that he'd given a lot of head, but he had a dick and he knew what he liked—and worked to wring every last drop of enjoyment from the experience for both of them.

Even before Marc approached his climax, Henry's mouth was full of his taste, his nostrils full of musk. Marc breathed and moaned, jerked and thrust. Then he tightened—thighs, abs, balls. Feeling the moment approach, Henry prepared himself, only to have Marc finally tug at his ear—back, not forward.

"Gonna come," Marc gasped.

"So come," Henry said, moving his mouth back down to swallow Marc's harder-than-hard cock.

Marc batted at his ear again, hips thrusting upward, legs trembling. Then, with a great cry, he came, and Henry worked to swallow every last drop, pumping with his hand, sucking gently. Keeping pace with Marc's climax—milking him and carrying him through.

Leaning back, Henry licked his lips and scrubbed his mouth against his sleeve. He hadn't missed much. He savored the taste—not his favorite, but he'd be lying if he said he didn't like it. The bitter tang was as much a part of sex as the scent of a man's balls, the sound of breathless cries, and hips obeying a rhythm commanded by nature.

Marc continued to shiver and jerk, breathing heavily. Henry tucked his polished and limp cock back inside his underwear and did up his suit pants. Then he bent backward to grab the icy-cold Coke from the center console and swallowed what was left in one gulp.

When he turned around, Marc grabbed the front of his shirt and tugged. "Come here."

Henry obeyed the command, allowing himself to be pulled forward, meeting Marc's lips in another of those unexpectedly sweet kisses. Catching his own flavor, Marc leaned back and hummed. "I taste good with Coke. Damn."

Henry's gentle laugh highlighted the situation in his own pants, the hardness that had yet to abate. Without thought, he ground down, then immediately felt guilty.

Beneath him, Marc moaned again. "Can't believe how good that feels."

Henry thrust again. "This?"

"Yes." Marc lifted his head. "I think I'm definitely gay."

Henry laughed. "Wow, I must be good. One blow job and you've switched teams."

"The BJ was phenomenal, but this…. Tasting myself on your tongue, feeling you hard against me. It feels…. Fuck. It feels right."

"You're just horny."

"No. I'm, well, yeah, I kinda am, even though you just blew my mind. Hey, what about you? I…." He paused again. Henry fought the urge to make a joke about verbal tics. Marc would laugh, he was sure, but he also liked this less-sure version of his idol. The man who trembled beneath him, stuttering and hesitating. "I don't know if I'm ready to—"

Henry silenced him with a kiss. Then, "Shh. You've been gay for five minutes. You don't have to blow me on your first day."

After a moment of contemplative silence, Marc said, "Maybe I've always been gay. It never felt like this with a woman."

"Maybe you just haven't met the right woman."

Marc studied him a moment. "No, it's you. I've never obsessed over anyone the way I have over you these past few months."

Wow. Henry's heart lurched. He grabbed at a breath. "Wanna give the object of your fascination a hand job?"

"That, I can do."

Rearranging themselves took about as much time as moving to the backseat and involved more laughter and more nuzzling kisses. The sweeter side of Marc began to feel less unexpected. Then Henry's pants were unzipped, nudged down, and pushed aside. His stiff cock jutted out into the cold. Marc grabbed him without hesitation, and Henry ceased to care if what they were doing made sense.

"You feel good," Marc said, sliding his hand up and down in much the same way Henry had done for him. Gauging his length, his thickness. Getting the feel of him. "You're not cut." Noticing that extra little slide.

"Nope."

"I thought you were Jewish."

"That is, like, the weirdest thing to say when you have another guy's cock in your hand."

"Not really. I mean, it's an observation, right?"

"I'm not Jewish. Auttenberg is a German name."

"So is your first name really Heinrich or something?"

On his birth certificate, and…. "That's my father, and I really, really don't want to talk about him right now either."

"Got it."

Obviously an expert at tugging on his own dick, Marc employed a pull and twist. Henry spread his legs, let his head drop back, and gave himself over to the experience of being fondled. Marc moved his hand up and down in a maddening, irregular rhythm at first, with a pause now and again to squeeze, or to run his thumb over Henry's slit, pressing, collecting slick droplets to add to the uneven friction. Then, just as Henry began to crave the unexpected, to move into it, need it, Marc spat into his palm and began jacking him with swift and steady strokes.

Henry thrust into that talented hand, aware he was gasping, grunting, moaning. Making a lot of sound. He grabbed Marc's neck and pulled him in for a kiss, mashing their mouths together. Their tongues met and tangled, and for a magical moment, it seemed they moved together, as if they were making love. God, how he'd craved this closeness—and it was so damned perfect, it nearly hurt. Then the urge to come jolted through Henry, claiming all his thought. His entire focus narrowed to the thrum in his balls, the need to push harder and faster, his impending climax.

"Coming," he warned, knowing he'd probably said it too late, but aware, just the same, that Marc had probably read the signs.

Marc continued stroking him until he came, then something soft landed over the head of his cock, the cold fabric pulling a yell from his throat. "Shit, what's that… ungh…." Whatever it was, it didn't matter. He was coming, and coming hard, body jerking and tingling, skin flushed and maybe even warm.

When he returned to reality, Marc was wiping him gently with the cold, and now damp, fabric. "It's one of my socks," he explained. "We're not freezing to death with sticky underpants, remember?"

Henry let out a shaky laugh. "I remember."

Marc kissed him again, combining hard and sweet, showing Henry yet another facet of his hidden self, this apparent need for confirmation on top of connection. When Henry started shivering, he drew back. "I could get really used to kissing you, Auttenberg."

"I could get really used to you calling me Henry."

Marc's quiet laugh fogged the air between them.

Another round of rearranging, this time tucking his spent cock back inside a few layers. Then they reset their hats, found their gloves, and retrieved Henry's coat. After, Marc reclaimed his seat, spread his legs, and opened his arms. "Let's not waste all the heat we just generated."

"I'd not have picked you for a cuddler."

Marc might have shrugged in the dark, his outline fairly indistinct but for his upraised arms. "Not fooled by my practical spin on it?"

Henry chuckled. "I can pretend."

The way Marc folded around Henry as they realigned belied any practicality. The closeness felt more important than trapping any heat. Henry found he liked it, this other hidden aspect of the man he was just getting to know properly. But as they lay together breathing quietly in the chilly dark, body heat trapped between them and held there by the spread of Henry's coat over his back, he couldn't help wondering if Marc's seeming affection had grown more out of circumstances than intent.

Marc kissed the side of his head. "I can hear you thinking, you know."

"If you don't want this when we get back to the office, I'd understand."

The circle of Marc's arms tightened. "I figured that's what you were thinking about. Pretty selfish of you when I could be lying here having a crisis."

Henry laughed. "Are you?"

After a pause, Marc gave a definite shrug. "A bit. Which is why I'm not going to forget this when we get back to the office, and not because you're my big gay experiment." He breathed out. "I don't know if now is the time to really get into it? I've got some thinking to do. But I don't regret this. I won't. I wanted it too much, and it's too good for regrets. It's better than I hoped."

Henry sucked in a deep breath. "I can help with the thinking. Even if you decide this isn't what you want, I can be a friend, or a friendly ear. Coming out isn't just enjoying a blow job, and it's not just telling one person."

"I know." Marc nuzzled his cheek. "That other guy—"

"We're past the 'hit first, ask questions later' stage, and I know if you blow me off, it won't be because I'm gay." Henry raised his head enough to look Marc in the eye. "You've known that for two and a half years, and you've only ever been civil. Mostly. When we weren't working together." He smiled.

"Not going to blow you off. I want your report on Hiddenger."

Henry snorted. "Nice."

He could just make out Marc's faint smile in the dark. "I don't know what this might be, but I'm interested in finding out. Are you?"

"Yeah." Henry's stomach disagreed, and an invisible fist wrapped around his heart. But Marc had said it clearly enough before, in terms he could understand. Risk equaled reward. And this? Even now, lying together in the backseat of a cold car, they seemed to fit.

"Next thing to figure out is what I'm going to tell my family."

Leaning forward again, Henry dropped a quick kiss onto Marc's lips. "I get the feeling you've avoided telling them a lot of stuff."

"You know, they really shouldn't be surprised by this. I've never been who they wanted me to be."

"I find that hard to believe. You graduated with honors, and you've got a great job."

"But I went to the wrong school and got the wrong degree. I'm living in the wrong city, working with the wrong company."

"Right."

"No, wrong." Marc's nose had cooled, and it made a chill spot on Henry's cheek.

"Boston is the right city. You have good friends, and you're definitely doing the right job."

"Thanks. Mostly I know that. But this is…. This is going to feel like another wrong choice."

"It's not a choice. This is who you are." And acknowledging it would be difficult at any age, at any time. The world could be a stupid and cruel place. When Marc didn't immediately respond, Henry pulled in a breath and held it. Prepared the right words to put himself out there, to demonstrate he really believed Marc was different, and that he was worth the risk. "I can be there, if you want."

"Thanks."

The small response felt like a letdown, but only at first—only until Henry considered what Marc had left out. Assumptions and promises. They'd already talked about what might or might not happen between them. Now they were talking outside of that. They were talking about the friendship they were building, regardless.

"So tell me about your family," Marc said. "Do you usually spend Christmas with them? Any German traditions?"

"Yeah, and not so much on the traditions. More when we were kids. My mom's not German, and my dad was born here. So it's not as if we sit around in lederhosen drinking beer and eating sausage."

"Pity."

Henry dug his elbow into the man beneath him, but the gesture was halfhearted. Knowing what Marc faced at home made him miss his own family more. By now they'd be worried. He'd called from Syracuse, but not since. They'd guess he'd been caught by the storm. For him, though, more than their concern over where he might be, was the fact this would be the first time he'd missed Christmas Eve.

"We do have this one tradition, but it's not a German thing. We always spend Christmas Eve together. My sister and her family, me, my mom and dad. We stay up late and play games. We watch—" Henry swallowed and was surprised by the size of the lump in his throat. He hadn't realized how much he relied on even simple tradition, spending this single night with his family, even as an adult. It made sense when he reflected upon it, though. His life was made up of touch points. Of things he could count, and count on.

"What do you watch?" Marc's tone was gentle.

"*The Sound of Music*. I know. It's stupid, right? It's my sister's fault. She saw the movie for the first time when she was, like, five, and we've had to watch it every year since. Sometimes more than once."

Marc didn't laugh. He did chuckle, but it was a commiserating sound. "What else do you do? Do you sing?"

"God no. Well, sometimes, and badly. That's when we know we've had too much to drink." Henry grinned. "My favorite part of the night is when we get to choose one present to open."

"We used to do that too."

"I'm sorry."

"Don't be. I'm their loss, right?"

"Right." But Henry's response felt thin, as if the tightness of his throat had tried to squash the life out of it. He shifted a little, worried he might be getting heavy, or that his weight atop Marc might start feeling metaphorical.

"If you keep moving, I'm going to get hard again."

Henry pressed down, right there, smooshing their sated cocks together. "You're definitely gay."

Marc hugged him a little closer. "Probably. And damned comfy." He sucked in a short but audible breath. "Thank you for taking me seriously."

Blinking, Henry stuttered, "Um… sure. You've proved yourself worth listening to, even before tonight."

Marc chuckled softly in response.

After that, they fell into the first truly companionable quiet of the day. Night. It was late and dark and cold. Definitely night. But though the air inside the car had dropped to well below comfortable, the sound of the wind outside proved oddly soothing, as did the rise and fall of Marc's chest beneath his. The whisper of their breath, the warmth of their aligned bodies. They hadn't had to shift much to get their legs sorted. They lay together naturally, Marc's shoulder making the perfect pillow.

It was only going to get colder, and he hadn't forgotten the danger of their situation. But Henry felt safe and secure tucked in close to Marc. As if, together, and only together, they might keep each other safe until morning, and maybe beyond. With that thought at the forefront of his mind, he gave in to the heavy blanket of sleep and let fear remain outside, in the provenance of night.

Chapter
EIGHT

A scratching noise intruded upon his sleep, matching the endless steps of some useless dream journey. Henry opened his eyes and blinked a few times, disoriented by the feel of *someone* under him and the not quite familiar scent of that someone pressed to the side of his face. The noise came again, accompanied by a flashing light. Henry looked up and the plume of mist erupting from his mouth filled in all the gaps in his memory. He and Marc were stuck in their rental car on the side of the road in the middle of nowhere, and now the ghosts had come.

Or maybe someone had found them.

A muffled voice called from outside the window. Pulling a gloved hand from the warm little nest he and Marc had made on the backseat, Henry pressed his palm to the window.

"What are you doing?" Marc mumbled.

"There's someone out there."

Marc's thoughts did not immediately skip to ghosts. "Oh thank God."

Together, they struggled until the easiest thing for Henry to do was slide off the seat and onto the floor. Marc sat up and depressed the window button. Nothing happened. A quick glance forward showed the radio had gone dark. Silent and icy blackness filled the interior of the car.

"Battery must be dead," Henry said.

Light flashed through the window again, revealing a speckled clear spot in packed snow. Had the storm buried them?

Marc opened the door and pushed. The bottom stuck in the ice and frigid air rushed through the crack.

"You all okay in there?" a female voice asked. "How many of you?"

"Two," Marc answered. "And we're fine."

"I got a plow out here. I can't get your car out, but I can give you a ride somewhere."

"That'd be great," Marc said. "Just need to get this door open."

"Yeah, it's stuck. I'd half plowed past you before I saw you. I need to clear a bit. Hold tight."

Henry scrubbed at his face. The cold air rushing into the car had equalized quickly with the internal temperature. He didn't want to think about how cold it actually was, and if they'd have woken up in the morning or been a news story. Their cocoon had felt warm, but any heat between them had quickly dissipated as soon as he moved. Shivers now racked his shoulders, pulling painfully at his muscles, and his feet were numb.

Shoes.

"We need to put our shoes back on," he said.

"Right, and maybe put our cases back together."

By the time their rescuer had cleared the door, Henry had found their shoes and packed their cases. "Pretty sure we're going to end up with each other's shorts and socks."

"We'll figure it out later."

Marc leaned against the door while the woman pulled, and together they managed to get it open. Marc scrambled out. Henry handed him his coat first, then the cases. He followed after, dragging his overcoat out with him.

Winter had claimed the world, turning it into a dark and icy wasteland. Forward from the plow, in the track of the headlights, he could see the road had been cleared once already. Banks two feet high leaned away from another six inches on the tarmac. "A plow already passed us?"

"Yeah. Your car is nearly off the road. They just about buried you."

"We didn't even hear them." Another chill raced down his spine.

Beneath her woolen hat, the woman's ruddy cheeks lifted in a grin. "My lucky night. I get to be the hero. Name's Betty, by the way."

"It's really good to meet you, Betty," Henry said. "I'm Henry and this is Marc."

"You two did real good snuggling up together in the backseat." She winked. "Looked mighty cute too."

Marc cleared his throat and looked away, but a smile tugged at his lips.

Henry simply blushed, and the color stung his cold cheeks. Clapping his hands together, he said, "So, um… where can you take us?"

"Let's try for Duanesburg. From there, we should be able to find you a ride to Albany."

They stowed the suitcases and climbed into the cab of her truck, Henry in the middle, Marc by the passenger door. The clock on the dash read 1:03 a.m. They'd left Chicago at one the previous afternoon, and despite having had maybe five hours sleep between then and now, it felt like the longest twelve hours of Henry's life. So much had happened, most of it unexpected. But right then, the warm air blowing from the vents felt more significant than any of it.

The rumble of the engine and motion of the plow quickly proved somnolent. Before Henry knew it, his eyes had closed again. He jerked awake, only to realize he'd leaned into Marc. He turned to look at him and met a sleepy smile that warmed him more than their now ridiculous layers and any heat blowing around the cabin.

"You boys local?"

"We're from Boston," Marc said.

"Well, you're not going to get there tonight. Storm's moved on, but it's going to be a while before the roads are clear. I'll bet most of the rentals are gone too, or buried on the side of the road." She turned a grin on them. "You need to make a call? I got a cell booster in the cab. Never know when you might need one out here."

Shifting away from Marc slightly, Henry dug in his pockets for his cell. After he'd pulled it out he noticed Marc hadn't reached for his own phone. He really had no one to call? Settling himself back against Marc's side, Henry dialed his parents. It was late, but....

"Heinrich?" His dad sounded old and quiet.

"Hey, Dad."

"I knew you'd call. I told your mother you'd call." And he'd waited up, would have waited all night if necessary. "Where are you?"

"Outside of Albany. We had to pull over when the storm caught up with us. Wait for a plow." That sounded better than sliding off the road and nearly being buried by snow, right?

"I'm glad you're all right. Want me to drive up to Albany and get you?"

"No, Dad. The roads might not be clear for a day or so. As soon as they are, I'll come right home, okay? I'll call Mom in the morning too, and again tomorrow night. Let you know where I'm at." He could feel color trying to creep across his cheeks, but he was so flushed from the warmth of the car and his clothes and Marc, the new blush barely registered. Besides, while it might seem as if his family kept a close hold of him, not everyone had a father who would wait by the phone and then offer to drive a hundred miles to pick him up. In a storm.

That was better than having no one to call.

Henry glanced over at Marc and spoke into his phone. "Hey, Dad?"

"Hmm?"

"I'm bringing a friend home for Christmas."

Marc's eyes widened slightly, but he didn't object.

Where Henry's mom would have had a million questions about this "friend," his father only said, "Of course! We'll see you when we see you."

"Will do. Now go get some sleep."

"I might just do that. Look after yourself, Heinrich."

"You too, Dad."

He tucked his phone away and looked back up at Marc.

"Your name *is* Heinrich," Marc said.

"I prefer Henry."

Marc's brow furrowed briefly. Was he counting excuses not to visit Henry's family? The way his expression quickly relaxed seemed to say otherwise. "All right, then. Merry Christmas, Henry."

Henry couldn't hide his smile. His first name, at last. It sounded good on Marc's tongue, and he looked forward to hearing it again. But more than that, he realized, he'd gotten his Christmas Eve gift after all. Two of them. A fantasy—which, but for the cold, had lived up to every expectation—and a truth, an aspect of Marc not very many people got to see. It had been an intensely personal gift, one just for him. Just for Henry Auttenberg.

He leaned back into Marc's warm side and smiled. He couldn't prepare for what might happen when they got back to Boston, but he was ready for it. "Merry Christmas, Marc."

Counting
STARS

I needed to end *Counting Fence Posts* where I did, even knowing their story wasn't finished. "Counting Stars" doesn't add much, except maybe to reinforce the feeling something has been started. Something both of these guys will want to see through. Writing this super fluffy short also gave me the chance to get into Marc's head for the first time, and to have him issue the invitation to a New Year's Eve party, thereby continuing the story.

Marc

*T*he chance to go home and hide in his crappy little apartment in South End passed by at a sedate fifty-five miles an hour. Marc watched the exit sign recede, his neck cracking as he turned. Two nights slumped across a lobby chair in the corner of a nameless motel on the outskirts of Albany had left a permanent kink in his spine. Facing forward again, he swallowed against the panic rising up from his gut.

Why had he said he'd go home with Henry?

As though hearing the thought, Henry glanced back at him. Wintry sunlight strobed across his face, picking out ruddy cheeks, gray eyes and the slight smile that almost—no, *always* plucked at something inside Marc. It was Henry's mouth. He had the sexiest damn mouth Marc had ever encountered. He couldn't exactly say why; whether it was the fullness of his lips or the angle of his smile. Maybe it was the fact his smiles were rare and each felt like a gift.

"Having second thoughts?" Henry asked.

"No." The denial was instinctive. Marcus Winnamore never had second thoughts. He picked a direction and followed it until the end.

"I can turn around. It's no problem," Henry's father said.

It'd been no problem to drive over a hundred miles along barely cleared highway to deliver his only son from the gates of frozen hell, either. Who did that? Heinrich Auttenberg Senior, obviously. Marc had no doubt Heinrich "I prefer Henry" Junior would have done the very same thing.

"I'm fine, really." Home might mean a long, hot shower and being horizontal for a while, but it also meant the small stack of unopened Christmas cards, a frozen turkey dinner and the absence of Henry. Which shouldn't be a big deal. Wasn't as if they were suddenly inseparable. The thing in the car might have been just that. A thing. They'd been facing frozen death, after all.

Henry wasn't one for empty gestures, though. For him, this invitation was personal.

For Marc—

"I'll drop you home later, hmm?" Auttenberg Senior said, nodding to indicate Marc should probably just agree with him.

"Thank you."

"Dinner will be worth the detour. Lissa is making everything fresh today. No Christmas leftovers for the weary travelers."

"Mom made two Christmas dinners?" Henry asked.

Auttenberg Senior shrugged one shoulder. "I helped. I made my cranberry relish and two pies."

"Two pies?"

"I couldn't decide on just one."

It was a very un-Auttenberg comment. The two men occupying the front of the car were definitely related, however, and it was nice to know there was a relaxed version of Henry in the world—even if Marc would never be able to deny the fact he liked poking little ripples into the still pond of Henry's calm.

"I'm looking forward to a proper meal," Marc said. His stomach would be unknotted by dinner time if he had to reach in there and align everything himself.

Twenty minutes later, they wove through the icy tunnels of suburbia under siege. With the snow stacked high in front of every house, the neighborhood was a maze. No doubt a proper architectural term existed for the squat and square houses that spread across Dorchester like a rash. Each had a square porch set against a cube of house with corners and angles and square windows. The color varied slightly from house to house, though often it was down to the age of the paint. Come home on a dark night, and it would've been difficult to tell one from the other.

Auttenberg Senior picked a driveway seemingly at random. As he climbed out of the car, stepping into a narrow drive carved between thick banks of snow, Marc thought he might have been able to tell the Auttenberg house from the rest of the pack. The decorations were as bright and garish as those dripping from every eave in the street, but there was something neat about the place. Orderly. In an odd way, it felt like Henry. Staid. Solid. Reliable. Welcoming. Warm.

Henry was wrestling Marc's suitcase out of the trunk.

"Why not just leave it there? I don't need anything inside."

"Mom will have everything washed and folded by the time we're done with dinner."

"She doesn't have to—"

"Of course she doesn't. She'll want to. It's how she is. When I moved out, she used to call me and ask if I had any clean underwear."

"Seriously?"

"Mmm-hmm. Trust me, if we don't take your case in, she'll ask where it is and come get it. And it's slippery out here."

Henry worrying about his mother slipping on the driveway during her quest to wash a colleague's underwear shouldn't be cute. But it was. Marc helped pull both cases out of the car and followed Henry to the porch. The door flung open, holiday scents spilling outward in a warm and cheery haze, and a woman who was hopefully Lissa Auttenberg attached herself to Henry like a multi-limbed parasite. Except in a much more loving and lovely way.

Thankfully, she didn't inflict the same damage on Marc. She took his offered hand and squeezed instead. "I'm so happy you could join us! Henry never brings friends home."

Marc shot Henry a *look*. Henry responded with the same one-shouldered shrug his father used in the car.

"I appreciate the invitation, ma'am."

"Call me Lissa, please." She let go his hand and leaned out sideways. "Heinrich, did you remember the cider?"

Henry's father groaned. "No, sorry. I'll go back out."

Because six hours on barely cleared roads wasn't enough for one day?

Lissa flapped a hand. "Don't worry about it. Was just a thought. Come on, let's get inside. It's freezing out here."

The warmth of the Auttenberg house was dizzying. Bright yellow lamps, colorful strings of tinsel, cards propped against every surface, a Christmas tree in full swag, the scent of turkey and dressing, cinnamon, the crackle of a fire behind a grate and the quiet murmur of caroling. And this was all in the first room.

Lissa was trying to pull his coat from his shoulders while Auttenberg Senior tugged at the suitcase in his hand. Somehow they were doing the same to Henry, at the same time. Henry handled the whole process with much more grace, meaning he submitted. Consciously relaxing his shoulders, Marc shrugged out of his coat and let the case be taken from his fingers.

"I'm sure you two would like a shower and there's plenty of time for a nap. You poor dears. Two days in a chair, not to mention the car and the storm." Lissa pressed a hand to her heart. "The snowplow driver who saved you is a hero! I hope she's commended by her department, or whoever sends out the plows! It's such a shame she couldn't join us today. She was just lovely on the phone. She can rest assured we'll be remembering her every year. I wonder if she'd like a picture of you two in front of the tree?"

What?

"I think the phone call was fine, Mom," Henry said.

The ride down from Albany had been accomplished in an almost comfortable bubble of quiet. Despite his effusiveness over the phone, in person Auttenberg Senior was as reserved as Henry. After a minute in Lissa Auttenberg's company, Marc was beginning to understand why the men were so quiet. They'd probably given up trying to get a word in twenty-odd years ago.

A smiling Lissa directed them toward the staircase. "Well, I've laid out some of Henry's old clothes for both of you."

"Thanks." Tipping his head toward the stairs in a "follow me" gesture, Henry led the way.

Marc followed. After turning the first corner, he leaned in to whisper, "Is she always like that?"

"Like what?"

Grunting, Marc continued to follow Henry up the stairs, instinctively ducking his head as the small house closed in around him. Henry abandoned him in a short, dark hallway, disappearing into an equally dark room. He reappeared a moment later with a short stack of clothing in his hands and raised it toward another door. "Want to go first?"

The weirdness returned, along with the feeling he'd missed his exit. He was in a strange house, and though surrounded by people, Marc suddenly felt... alone. These weren't his people. The clothes folded over Henry's arms weren't his clothes.

Why exactly was he here?

Was he really gay?

Curling his fingers around Henry's biceps, Marc leaned in, nosing Henry's almost smooth cheek. In contrast, he had three days' growth and it itched. He inhaled Henry's scent—those same three days plus the now familiar presence of someone he'd been intimate with—and hummed softly. It was still there, the insistent itch of attraction. Whether it made him gay or not, he still wanted Henry.

"Showering together might be more efficient," he murmured.

Henry turned his cheek, lining up their mouths, and spoke against his lips. "Not in my parents' house."

"They sent us upstairs together."

"Assuming we were adults."

"Which is why they shouldn't be surprised—"

Henry silenced him with a kiss, his lips latching softly onto Marc's before questing for more. His tongue broke barriers, aggressively deepening the connection. Groaning, Marc stepped closer, bringing their bodies together, reaching for more of Henry with his other hand. The sound of their kisses echoed quietly in the enclosed space. Quick breaths, the moist drag of lips and tongues. Groans that sounded like bruises. Grabbing the back of Henry's hip, Marc stepped away, pulling Henry toward the bathroom.

This, exactly, was why he was here.

He needed more Henry. He wanted more Henry. A fantasy unfurled quickly in his head—Henry up against a wall. No, Henry in the shower, completely naked, skin shining beneath a cascade of water. His cock jutting out, thick and fully hard. Buttocks flexing. Fingers roaming. The wonderful inevitability of that moment before climax. Sweet surrender.

Henry followed him into the light… and stopped. Then he leaned back, grinning, and stepped back into the hall. The door swung shut between them.

"Don't use all the hot water." Henry's voice was muffled by wood and several layers of paint, but Marc could hear the laughter beneath his words.

Henry had managed him. *Managed* him. Marcus Winnamore. Worst part? Marc stood there, staring at the back of the door with a stupid grin on his face.

Henry

Marc denied him a kiss after the shower. Dark brown eyes twinkling with humor and challenge, he lifted his chin as Henry leaned in. "Your turn."

God, Marc smelled good. Warm and steamy. Sexy. Had he jerked off in the shower? If he had, he'd been quick. Not that self-love ever took too long in Henry's experience—which would be why the solitary act so often left him unsatisfied.

Determined not to lose ground, Henry blocked the doorway as Marc tried to pass. Grinning, Marc pressed close. "Water pressure is great. Felt like fingers on my back, down my spine. Little sensitive on the front parts, though." Front parts? "Had to shield my dick with my hand if you know what I mean." His tongue flicked out, catching the shell of Henry's ear. "Could have been your hand. Front, back..."

A groan escaped Henry.

Marc cackled.

"Please tell me you didn't jerk off in my parents' shower."

"I didn't jerk off in your parents' shower."

After pressing a light kiss to his cheek, Marc slithered past, into the hallway, and shut the door against Henry's back. Served him right, really. If anyone would be into games, adept at upping the stakes, it would be Marc.

Henry quickly shed his clothes, wincing at the odor of nearly three days on the road. The stink had been more attractive on Marc, for sure. Then he stepped under the shower and indulged in five minutes of nothing. Of standing. Of appreciating superior water pressure. Of being home and on the way to being fed. Of the fact a man he'd lusted after forever stood in the hall outside, dressed in an old pair of his BU sweatpants and a flannel shirt that should have been sorted into the donation bag five years ago.

And that the want between them remained intense. Whatever they'd shared on the side of the road in upstate New York hadn't been left beneath four feet of snow. It had traveled south with them, followed them up the stairs and nearly tempted him to have sex in his parents' house.

"Marcus Winnamore is in my parents' house."

The thought tugged him toward the swirl of water around the shower drain. What the heck was he doing inviting someone like Marc to his parents' house? And why had Marc accepted the invitation? Surely he'd rather be elsewhere… anywhere.

More likely, he was reacting. That was what people like Marc did. They bent with the winds of change, only thinking about it after the storm had passed. When he did get home, would Marc regret having spent time with Henry and his family?

Would he deem his experiment over?

Henry's thoughts stopped swirling. Paused. Rolled back over the past few days to the backseat of the rental car. To the intensity of Marc's kisses and the sound he made when he came. His enthusiasm while returning the favor—the feel of his hand on Henry's dick. Sure and definite. Not hesitant, not experimental.

Henry reached for the soap, thinking about jerking off in the shower, but confined himself to some seductive touches without imagining his hands were in fact Marc's hands and that…

He jerked off in the shower, cheeks flaming with arousal and guilt.

The quick tug left him warm and satisfied, though. His skin tingled and his mouth wouldn't stop quirking into a smile—until he wondered what Marc might be doing at that very moment and further imagined him downstairs chatting with his mother and father, sharing the full story of what they'd gotten up to in that rental car in upstate New York.

Cold air stung his hot skin as he flung the shower curtain aside. The sweatpants clung to his still damp calves. Henry tugged them so hard, the waist cord retreated into its hole. Dammit! He put the shirt on inside out and fell into the door trying to wrestle a pair of his father's thick woolen socks over his feet. The smell of Christmas hit him again in the hall, wrapping around him with a comforting snug. Then he noticed the door to his old bedroom stood ajar.

Oh no.

Marc was in there. Thankfully, he wasn't sitting on the bed with the contents of Henry's nightstand strewn across the quilt. Marc *was* on the bed. He lay on his back, head pillowed by folded arms, eyes closed, face slack with sleep.

It was weird seeing someone he'd been intimate with on his old bed, the one that somehow remained pure and innocent, despite some youthful fumbling. Kissing, mostly. A couple of touches. He hadn't actually gotten naked with a guy until college.

Again, he was struck by the fact Marc was here, in his parents' house. In one sense, he wanted to chide himself for being so affected by it, by the sight of Marc asleep on his old bed. He also wanted to cherish the feeling as precious. This was someone he could see himself caring about in a true and deep way. A man he'd looked up to and had tried to emulate. Not all of his fantasies about Marc had included sex.

He stood there a moment longer, pulling at the cuffs of his long sleeve T-shirt. If he wanted a nap, he could use his sister's old room. Or the couch downstairs. But… Marc was on his bed. *His* bed. And he'd left a space to his left, as though expecting Henry to join him. He looked warm and cozy. And...

Borrowing a little of Marc's forward momentum, Henry picked up the quilt folded at the end of his bed and drew in a deep breath that ended in a jaw-cracking yawn. Then he laid down beside Marc, spreading the quilt over the both of them, and closed his eyes. The room spun crazily in the crackling dark behind his lids. God, he was tired. He could smell Marc again, warm and clean. The familiar scent of his mother's laundry detergent rose between them. Christmas wafted through the door he'd forgotten to close properly. Happily, muzzily, Henry curled his toes, smiled and gave into the deep tug of sleep.

Marc

Marc swam toward the surface of consciousness slowly. He felt as though he'd been asleep for a month, but his internal clock indicated only a couple of hours had passed. That and the late afternoon light filtering through his closed lids. He was warm and cozy and... someone was breathing next to him.

He opened his eyes to an unfamiliar ceiling. Dingy white and cluttered with the faint, off-yellow outlines of glow-in-the-dark stars. Remembering where he was, Marc smiled. Of course Henry had stars on his ceiling. He probably made wishes on them. Which was kinda sweet, actually.

Sweet not being Marc's thing, he slithered toward the edge of the bed, taking care not to disturb the quilt that had mysteriously been tucked around him, and sat up. He scrubbed sleep from his eyes and made an attempt to smooth his hair. He'd fallen asleep with it wet and could feel the damage at the back of his head. He turned around to look at Henry and that stupid smile caught him again—because damn if Henry didn't look *sweet* all snuggled under his colorful quilt. He had that wholesome and entirely too sexy combo going, and that shouldn't be his thing.

Except, apparently it was.

Tearing his gaze away, Marc checked out the room. He'd meant to poke around before falling sleep, but the bed had been wide and flat and just *there*. Three days without a bed had started making a free patch of floor look good. The happy clutter of adolescence filled every corner of Henry's bedroom. Books, posters, a chair piled high with teddy bears—and if Henry hadn't thought to hide that pink unicorn before collapsing into a nap, all the better for Marc. Grinning, he crossed the room and picked it up. Damn it was soft. Of course, he was hugging the damn thing when Henry woke up.

"Soft, isn't it?"

"And pink. Very, very pink."

Henry shrugged away the quilt and stretched his arms over his head, yawning and blinking. When he looked human again, he said, "And soft."

"You should put it on your desk at Beck and Meyer. See if a senior partner is suckered into picking it up."

Chuckling, Henry sat up and rubbed the back of his head, wincing as he discovered the inevitable mess. "Ugh. I should have dried my hair before lying down."

"No kidding."

"Not all of us can look perfect all the time."

Snorting softly, Marc tossed the unicorn back toward the chair and zeroed in on Henry's desk. He picked up one of the three framed pictures. It was Henry at his graduation from BU; capped, gowned and pressed in on both sides by the wide smiles of his mother and a younger version of Lissa, who must be Henry's sister. Auttenberg Senior stood just behind Lissa and another man stood behind the sister, holding a toddler in his arms.

Swallowing an annoying and somewhat prickly lump, Marc turned. Henry was standing right behind him. Marc held up the frame. "This is a great photo. I'm surprised you didn't pack it for your apartment."

"I do have it there. A larger version. Housewarming gift from Mom, along with six casseroles for my freezer, a set of matching towels and ten packs of underwear."

Marc laughed. He set the picture down and picked up another of

Henry and the younger woman from the first photo. "Is this your sister?"

"Yep. Mel." Henry's smile widened. "Short for Melissa, which is my mother's name."

"Your parents named both of you after themselves?"

"Pity in the form of cash would be most beneficial."

Scoffing, Marc set the picture back down to pick up the third and final frame. "This is Mel's wedding?"

"Yeah and I have a larger version of that at my place too. Along with yearly portraits of her kids in frames with multiple little windows I can fill every year when she sends me the new photos."

"So, basically you never left home."

"Nope."

A tingling burn spread across his chest. Swallowing, Marc set the last photo down and ran a finger along the jumbled book spines. He recognized the tight warmth as jealousy, which he hadn't felt for a while. Which he shouldn't feel here in a tiny house in Dorchester. His bedroom had been four times the size of Henry's. His bed larger. The wallpaper had never been old enough to peel from the corners the way it did in this house, and if he'd looked out his window, he'd only have seen their neighbors through a screen of trees. Here, the house next door stood so close, they could hear the neighbors' toilet flushing.

His room had never been this personal, though; nor had it ever been as full of tokens. Reminders that he was part of a family. Loved. Cherished. The first time Marc had visited his parents from college, it had been to discover his bedroom had been packed away, the few boxes of his childhood neatly labeled and stacked in the attic.

Henry was folding the quilt, which looked as though a fabric shop had thrown up on it. His grandmother had probably made it. Or an aunt. Someone who knew Henry should be surrounded by bright color and familial warmth.

Suddenly irritated, Marc nodded toward the door. "Think we could get a snack?"

"Sure." Henry caught him by the arm just before he got there. "Hold up."

"What?" He hadn't meant to snap, but he had. Marc pressed his lips together and looked pointedly toward the door.

"Everything okay?"

"Yeah." He softened his tone. "Just hungry."

Henry inspected his face a moment, expression pensive, then nodded. "All right."

"Do I have your permission to go downstairs?" Marc tried for light tone and probably failed.

"Not if you're going to be rude to my parents."

Yep, failed. "Listen, Auttenberg—"

"Henry."

There it was, the fire of intractability that made Henry so desirable, and now Marc knew where it came from. Henry might be somewhat reserved, but he was solid. Implacable. He had *this* behind him—a room full of cherished memories and a family who supported his choices. His very self.

He had substance.

Marc was supposed to be the one with substance. Instead he stood there questioning everything, and questions made him moody—particularly when he hadn't had time to figure out all the answers.

He looked at Henry, looked for answers. Just one would do. Henry's gorgeous mouth curved into a small smile. Breathing out, Marc leaned in and kissed him—not tentatively, not asking for permission. He claimed Henry's lips as though they already belonged to him, backing Henry into the closed door before reaching up to frame his face, grip one shoulder and lean in harder, more intently. Henry met his kiss with equal force, his tongue again the aggressor. He grabbed the back of Marc's hips and pulled him closer. Groaning, Marc deepened the kiss, surprised he could, that they still had somewhere to go. Desire licked across his skin, burning a path to his groin. His fingertips and toes tingled. Henry tasted of toothpaste and sleep. He smelled of soap and this house. Of Christmas and good things. And he was so very male—his skin soft, but not quite pliable, his lips a little rough. Stubble tickled the tips of Marc's fingers and the body against his was hard. Strong.

Marc reached down, trailing his fingers over the fabric of Henry's long sleeve T, until he got to the waist band of his sweats. He wanted to feel Henry's other hardness. Meet it with his own. Henry gasped into his mouth. Moaned. Rocked into him. Clutched at his hip. Then he was pushing Marc away—the parting of their lips almost painful, the loss of heat between them awful.

Between heavy breaths, Henry said, "We can't." But he wanted to. Marc could see the want and need in every fiber of Henry's being. Closing his eyes, Henry tipped his head back toward the door and breathed again. Panted, really.

Marc stepped away. Much as he'd like to push, tease and… push, he also wanted to respect Henry's wishes. Respect his family and home. It was a small thing, really, but as he sought to calm the southward flow of blood, he acknowledged that doing this for Henry, backing off, felt right. He liked the fact Henry could make a demand of him. It was new and different, something he hadn't known he needed, and a sure sign he'd met his match.

Heavy footsteps on creaking stairs gave them plenty of warning before the knock at the door. "You two awake in there?" Auttenberg Senior. "Mel is here and Lissa is getting ready to serve dinner."

"We'll be right down, Dad." Henry stepped away from the door, tugging at his sweats.

He was still half hard. So was Marc. He met Henry's soft smile with a wink and grinned as color flushed Henry's cheeks. Leaning in, he brushed his lips to heated skin and whispered, "Count something, Auttenberg."

Silence, then breath tickled his ear. "Counting our kisses was totally the wrong choice, just so you know."

Marc's heart simultaneously jerked and held. Sweet shouldn't be his thing! Except, in Henry's case, it totally was.

Henry

*D*ownstairs the house rang with noise and color. Mel and family had arrived and Henry's nephew was shaking the small pile of gifts stacked next to the tree, trying to guess what was inside. His niece burbled quietly from one of those car seats that looked secure enough to withstand atmospheric reentry.

Mel wrapped him up in a hug. "I'm so glad you're okay!"

Henry exchanged the usual handshake with her husband Jerome, each assuring the other it was good to see them.

Introducing Marc felt weird. Henry settled on "a colleague from Beck and Meyer," keenly aware of the fact Marc was wearing his clothes. Had just been asleep in (okay, on) his bed. Then there were the roadside shenanigans in upstate New York. *This is Marc. He thinks he's gay, so we fooled around during a blizzard. I'm an idiot, so I figure we're going to try it again sometime.*

Yeah, no.

He could feel the weight of Mel's curiosity as she shook Marc's hand, though.

For his part, Marc slipped easily into his usual role: Marcus Winnamore, rising star of B and M. His outfit no longer mattered. His smiles dazzled and his wit charmed. Within minutes, both Mel and Jerome were chuckling and following Marc toward the dining room as though they were his guests, not the other way around.

Marc remained admirably cool throughout dinner, entertaining everyone with stories from both college and his career at the firm. He asked questions, too, and listened attentively as Henry's father talked about his hardware store, H&H.

"It's been in the family two generations already," Heinrich said proudly.

Marc darted a glance toward Henry before asking, "What does the other H stand for?"

"My grandfather," Henry replied with a grin, then answered Marc's next question before he could ask it. "If I have a son, I have to call him Heinrich. Officially, he'll be Heinrich Auttenberg the sixth. It's a long and illustrious line."

Mel snickered. His father laughed.

"If you have a daughter, do you have to call her Melissa?"

"I'm going to call my dog Melissa."

More laughter. Mel kicked as many ankles as she could reach beneath the table. Then a warm hand crept over his knee and squeezed. Henry glanced over at Marc and met a quick and sneaky sorta smile. He blamed the sudden flush of his cheeks on the wine.

His mother spoke up. "If Henry has children"—oh God, she was giving Marc a meaningful look—"he can call them what he wants. We already know he's not going into the hardware business with us." She did the books for H&H. He'd had to get his aptitude for numbers from somewhere.

"Maybe when I retire." Henry's cheeks were burning now.

His father reached around the table to clap him on the shoulder. "You'll be what you want to be, Heinrich."

It'd be easier to just lean over a candle. Give his cheeks a permanent burn.

Marc's smile was less sneaky, more wistful, and Henry remembered the same look from the car. It spoke to him, this quieter expression. It was louder than the cut of Marc's cheekbones, the depthless gaze of his eyes. His mouth, so kissable. His sharp nose.

The package of Marcus Winnamore, handsome and successful. He hadn't expected it, but he liked it. Marc's inner vulnerability made him all the more attractive and it changed the focus of Henry's winsome crush. Tempered his fears. Made him want Marc even more.

After dinner, everyone wanted Henry to open his gifts. Cheeks still uncomfortably hot, Henry sorted through the pile. His eyebrows nearly leapt from the top of his head when he saw a tag labelled "Marc." Wordlessly, he handed the small package over and picked up the one his nephew had obviously wrapped, knowing that was the one he had to open first. He looked up to smile at his nephew and noticed Marc hadn't touched the gift in his lap. Well, he'd touched it. His fingers were resting lightly on the corner of the box, and if he stared at the paper any harder, he'd set it alight.

Henry tore the paper from the package in his lap, revealing a set of graphic novels he would definitely read. Grinning, he thanked his nephew and reached for the next box. Marc was still picking at the paper on his.

Lissa clucked her tongue. "We don't need to reuse the paper, Marc."

Curious now—and hoping his mother hadn't bought his almost-maybe-sort-of-boyfriend a package of underwear—Henry waited with everyone else for Marc to finish opening his gift.

It was socks. Henry wanted to die until Marc shook out the first pair, adorned with Santas stuck in chimneys. The second pair featured an intersecting pattern of Rudolph heads. Marc was laughing by the time he unfolded the third. Pie wedges. Pumpkin and apple. "These are great. Thanks."

The fourth was the most discrete: snowflakes.

"You could almost wear those ones to work," Henry said.

"I'll be wearing all of them to work." Mark picked up the card from the bottom of the box and opened it. A green piece of paper fluttered out of the fold. Henry recognized it with an audible groan.

His parents didn't do gift cards like everyone else. They gave cash. Fifty bucks a card. How embarrassing.

Marc leaned over to pick it up and tucked it behind the card as he read, "Because you never know when you'll need a little something extra."

"It's to put in your wallet and forget about," Heinrich explained. "Life has enough surprises, hmm? All our kids carry an extra fifty, just in case."

Marc's smile wavered only slightly before he nodded. "Thank you. That's... Thank you." He tucked the fifty into his wallet and went back to messing about with his socks.

The rest of the evening passed too quickly. Henry could have wished for a quiet moment with Marc, but in all honesty, he was enjoying the company of his family too much to look for opportunities. Then there was the fact Marc looked to be having just as comfortable a time. He was enjoying himself, even when chatting with Henry's nephew.

When Marc stood up, covering a yawn, and asked if he could call a cab, Henry's father and sister both objected.

"I can drive you."

"Jer and I can drop you off on our way."

Marc was polite in his refusal of a ride and no one pressed too hard. He wasn't allowed to leave without a suitcase full of freshly pressed laundry and several Tupperware containers of Christmas leftovers, however. Thankfully, the entire family didn't insist on waiting on the porch with them for Marc's cab to arrive.

"Do you regret coming over?" Henry leaned against the rail, curling his fingers over the edge to steady himself as he looked up. The ambient light of Dorchester reflected dully from a ceiling of murky grey. The stars were rarely visible this close to the city.

The rail creaked quietly as Marc leaned next to him, facing the other way, looking back toward the living room window. "No." His voice was quiet and contemplative. "Might have been the nicest Christmas I've ever had."

"Should I apologize for the socks?"

"Actually, I could have used some new underwear."

"God, don't tell Mom. She'll send you a care package."

Marc didn't answer that, and Henry didn't press for more information than his silence already gave. Instead, he leaned out again, looking up at the sky.

"Looking for stars?" Marc asked.

"In the summer I used to climb out my window and lie on the roof, waiting for the stars to come out. I don't know if I ever really saw them or not. It's hard to tell if my memory of starry skies comes from trips to the country or movies or maybe some miracle glimpse from this close to the city. But I always imagined them up there, you know?"

"Did you count them?"

"Huh?"

"The stars." Marc turned around and leaned out, looking up. "How many are there?"

Henry swallowed a short laugh. "One summer I got to three hundred and twenty-six before I lost count."

"I knew it!"

"I used to pretend the planes were stars too. Falling stars. I wished on every one." Why would he share something like that?

"Of course you did."

Henry snorted softly.

"I saw the stars on your ceiling. Upstairs. I figured you used to wish on those too."

That he had, sometimes, would never be shared, even under the most excruciating torture.

Marc leaned closer and murmured, "What did you wish for, Auttenberg?"

"For someone to call me Henry." He turned, met Marc's gaze and lifted one eyebrow in question. "What about you?"

"I don't wish on stars."

"Yeah, you do. Everyone wishes on a falling star, airplane or not, at least once in their life."

They were close enough for a kiss to happen and the delicious tease of proximity and promise was almost better than a brush of lips. Marc seemed to think so as well. He remained still, smiling, eyes sparkling in the reflected light of the window behind them, the streetlights outside the porch and some inner glow of certainty and amusement.

Then the kiss happened. Henry didn't initiate it, neither did Marc. They simply came together, lips touching, moving, whispering. Exchanging wishes and secrets. It was a warm and affectionate kiss. One of the nicest kisses Henry had ever had.

"What will you wish for tonight, Henry?" Marc's words tickled his lips.

His name could have sounded ironic. Instead, it felt like another gift, which was really, really stupid. As was his answer of *you*.

Licking his lips, Henry drew back a little. "What would you wish for?"

Marc smiled. "A date."

"A date?"

"With you."

"That's not a wish."

"New Year's Eve. Come to Shelly Flore's party with me."

A date with a man he really wanted to spend time with at a party he'd never attend alone.

A date with Marcus Winnamore.

Henry squinted up at the sky, looking for a sign. A single star, a trail of light. Something. He saw nothing. This one was up to him. He looked back at Marc and drew in a fortifying breath. "Okay."

A cab crunched to a halt against the snowbank lining the sidewalk and honked once. Marc shrugged into his coat and picked up his suitcase. "See you tomorrow?"

"Yeah. Be…"

"Be what?"

"Be safe, okay? Roads are still messed up."

"You're sweet, Auttenberg." He grinned. "Just like your family." It could have been an insult, but it wasn't. From Marc, it was a statement of fact. He leaned in to peck Henry's lips once more. "Night, and thanks."

It was only as the cab moved away that Henry realized they hadn't actually exchanged wishes. Not real ones. He had an idea of what Marc might want, though, and figured they wanted the same thing. Security. Family. Someone by their side. To personalize that dream any further would require a real star—not an imagined one, or a glow-in-the-dark sticker. Henry was tempted to do it anyway. Wish it for Marc, wish it for himself. Instead, he counted the dark patches in the clouds, pretending they were stars, and imagined each one was a chance to make one of their wishes come true.

Counting
DOWN

*I*t's been a week since a Christmas Eve blizzard changed the course of Marcus Winnamore's life. Plan A is now Plan B, and the first item on his new agenda is taking Henry Auttenberg on a date. They've been invited to a New Year's Eve party, and Marc is counting down the hours until midnight... until he can kiss Henry in front of his colleagues and friends.

Things don't quite work out to plan. Finding the elevator out of service, Marc and Henry check the stairs, only to choose the wrong door and become locked in the basement. Close quarters once again make for close conversation, and as they explore every avenue of escape, they also explore the deepening attraction between them. For Marc, this isn't an experiment. Will he still feel that way when he has to admit to someone other than Henry that he's gay?

Chapter
ONE

He had his hand on another man's leg. He, Marcus Winnamore, had his hand on another man's thigh, and if he moved it up a little, he could graze something else he never thought he'd touch—willingly, longingly—another man's junk. Not just anyone's either. Next to him sat Henry Auttenberg—the guy who had fascinated him for six months. Mostly, it had been his mouth. His sinfully full lips. His eyes too, with their mutable color. Were they gray or green? Then there was Henry's laugh, so rare and precious.

A week ago, Marc's life had been following Plan A. But after spending the Christmas Eve blizzard trapped in a car with Henry—where he'd given in to the lure of Henry's mouth and more—Marc had to formulate a new plan. For consistency, he called it Plan B.

He liked Plan B. It felt right. It felt damned good when he wasn't questioning the fact this new plan had been formed over a kiss.

At least he had a plan.

Floating free and reckless, under the spell of the mouth and eyes of the guy he'd been secretly fantasizing over for six months, might work in a snowstorm. Under threat of frozen death. Now they were back in the real world. About to attend a New Year's Eve party given by one of the firm's partners. Their first date.

It was okay to be nervous, wasn't it?

Marc moved his hand a little higher.

He felt rather than saw Henry turn his attention from the passing vista of Boston at night. "Any higher and I'm going to have difficulty getting out of the cab."

Marc's gut tightened. His jeans did too. Just the thought of Henry hard at his touch. "We should have skipped the party." The light tone he'd tried for didn't come off. Marc cleared his throat. "We could have stayed at your place."

"It was your idea to go to this party."

"Right." Marc resisted the urge to clear his throat again. Anxious wasn't his thing. Onward, upward! Attending this party—with Henry—was a necessary step.

Henry nudged his shoulder. "Have you got a plan?"

"What? No. Why would I—"

"Marcus Winnamore always has a plan." Henry offered one of his sly smiles.

"Forward momentum requires forward movement." Honestly, he didn't know where he found this shit sometimes.

Henry's smile widened. "You're going to use this party to announce *us* to the office, aren't you? That we're more than colleagues, and that you're into kissing guys."

Marc huffed in annoyance. Was he that transparent? Probably. Either way, kissing Henry at midnight in front of friends and coworkers from Beck and Meyer would be as good as issuing a memo. It'd be done. "I thought a social situation would be preferable to someone finding us in the copy room."

Henry chuckled, the sound disturbingly low and sexy—probably because they'd already violated the copy room. The offices of Beck and Meyer were very quiet between Christmas and New Year's. Marc twitched his hand away from Henry's crotch. Henry captured his fingers before he could get too far. "You're cute when you're anxious."

"I'm not anxious."

"Of course not."

Marc straightened his spine. "And you can keep your *cute* comments to yourself."

"Yeah, wouldn't want to soften the image."

Henry's smile might have had an ironic twist, but his tone conveyed nothing but warmth. Marc was unused to seeing him like this. Relaxed and making jokes. Henry came across as the quiet type. Marc had always sensed there was a lot more going on beneath the staid exterior, however.

The cab coasted to a stop outside the apartment building of senior partner Shelly Flores. Marc had visited twice before, for previous parties. The apartment occupied the entire top floor, including a patio that would not be usable tonight—unless you liked pretending you were visiting the Arctic Circle. Either way, the endless windows would offer up a good view of the fireworks over the harbor.

Marc paid the fare, and they tumbled out into the remains of the blizzard that had brought them together. Banked snow three feet high hid the sidewalk, with gaps every twelve feet or so allowing access to the buildings behind. Marc reached back for Henry and clasped his fingers before picking his way through the short and icy tunnel.

When he got to the other side, Henry leaned in close. "Now that we're safely out of the cab and at no risk of spending New Year's Eve stuck in a snowbank, I'm going to comment on the fact neither of us is wearing gloves. Again. What is it with us and not dressing for the weather?"

"I've got gloves in the pocket of my coat."

"Of course you have." Henry grinned, the shoulders of his wool coat hitching up beneath his ears. Yep, Henry was adorable when he smiled, especially when he grinned. His whole face changed. A switch got flipped inside him. He morphed from serious, possibly shy, and somewhat aloof, into someone eminently approachable.

Marc pressed a quick kiss to Henry's cold lips, delighting in the thrill of kissing a man—kissing Henry—and doing so openly. "Let's get inside before someone abducts us. I am not spending our first date locked in the trunk of a car with you."

Henry's hand tucked securely in his, Marc led the way inside the building. The style of the lobby belied the wealth required to own one of the apartments above. The tenants probably preferred it that way. Not everyone liked to advertise. The lack of a doorman made Marc a little uneasy—they were in the city after all—but the marble floor shone beneath muted lighting, and there were no bums lurking in the corners. Place didn't smell like a bus terminal.

A sheet of paper taped to the buffed brass elevator doors stood out against the otherwise tidy space. Marc peered at it while Henry read the message. "Elevator out. Use the stairs."

As if to confirm the irritability of systems within the building, the lights in the lobby chose that moment to flicker.

Marc looked up and around, trying to follow the direction of the bent arrow on the sign. "Over here," he said.

Henry tugged his hand. "Not this way?" He nodded toward the front of the building.

"Stairs will be back here somewhere." Marc led the way behind the square wall of the elevator housing to the rear of the lobby where they met with two doors, neither of which was marked stairs. One did have a sign. *Maintenance*. Marc pushed the other door open. The lights dimmed again. "Not going to be much of a party if the lights go out," he remarked.

"I dunno." Henry moved up close behind him, his breath tickling the back of Marc's neck. "After that tease in the cab, I kinda like the idea of finding a dark corner."

Marc's pulse kicked up, sending his blood zinging throughout his veins. First the cab, now this. Every time he got close to Henry, he lost the ability to think and breathe and function like a rational being. Plans got changed.

He half turned, keeping the door open with his shoulder. "We could still get a cab back to your place. Mulligan's would have been a public enough venue to announce *us*."

"Me at Mulligan's?" Henry had the crazy idea he needed a personal invitation to the weekly office outing at the nearby pub. Just one of his idiosyncrasies.

Marc smiled. "Your attendance is required from now on."

"Required, huh?" Henry pushed him through the door and into a dark hall. "Maybe we should negotiate terms before going upstairs."

The door shut behind them, plunging them into darkness. Pulse hammering, Marc allowed himself to be nudged back against a wall, already lifting his chin as Henry coasted along his jaw. A hand— presumably Henry's—snuck around behind his neck, warm fingers angling his head forward as lips captured his. Marc fell into the kiss, the taste of another man's mouth. Henry's mouth again, and as exciting as the feel of Henry's thigh beneath his palm.

A moan built up in his throat. He released it and shivered as he felt it returned, Henry trembling against him. Marc caught Henry's lower lip and sucked. He tucked his hands inside Henry's coat, seeking skin. Layers of clothing frustrated him. Marc rocked his hips forward, needing the pressure of something against his constrained erection. Another moan from Henry evidenced a similar need.

Then Henry was pulling back, his hands to either side of Marc's face, palms cool against Marc's cheeks. "Fuck."

As a rule, Henry didn't curse. Neither of them did. His use of that single word nudged Marc's temperature a little higher. "You said it."

Henry leaned in to kiss him again, quickly, almost chastely, before he backed away entirely. "We should go upstairs."

"Yeah, we should."

"To the party."

"Right. The party."

Snorting softly, Henry moved back another step and tipped his head toward the dimly lit end of the hall. "C'mon."

There were stairs back there, but instead of leading up they dropped down into the basement and the only source of light. Frowning, Marc poked his head into the stairwell. "Do you think we have to go down before we go up?"

"Maybe?"

Henry withdrew, leaving a cool space beside Marc, and went back to the lobby door. A flat click echoed down the dark hall. "Um…." Another click and rattle. A thud, a mutter. "I think it's locked."

Chapter
TWO

*W*hat?"

"The door is locked," Henry said. "It's like a security door. We can't unlock it from this side without a card." He pointed out the small black card reader neither of them had noticed before.

"How did we even get it open?"

"Dunno. Maybe someone else tried to come this way and didn't pull it closed properly." Or let it slam behind them as they focused on a kiss. "Let's just go see if there's another staircase at the bottom of the other one. Sometimes these old buildings have crazy architecture."

Marc licked his lips. "Okay."

An awful tight feeling low in his gut hinted they'd find nothing at the bottom of the stairs but the bottom of the stairs. Still, it was worth a try. Every plan had a backup. Henry was already angling past him. Marc stepped ahead. He was a take-charge kinda guy. A locked door wasn't going to be the end of his night.

The stairs terminated in another hallway lined by four doors.

Henry issued a choky sort of chuckle. "We're going to spend our first date locked in a basement on New Year's Eve, after spending Christmas Eve stuck in a car during a blizzard."

It wasn't time to panic. Not yet. "Nah, we're still coming up with ideas for a new reality show. First one was called *The Freezer*, right? Survivors get shunted to *The Basement* for season two."

Henry tried one of the doors. When it opened, he stuck his head in. "Or *The Laundry*. Where all dirty secrets come clean."

Marc groaned. "That is so bad."

"Yep." Henry let the door close and wrapped his arms around himself.

"Cold?"

"No, just...." Henry shook his head. "Let's try the other doors."

Two were locked. The last opened to the odor of wet cardboard and old banana skins. Marc fumbled for a light switch and found it. A rusted trash compactor the size of a Dumpster took up half the concrete room. Stacked boxes vied for the rest of the space, leaving just enough for the door to swing open.

Marc shut off the light and closed the door. "Okay, we're not going to be the only guests who make this mistake. We'll just camp out up by the lobby door and wait for someone else to open it."

Henry produced his cell phone. "Or we could call for help." His brow furrowed. "Except I have no signal."

A deepening sense of déjà vu enveloped Marc as he pulled his cell phone out. He noted the time first. Just after nine o'clock. Three hours until midnight. Maybe their first public kiss wouldn't be public at all. "No signal here either." He resisted the urge to tap the screen. "Must be all the marble in the foyer or just being in an old building. We might have better luck up by the door."

Getting back to the door suddenly felt imperative. It could have been opened three or four times while they'd been poking around down in the basement. Without a key? Probably not, or there would be more contestants for *The Laundry* clomping down the stairs.

They returned to the hall where the lobby door remained locked despite several attempts to toggle the handle. It did not give to a gentle touch or a rough rattle. Marc pressed his forehead to the painted metal and breathed in and out slowly. He was tempted to count, but that was Henry's thing. Guy had apparently counted the fence posts between Syracuse and Boston. Who did that?

In the back of his mind, a digital display blinked into the darkness, showing the time ticking away toward midnight. Marc accepted the image with a mental smile. Everyone counted down the hours to midnight on New Year's Eve.

Henry touched his back firmly enough for Marc to feel the pressure through his coat. "Someone will come. What time was the party supposed to start?"

"E-mail said eight."

"Okay, so we're only an hour late. Bessler will be later than we were. He has no sense of time whatsoever."

True enough, but Luke Bessler wasn't at last year's party. Marc turned around. "You weren't at the party last year."

"No."

"Have you ever socialized with anyone from the firm?"

"I spent Christmas Eve trapped in a car with Marcus Winnamore."

One side of Marc's mouth lifted in a sideways grin. "Ass." He pulled his phone out and checked for a signal. Nothing. "Dammit. Check your phone."

Light flashed across Henry's face as he woke his cell. "One bar. Who should I call?"

"Shelly Flores. It's her building and her stupid sign on the elevator. She can send someone down to rescue us."

"What's her number?"

Digits related and entered, Henry dialed and pressed the phone to his ear. His expression brightened, then dimmed in the low light. He pulled the phone away and peered at the screen again. "Lost my bar."

They messed with both phones for ten minutes, each minute measured by an ominous tick in Marc's head. The phantom display read nine thirty in big, creepy luminous digits by the time they were done. Two and a half hours until midnight, and no one had tried the door.

With a short sigh, Henry slid down the wall to a seated position on one side of the hall. Marc copied him, sitting on the other side. Their legs intersected in the middle. Henry closed his ankles around one of Marc's for a second before letting go.

"So," he said.

"So." Marc played with his phone. Lighting the screen, shuffling through his apps, staring through all of it.

"Not going to say this is my worst first date ever. It's not over yet."

Marc looked up with another smile. What was it about Henry? He was as unassuming as they came. Good-looking, but not showy with it. He had the wholesome thing going, and having met his family over Christmas, Marc could see why. The Auttenbergs were all like Henry. Quiet, but in a warm and cozy way. Any lack of conversation was due to an ability to exist comfortably in one another's presence.

"You've had a worse date than this?" he asked.

Henry made a small noise in his throat. "Heck yeah. I told you about the guy who nearly broke my jaw, right?"

"You mentioned it. Someone who wasn't quite straight, but not ready to be gay?"

Sighing, Henry rubbed the side of his face. "Tell me about your worst date."

"Hmm, worst date." Marc consulted the clock in his head before dredging up a seven-year-old memory. "Kate Merton. That was New Year's Eve too. I made the mistake of going home for the holidays, and my parents told me I was taking Kate to the party at the country club."

"Told you?"

"Mr. and Mrs. Winnamore request your presence...." Marc scoffed. "That's an invitation to breakfast."

"Chummy."

"You have no idea."

Henry's ankles closed around his again and held this time.

"I already knew Kate," Marc continued. "We grew up together in a way. I mean, I didn't do a lot of growing up at home. I was shipped off to prep school as soon I was old enough."

"How did you get from prep school to BU?"

"My one act of rebellion." With a quick smile, he returned Henry's ankle hug. "Or my first, I guess. Staying in Boston and choosing my own career does not sit well with Mr. and Mrs. Winnamore."

Henry snorted softly.

"So, Kate. We saw each other some summers. She's.... If I had to get married, she'd be a good choice. Even my parents agree on that one."

"If you had to get married."

Marc shrugged.

"The date?" Henry prompted.

"I was pissed at my parents, so I got drunk. Sailed right past friendly to nasty. Or maybe friendly wasn't an option that night. I was loud, abrasive. Rude."

"You, rude?"

"Heh. Seriously, you have no idea what an ass I can be."

Henry's silence suggested he might.

"Worst part was that Kate tried really hard to enjoy herself. She made excuses for me and managed to pull me away before at least one fight erupted."

"Wow. How drunk were you?"

"I tried to have sex with her on one of the pool lounges. In full display of the dining room windows."

"I think you're describing Kate's worst date ever."

"Probably."

"How far did you get?"

"With what?"

"The sex. Did you moon the dining room?"

A laugh pushed out of Marc's throat, surprising him. "You know, I don't recall. Though I do sort of remember the feeling of a cool breeze on my ass. So it's entirely possible I did. But with the inside being lit and the pool deck dark, it was probably a pretty private affair."

His parents had certainly never mentioned it. Thank Christ.

Another silence from Henry, this one weighted with questions. Marc nudged his foot.

"Did you know, then, that you might be gay?" Henry asked.

Marc shook his head. "No. I mean… no. It wasn't that I was in denial. I didn't secretly watch gay porn or anything. Not then." That habit had started after Henry arrived at Beck and Meyer. "I was just angry. I wanted to like Kate. I did like her. I've liked a lot of the women I've dated. But none of them…." Marc paused again as a blush crawled up to his cheeks. None of the women he'd been out with, or slept with, excited him the way Henry did. He'd never obsessed over the physical characteristics of any of the women he'd dated, and the act of sex had always felt mechanical.

"Can you hear voices?" Henry had his head tilted toward the door.

Marc couldn't hear anything but the thrum of his own pulse. Still, he tipped his head to a like angle—as if both of them leaning toward the door would focus the sound—and listened. Faintly, through thick masonry and fireproof steel, he heard something.

Pushing to his feet, he pounded on the door. "Hey!"

His voice echoed back at him, loud and flat in the enclosed space. The sound of his fists against the door seemed equally one-dimensional. The locking mechanism rattled, but only on their side.

The door remained solid. Immovable. He was sure that from the lobby, his cries for rescue would be muted.

Henry joined him, banging and yelling, and for a second, Marc felt like grinning. They'd look ridiculous if someone opened the door. Hands raised, mouths opened. Gratitude would make them sillier.

No one opened the door. Marc stopped pounding and yelling, then reached over to grab Henry's arm, indicating he should do the same. He pressed his ear to the cold steel and listened. Nothing. "Dammit."

"Someone else will come."

Henry was an optimist. He'd been sure they'd be rescued by a snowplow too. And he'd known how to survive the cold until then. Did he have a plan for this situation? "Anything in that survival book of yours about being locked in the basement?"

"No."

"Maybe we should check out the other rooms again. Those other doors. Maybe there's an internal phone or call button or something in the laundry or the trash room." An exit behind the compactor?

"I dunno. What if someone opens the door while we're gone?"

"Do you want to stay up here?"

Henry's frown wasn't visible. Marc's eyes had adjusted to the low light, but his read on Henry mostly came from his silences. Thinking about it, he realized he'd been doing that for a while— even before they'd gotten together. Henry was so often quiet at the office that Marc measured him more by what he didn't say.

Henry turned, and the light from the stairwell caught his face. He *was* frowning.

"What's up?" Marc asked.

"I'm thinking."

"What's to think about? Two of us, two avenues of discovery. Divide and conquer."

"There you go with the glib sayings."

"What?"

"Nothing, I just…." Henry raised his hands. "I'll wait here."

"Okay." Marc moved away from the door, uncertain he should leave at all. Henry's sudden change of mood was weird. Should he ask? Were they that far into their relationship? Though this was their first date, they'd technically been together for a week. He'd already met Henry's family. They'd spent a holiday together. Sort of. And they'd had sex—or what Henry described as sex. What with being stuck in Albany for nearly two days with no privacy and limited time together since their return to Boston, they hadn't gotten the chance to use condoms yet, so Marc's jury was still out. Not that he didn't like what they did together. The feel of Henry's hand, mouth—

"Are you going?" Henry wrapped his arms around himself again.

"We'll get out of here. I promise."

Because no one died in the basements of buildings in Boston. Not in this neighborhood, anyway. At worst, someone would come to do their laundry tomorrow. Or the next day. The clock in Marc's head flickered, racing forward through two days of time. His breath quickened, and his pulse skipped all over the place.

He gripped Henry's arm. "I'm going to find a way out, even if it's just so I can kiss you in front of everyone at midnight."

Henry smiled and nodded. Marc released his shoulder and continued down the hall.

The compactor room was a bust. There was a door behind a stack of boxes, but even without the chunky chain and padlock barring access, Marc figured the thick paint surrounding the edges had had enough time to harden into concrete. They'd need a chisel to get the door open. Still, he picked at the paint—just to test his theory—and ended up with a stupidly sharp sliver beneath his nail.

Twenty years and bloody nails might see them free.

Sucking on the injured finger, he checked the two locked doors again. Just in case. Both rattled in their frames, but neither gave him the feeling something more than a room lurked beyond. Marc couldn't explain the sensation. He didn't think of himself as a particularly metaphysical person. But Henry had changed some of his perceptions.

Muttering to himself, he ducked into the laundry room and flipped on the light. A neat row of washers, three large dryers set into the wall, a folding table, a TV mounted high up on a stand, and two folding chairs tucked into a corner beside a laundry tub. No other door—though, if his mental map was right, the wall of dryers should face the back of the building.

He looked up.

Set into the ceiling over the row of washers was a large vent. Huge. Big enough for a guy to squeeze through—if he were so inclined. They'd have to pull the cover off, put a chair on top of the machines to climb up, and if the vent went straight up, well, that'd be as far as they got.

Marc leaned out of the door. "Henry?"

No answer.

He tried again from the bottom of the stairs. "Auttenberg!"

Footsteps, then a dark head poked around the corner. "What?"

"Get your ass down here. I want to try something."

Henry descended the stairs at a cautious pace. "Now's not really the time—"

"Not that." His grin was automatic. "Not right this minute."

"What makes you think I'm going to bottom for you, anyway?"

Marc shifted in place, caught between the urge to clench and thrust while standing still. He was face-to-face with Henry, meeting him eye to eye, because they were pretty much the same height and not that different physically. The idea of Henry under him appealed greatly. Being the one on the bottom, though…. He'd thought about it. Of course he had.

Leaning forward, he spoke near Henry's ear. "Someone's gotta show me what to do."

Henry's breath caught, held, and rushed back out. "Nothing like learning from doing."

And there it was again, the hidden *something* that made Henry so fascinating. The way he refused to be cowed. The way he returned every poke with equal force.

Capturing Henry's ear between his teeth, Marc nipped, then kissed. Henry's skin tasted good. He didn't use flowery soap or cologne, and the scent of his shampoo was oddly familiar. Not the same as Marc used, but something like it. Henry's cheek moved past his, smooth and freshly shaven. Their lips met, mouths opening instantly. A moan built quickly in Marc's throat. Again. Couldn't he kiss Henry without voicing need?

No, he couldn't.

Tongues tangling, the taste of Henry claiming him. The feel of Henry's hands sliding beneath his coat. Marc forgot they were standing in a hall. Forgot the numbers ticking over in his head, counting down to midnight. Forgot whether he wanted to thrust or clench. Did both. Backed Henry into a wall and kissed him with a fevered intensity. Henry's breath cooled his lips as their mouths moved and realigned, and quick pants echoed between soft moans and groans.

A gentle rock forward brought their hips together—groins connecting. Hardness to hardness. Marc reached down to trace the ridge beneath Henry's fly. Henry caught his lip and bit it—gently. All of Marc's breath left him in a rush.

Henry let go and stepped back. "The door...."

Marc nipped at Henry's kiss-swollen lips. "Huh?"

"The door. We're not watching the door."

Whoops. Marc looked up and listened. For a second or two, he heard nothing but the pounding of his own heart and the swish of blood behind his ears. Leaning forward, he nosed Henry's cheek. "I think that kiss was worth being trapped a little longer."

Henry's cheek moved. He was smiling. "Maybe." Quietly, he cleared his throat. "So why did you call me down here?"

"Oh." Marc straightened and stepped back. "There's a vent in the ceiling of the laundry room. I thought we could check it out."

"Hmm."

"What does that mean? Hmm?"

"I'm trying to decide if crawling through a building's ventilation system would be better or worse than spending New Year's Eve sitting by a fire door."

"It could be an old laundry chute."

"Is that supposed to be a compelling argument?"

Marc chuckled. "I was just thinking out loud."

"All right, let's check it out."

Once inside the laundry room, Henry repeated his *hmm*. Looking up, he squinted at the vent cover and dug something out from under his coat. It looked like a pair of pliers folded in half.

"What is that, like a Swiss Army Knife?" Marc asked.

"Leatherman. Fewer tools, but stronger."

"And you carry it because...."

Henry glanced at him, his expression blank. "It's useful?"

"Is this something you got from that book?"

"Why are you so hung up on the fact I read a survival book?"

"Because you live in Boston, not Syria."

"It helped us out in the blizzard."

Snorting, Marc pointed upward. "Okay, Gadget Man. See if you can loosen that vent."

Henry climbed on top of the washing machine. "You know, waiting for someone to open the door is probably easier."

"If someone opens the door."

"We did."

"We also tried to drive through a blizzard."

"That was all you, Marc. All you."

Henry poked at a corner of the vent, then chose the appropriate tool. He'd just put it to a screw when a faint peal of laugher rolled down the hallway outside, followed by a quiet boom that echoed through the walls and floor.

Marc looked up just as Henry looked down. Their gazes met. They spoke at the same time.

"Dammit."

"The door."

Chapter
THREE

*M*arc abandoned Henry on top of the washing machine and ran into the hall. "Wait!" he called, knowing it was too late.

He tripped on the bottom step and spilled forward, catching himself with the heels of his palms. The gritty concrete dug into his flesh before he pushed away and continued up the stairs. Running was futile. The boom had been the door closing, but he couldn't make himself slow or stop until he reached the end of the hall, the dark mass of the fire door, and the echoing quiet. He breathed into the pause, listening for voices on the other side. He heard only Henry running up behind him.

"Bang on the door," Henry huffed.

"They're gone."

"Try anyway!" Henry pushed up beside him and attacked the door with balled fists. He even kicked it a few times. "Why aren't you helping? We can make more noise together."

Crossing his arms, Marc leaned back against the wall. "Because it's too late. They were gone before I even got out of the laundry."

Henry continued to flail at the door, as if he were experiencing a fit. Marc wondered if he should interrupt or let whatever it was run its course. This was a Henry he hadn't seen before.

When Henry showed no sign of calming, Marc put a hand on his arm. "Henry."

Shaking off Marc's hand, Henry backed away and leaned against the opposite wall. Marc's eyes hadn't fully adjusted to the darkness again, so he couldn't read the expression on his face, but the sudden quiet snapped with tension.

What should he say? If Henry were female, Marc would try a gentle comment. Even as he thought of it, though, he wondered if such a thing would be wrong in any situation. If Henry's gender should or should not dictate how Marc interacted with him. This was a part of being gay he hadn't considered. With both of them being guys, would that mean they didn't talk about feelings and stuff? They'd been pretty open in the car Christmas Eve. It had taken a while, and they hadn't suddenly started sharing their most intimate secrets, but they'd talked.

"How come you weren't as upset when we were trapped in the car?" Marc asked.

"I'm not upset."

"Henry—"

"This is my fault."

"What?"

Henry gestured toward the closed door. "This. If I hadn't pushed you in here to kiss you, the door wouldn't have shut."

"I'm not blaming you." Marc stepped forward. "And even if we did decide your actions were responsible, it's over and done with. The door is shut. We can't open it. Assigning blame isn't going to change our situation."

Henry's only answer was a sharp sigh.

"What is this really about?" Marc asked.

"I don't like being locked up."

"I think we've established that."

Henry's breathing slowed to a normal pace, but anxiety still rolled from him. Marc had never seen him this tense—and he had no idea what to do about it.

"I was locked in a basement when I was a kid," Henry finally said, his voice quiet. "I haven't thought about it in years. I didn't really figure I had an issue with basements." He shrugged in the dark. "I guess I do."

"What happened?"

"I don't think I want to talk about it."

"Is it because you don't like to talk about it or because I'm your date?"

Henry looked up sharply. "What kind of question is that?"

"I was just thinking about how different it is to be with a guy, like in ways I hadn't expected. Like, should I open doors for you, or should you open them for me, or is that just weird?"

He could feel Henry staring at him in the dark.

"Or, like right now. You're upset and I'd like to comfort you. But I'm not sure how. If you were a woman, I'd, well, I'd probably pat your shoulder, or maybe hug you or tell you a joke, or offer to listen."

Henry didn't answer, and Marc let the silence grow between them, unsure what his next step should be. Slowly, his eyes grew accustomed to the dark, and he could see Henry was staring at the floor, forehead creased.

He looked up. "It was my uncle. I used to visit his farm for a couple of weeks every summer when I was younger. The year I turned thirteen, he caught me kissing a boy down by the pond and shut me in the basement as punishment. Left me in there overnight but didn't leave me alone. He read the Bible through the door to me for hours on end, passages interspersed with his own sermons on the evils of sodomy. He ate dinner there, describing everything he was eating, what I was missing out on."

Marc could feel his lower jaw unhinging. You read about shit like this, but the stories were just that, weren't they?

Grow up, Winnamore. You know full well this sort of abuse happens. Small incidents, larger ones. And this wasn't the only episode Henry had shared with him. There'd also been the guy who'd nearly broken Henry's jaw.

"It was a long time ago, and I don't think about it. Not really. I didn't even tell my parents about it until the next spring when they asked if I wanted to visit Uncle Jeb that summer. That's…." He barked out a laugh. "That's how I came out to them. Fun, huh?"

"But they were okay with it, right?"

Henry's family seemed to have no qualms at Christmas about Henry rolling up with a male friend who was quite obviously *more* than a friend. They'd welcomed Marc warmly.

"They were great. Mostly. My mom cried, but Dad was really cool. He just thumped me on the back and said, 'You are who you are, Heinrich.'"

Marc swallowed. "Would it be wrong to say I feel fortunate to have missed out on the juvenile gay experience?"

"No." The back of Henry's jacket whispered against the wall as he shrugged. "Sounds like you had your own stuff to deal with, anyway."

"I was never locked in the basemen by a Bible-bashing madman. Where was Jeb's wife? Was he married?"

Henry laughed without mirth. "No, never married. I actually think he was gay."

Marc felt his upper lip curl. "I'd feel sorry for the old coot if not for that story, then."

"Old coot?"

Marc took a turn at shrugging. "I've got a mental picture of him. Check shirt, suspenders, coonskin hat."

"Not all farms exist in the 1950s."

"S'pose not. So…." Marc angled his head a little to peer into Henry's eyes. "You good?"

Henry met his gaze. In the dim light, Marc couldn't see the color, but he just about had it memorized—Henry had mostly gray eyes, and they were kind of beautiful.

"You can open doors for me if you want. If you get to them first. I'd do the same for you," Henry said.

"What about the hugs?"

"I'd never have figured you as the hugging type."

"You don't know me very well, do you?"

"No."

Henry moved away from the wall, taking a step toward him. Marc closed the distance and pulled Henry into an embrace that quickly surpassed casual. With them being of similar height and build, Marc had supposed hugging Henry might feel awkward. It didn't. Henry fit against him and, with a small adjustment for shoulders, into his arms.

"This isn't how I imagined it," Marc said.

"What?"

Henry made to pull out of his arms, and Marc tightened his grip. "No, I like it. It's just different. I don't think I've ever hugged a guy before."

"It's not a requirement, you know. For being gay."

A chuckle bubbled up in Marc's chest. He released the hug, pausing to kiss Henry's temple as he let go. "You're such a dope."

"What makes you say that?"

"It's just, like, I'm trying all this stuff out. Holding your hand, kissing you in the street. Hugging you. Molesting you in the copy room and…." Marc's thoughts caught up with his tongue.

With the exception of the kiss that had trapped them behind the fire door, he was the one making most of the advances. Henry seemed to appreciate his eagerness, and he returned every kiss, every caress. He'd been the one sucking cock in the copy room—but had he dropped to his knees, or had Marc pushed him down there?

Wait, stop. Henry knew how to say no. He was full of pushback. Guy was as contrary as they came.

But….

"You're into this, right?" Marc could have wished for a more confident tone, but the question was out there now.

"What do you mean?"

Was he imagining it, or was Henry's habit of answering his questions with another question some sort of deflection? "Are you still hung up on the whole experiment thing?"

"What? No." Henry huffed out a sigh. "I'm trying to find the place between helping you figure stuff out and more."

"More?"

"This isn't the time."

"I don't understand."

"This isn't the time for a relationship talk. It's been a week, Marc. We're barely walking, and we're stuck in a hole in the ground. Maybe we should be trying to find a way out of here instead of figuring out if the gay is going to stick."

Marc sucked in a breath. "You do think I'm just experimenting."

"Is that so unreasonable?"

"No. Yes. I mean…. Jesus. I…." The hammer of his heart did not feel good or exciting. Instead of desire, anger burned through his veins. And something else. Not humiliation, but close enough to it. Marc closed his eyes and watched the patterns whirling through the dark behind his lids for a moment. The blotches of orange and red resolved into ticking numbers. Opening his eyes, he pulled out his phone to check the time. Just after ten. Two hours until midnight—two hours to something that felt as nebulous as their escape from the basement.

Marc tucked the phone back in his pocket. "You're right. Now isn't the time. So, should we camp by the door or try the laundry vent?"

Henry looked at the door, then turned to gaze down the hall. A heavy sigh pulled his shoulders down. He seemed to make a careful study of their shoes before glancing up again. "I'm sorry."

"It's cool."

Henry opened his mouth and closed it. Nodded. "Let's wait by the door for a while. Until maybe eleven. If we don't hear anyone come or go or whatever before then, we can try the laundry chute."

"Okay."

One of Henry's eyebrows quirked upward, and the hint of a smile pulled at his mouth. "It's going to kill you to sit still, isn't it?"

Marc gave in to the smile Henry was fighting. "Probably." He didn't add *But I'll try, for you.* Sorta went without saying.

Silence could be deafening. Marc had noted the phenomenon before—usually while in the company of his parents. How many dinners had he shared with them where the only sound to break the heavy quiet was the click of silverware or the occasional clank against china? Even then, too much noise had often earned a sharp look from his mother.

When he was younger, he'd often imagined that the world ended while they ate. That outside the starched silence of the dining room, the nation's capital was reduced to a smoking ruin. The president was dead, or buried in a bunker, and lawlessness brooded across the land. And there he was, stuck in a dining room with a man and a woman thoroughly disconnected with anything that mattered, being admonished for scraping his knife across a plate.

Of course, the silences had been easier to bear than the forced conversation. Sometimes his parents exchanged quiet words about their day before asking him about his. They weren't really interested. They were simply being polite. Teaching him to be polite. The only time their conversation rang with something other than emptiness was when they had something to say to him—

usually a complaint. The school had called, or was he sure he didn't want to play lacrosse this year. Why hadn't he called the Kinney girl? Had he filled out the application to Harvard yet?

Bullshit. All bullshit.

They'd never wanted to hear about his contributions to the school paper. The silly comic strip he loved creating. He should be running for class president instead of wasting his time with the AV club.

He tried it their way. Junior and senior year of high school, he picked up every elective his father suggested. Played lacrosse. Dated the daughters of his mother's friends. Ran for the student council. He'd never been more miserable.

His act of rebellion? Turning down a place at Harvard for a partial scholarship to BU to study what interested him. A career in finance. He wasn't interested in law—outside of securities regulations. He didn't want to counsel people. He didn't even really want to make a lot of money—just enough to guarantee his freedom. A sum of success he could show his father one day.

Henry's foot nudged his, and Marc looked up from the tangle of his fingers, let the complicated vines of his thoughts fall apart, remembrance and history recede back into the corners of his mind. They were seated on the floor again, each on their own side of the hallway, legs and ankles intersecting in the middle. Henry had his arms crossed over his knees, his chin resting on the shelf they formed. "You're thinking pretty hard over there."

"Why did you go into financial consultancy? Mergers and acquisitions in particular?"

Henry's brows rose, and he lifted his chin, sat back against the wall.

"I don't need the qualifying answer. It's not an interview question. I just wondered why you picked this career over all others."

"I drifted toward it in college. I've always liked numbers and figured I'd get into accounting. Then I attended a lecture on strategic mergers and became fascinated by the idea of taking two separate business entities and combining them into one. It was like a puzzle. Sometimes the pieces all fall into place. It makes sense, and you don't understand why everyone else can't see the solution. And finding the perfect match, making it work. But even when it doesn't make sense, I enjoy the challenge. Then there're the situations where you're saving a company. Breathing new life into a business that's still viable but just being mismanaged." Henry nudged his ankle again. "Why do you want to know?"

"I was just interested." Marc lifted his chin to indicate the apartment upstairs. "Shelly Flores? She hates her job. I think that's why she's so ruthless. I've been on her team for three mergers, and they've been bloody. It's like she has to punish everyone for making her do something so detestable."

"Weird."

"Yeah."

"So what about you?"

Marc thought it over for a second, but Henry's answer so clearly matched his, he didn't have to dig far. "The puzzle. Like you said. My starting angle was different. Forensic accountancy. I had this idea of...." A soft snort tickled his upper lip. "My dad's a criminal lawyer."

"Ah."

"A couple of his cases have been pretty sensational. Death threats and the like. After reading about one of his scumbag clients in the paper, I remember thinking they really needed someone to rip apart his finances. The proof would all be there."

"So your entire career is based upon a need to humiliate your father."

"When you put it like that...." Marc exhaled and leaned back against the wall. "I know you think I'm what, a go-getter? Direct? A Shelly Flores." Henry opened his mouth, but Marc overrode him. "I like building stuff. I feel like that's what we're doing. Fixing problems and making companies stronger. No, it doesn't always turn out that way, but when it does? When it's that perfect match you described, well, it's like a high, isn't it? When it all works."

"Yeah."

"And the money's good."

Henry chuckled. "Yeah, it is. Or will be when I finish paying off my loans."

"Smart guy like you didn't get a free ride?"

"Not to BU. Another school. But... I wanted to stay here."

Marc smiled. "You didn't want to leave home, and I couldn't wait to."

Henry said nothing to that, and the quiet returned, creeping gently between them with cool fingers. Marc shifted, acknowledging as he did that his buttocks were going to keep going numb as long as he continued sitting on the floor.

Then Henry spoke again, his tone quiet and confidential. "Are you going to tell your parents you think you're gay?"

"I don't think I'm gay. I know I am."

Henry made an odd sound.

"Look, I know you think I'm feeling my way here and maybe using you along the way, but it's not... that's not what I'm doing. It's like a veil has been ripped away. Like the black-and-white movie of my life has suddenly met Technicolor. I'm not scared of this, and trust me, I know all about fear. Every confident guy you meet—the go-getters? We're all hoping you buy the act. That you don't look beyond the veneer."

"What's behind the veneer?"

Good question. Marc licked his lips, recognized the nervous habit he'd worked hard to forget, then fought against the urge to press his palms to his eyes or tug at his hair. He'd started this conversation. Couldn't say why, but he'd been the one to ask the first question.

Then the answer came to him, and like the silence preceding their conversation, it rang loudly. "Me. Just me."

Henry didn't mock. Instead, he nodded. Glanced at the door and looked back at Marc. "This is pretty deep for a first date."

"It's how we roll."

"We're kinda beyond first date material, anyway."

"Yeah."

Henry kicked at his ankle and smiled. "I'm glad you're not scared. Of this. Maybe you can talk me out of it as well."

With those words, it all fell into place. Marc welcomed challenge and change. It meant growth. He wasn't in a hurry to share this new change with his parents, but not because he feared their reaction. More, he wanted to keep it to himself. Cherish perhaps the most important discovery about himself for a while. But Henry was afraid, and that could only mean one thing. He thought Marc might hurt him—intentionally or otherwise. It wasn't a foolish notion. Marc might very well mess this up. He'd already blundered noisily and messily.

It was the reason behind Henry's fear that plucked at the center of Marc's chest, though. Henry could be hurt by what they were doing because he was invested. So was Marc—not that that was news to him. Curiosity aside, his attraction to Henry was more than physical. Feelings were definitely involved... and it was way too early to talk about them.

But, hey, if every date included a disaster scenario, they could put off getting any deeper than this for quite some time.

He kinda hoped every date wasn't this much of a disaster.

Chapter
FOUR

*I*t's coming on eleven." Henry tapped at the screen of his phone again and held it to his ear. After a couple of seconds, he pulled it away with a frown. "And that one bar is still teasing me."

"Think we might have any more luck sending a text?"

"Couldn't hurt to try." Henry started tapping again.

Marc woke his phone and sent a quick note to Shelly. "Okay, one of these has got to get through."

"Now we just have to hope she checks her phone."

"Who doesn't check their phone every three seconds for an update on life?"

"Me."

Chuckling, Marc tucked his phone back into his pocket and pushed up off the floor. "My ass is numb." He pressed his palms to cool denim and rubbed.

"I'd offer to warm it for you, but we should use lube your first time." Henry's grin brightened his entire countenance.

"Just the first time?"

Henry laughed. "Let's not go there right now. This corridor is not where I want to have the sex discussion."

"There's going to be a sex discussion?"

Pushing to his feet, Henry shook his head slowly. "Doesn't need to be, beyond us deciding what we want to try. Unless you want to talk about it. At another time and in another place."

"Like when your finger is in my ass?"

Henry made a choking sound. "Are you totally sure you're new to the gay thing?"

"I watch porn, remember?"

Henry shook his legs out and did a little ass massaging of his own. Cocking his head, Marc made a show of watching until Henry waved him off. "Stop."

"Can I just say one thing?"

"One. Just one."

"You turn me on like no one I've ever met before."

Even in the low light, Henry's blush was visible. It must have stung his cheeks. "You really do give everything your all, don't you?"

"Only the important things."

Henry smoothed his hands over his thighs. "So, wait by the door or check out the ductwork over the laundry?"

"Are you good with heading downstairs to check out the laundry?"

"It's forward momentum, right? Besides, we haven't heard anyone enter the building for over half an hour."

"Yeah. C'mon, let's go."

The ductwork might not prove an avenue worth exploring, but as Henry had indicated, checking it out would be doing something. Once back downstairs, Henry climbed on top of the washer again, grinning as Marc helped with judicious groping. Henry's ass felt pretty good through his jeans. Cold but strong. Masculine. Marc stood back to watch as Henry unfolded his pocket tool again and began unscrewing the vent.

"Wanna come up here and hold the vent so it doesn't drop when I'm done?"

Marc climbed up beside Henry, put two hands to the vent as Henry continued loosening the screws, and became absorbed by Henry's expression of concentration. The small crease between his brows, the tightness along his jaw. His tongue tip teased his lips now and again, and his eyes were laser focused.

"If you tell me I'm cute when I'm concentrating, I'm going to call this whole thing off," Henry said.

Marc grinned. "Okay, I just won't say it out loud, then."

"You're impossible."

"You enjoy the challenge."

Henry glanced down, meeting his gaze. They were close enough to feel each other's breath. Close enough to kiss. One corner of his mouth tugging into a grin, Henry looked up again. "Last one."

The vent dropped into Marc's hands. With Henry's help, he lowered it to the top of the adjacent washer. Then he looked up. The duct was as wide as the vent and looked like a straight shot to the top of the building until he shone the light of his phone into the hole. "It turns two feet in," he said.

Henry nodded. "Two questions. How do we get in there, and will it hold us?"

"Really only has to hold one of us and we should be good. It's in the ceiling rather than suspended beneath it."

"Okay, which one of us is going to check it out?"

"I'll go." Marc shrugged his coat from his shoulders and dropped it on top of the discarded vent.

"You sure? I'm good to go if you're not."

"I'm sure. Here, let's get one of these chairs up here for me to climb up on."

"I could just try to give you a boost."

Henry cupped his hands down by his knees. After making sure he was positioned well, Marc stepped up and reached for the top of the vent as Henry hoisted him upward. His fingers grazed the metal side, echoing and banging. He thought he was going to miss and drop back down. Then he caught the lip with his other hand and pulled.

"Going to need another lift to get myself over the bend," he called down.

"Cool. Let me know when."

"Now would be good."

Henry poked his head between Marc's thighs, confusing him until he stood, lifting Marc onto his shoulders. The motion was so sudden, Marc banged his head on the cross duct. White spots danced in front of his eyes.

"You okay?"

"It's very bright in here all of a sudden." Marc resisted the urge to rub the top of his head.

"Very funny. Can you get over the edge?"

"Yep, pulling forward now." He angled forward and began crawling. Henry helped by pushing, and after much grunting and groaning, Marc found himself on his belly in the cross duct. "Okay, I'm in." Over the echo of his voice, a faint snicker floated up from below. "Are you laughing down there?"

"I wish I was recording this."

"Ha-ha."

"What, you had your ass groped and ended up in a dark hole. It's all very Freudian or whatever."

"Really, it's not. Also, you groped my ass in the copy room yesterday."

"So I did. Which was more fun?"

"The blow job, duh."

Henry's answering chuckle was muted, and Marc breathed into the relative quiet a moment before speaking again. "Okay, duct hasn't collapsed beneath me, but I've encountered our first unforeseen problem. I'm going to have to slither like a snake up here to get anywhere."

Another snicker from below. Or maybe it was a giggle.

"I'd never have guessed you had such an absurd sense of humor."

Henry was openly laughing now. Between gasps, he managed, "Let's just say I'm punchy."

"Good to know."

Slithering was weirdly difficult. Marc couldn't figure out if he should use his arms or legs. He settled for mashing his palms against the sides of the duct and pulling while kicking with the aim of propelling himself forward. It worked after a fashion, but it felt slow and clumsy. Wiggling his hips helped. Every time he did it, he thanked providence for the fact he was hidden from view. Crawling through a duct to rescue his date would make a great story, and whether he succeeded or not, he'd be telling this one at Mulligan's. That was his job every Thursday, entertaining his colleagues at the pub across the street from their offices. Team Building 101.

It'd be different with Henry there. Better, Marc hoped. He didn't want to overexpose his personal affairs, but neither did he want to hide his preferences. The idea of sitting in a booth next to Henry, one arm casually looped about his shoulders, held a lot of appeal.

His head brushed the end of the duct. Marc lay in a sweaty, heaving heap for a minute, catching his breath.

"How's it going up there?"

Henry's voice sounded closer than it should. Marc tried to peer over his shoulder and whacked his head against the top of the duct again. "Ugh."

"You all right?"

"Yeah, it's just cramped in here. Are you in the duct?"

"I'm standing on a chair."

"Be careful."

Henry answered with a soft snort.

Folding his arm back down by his side proved as difficult as glancing over his shoulder. His elbow connected with the duct several more times than necessary before he managed to get his phone out and pointing in a somewhat sensible direction. He activated the screen and turned it around to shed light on his situation. The duct turned again, angling directly up from his position. Another round of bruising maneuvering got him rolled over onto his back. Marc pointed his phone upward. "Hit a bit of a snag here."

"What's up?"

"The duct bends upward from where I'm at. I'm guessing I'm over near the wall? And it's a straight shot up the wall. I can see some light up there, which might be a vent. Maybe into the lobby? But I don't know if I'm going to get around this corner, and even if I can, if I can reach that high, or climb or whatever."

"Damn. Would it help if I got in there too and pushed you up?"

"If I can get around the corner and if we don't bring the ceiling down… maybe?"

"That's a lot of ifs."

"Yeah. We might be better off watching the ball drop on that dinky little TV in the laundry while we wait for someone to come rescue us. Hey, did you check to see if your text went through?"

Shuffling echoed along the shaft. "Not yet, but it probably won't while I'm down here. Maybe I should leave my phone up by the door?"

"Couldn't hurt."

"Okay, hold still. I'm going to go do that. Then I'll come back down and we'll reassess."

Marc didn't do much while he waited for Henry to return. He simply stared up into the darkness and waited for the duct to fall through the ceiling. Then he heard Henry reenter the laundry and climb back up on top of the washing machine.

"Right, going to try and get into the vertical shaft."

Another snicker.

For Christ's sake. He was dating a twelve-year-old… and, as newly out, shouldn't he be the one snickering at all the sex jokes?

Marc managed to backward slither into a sitting position. "Okay, sitting. Wondering how in hell I'm going to stand up without breaking my knees."

The sound of Henry's struggle to get into the horizontal shaft distracted him for a while. The shaft shook alarmingly beneath him a couple of times and then fell still. Marc angled his phone back toward the laundry room and woke the screen. Henry was in the shaft, some distance away, huffing and puffing.

"Okay, good news and bad news," Henry said.

"Good news is you're in the shaft, right?"

"Basically."

"What's the bad news?"

"I managed to kick the chair off the top of the washing machine, so it's a long way down if we have to go out this way."

"I'm starting to think this wasn't such a good idea."

"No kidding. It's about as dumb as looking for a farmhouse in a snowstorm."

"You were the one who ran off down the road."

"After you!"

"Yeah, well...."

After a pause, Henry said, "I was going to say that for our third date, we should just stay home. But knowing our luck, terrorists would decide to take the entire building hostage."

"So we're counting the blizzard as our first date now?"

"Terrorists, Marc!"

"I heard you."

Henry seemed to have an easier time moving through the shaft, probably because he could see where he was going. It was an interesting perspective on the guy, for sure. Watching his brow crease intermittently as he pushed forward in fits and starts. Marc almost laughed when he noted Henry abandoning the hip-wiggling motion as quickly as he had.

Coming to a stop about six inches from Marc's shoes, Henry dropped his forehead to the bottom of the duct and blew out a breath, then coughed. He glanced up, expression wry. "It was like once I got in here, the only sensible thing to do was crawl up to where you were. Even though I know we're probably even more stuck than we were before. Why is that?"

"You're a team player?" Not every guy would have wormed his way through the shaft to help Marc up to the next vent.

Henry chuckled softly. "Okay, I suppose we should see if you can actually manage to stand. Which is something we should have figured out before I got in here."

"Yeah, well, misery loves company. Here, hold this." Marc passed his phone to Henry and prepared to try to stand inside the duct.

The problem would be his knees. If he were double-jointed, he might gain enough flexibility to get them around the corner. Escape wasn't worth dislocating them, though. Pushing his hands against the wall behind him, Marc began easing himself upward and stopped. He wasn't a freaking snake. He tried dropping his knees sideways next. Promising.

The sound of his efforts—short breaths and the scuff of shoes and denim against metal—echoed loudly through the duct. A cramp gripped his left thigh, pulling a hiss from his lips. Still, Marc struggled and pushed until he got halfway upright with just one knee caught on the bend.

"Push my knee, will you?"

Henry shuffled forward and put a hand to his leg, just below the knee. He pushed and Marc pulled. His legs looked like broken pretzels, and he had to squash down panicked thoughts twice. With a pop, his right knee slipped through and he was in the vertical shaft. He stood quickly on shaking legs and leaned forward, resting his cheek on the cool metal. "Holy crap."

"If the duct falls now—"

"Don't even. Seriously, not going there."

"Can you reach the vent?"

"Hold on. Just need to convince myself my legs aren't broken or twisted or permanently damaged in any way." Marc breathed the close, dusty air for another few seconds, thankful for the slight breeze from the vent behind him. A weird sound tickled his eardrums, a long, low groan. At first he thought he'd made the sound. Maybe his stomach had rumbled? Or Henry's. Then a whoosh of hot air blasted down the back of his neck.

Swallowing a yelp, Marc called down to Henry. "Well, we know the system's in use. Heat just came on."

"Lovely. So if we do get stuck in here, we won't freeze to death."

"Right, turning around to try the vent. You brought that tool with you, right?"

Henry fumbled and shuffled. The tool emerged into the space where the duct folded upward, hovering over Marc's shoes.

Marc stared at it a second before laughing. "Oh, man. Why didn't we think of this before I tried to dislocate my knees?"

"Because we're a pair of idiots. Seriously, I'm starting to doubt our cognitive function."

"I'm blaming your hotness."

"Don't discombobulate me while I'm trapped in an air shaft."

"Okay, before our next date, we need to come up with a serious plan. Contingencies and so on. An emergency call list."

After a while, Henry answered in a quiet and thoughtful tone. "The hotness comment gets you another date. But maybe we shouldn't tempt fate or terrorists with an emergency plan."

Marc started bending toward his feet. "I'm not going to be able to get all the way down there. If I shuffle to the side, can you roll over and sit up?"

"We're doing tricks now?"

"Very funny."

Marc revisited the countdown in his head. The large red numbers flickered somewhere between eleven and twelve. They might not make it upstairs for that promised kiss, but he'd have his lips on Henry's at midnight, dammit. Even if it had to happen in this shaft.

Henry managed to roll and sit. He held up the tool, and Marc grabbed it. "Shine the light up here?"

The feeble glow of his phone barely illuminated the vent, but it was enough for Marc to see they had another problem—and it was something else they should have figured out before crawling into the ducts. "The screws are on the outside."

Henry's head banged against the duct. "Dammit." He looked up. "Try pushing it out?"

Marc rattled the vent, but it was stuck fast. He tapped the vent with the tool, producing a sharp rapping sound. He yelled. He slapped at the vent with his other hand and even kicked the shaft, producing a low, echoing boom. Hot air continued to flow around the nape of his neck. Sweat rolled down his back, making his shirt stick to his skin.

Frustration fizzed and snapped through his veins. Being stuck—and now hot and sweaty—was finally starting to piss him off. "Fuck!"

"Okay, we're done here," Henry said. "Back to the laundry?"

Marc slumped against the side of the duct. "Yeah. I guess." He turned around and looked at the bend behind him, the next horizontal sweep of ductwork, and wondered if it was worth the effort of trying to get up there. A sense of defeat rolled out of the darkness with the steady stream of warm air. Shaking his head, Marc turned away and looked down. Henry had disappeared, and he could just hear him shuffling backward along the lower duct. Returning to the laundry was the safest bet.

Someone would find them soon, right?

Chapter
FIVE

*E*xiting the HVAC ductwork proved anticlimactic. No worrying creaks, falling plaster, or skin torn from palms. No broken limbs. Just two dusty and disheveled men patting themselves down in the laundry room. Marc handed the tool back to Henry and received his phone in exchange. He checked the time—11:41.

Depression settled down around his shoulders. In the vent, a happy ending had still seemed possible, even if The Kiss—now in capitals and blinking in his mind like that damned countdown to midnight—had to happen up there, when they were cramped together in a weird place, breathing on each other's faces. Here, in the laundry, it just felt like he'd got lost on the way to something wonderful.

And he was dirty, sweaty, and hungry.

First two he could do something for. Moving over to the tub, Marc washed his hands and pressed a dampened paper towel to the back of his neck. Henry followed suit, washing his hands and splashing water on his face before catching some water in cupped hands for a drink. Leaving him to it, Marc picked up the fallen chair, shook it open again, and set it down. He flopped into it and leaned his head back against the washer behind him, closing his eyes. Footsteps and a rattle indicated Henry had grabbed another chair and settled beside him. Marc didn't open his eyes. Instead, he watched the ticking numbers behind his closed lids while misery churned in his gut.

He'd been on some crappy dates. New Year's Eve with Kate might sound like the worst, but only because it made an interesting story. He couldn't count the number of dates he'd had since— mostly because his memory of them was a blur. None really stood out of the tedium of following a script toward an uncertain conclusion. The dates that hadn't ended in sex were no less disappointing than the ones that had. He'd been playing a role. All this time, he'd been searching for something, and he'd been looking in the wrong damned place.

Until his date with Gabrielle from the secretary pool at B and M.

When he went to pick her up, he saw Henry jogging along Hull Street. It was the first time he'd seen Henry out of his corporate uniform. The expression on his face caught Marc more than the lean figure in jogging shorts and tank, though. The faraway look, the relaxed smile. It was a different Henry. Not the sober and quiet guy from the office. Suddenly he was more interesting and complicated.

He was… attractive.

Marc couldn't remember anything about the date with Gabrielle, except a fascination with Henry that had continued for months until they'd ended up stranded in a blizzard together. Now, finally, he was on The Date, counting down to The Kiss.

And the evening was a complete and unmitigated disaster.

Maybe he should forget being gay.

Forget his obsession with Henry.

Could he have a midlife crisis at twenty-eight?

Something touched his hand, and Marc jumped. The yelp he'd swallowed earlier fought its way out. The sound was pathetic in the small space of the laundry. Or maybe that was just his mood. He opened his eyes.

Henry was touching the back of his hand. "Everything okay over there?"

Marc moved his hand away, indulged in a little palm-to-eye action, pressing his lids closed again. "Yeah, sure." It was instinctive, the urge to lie. "Just beat from our adventure in the ducts."

"I'm sorry we couldn't find a way out."

"Not your fault. If we'd stopped to think…. Well. We probably wouldn't be down here at all." He let his hands drop to his lap and peeked over at Henry. "This your worst date ever, yet?"

"No."

"I think it's mine."

Henry gave a half smile and leaned back in his chair. "It's not so bad. Company is fine."

"You wouldn't rather have stayed home?"

"Nope."

"Even though we're shut in a basement."

Henry's shoulders hitched into a little shrug. "For the past couple of hours I've been too busy to dwell." He smiled again, this time more than halfway. "And the boy I'm kissing is locked down here with me."

The boy he was kissing. Henry made it seem so sweet and natural. Something loosened in Marc's chest. "You ever see him again, the boy your uncle caught you with?"

"Nope."

Marc reached for Henry's hand, pulling it into his own. "I'm sorry this is such a sucky date."

Henry squeezed his fingers. "You know, if we'd made it to the party upstairs, we probably wouldn't have seen each other all night, anyway. You'd have been surrounded by your groupies, and I'd probably have snuck off to check out Shelly's library. Or found her porn collection."

"I don't have groupies."

"You know what I mean. Your circle at the office."

Marc grimaced. "My followers." Usually he enjoyed being the center of attention. Now he couldn't think beyond the man holding his hand.

Marc's thoughts took another whirl around the inside of his head, pausing over the small collection of memories he'd already built with Henry. Kissing, touching, getting off. The conversation from this evening. The easy banter they fell into when they weren't answering the big questions. "Maybe this was a bad idea."

Henry's brow wrinkled. "The date or the destination?"

"The destination. I wanted a date with you too badly to regret even this. But you're right. Even if we had made it upstairs, I don't think it'd have been the evening I wanted. I was so damned focused on kissing you at midnight, I hadn't thought about the rest of it."

Why had he needed that kiss so badly? Beyond needing to have a plan, Marc could only come up with answers that disturbed him. He'd set himself a task, a test. The kiss was to be the proof of his attraction to Henry. That it was real and something he wanted to declare.

"Hey." Henry tugged on his hand. "We're going to miss the fireworks, but it's not so bad down here. We've got heat. Chairs. We've crawled through a duct together. Not many dates get into ductwork. Sad fact. Oh, and we nearly had our first fight." Henry's smile widened, and once again, the transformation took Marc's breath away.

He remembered why he'd wanted this date so much.

"I wanted to take you home, Henry. After midnight. I… dammit." He pressed his hands to his eyes again, then pushed them up over his forehead, as if he could massage his thoughts into sensible words. "It feels stupid now, that I wanted to stamp the beginning of the year I decided to be gay with this huge event, this big kiss. Then take you home and seal the deal. Have gay sex and—"

"Marc." Henry reclaimed one of his hands and pressed it to his lips.

The sweetness of the gesture, and the difference of it, slowed Marc's thoughts once more. "It's so different with you. I keep trying to figure it out, but I can't."

"Not everything is about rules and choices," Henry said. "Sometimes things just happen. It's how we react that defines us. You're processing a lot, and most of it can't be set down on paper and analyzed like a financial statement. All things considered, I think you've been cooler about the whole deal than I would have."

"You've known you were gay for a long time. I just found out."

"You weren't happy for a long time. Now you can see how you might be, and it scares you."

He could be right. "But why? Why would anyone be scared of happiness?"

"Because it can hurt when it's taken away."

A sigh of... everything... left him. Marc slumped back into his chair, his and Henry's joined hands dangling between them. "You know, in my fantasies, before Christmas Eve, I figured if I ever acted on my attraction to you, it would be all about the sex. I even went to a gay bar one night."

"I bet you got a lot of looks."

"I did, and they made me really uncomfortable." He tapped his chest and glanced over at Henry. "Me. Uncomfortable. I was curious, but figured if just being looked at made me feel weird, then maybe I wasn't gay. But I still couldn't get you out of my mind."

Henry didn't say anything to that. Really, what could he say? A flippant response would change the timbre of their conversation, and the fact that Henry seemed to realize that only made him more attractive.

"I don't think I've ever talked so much to a date before. Or anyone. Even in the car we talked."

Henry's lips twitched. "Yeah."

"I think I'm beginning to realize why you were hesitant to take me on."

"Because you talk too much?"

Marc returned the lip twitch, then let the grin happen. Then he squeezed Henry's hand again. "This is good. I like this. I don't want to bare my soul every date, though. It's exhausting."

"Okay."

Marc raised their hands and pressed Henry's knuckles to his mouth. "You fascinate me. I can't wait to get you naked."

Henry unleashed a laugh, bending his head back to do so.

Marc leaned in to kiss the column of his throat, humming as barely there stubble tickled his lips. Instantly, he was hard. That one touch—or maybe it was the taste of Henry's skin, the tang of salt and hint of shaving soap, the whisper of familiarity and difference that tied him into a complicated knot of *want*.

Henry's chin dipped, and Marc kissed the brilliant smile, the beautiful mouth he'd fantasized about. The part of Henry that proved again and again how distracting it could be. Henry's fingers tightened over his. Marc slipped his other hand behind Henry's head and drew him closer. Their lips fell into the synergy he'd only found with Henry. It was as if he'd been born to kiss this man. He answered the invitation of Henry's tongue and... fell.

Time slipped—midnight could have come and gone. All that mattered was Henry. The scent of him, the feel of his skin, that tiny prickle of roughness catching his lips as he wandered in and out of the kiss, exploring the line of Henry's jaw, sampling an earlobe, darting back to kiss him again.

Every moan had his skin tingling. Every groan reverberated through him. He could barely feel his hands, and he'd lost touch with his legs. All of his blood, all of his being, was centered at his groin. His erection pulsed and throbbed, painful behind his zipper. He savored the ache and the anticipation.

Henry pulled out of the kiss, and Marc's entire body protested the loss. *More, more*, his synapses screamed. "Want you, all of you, so bad." He curled his hand around the back of Henry's neck. "But—"

"Shh." Henry quieted him with a quick kiss. He pulled away, stood, and held out a hand. "C'mon. These chairs are doing some ominous creaking."

That's what that sound was.

Marc got up and followed as Henry led him along the row of washers and nudged him up against the wall, pressing a knee between his thighs. Groaning, Marc let his head flop back. His view of the ceiling shifted and blurred as Henry pressed kisses to his neck, lips tickling, teeth grazing. He let his hips rock forward, the pressure of Henry's thigh between his somehow exciting. Weird, because he couldn't figure out why he liked it so much, but…. Oh. His balls met resistance, pushing up beneath his straining cock. "Oh God."

Henry leaned into him, grinding their hips together. Marc could feel the heat and hardness behind Henry's fly. One of his hands fluttered down there, completely without his permission. But really, he wanted to feel that heat against his palm. Stroke Henry's erection. Have Henry's hand on his.

A tug at his belt had him looking down. Henry's lips found his, and they kissed through the loosening of his jeans, zip going down, Henry reaching in to caress the outline of his cock through the cotton of his briefs.

"You good?" Henry's breath tickled.

Marc answered by pushing into Henry's hand. Then he reached for Henry's belt. "Want to feel you too."

"Not gonna say no."

Henry dropped small kisses along his cheek as Marc bent to the task of unbuckling Henry's belt and unzipping his jeans. He grasped the bulge he found there, marveling at the heat for a second. How often had he had his own cock in his hand? He knew this heat and hardness, the ache of a dick straining toward some sort of release. But the dark circle of moisture on Henry's boxers was someone else's excitement. It was because of him—his hand, his attention.

Stroking a woman had never felt quite like this. He hadn't felt... was there such a thing as sexual empathy? He squeezed Henry's dick and felt a reciprocal pressure against his own. It seemed they pulsed in sync, pushing against each other's hands.

He wanted more than a handful of hot cotton. Pulling his lips from Henry's—when had they started kissing again?—Marc glanced down long enough to pull Henry's boxers down and over the head of a very happy cock. He quickly grasped the warm, rigid flesh awaiting him and squeezed.

Henry's groan punched through his chest, as if he'd made the sound himself.

Henry pushed Marc's jeans and underpants down, taking less care with the out and over so that Marc's erection snapped out of its confines with an almost painful jerk. Then warm fingers had him too and they were stroking in time.

This was new—the closest yet they'd come to what Marc called *sex*. Henry had sucked him off twice. Moving together felt different. Almost as though they were making love. Already, their hips and hands had acquired a rhythm. Already, his impending climax clutched his nuts.

Henry bit his ear, and Marc shuddered. A whisper of stubble across his cheek—already sensitive from repeated brushes of not-quite-soft masculine skin—had him shivering. He couldn't think. Myriad sensations robbed him of coordination, speech, the ability to do anything more than twitch and moan as he pushed through the clasp of Henry's hand. Was he giving as good as he got? Did he still have his fingers wrapped around Henry's cock? Yes, and oh God, it was so hard and heavy against his palm. Marc squeezed, and Henry's hips stuttered into his... and there was his thigh again, pushing insistently between Marc's legs.

Why did that feel so good?

Henry's fingers pulled and twisted, catching the head of Marc's cock just right. With a swipe of his thumb, he spread precome down the shaft and stroked again. Marc tried to do the same, but his concentration was scattered—and he was going to come soon. Dammit, he didn't want to come so fast. Being with Henry felt too good.

"Wait…. Oh, shit."

Henry nipped at his earlobe and pushed his thigh between Marc's legs. Marc bucked and shuddered and came, his entire self flowing down and out, spurting through his dick. His knees shook as he mindlessly humped Henry's leg, pushing his cock through the hot and wet pocket of Henry's hand. His voice cut into small words. "Oh, oh, oh…."

Then he was slumping forward, chin hooking over Henry's shoulder as he nestled into the embrace of his arms, and they felt so good around him. Protective and sweet. The small kisses and murmurs dropped around his ear and hair stirred the gentle poke of feeling in the center of his chest.

Was he too old to be "in like" with someone?

Lifting his head away, he kissed Henry's cheek. His jaw. The corner of his mouth, his wonderfully inviting lips. Huffing breath kept him from engaging in a deep kiss, so he pecked and licked. Whispered against Henry's mouth. "So, so good. You make me feel so good. God, being with you… it's just so good."

He'd been turned to a puddle of mood goo by a hand job.

And Henry was still hard and still in his hand. Jesus, he'd forgotten to reciprocate.

"S-sorry," he stuttered, giving Henry's cock a quick stroke. "But totally your fault. I got lost somewhere along the way."

Henry grinned into the wordy kiss. "'S okay. Not like you're going to walk away and leave me wanting, right?" He pushed into Marc's hand, and that damned thigh nudged between his legs again.

"Why does it feel so good to have your leg between mine?"

"You never humped a leg before, never had someone between your legs?"

"No… I don't know. Ask me later. I want to get you off first."

"Mmm." Henry bucked into his hand again. "I'm close."

The scent of semen wafted up, combined with warm skin and Henry's arousal. What would he taste like? Surprisingly, Marc's mouth watered. A brief imagining of the feel of Henry's hard shaft against his tongue teased—and then became an itch, an insistent niggle. More than an idea. A want. A *need*.

"I want—" Marc clamped his mouth shut. Sudden embarrassment stung his cheeks. His hand stilled.

"What?" Henry kissed the corner of his mouth. "Tell me what you want."

Words left Marc in a rush. "You, in a bed. Naked. I haven't seen all of you. I want to feel your skin. Figure out where you like to be touched. I want you beneath my hands. Your hips bucking. The muscles of your legs and arms. Your… guy-ness. That's what I wanted to do tonight, after the party. Take you home and talk you into bed. I want more than this. I want to make love to you, however it works. Come together." He was babbling.

And Henry's hard cock was still pushing through his palm. Most awkward sex talk ever?

"We'll get there."

"I want to suck you."

"Jesus, God…. Marc…." Henry's breath puffed across Marc's face as he groaned and shoved against Marc's palm again. "You don't have to."

"I want to."

"Are you sure?"

No, but Marc Winnamore didn't back away from a challenge. Ever.

After delivering another stroke, Marc let go of Henry's cock and tried to kneel. Somehow his head hit the wall behind him, probably because his jeans and underwear were still down around his thighs.

"Hold on." Henry pulled away from his grasp, and the sense of loss was weird. Almost terrible. How could a hand feel bereft?

Marc groped after Henry, then followed him to the sink. He sighed jerkily as he figured out what Henry was up to. Washing his sticky hands. Henry passed a dampened towel over his shoulder, and Marc attempted to clean himself up a bit. He was half-hard again. Would he shrivel or plump as he blew Henry?

Was he really going to suck another man's dick?

Nerves fluttering in his belly, Marc pulled up his underwear and jeans. He looked up to find Henry waiting for him, sensuous mouth crooked into an easy smile.

"You're thinking again, aren't you?"

"Good thoughts." Marc advanced upon Henry, putting a hand to each shoulder, and backed him toward the wall. "Thinking about how much I want to taste you, feel the weight of you on my tongue."

"Mmm. Very good thoughts."

They kissed again, slowly, almost languidly. Marc moved to nuzzle Henry's cheek, tucked his nose beneath Henry's chin. Kissed his neck. Tasted his skin. Moving down, he pressed a kiss to the collar of Henry's shirt. He tugged at the buttons, got one undone, and slipped a hand inside. Found cotton.

"Dammit, you're wearing an undershirt."

"It's winter."

Marc tweaked a nipple through the soft cotton. "Do you like that?"

"Mmm-hmm." Henry rocked forward, poking him in the thigh with his very hard cock. "But my dick is starting to think you've forgotten about him."

Marc's instant grin wavered only a little as he dropped to his knees in front of Henry. He took a moment to admire the jut of rigid flesh. Henry's uncut cock was *nice*. No, fucking sexy. Well-proportioned without making Marc feel inferior. He inhaled the aroma of arousal and sex. A pearly bead of precome rolled down the slit, paused, and dropped toward the floor on a gossamer thread. Before he could get caught in the gridlock of thought, Marc stuck his tongue out. He missed the drop and licked the underside of Henry's cock instead—right where *he* liked to be touched.

Hissing softly, Henry curled his hand behind Marc's head. He didn't pull or jerk; he simply clutched at Marc's hair and waited, his legs—his presence—tense and taut.

Marc wrapped his hand around Henry's shaft and pulled back a little, causing Henry's foreskin to retreat fully. He opened his mouth, moved forward. The absurdity of his situation poked at him. For a second he hung there, Henry's cock just inside his mouth but not touching his lips—like a snake poking its head into a hole that was much too big. Or something.

Do it, Marc.

Marc closed his mouth and gave an experimental suck. Henry jerked lightly between his lips. He curled his fingers a little tighter into Marc's hair. Marc acknowledged these things while being swept away on another wave of *new*. The taste of sex, the heat against his tongue. The very fact of having a cock in his mouth.

He knew what to do next. It was instinctive as well as informed. He'd been on the receiving end often enough. He sucked his way down Henry's shaft until the tip nudged the back of his throat. After pulling back a little, he did it again, then again, stopping short of choking each time. Once he had a rhythm established—one met by gently enthusiastic thrusts of Henry's hips—Marc experimented with his tongue.

Swirling was hard. How had Henry managed that with such dexterity and ease?

Marc rewrapped his fingers around the base of Henry's cock,

steadying the shaft, and tried again, pressing his tongue to the underside before sort of letting it slip up and over.

"Yes, like that."

Emboldened by Henry's approval, Marc did it again, just *like that*. He found that grinning while sucking made for a sloppy connection. Humming made Henry groan and shudder. Using his hand helped him cover more territory, and enthusiasm had him sucking too hard and fast. He backed off before he choked and pulled away entirely.

"Sorry."

"You're doing fine. I'm really close."

"Really?" His mouth felt weird. Also, talking up at a guy while a cock stared him in the eye? Very strange.

Marc started again, and the weird feeling became an overstretched feeling. His jaw ached and his cheeks hurt. He wouldn't be letting a little thing like that stop him from finishing his task, though. Nope. He sucked and slurped and hummed. Stroked up to meet his lips and back to Henry's balls. Reached between Henry's legs to play there, nudge his tight sac.

Then Henry was pushing at his shoulders. "Stop…. Marc!"

Marc had felt the hitch in Henry's balls. The jerk in his cock. It was time.

Oh my God. I made a guy come with my mouth.

For all his enthusiasm, he didn't think he was ready to taste or choke on Henry's spunk, though. Moving aside, he continued stroking with his hand until Henry tensed, cried out, and shuddered into his release, shooting over Marc's shoulder. Now Marc knew just what to do—how much handling would feel good, how much would be too much. He carried Henry through his orgasm, standing so he could kiss lips parted by happy grunts and sighs.

His mouth still felt weird.

"My cheeks hurt," he murmured.

Henry huffed out a laugh. "All to a good cause."

"Lemme get you a towel."

"Hold on."

Henry pulled him in for another kiss that quickly deepened into something that was suddenly necessary. When Marc thought to come up for air, he still had Henry's dick in his hand and his other arm around Henry's shoulder. Henry held him just as closely and was nuzzling his neck, just below Marc's ear. Man, he liked being this close, this involved. Cuddling had never felt so good.

Marc didn't know what pulled him out of the sweet and lusty trance. A whisper of air at the back of his neck. The feeling of being watched. By the time he heard the throat clearing, it was too late to jump back, tuck Henry's cock away, or worry about the mess on the floor or the pungent odor of sex in the air.

"Not sure you two really need rescuing."

Marc glanced over his shoulder. Luke Bessler stood in the doorway to the laundry, Henry's phone in his hand.

Chapter
SIX

*H*eat prickled across the back of Marc's neck. His scalp itched. His cheeks burned. Breathing suddenly became difficult. Passing out a distinct possibility. A tug across his palm pulled Marc's gaze down. Henry putting his cock away. Okay, good.

Had Bessler seen Henry's junk?

How long had he been standing there?

Marc couldn't pin down a single emotion in the maelstrom sweeping through his head and chest, but the fleeting hint of fear in Henry's expression suggested he hadn't quite embraced the spectrum yet.

Should they be afraid?

Henry recovered first. Buttoning himself up, he aimed a sober smile at Bessler. "I see you found my phone. Did Shelly get my text?"

Even while listening for the answer, Marc couldn't shift his gaze from Henry's reddened lips. Someone had kissed this man stupid. He had. He'd been caught kissing a man. A cold shiver replaced the warm prickle. Marc took a step back. One of Henry's eyebrows flicked up briefly, but Bessler drew his attention.

"Yeah, a few minutes ago. Grace is holding the door open." Bessler turned the phone over in his hand before holding it out.

"When she hears about what I walked in on, I'll owe her lunch for the next six months."

Snickering softly, Henry reached for his phone. "Thanks for the rescue."

"Sure, no problem." Bessler looked at Marc. Looking away would be childish, wouldn't it? "I didn't know you were—"

"G-ay." Brilliant. His first public word for the New Year and he'd botched it.

"I was going to say with Henry, but gay works, I guess." Bessler shrugged as if they were discussing something other than Marc's sexuality—like, say, the color of the floor. "So, I'll, ah, give you guys a minute or two to get organized?"

"Sure," Henry answered. "We'll follow you up in a few."

Marc still hadn't managed to draw a full breath, and there was a high-pitched whine centered between his ears. Was it him screaming inside his head? Bessler's footsteps retreated down the hallway until the only sound was the ringing in Marc's ears and the crash of his world tumbling down around him.

So this was what it felt like to be *out*. Someone other than he and Henry knew he was g-ay. Gay. There, he'd thought it without the hitch.

Marc backed up to one of the chairs and sat down. He propped his elbows on his knees and dropped his face into the waiting cup of his hands. "Oh God." His stomach clenched. "Oh… God." Would throwing up be better or worse than passing out?

The chair beside him creaked. Henry sitting. A warm hand hovered over his shoulder a moment before landing, as though Henry were afraid to touch him. Maybe he should be? Marc felt a bit like an unexploded bomb. Or should that be an uncertain bomb?

"If you need some time, I can go try to prop the door open. Or we could just head out and get a cab."

Swallowing, Marc shook his head. "No, I mean…. Fuck. I don't know." He glanced over at Henry. "I'm sorry."

Henry's smile had a bittersweet twist to it. "Don't be."

"How could I have thought I could kiss you at midnight? How could I have not known it'd feel like this?"

"Ever told anyone you were gay before?"

"No. Well, you."

"Then you couldn't have known."

Marc made an attempt to straighten his spine. "I thought I was ready. I was excited, dammit. I've been thinking about nothing else for days. I had the whole moment in my head. Taking your hands. No! I was going to touch your face. Wait…." He'd imagined the kiss so many times, and each iteration now flashed through his thoughts, adding to the spinning storm. "I wanted this, Henry. I wasn't afraid!"

"I know." Henry's smile had faded, but not to anger. The compassion in his expression was somehow worse. He squeezed Marc's shoulder, then pressed his palm behind it and rubbed, his hand the only warm spot on Marc's body.

"Why do I feel like this?"

"Because of what could have happened, maybe? Luke might not have been cool. Not everyone upstairs would have been cool with the kiss. Maybe you're just realizing that."

Marc shook his head. "Well, yeah, I guess, but it's more…." Looking up, he sought Henry's gaze, those somber gray eyes. "I feel sick. I'm scared and I feel sick and I don't understand why."

Oh, and he'd started to shake too.

Wonderful. Fucking wonderful.

Henry patted his shoulder. "I'm gonna go call us a cab."

"No."

"You don't look like you're in any—"

"I'm not going to run away from this."

"Marc, this isn't—"

"I need to see this through."

"Can I say something without you interrupting me?" Henry's tone had acquired an edge.

Marc nodded.

"There's a lot going on in your head right now, and I think you should take some time to deal with it. Going upstairs and facing an apartment full of people probably isn't the best deal. If you want, we can ask Luke to keep what he saw to himself. Say you're not feeling good." Marc opened his mouth, and Henry increased his volume. "Or I'm not feeling good, or we're just pissed off about the whole being locked in the laundry thing. Hell, I don't know. One of us got cut up in the ducts or something. Point is, we don't have to go upstairs. You don't have to do this now. Take some time, think it through."

Henry was probably right. The idea of tucking tail and running, though…. Marcus Winnamore didn't turn away from a challenge. Ever. He also stood by his word. In their line of work, that meant everything, and Marc had adopted it as a personal mantra.

But a man could change his mind. That was courage, right? To be brave enough to say you were wrong.

Was he wrong about this?

Marc locked eyes with Henry again, searching the gray depths for answers. Hell, he'd settle for clues. What he saw was Henry. His chest tightened, and his pulse kicked up another notch. All the good feeling surrounding Henry formed a warm sphere beneath his panic. He knew, looking at Henry, that whatever route he chose from here, this man would support his decision with empathy and grace. He also understood that Henry's power came not from the depth of character beneath shrewd ambition, but from that warmth. He was a good person working in an industry crowded with assholes.

And that, more than anything else, was what made him attractive.

When picturing his future, Marc had always assumed he'd eventually find a wife who suited his parents' ideal. That she'd be beautiful and smart but something like an accessory. A thing he eventually had to acquire. He'd hoped they would be friends. That was his ideal.

In Henry he saw a potential partner. Someone he could....

Drawing in a quick breath, Marc broke away from Henry's gaze and pushed to his feet. "C'mon, we don't want to keep Luke waiting." He walked to the sink and started washing his hands. Again. The cleaner his hands got, the more aware he became of the stickiness inside his shorts. That'd have to wait until he got home. This laundry (and the world) had seen enough of his junk for one night. He cupped his hands under the water and drank. Swallowed the faint taste of Henry and remembered the feel of Henry's cock in his mouth.

His stomach didn't hitch.

While Henry cleaned up, Marc shrugged into his coat. The heavy weight of felted wool settling around his shoulders had a feeling of finality about it. As if he'd wrapped up this adventure and prepared to go home.

Was that what he wanted to do?

He handed Henry's coat over and watched him button it up, faintly obsessed as always by Henry's long fingers. The shape of his hands. When he glanced up, it was to find Henry looking at him.

"You okay?" Henry asked.

Marc shook his head. "No, but I will be."

Henry's uncertain smile returned, but he followed Marc into the hall.

Luke and Grace awaited them at the doorway, heads bent close together in conversation. Watching them as they approached, Marc realized they were the sort of team he wanted to be a part of. A couple who were friends, allies, partners. Probably helped that they worked for different firms.

Grace heard them and looked up with a tentative smile. "Hey!"

Marc returned her smile, his feeling as strained as hers looked. Then he thrust out his hand. "Good to see you, Grace. Happy New Year."

She gave his hand a firm shake. "You too." Her gaze flicked toward Henry.

Marc touched Henry's shoulder, drawing him forward. "Henry Auttenberg, meet Grace Bessler. Ah, Luke's wife. She's with Bahvan Consulting."

Smiling, Henry said, "Happy New Year." He shook hands with Grace and Luke. "And thanks again for the rescue."

Luke offered his hand to Marc next, and Marc hesitated before shaking and murmuring, "Happy New Year."

"So, you guys coming up or...?" Luke looked from one to the other.

"I think we're—" Henry started.

"Coming up," Marc finished.

Henry's eyebrows lifted.

Marc moved his hand over next to Henry's, drew in a hitched but quiet breath, and grabbed hold. Took another man's hand in his own. The dizziness returned.

Everyone looked down at their hands. Luke, Grace, Henry, and Marc. Henry glanced up first. "We don't—"

Marc squeezed Henry's fingers. "I want to."

"This interrupting me thing is turning into a habit." Henry looked adorable with his brows crooked together, a wrinkle between.

"If you guys need another minute—"

"No." Marc tugged Henry's hand forward. "We don't."

"Actually, we do." Henry didn't budge.

Grace pulled Luke away from the door. "If we don't see you guys upstairs, have a good night. Happy New Year!"

Luke followed his wife around the corner, leaving them alone. Marc turned to Henry. "What?"

Henry pulled his hand out of Marc's. "I'm not a token or a trophy, Marc."

"I didn't—"

"I know this is a big deal for you and tonight was a part of your big plan. I also know you're a master of recovery. It's why you do so well in this business. You can replot on the fly. You know every point in every file. Every figure. You've probably thought out every contingency before we ever get to the meeting table. But this isn't business. I'm a person, not a column of figures. If you want to replot me, you need to let me in on the plan. Not just tuck me under your arm like a file and pull me out when you need to make your best argument."

Marc felt his jaw unhinging. "I thought going upstairs was the right thing to do to show you I was committed to this thing. To show myself."

"This thing?"

"I'm trying to forge ahead."

"Just stop, please."

"Are you saying what I think you're saying?"

"What I'm saying is… I'm not a gesture. Look, coming out isn't something you can do to a schedule. It's not going to happen when you expect it, and when you plan for it, it's going to go wrong. Not everyone is going to understand, and some people just won't fucking care. But you seem to be forgetting the other half of the equation. Me."

Because Henry was a person, not a file. Right, got that. Except…. Oh.

Marc let his chin dip, carrying his gaze toward the floor.

Oh.

He scrubbed the back of his neck, ordered a few more thoughts— Henry being *right* foremost among them—and looked back up. "I'm sorry."

Henry's jaw tightened.

Marc cleared his throat and tried again. "I would like to go upstairs for a little while. I could seriously use a drink. Also…." A rough exhale left him feeling weak-kneed once again. "I don't know if we should go home together tonight. That was a part of my plan, as you know. Now? I think we both have a lot to think about. But I'm not ready to let you go yet. I need to salvage something from this—" Spreading his arms, Marc gestured around them. "—from all of this."

Retracting his arms, he breathed out another sigh. "Yeah, I figured going upstairs would be showing everyone I'm not afraid of what they think or who I am. Even though I can't get my knees to stop trembling. I also figured it was a way to grab some more time with you before our date finished. Before it became your worst date ever."

"Not yours?"

Marc shook his head. "No. It should be. If we plotted this out, scored it, it would be the worst date in the history of romance. But I don't regret a minute of the time I spent with you. Well, except... okay, we can forget all the parts where I was being a selfish prick, an idiot, and totally clueless."

"So about 95 percent—"

"Wow."

One eyebrow quirked. "Every time you interrupt me, the percentage goes up."

"Was it really that bad?"

Henry's expression gentled, his mouth settling into a smile. "No. I knew what I was getting into with you."

"Meaning?"

"You're the guy who tried to drive through a blizzard. Of course you were going to try your darnedest to have me right where you wanted me at midnight."

Quickly putting aside Henry had just used the word *darnedest*, Marc answered, "You could have stopped me at any time. We could have had this conversation in the cab."

"Maybe I wanted to be a part of your plan."

"But... not so much now?"

"I'd have liked to have been asked before being drafted for the recovery effort."

"Ah hell." That's what he'd forgotten. "I am an idiot. And a prick. And the other thing I said."

"Yeah, you are, but they're some of your most endearing qualities."

Marc laughed. "Seriously?" He studied Henry again and thought about what he'd said—about plans and replots and numbers and them. "What do you want to do?" he finally asked.

"I don't want to end our date here in the lobby."

"So it's upstairs or share a cab."

Henry nodded.

"Your choice," Marc said.

Henry smiled. "Let's go upstairs."

At first, the answer felt like a bucket of disappointment. As Marc considered it, though, he realized going upstairs was the better choice. They really weren't ready to go home together yet. Him and Henry. Tonight had been full of revelation. The high points had been ecstatically high. Upon reflection, the low points were more frustrations than anything else. And a surprise or two. Being gay wasn't turning out the way he expected, nor was Henry. In his gut, though? Marc couldn't deny his excitement at that discovery. Why should Henry follow a path ordained by anyone but Henry?

Nodding, he reached for Henry's hand again. Their fingers met and slid together, the motion already practiced and familiar. As Marc closed his hand around Henry's, a sense of rightness slid beneath his skin, calming some of the twitches, warming the icy prickle of fear.

"I'm not going to say I totally get it now, but only because I think I've finally figured out how much I just don't get. That's what scares me. Not having a plan. Not knowing what I'm facing."

"I know." Henry smiled. "But you have more of an idea now, right?"

"Are you sure you want to do this with me?"

Henry took another minute to think. He didn't seem to be questioning his answer, though, merely searching for words. Or so Marc hoped. "I like a challenge as much as you do."

Marc laughed at the mischievous spark in Henry's eyes. "Oh man. I think I've met my match."

"Maybe." Henry grinned, then sobered a little. "There's something between us. Something more than simple chemistry. I want to see where it goes."

"Me too." Marc leaned in to taste Henry's lips, wondering as he did so if this would be their last kiss of the night. Did he really need to demonstrate his newfound gayness upstairs? Share it with everyone who supposedly mattered?

Not really. Because the only person who really counted was standing right here with him, lips pressed to his.

Drawing back, he nosed Henry's cheek. "Ready to go upstairs?"

"Yeah." Henry turned his head so their noses bumped together. "Just gonna say right now that I do not want to check out the rooftop patio. We'll end up locked out there. Also off-limits are any rooms with doors and the elevator, even if it's been fixed."

Marc chuckled. "Maybe we should just go."

"Nope, we're going to go upstairs and introduce gay Marc and his gay boyfriend to everyone."

"Boyfriend?"

"We've crawled through ductwork together, and you've had my cock in your mouth. I think I qualify."

"I was blowing you at midnight, wasn't I?"

"Actually, I think you were shooting across the laundry floor about then." Henry grinned.

"I started my gay new year by giving you a blow job."

"We don't have to preface everything with gay. Just so you know."

Marc squeezed Henry's hand, then lifted the knuckles to his mouth and kissed them. "Okay. So, upstairs?"

"Yes."

"Wait." Marc pressed another kiss to Henry's full and inviting mouth. "Happy New Year, Henry."

Henry smiled against his lips. "Happy New Year, Marc."

Counting
THE DAYS

With two months to fill between *Counting Down* and the conclusion to Henry and Marc's story, *Counting on You*, I decided to do something a little different. This short story is comprised of texts I imagined the guys sending back and forth over that period.

People don't really pay attention to grammar when texting. I know I don't—and even when I do, my phone plays tricks on me, substituting words and turning commas into everything but.

For this story I decided to stick to the rules, mostly, for the sake of readability. Also, maybe it's an old person thing, but I tend to text in full words because I find them easier to type (or Swype) than an abbreviation. Marc and Henry probably know all the shortcuts, but we're going to pretend they're business-minded young individuals who value clarity over brevity.

Some of you will notice that I've often dropped the period off short phrases and the final sentence in a paragraph. I did this because that's how texting tends to work. I actually scrolled through my own texts to verify this and was sort of astounded to notice all the periods I *did* use. I don't usually remember using them. But I guess I do—and that's probably a good thing. ;)

Finally, Marc is always on the left and Henry is always on the right.

Okay, that's it! I hope you enjoy this extra peek into Marc and Henry's life.

JANUARY 5

Marc
8:47 PM
So, I was thinking about the BJ in the laundry

Henry
8:48 PM
Hey, Henry. How was your day?
You still there?

8:55 PM
Waiting for you to answer your question

8:55 PM
What question?

8:56 PM
How was your day?

8:57 PM
You're so weird

8:57 PM
You're the one who answered my text by
saying hello to yourself and asking
yourself how your day was

8:58 PM
Because that's what you usually say when you
haven't talked for 3 days.
Not: I was thinking about the BJ in the basement

8:59 PM
Laundry

9:06 PM
Hellooo
Auttenberg

> 9:08 PM
> I was bashing my head against a wall

9:09 PM
Not recommended

> 9:10 PM
> What about the BJ in the LAUNDRY?

9:11 PM
I was more thinking about after. When Luke walked in

> 9:11 PM
> Yeah?

9:12 PM
How I freaked out

> 9:12 PM
> I was there

9:12 PM
It's not that I was embarrassed

> 9:13 PM
> We talked about this. It's cool. I get it

9:13 PM
I just hadn't been in that situation before

> 9:14 PM
> Believe me, I know

9:14 PM
What do you mean, you know? Was it really that bad?

> 9:15 PM
> No

9:15 PM
You can tell me if it was

9:16 PM
Marc

9:16 PM
What?

9:16 PM
Not doing this right now

9:16 PM
Not doing what?

9:17 PM
Just tell me what you've been thinking about.
We can critique your technique another night.
When it's *not* night and I'm not tired

9:17 PM
Not a great day?

9:18 PM
Not really

9:18 PM
Want to talk about it?

9:18 PM
No, I'm fine

9:19 PM
Maybe this isn't a good time
Are you banging your head against a wall again?

9:27 PM
No, I was just thinking

9:28 PM
I'm doing this all wrong. Going to start again:
Hey, Henry. How's things?

9:29 PM
Things are good. Long day.

Was just about to go to sleep when
this guy started texting me

9:30 PM
You think you're funny. Also, seriously? It's like 8.
Why were you going to sleep?

9:30 PM
It's now *like* after nine and I'm tired

9:31 PM
Let's chat tomorrow, then

9:31 PM
We can do that

9:31 PM
Night!

9:31 PM
NN
9:45 PM
Unless you really need to tell me
something about the laundry

9:45 PM
Go to sleep. We can talk tomorrow

January 6

Henry
6:14 PM
Hey

Marc
7:23 PM
Hey! Sorry, was at the gym

7:48 PM
Working out?

7:50 PM
Practicing my lock picking skills

7:50 PM
??

7:51 PM
Yes I was working out!

7:51 PM
Did you silently append moron to that statement?

7:52 PM
Why would I do that?

7:52 PM
It's your tone. I always imagine you mentally
insulting me after you state the obvious.

7:52 PM
Hah. I guess I might. Sometimes.
I don't think moron, though. More like, duh

7:53 PM
Huh

7:53 PM
So what's up? Got time to talk, or are you already in bed?

7:53 PM
Haha. No. I'm always tired on Mondays.
Even more when I have to travel

7:53 PM
Hell yeah. I know what you mean. So how's Charlotte?

7:54 PM
Surprisingly not warm

7:55 PM
January

7:57 PM
Yeah. Client feels good, though.
You know how sometimes you get this feeling
they're not going to work with you? Not getting
that here. Even had a desk set up for me and a PA
I can share. He's an idiot and it's sad because he's
probably older than me. But what can I say,
he's gainfully employed

8:00 PM
I ever tell you about the woman who insisted on
getting lunch for me when I was in NYC last year?
First day I was like, sure, and gave her my order
and maybe an HOUR later she gets back to her
desk with a muffin. She's peeling the wrapper
back and looking at the thing like it's going to
come alive when I ask her about my sandwich.
She forgot. Offers me the muffin.
So, 2nd day she asks again and I'm thinking,
she can't forget 2 days in a row?

I ask for tuna salad and she brings back chicken salad.
Chicken salad!

> 8:00 PM
> I like chicken salad

8:01 PM
Chicken salad is disgusting
3rd day I head out 15mins early and get a
tuna sandwich. I get back and there's a muffin
on my desk. A muffin. And the damn wrapper
is peeled back on one side

> 8:01 PM
> Ew

8:01 PM
Right? She was old, like grandma old.
I never saw her do any work

> 8:02 PM
> The PA is maybe 30 something? I dunno. I'm bad with ages.
> He seems to work for the whole floor.
> I probably won't use him

8:03 PM
That's because you're a nice guy.
I'd have him getting me sandwiches
and muffins and files I didn't need.

> 8:04 PM
> Yep

8:04 PM
Because I am NOT a nice guy.
It's okay, you can agree with me

> 8:07 PM
> I was trying to think of a way to say
> you're nice without using the word nice

8:08 PM
Because...

8:09 PM
Don't worry about it. Hey, I need to
catch up on some work. Chat later?

8:10 PM
Sure. Night!

8:11 PM
NN

JANUARY 7

Henry
Jan 7, 2:35 PM
So about the BJ in the laundry...

Marc
3:07 PM
OMG, I was in a meeting with Shelly.
Nearly LOLed

3:31 PM
Hah! Too funny
Got time to chat?

3:45 PM
Sure. Let's talk BJs on B+Ms time.
Did you send your PA out for chicken salad?

3:46 PM
No. Got my own lunch
So, the laundry. Sorry I forgot last night

3:47 PM
It's cool. I was just, you know, thinking stuff through.
Like, what was going through my head when Luke
showed up. Or what wasn't? Complete stand still.
Sort of. And then being such an ass

3:47 PM
Which is kind of like you

3:48 PM
Yeah. Anyway, I was thinking more about
what you said. About how going upstairs

probably wasn't a good idea. But I wanted
to do it anyway

3:49 PM
We did go upstairs

3:50 PM
It's been bugging me that we went upstairs.
Should we have just... not? You were really
quiet after that. Then we didn't talk for 2-3 days?
So...

3:51 PM
It was my choice. I said we should go upstairs

3:52 PM
Was it really your choice?

3:52 PM
What are we talking about?
You thinking you bullied me into going to
a party we nearly missed because of a
broken elevator? Or the fact someone nearly
caught you with my dick in your mouth?

3:53 PM
Both. And me using the B word

3:53 PM
B?

3:54 PM
Boyfriend
4:07 PM
Hellooo?

6:23 PM
Hey, just got back to the hotel

7:47 PM
And it's nearly your bedtime

8:05 PM
Ass. Listen, about before. You're
not the asshole you think you are.
Okay? And I might be... Quiet.
But you can't make me do anything
I don't want to do

8:07 PM
You spend all afternoon figuring out a way to
tell me I'm nice without using the word nice?

8:10 PM
Sending you the bill for the dent in this wall

8:10 PM
Aw. Did you bash your head again?
I'll kiss it better for you
xx

January 9

Henry

2:57 PM

Hey, looks like I'll be out of here

tomorrow afternoon.

Marc

9:10 PM

Awesome.

Want to catch up on Sunday?

January 10

Marc
8:10 PM
Not sure when you'll get this.
I'm packing for Atlanta.
Flying out tomorrow. Earlyish.

Henry
12:54 AM
How early is earlyish?

1:35 AM
You still awake?

1:47 AM
Just got home from the airport.

1:53 AM
OMW over.

January 12

Marc
4:50 PM
Okay, you've had two Winning BJs now.
Can we talk technique?

Henry
7:31 PM
Capping Winning wasn't a mistake, was it?

7:45 PM
You've met my ego.
7:47 PM
So...?
7:57 PM
Are you thinking of ways to say nice without saying nice?
Coz if you are, don't. BJs aren't supposed to be NICE.

7:57 PM
It was really nice.

7:58 PM
OMG

7:58 PM
What is your deal with nice?

8:00 PM
Honestly don't know. Just...
I dunno.
8:05 PM
Throw me a bone here.
This is all new to me and I want to know if I'm doing okay.

8:06 PM
Because I get BJs every Sunday morning at
2:30 AM. Lots to compare, right?

8:07 PM
Hey, I don't know what your social life is like.

8:08 PM
Yeah, you do.

8:08 PM
Okay, I guess.
You should go out more.

8:10 PM
Well, I would?
But I have a boyfriend.
8:15 PM
What was that? Did you try to send me a picture?

8:15 PM
Yeah. Doesn't your piece of crap phone do pictures?

8:16 PM
Always gets messed up on text for some
reason. Send an email?

8:16 PM
Don't worry about it.

8:16 PM
What was it?
Oh God. Did you try to send me a dick pic?
Don't send that to my B+M account.

8:17 PM
Did you append moron to that statement?

8:17 PM
FU. What did you send?

8:18 PM
It was nothing. So, are we going to talk BJs?

8:18 PM
What did you send???

8:20 PM
I'm sighing so hard over here the whole hotel
can hear me. Concierge is banging on the door
asking me to quit sighing so loud. Seriously.
I made the hotel sway.

8:20 PM
Okay...

8:21 PM
It was a picture of me smiling.

8:21 PM
Now I really want it.
Email it to me. Use my gmail account.

8:21 PM
nosociallife@gmail.com?

8:22 PM
Heyauttenberg

8:22 PM
It's a stupid picture.

8:25 PM
It's a great picture! Why are you smiling?
8:35 PM
Hellooooo?

8:45 PM
Bec you said you had a boyfriend.

JANUARY 14

Henry
12:30 PM
So, BJ technique.

Marc
1:04 PM
You knew I was in a meeting, didn't you?

1:15 PM
I thought you might be at lunch.
I did think about texting you at 10. ;)

1:16 PM
And you call me an ass.
7:35 PM
Hey.

7:36 PM
Hey! Just picked up my phone.

7:37 PM
Busy day?

7:37 PM
So so. You?

7:38 PM
Kinda whipped.

7:39 PM
O.O

7:39 PM
Whipped. Wiped. Same thing.

7:40 PM
Not really

7:40 PM
And you would know?

7:40 PM
Because all these random BJs I'm getting
usually start with a little bondage.

7:42 PM
Know what I'm really interested in?
Why your mind went there.
Right there. Instead of thinking I just
felt like I'd been whipped. Which I kinda
did in a metaphorical sense. Or thinking
autocorrect might have been playing dirty with me.

7:43 PM
So are you into that sort of thing?
Just, you know, if you are,
we should maybe talk about it.

7:44 PM
Are you?

7:44 PM
I asked first.

7:45 PM
Fine. No. I dunno. No. I mean...
No.

7:46 PM
I'm sensing some hesitation.

7:46 PM
Really?

7:46 PM
Hehe. So, no?

7:47 PM
Let's go with no.

7:48 PM
But you've thought about it?

7:48 PM
I guess. In an abstract sense?
What about you?

7:50 PM
My mom and my sister went to see that movie.
The 50 Shades one.

7:51 PM
And you snuck in there with them.
Lurked in the back?
Did you touch yourself?

7:51 PM
Who did you sneak in with?

7:52 PM
I would rather choke on a dildo.
Which I can't imagine would be all that pleasant.
Wow, can you imagine having to go to the
ER with a dildo stuck in your mouth?
If you got that far. Like, you'd probably die first.
8:02 PM
You there?

8:02 PM
Sometimes it's like I don't know you at all.

8:02 PM
We don't really know each other very well.
Not yet.

8:03 PM
I do know you can be...
Nice.

8:04 PM
OMG. Duck you. &*^%$$$.
You're laughing, aren't you?

8:05 PM
:D :D :D

JANUARY 16

Marc
8:04 PM
So, are we ever going to talk about
my Winning Technique?

Henry
8:14 PM
When you stop using the word Winning.

8:14 PM
Aw. Also, we never finished our 50 Shades discussion.

8:15 PM
We were having a 50 Shades discussion?

8:15 PM
As one does.

8:16 PM
Hehe. Okay, answer is NO.
I did not sneak in. But I heard ALL about it.
Dad and I were... Sunday lunch isn't the
place to talk about stuff like that.

8:16 PM
I can so picture it. Your mom. Your dad.
LOLOL

8:17 PM
Right? They're pretty free thinking, but. Yeah.
Anyway, no, it's not my thing. Abstract sense?
Maybe. Like, I think I can see what it's about.
But I'm pretty content as I am.
I just want... to be with someone.

8:18 PM
I hear you. Same.

8:18 PM
Boring can be good, right?

8:18 PM
Boring can be really NICE.

8:19 PM
We have so ruined that word.
Meaning we should talk about
your BJ technique now.

8:19 PM
Yes. By all means. Tell me how LOVELY it all was.

8:20 PM
You're a riot.

8:20 PM
TY

8:21 PM
Both times have been really, really good.
First time I came so hard I thought I
was going to pass out.

8:21 PM
That's kind of hot.
It'd probably been a while, tho.

8:21 PM
Why do you do that?

8:22 PM
Do what?

8:22 PM
Talk yourself down or whatever.
It's not very Winning of you.

8:22 PM
Heh. I know. I don't know. I'm anxious.

8:23 PM
Yeah, it'd been a stupidly long while,
but that wasn't it. It was you, Marc.
On your fucking knees in front of me.

8:23 PM
How come your phone says ducking. Fucking!
Fucking phone. I had to add that to my dictionary.

8:24 PM
I know. So dumb.
Like they think if the phones come with no language
in the dictionary no one will swear. Ever.
Stupid fucks.

8:25 PM
You don't really swear. Much.

8:25 PM
Neither do you. Much.
For someone who wanted to talk technique,
you sure change the subject a lot.

8:26 PM
So me on my knees...

8:26 PM
You have to know what that's like.
To look down at someone.
See their mouth wrapped around your dick.
I don't know what it is. The kneeling.
The looking up.
The whole deal.
It's hot.

8:27 PM
So it could have been anyone down there.

8:28 PM
So insecure.

8:28 PM
All part of the Winning Technique. ;)

8:35 PM
Okay, this might sound stupid or whatever.
I haven't been with a lot of guys. Not because I'm shy.
So shut up. Because I've been too busy trying to be you.
Remember that conversation? But for me it's always
been about the person I'm with more than technique.
If I cared about the person, a sloppy BJ would still be
better than doing it with some random dude who
sucked on billiard balls all day as practice. Before you
get your nuts in a twist over the sloppy comment...
that was not you.
You were good. I knew you'd be good. You were hungry
for it and you were curious and you have a cock.
You know what feels good.
It was good, Marc.
Really good.
Second one was even better.

8:36 PM
TY

8:37 PM
YW

JANUARY 15

Henry
7:30 PM
You ever go to karaoke when you're out of town?

Marc
7:45 PM
No one does karaoke like Mulligans.

January 16

Marc
8:46 PM
So that's another week done.
Got plans for the weekend?

Henry
8:51 PM
I'll probably visit my folks.
Mom hasn't done my laundry for a while.
She's probably in withdrawal.

8:52 PM
LOL

8:52 PM
You?

8:52 PM
Probably work. This hotel sucks.
Three cable channels with good reception.
ALL ESPN.
Kill me now.

8:53 PM
Is there a porn channel?

8:54 PM
On demand. Dare me to?

8:55 PM
How would it show up on the bill?
Can you expense porn?

8:55 PM
Good question.

I'm going to do it. See what happens.

Worst they can do is say, don't expense porn.

I'll pay for it. Done and done.

8:59 PM

Ugh, this selection is really bad.

Like... so bad.

And none of it is even remotely gay.

> 9:00 PM
>
> Well, duh.
>
> That's what the internet is for.

9:01 PM

Obvs. So what are some of your fave sites?

> 9:02 PM
>
> I don't have a fave.
>
> Read the titles you have on demand.

9:03 PM

They're dumb. Let's both watch something
from your fave site.

> 9:05 PM
>
> I love how you keep assuming I have a favorite.

9:05 PM

Still waters.

> 9:06 PM
>
> Mm-hmm. Sending you a link.

9:08 PM

Okay. Wow.

I got hard looking at the front page.

This stuff is seriously hot.

Do you pay for it?

9:09 PM
No, I don't watch enough.
I usually just look around at the clips.
Use my imagination and hand for the rest.

9:09 PM
Have you got toys and stuff at home?
OMG, do you travel with... stuff?

9:10 PM
No I do not travel with STUFF.

9:11 PM
So when we're talking stuff,
what are we talking about?

9:11 PM
You're the one who brought up stuff.
What are you talking about?
9:15 PM
Hmm?

9:18 PM
I'm researching so I don't sound like a total
idiot when I list all the STUFF I don't have.
Also really turned on right now.

9:18 PM
Yeah?

9:19 PM
You're right. I don't need to watch any of this.
Just thinking about it. Thinking about you.
Are you hard?

9:22 PM
Yeah.

9:23 PM
You're touching yourself, aren't you?

9:24 PM
Yes.

9:24 PM
Shorts on or off?

9:25 PM
Pushed down.
You?

9:28 PM
Pants off. Shirt off.
Take your shirt off.

9:30 PM
Done.

9:31 PM
One hand on your cock. Other hand on...
Stomach. Move your fingers up and down.
Obvs. on your cock. On your stomach too.
Up to just under your pecs.
Down to your hips.

9:33 PM
Not getting why this feels so good.

9:34 PM
Because you're not touching what needs to
be touched. Except your dick. How are you
stroking? Short and fast or long and slow?

9:35 PM
Long and slow.

9:36 PM
Thinking about your hood.
Sliding up and back.
Squeeze there.
Play there.

Up and back. Just there.
Cup your balls.

9:37 PM
What are you doing?

9:38 PM
Same. With my naked dick. Fuck.
Pretending it's your hand.

9:40 PM
Me too.

9:42 PM
Playing with my nipples now.
Guy nipples are so tiny.

9:43 PM
Pinch one.
That's my teeth.

9:44 PM
This would be better on speaker phone.

9:46 PM
Next time. I'm too close.

9:49 PM
Me too.

10:10 PM
That was hot.

10:14 PM
I know. Fuck. Never come that hard on my own.

10:15 PM
Me neither. I'm going to pass out now.

10:16 PM
Me too. Night.

10:16 PM
NN

January 25

Marc
12:30 PM
Did I leave my iPod at your place?

Henry
12:45 PM
I didn't see it. Did you check the front
pocket of your case?

1:30 PM
Aha! How did you know it would be there?

2:57 PM
Saw you put it in there when
you got out of the cab.

3:12 PM
You watched me get out of the cab?
3:23 PM
Like, from the window.
3:47 PM
Were you waiting by the window for me to arrive?
3:49 PM
Or just randomly passing by?

4:45 PM
I admit nothing.

5:12 PM
You were totally waiting.

January 26

Marc
10:03 PM
That was...

                                        Henry 10:05 PM
                        Even better on speaker phone.

10:05 PM
Who said we needed to be in the same city?

                                            10:06 PM
                        It'd be better in the same city.
                                Same room, even.

10:07 PM
So now I'm picturing us sitting on opposite
sides of the same room, jerking off, but
telling each other what to do.

                                            10:08 PM
                And you're not thinking that would be weird?

10:08 PM
No. It's not like we couldn't touch if we didn't
want to, but not being able to touch, telling
each other what to touch, could be a real turn on.

                                            10:08 PM
                        Yeah, okay. I could see that.

10:009 PM
Just thinking about it is making me hard.

                                            10:09 PM
                        Again? You just nutted.

10:09 PM
I'm picturing you sitting on the bed, dick in hand.
Just the idea I can't touch you is getting me there.

10:10 PM
Tell me what to do.

10:10 PM
Lean back. Like on your elbows.
Spread your knees.
Long strokes on your cock.
Root to tip.

10:12 PM
Can't believe how hard I am.

10:13 PM
Are you leaning against the headboard?

10:14 PM
And trying not to think about who
else has leaned here. Naked.

10:14 PM
Not now, Auttenberg.
Spread your legs. I want to see your balls.
Under there.

10:15 PM
You mean my ass.

10:17 PM
Yeah.
What should I call it?

10:17 PM
My ass.

10:17 PM
Isn't there, like, a word?

10:17 PM
Ass.

10:18 PM
You're a lot snarkier over text
than you are when we talk.

10:18 PM
It's my super power.

10:18 PM
LOL.
Okay, Super Snark. Show me your hole.

10:20 PM
Fuck.

10:20 PM
Touch it. Just your fingertip. Circle.

10:21 PM
Am I still stroking myself?

10:21 PM
Yep.
Is this what you do at home?

10:25 PM
And in random hotel rooms.

10:26 PM
You've got lube with you, right?

10:28 PM
Yeah.

10:28 PM
You know what to do.

10:30 PM
Don't want to get my phone all greasy.
Text you in a bit.

10:31 PM
I want ALL the details.

10:31 PM
We could do another call.

10:32 PM
No. I want it in text. How you touched yourself.
What you were thinking about.

10:55 PM
I had to lay back. I did that, knees up and spread.
Wide. I imagined your voice guiding my finger.
Lubing it up. Touching myself in slow circles until the
flesh around my hole puckered tight.
Pushing inside. Feeling the grip and give.
Do you know what that feels like yet?
Have you touched yourself? You have, I know you have.
I pushed in slowly. Just one finger. Still stroking.
Up and down. Up, twist and squeeze, down. Squeeze.
I got so close. You told me to use a second finger, so I did. ;)
Came hard.
Feel like a flat plastic bag right now.
Which isn't... sexy. Whatever.
DED.
Also, if there's an emergency in the night
and I die in my bed because I was too fucked
to hear the alarm, I'm coming back to haunt you.

10:57 PM
BEST. BOYFRIEND. EVER.

January 27

Henry
2:53 PM
When you get back to your room, shower thoroughly.
I mean thoroughly. Soap up a finger and clean everything.
Then get on the bed. On your back. Naked.
Lube and a hand towel beside you.
Lie back, knees up and spread. WIDE.
Wait like that for five minutes. Imagine I'm looking at you.
Telling you what I like. What I want to do.
I want to suck you. Suck your balls.
Lick your hole. Stick my tongue inside.
Think about that. But DON'T TOUCH YOURSELF
FOR FIVE MINUTES. Then lube up a finger.
Circle. Push.
You've done it before. I know you have.
Even before we went to Chicago together,
you were touching your ass. You wanted to
know what it felt like, didn't you?
Pushing your finger inside.
Stroke your cock. It's really, really hard, isn't it?
Call me when you're done.

Marc
4:10 PM
Holy fucking shit, Auttenberg. I nearly busted a nut in my meeting.
Call you later.

February 2

Henry
6:30 PM
Hey, I'm kinda tired tonight. Going to call it early.
Chat to you tomorrow.

February 4

Marc
9:37 PM
Just so you know, I haven't jerked
off this much since high school.

Henry
9:45 PM
This is more fun tho.

February 10

Marc
7:37 PM
I am wiped.
Notice I did not say whipped.
Can't remember if I called you
last night or if you called me.

Henry
8:10 PM
Check your phone log. I called you.

8:12 PM
So you did. Hey, feel like just chatting tonight?
Not sure I could get it up if you were standing
naked in front of me hard as the proverbial
whatever and a list of instructions ten pages long.

8:12 PM
Hehe. Sure. I'm kinda wiped too.
Notice I did not say whipped.

8:13 PM
How's it going over there?
Where are you again?

8:14 PM
Back in Boston this week.
Probably for the rest of the month.

8:15 PM
I can dream.

8:15 PM
You're back in Atlanta?

8:15 PM
Yeah. I think they sent me your PA.
Wasn't he down here somewhere?
Late 30s. Looks like he plays D&D in his spare time.

8:15 PM
I used to play D&D.

8:16 PM
Did you go to the park with your dorky
friends and swing a sword around?

8:17 PM
That's LARPing and one does not LARP in Dorchester.

8:17 PM
I have no idea what you just said.

8:17 PM
LOL.
8:19 PM
My friend and I dressed up for a ren faire once.
It was cool. Do you ever wonder what it might have
been like to live back then?

8:20 PM
Then? I'm assuming you mean like medieval times.

8:20 PM
Sure.

8:21 PM
We wouldn't have been able to sleep together, right?

8:23 PM
I dunno. I sometimes think people are more
hung up on stuff like that now than they were back then.
I mean, sure, there's been periods of history where
homosexuals have been killed and tortured for
even thinking about it. But there have also been

times when people just didn't care, right? When it
was natural to love your best friend in all the ways
because life was short and it was up to you to find
comfort where you could.
Because that's what it's about, right? Being who
you are. Why should that upset anyone else?

8:23 PM
Because people are fucked up. Especially men.
We have this idea of what it means to be a man
and it's... when you pull it apart and lay the
pieces down, it's ridiculous. It's stupid.
Women have their rules too and... I get it?
I mean, I know I'm a product of my society
and a lot of what I think is stuff I've been
taught to think, you know? It's really hard
to deconstruct some of that.

8:25 PM
Yeah.

8:27 PM
So what did you dress up as?

8:27 PM
Huh?

8:28 PM
For the ren faire.

8:29 PM
Traveling bard. I wore purple pants. PURPLE.
And carried a lute that was a seriously butchered
guitar I bought from a thrift shop.

8:30 PM
Got a picture?

8:31 PM
I'm sure my mom does.
She has pictures of everything.

8:31 PM
I want to see it.

8:31 PM
I'll ask her this weekend.

8:32 PM
Do you visit your folks every weekend?

8:38 PM
Not every weekend, but a few times
a month. Is that weird?

8:42 PM
Nope. If I had folks like yours I'd live with them.

8:42 PM
No you wouldn't.

8:42 PM
Would. Get that picture for me.

8:43 PM
Yes, sir!

FEBRUARY 14

Henry
6:30 PM
I can't believe you sent me flowers.

Marc
6:57 PM
Happy Valentine's Day.

7:30 PM
Thank you. Sorry I didn't send you anything
except that stupid gif this morning.

7:37 PM
I liked the stupid gif and it's the thought that
counts, right? I should have told you to take
a picture of your face when you saw the flowers.

7:41 PM
Why?

7:42 PM
The only picture I have of you is 14-year-old
Henry wearing purple pants.

7:43 PM
You have it on your phone??

7:44 PM
It's my wallpaper.

7:44 PM
Please tell me you're lying.

7:44 PM
I wish I could.

7:45 PM

...

7:47 PM
14-year old Henry is adorable. You weren't
kidding about that guitar, though. Looks
like someone sat on your lute and tried to
glue it back together.

7:48 PM
Yep.

7:51 PM
Send me a picture of you now. Smiling.

7:52 PM
I just got back from a run.

7:52 PM
In February? Are you nuts?
It's dark out there.

7:53 PM
It's never dark in the city and yeah I'm nuts.

7:55 PM
Still waiting for my picture.
7:58 PM
I said smiling.
8:03 PM
This one is worse. You look like someone
stuck a finger up your ass.

8:04 PM
No I don't.
Unless it was an ice-cold finger.

8:07 PM
That's better.
You look like someone told you to smile, tho.

8:08 PM
And that would be because…

8:08 PM
Okay, go take a shower and try again.
8:25 PM
Hey, I like that one. Yes! Your smile is great.

8:27 PM
I look like a dork.

8:28 PM
Newsflash: you are a dork.
Purple. Pants.

8:29 PM
Don't make me regret sending you that picture.

8:31 PM
Aw. Don't be like that. I wouldn't have made
it my wallpaper if I didn't like it.

8:32 PM
I'm really hoping you're lying about the wallpaper.

8:34 PM
Check your email.

8:36 PM
OMG MARC.

8:36 PM
:D

8:36 PM
Dying.

8:37 PM
I hope that's laughing dying and not
throwing yourself out the window dying.

8:38 PM
I'm imagining you explaining your wallpaper

to someone who doesn't know me. Or even
better, someone who knows me. OMG.

8:39 PM
Hehe. Okay, contact picture set.
You are no longer Mr. Anon Gray Head.

8:40 PM
Yay?

8:40 PM
You still have that picture of me?

8:40 PM
Yep.

8:41 PM
Is it your wallpaper?

8:41 PM
No, it's your contact picture.

8:42 PM
So it's my face on your phone when we're jerking off.

8:42 PM
And when we just talk. Yes.

8:43 PM
:)
So, wanna play?

8:43 PM
Seeing as I can't thank you for the flowers in person...

February 16

Marc 6:45 PM
Thanks for the book. You're such a dope.

Henry 6:57 PM
Read it cover to cover. There will be a test.

6:59 PM
Reading the kidnapping chapter now.
7:05 PM
Why would anyone need to know that tanks
have a blind spot? It's kind of obvious, tho.
Jesus, the main gun can kill with percussion only?
Henry, why do you read books like this?
7:09 PM
Hah! Found the trapped in the snow chapter.
You were right about the seat covers!

7:09 PM
;)

7:14 PM
The self-defense chapter is really informative.
Do you have any training?

7:16 PM
Not really. Judo in high school?

7:17 PM
We should do a class together.

7:18 PM
If we're ever in town at the same time, you mean?

7:18 PM
I'll happen, Auttenberg. We just need to
get through whatever hell this is. Shelly
knows I want you on my team.
We'll make it happen.

7:20 PM
Have you thought about why we've been
sent everywhere separately since NYE?

7:21 PM
I have.

7:21 PM
Do you think Luke said something about
what he saw in the laundry?

7:22 PM
I don't care if he did. We were on our own time.
7:30 PM
Are you having 2nd thoughts?
I thought we were having fun.

7:31 PM
We are. Shelly is probably just
clearing our schedules, right?

7:32 PM
She's testing us. It's what she does.
We'll prove we're up for it.
Whatever, wherever.

7:32 PM
Over, under, around or through?

7:32 PM
You know it.

7:33 PM
I'll look into classes.

7:33 PM
You do that.

FEBRUARY 20

Marc
9:55 PM
Hey

Henry
9:55 PM
Hey. :)

9:56 PM
That was...

9:56 PM
Yep.

9:57 PM
Ever thought about trying to do it over
video chat?

9:58 PM
Yeah, but then I get all paranoid about
someone hacking our laptop cameras
or whatever.

9:59 PM
I wondered about that too.
10:02 PM
Just want to see your face when you come.

10:03 PM
Me too.

10:05 PM
Lots of people do the long-distance thing.

10:07 PM
Is that a question?

10:08 PM
It's me trying to figure out what we're doing.
10:15 PM
You still awake?

10:17 PM
We're doing what we want to do, right?

10:18 PM
Are you asking if I want to do this?

10:18 PM
Maybe we should talk about it when
we don't have fuzzy orgasm brain.

10:19 PM
We could. Or I could just say right now
that this isn't what I want. It's what I
have right now.
10:20 PM
That sounded bad. Sorry.

10:28 PM
So, you're the one who usually does this.
I'm probably going to mess it up. But...
this isn't how it's going to be forever.
I believe that. B+M likes us and when
a company likes someone, they work
to make them happy. We get good results.
We just need one job together to show
them what we can do, and we'll be a team.
You know this. I know this.
Shelly Flores knows this.
Just one job, Marc. Until then, we have this.
It's not perfect. It is what it is. But it's more
than I've had in a long, long time.

Even when we're not jerking off,
I like chatting with you. I feel like...
We're friends. And that's important to me.
I really like being your friend, Winnamore.

10:28 PM
What happened to the B word?

10:28 PM
Boyfriend.

10:29 PM
Do you like being my boyfriend?

10:30 PM
I just made a gesture here. My thumbs
are sore from all that gesturing.

10:31 PM
You should use swype.

10:32 PM
Are you trying to piss me off?

10:34 PM
No. Sorry. I'm...
Processing.

10:35 PM
Process away.

10:38 PM
I like this too. You're right. About all of it.
I've never talked to anyone as much as
I've talked to you over the past couple of
months. And I like it. It's weird, but I like it.
I like playing with you too. I just want more.
But you're right about that as well.
Damn I hate it when someone else is right.

10:38 PM
Because you're a Winner?

10:39 PM
Hah.
10:45 PM
Hey.

10:46 PM
I was nearly asleep.

10:46 PM
Sorry. Just wanted to say goodnight.

10:46 PM
NN

10:46 PM
And thank you. For listening. For talking.
For doing this with me. For all of it.

10:47 PM
YW

10:47 PM
I'm kissing you softly. With tenderness
that's stupidly embarrassing, but it's just us.
Only you know I'm kissing you like this.

10:48 PM
Pulling you close. Letting you snuggle with me. xx
10:49 PM
Night, Henry. xx

10:50 PM
Night, Marc. xoxo

Counting
ON YOU

*H*enry and Marc can't seem to catch a break. They've had two disastrous dates—the first trapped in a car during a blizzard and the second locked in a basement—followed by nearly two months apart. Even though they work for the same firm, their relationship is held together by flying visits, phone calls, and text messages. A joint assignment in Washington DC might be more togetherness than they can handle, however.

Henry is still battling insecurity, and this assignment is too important to his career to mess up. Marc is committed. He's falling for Henry and looks forward to having him permanently on his team and at his side. But the real test isn't the assignment. When Marc finally lays his heart on the line, can he count on Henry to be there for him, in every way that matters? And can he do the same for Henry when Henry needs it the most?

Chapter
ONE

February

The wind didn't tug at Henry's sweats—it pushed right through them to blast his skin, leaving his thighs tingling, then numb. He pulled the loop of his scarf up over his mouth and grimaced as damp wool tickled his lips. The press of cold air obliterated the drone of his own voice from the buds in his ears.

Why was he jogging outside?

Better question might be why he was trying to listen to a case file. Between worrying about the fact he'd lost touch with his hands and feet and wondering whether he should call Marc, he hadn't heard a word of it.

He couldn't remember when he and Marc had started taking turns, switching off the days to call or text, but sometime over the past two months, a routine had fallen into place. Unlike the cruel wind slowly transforming him into a human icicle, the routine was comfortable.

Henry stumbled and caught himself on a nearby lamppost. Even inside a glove, his fingers were too numb to save him. He slid across the post and down, landing face-first in a hard-packed snowbank.

I love Boston. I like the snow. I love Boston. I like....

Coughing, Henry pushed up to his knees and tried to grip the post again. Only after he had the cold steel wrapped in a bear hug did he manage to regain his feet. He rested there a moment, catching his breath. Would he actually know if he'd broken something until he thawed out?

The drone of statistics in his ears was cut off by Marc's ringtone. Henry bit the fingertips of his left glove, extracted his hand, and reached inside his jacket for his phone. A quick swipe, and he was desperate to get his glove back on before he lost fingers. Instead of saying hello, he coughed. The sound crackled and echoed through his earbuds.

"Hey!" Marc answered. "You sound terrible. Are you sick?"

Marcus Winnamore had a good voice. Warm and convivial. He could speak in a confidential tone, making you think you were the only one to hear this particular secret, and he could speak in a confident tone, convincing you that whatever he said was true.

He also had a seductive voice—and right then, it spread beneath Henry's layers of cold and numbness, reaching inside to light the fire of attraction that continued to burn after a couple of months of the most unconventional relationship either of them had ever had.

"Not sick," Henry said. "Just regretting the brilliant idea to jog outside."

"Is it snowing again? Why are you outside? Your building has a gym."

Once, he'd have appended Marc's outburst with a mental "you moron!" Now Henry simply recognized the questions and statements as Marc's way of establishing fact and asking why Henry was deviating from the plan.

"Not snowing and the gym is in the basement," he explained.

Marc chuckled. "Which I'm assuming you have a key to. Not every basement is out to get you, you know."

"Yeah, but Betty White lives in this one." She didn't, really, but her doppelgänger did, and jogging next to a little old lady always made him feel weird. Also the row of mirrors in front of the treadmills, the low ceiling, and… okay, the fact it was a basement. After his New Year's date with Marc, he was considering developing a phobia against basements. Would fit in nicely with his phobia regarding blizzards, rental cars, and getting involved with guys who didn't really want to be gay. "Listen, I need to get inside before I fuse with this lamppost."

"Huh?"

"I'm currently hugging a lamppost, and if I stand here much longer, they'll be chipping me away with ice picks."

"You miss me so much you've taken to hugging random poles?"

"Not random."

"So you picked this post specially. Here's a tip. Don't try kissing it. You might lose a lip or two."

"I picked this post because I fell in all this stupid ice and snow. Why do we live in Boston, Marc? Why haven't we made plans to move to New Mexico?"

"It gets really cold in New Mexico."

"Florida, then."

"Sinkholes."

"California?"

"San Andreas fault! Geez, Henry. Aren't you keeping up with potential disasters?"

Chuckling, Henry pushed off the pole and took a tentative step forward. When he didn't slip, he resumed his jog. "I tried to call last night."

"Yeah, sorry. I got tied up, and not in the fun way."

"According to you, there is no fun way." Two months of little more than phone conversations (that sometimes went beyond conversation and into lube and hand towels) had given them ample opportunity to chat about sexual preferences. And lube and hand towels.

"I could be persuaded. Maybe. I wouldn't want to be done up in one of those fishing net arrangements. But you using your ties, or no, my ties, to hold my wrists up against bedposts or something, would be…."

A heavy breath pushed through the phone. Henry could almost feel it on the back of his neck. He could definitely feel it darting beneath his skin, heading southward, along with blood he really needed elsewhere. "Please don't make me jog with a hard-on."

Marc laughed. "Okay. Anyway, sorry about last night." He paused. "I missed talking to you."

Ah, sweet Marc. Henry missed him, and all the other Marcs. "Do you have plans tonight?" he asked.

"Yeah, about that."

Henry shivered, and all signs of arousal retreated.

"I'm calling early because I'm packing. I've got a flight to catch."

Henry's shoulders slumped as the recognizable twist of misery moved through him. Talking with Marc was good. If pressed, he'd say their relationship had grown out of talking. Being trapped in a car during a blizzard and then in a basement laundry together had given them ample opportunity to clear several conversational hurdles. They now chatted like old friends. But he'd really much prefer to touch Marc while they were talking—or too busy to talk. Fate, however, who was obviously a bitch with a warped sense of humor, had seen fit to give them only four days and two nights together since New Year's Eve—none consecutive. Instead, he and Marc had been traveling. Marc more than him, and always separately, attached to different teams.

They'd discussed the possibility upper management weren't happy about their relationship. But none of their assignments had felt like a punishment. They were good and rewarding cases, the kind of work they both relished, and before the blizzard, before the laundry, two months wouldn't have seemed much of anything. Then, they'd only been colleagues.

"You still with me?" Marc asked.

Henry shook his head, pulling himself out of a deep thought funk just before he passed the steps to his building. "Sorry, I'm here. Where are they sending you?"

"I'm coming home, Auttenberg."

Gaping—not a good idea when the ambient air temperature could be measured in kelvin—Henry reached for the handrail beside the steps. "Home as in Boston?"

"Yeah." The warmth was back. Marc was smiling, no doubt.

"Tonight? What time?" Thankfully, his jaw froze in place before he could offer to go out to Logan to meet him. Were they at that stage of their relationship? Was there ever a stage where you trekked out to the airport to meet a boyfriend? More questions unfurled in a rush. Would he catch the T or get a cab? What would be less weird? Why was he suddenly in such a rush? What if he got out to the airport and Marc was embarrassed, or not pleased, or—

"I'm catching the red-eye. I'll probably land with enough time to change my shirt before I head into the office."

"Oh."

"You okay? Inside yet?"

"Getting there. So how long will you be in town for?"

"Only Shelly Flores and the good Lord know," Marc said. "Given it's already Wednesday, I'm hoping I'll be around for the weekend." That would be four days together. Four consecutive days *and* nights. "There's some talk about a client in Atlanta."

"Gernicky and Sons? I was just listening to my notes on that one." Henry's heart leaped into his throat. Four days and a job together? Had Fate become distracted by someone else?

"You've been examining the case files?"

"Shelly asked me to go over the financials."

"Awesome. If I go, I'm going to ask for you to be on my team. Because this job would be a total favor for Shelly. It's from her overflow bin."

Another gust of wind pushed Henry sideways. Gripping the rail for support, he hauled himself up the stairs and fumbled in a pocket for his key. "I'm not going to get excited."

"Neither am I."

"I'm already excited." Oh God, he'd said that out loud, hadn't he?

"Same."

Henry grinned as Marc's chuckle echoed down the line, stupidly relieved he wasn't the only one excited. He lifted his gaze heavenward and got a gust of wind in the face. Squeezing his eyes shut, he offered up a quick and useless prayer. *Let him be as into me as I am him.* It felt like Marc was as invested. The fact this was Marc's first relationship with a guy formed a constant buzz at the back of his head, though. With them being apart so often, Marc didn't really have to think about being gay. Would that change if they ever got the chance to spend real time together? If they took an assignment together?

Looking down, Henry opened his eyes. He couldn't feel his face. Nevertheless, he forced his lips to work. "We're professionals, right? We're going to make this work."

"Absolutely," Marc cheerily assured him. "Hey, I need to get out of here, pack my stuff, and organize a ride to the airport. See you at the office tomorrow?"

Henry pulled open the front door and ducked into the lobby. The absence of wind and biting cold was nearly overwhelming. "Yes."

"Are you inside yet?"

"Just."

"Cool. I can hear you better now. Wind sounds wicked today. Go get warmed up. Take a bath or something. Imagine I'm in it with you."

If only. "I will, and Marc?"

"Hmm?"

"I—" The words caught in his throat. Henry swallowed them. Replaced sentiment with practicality. "Travel safe, okay?"

"Hey, I've read the book. If this plane goes down, I'm in the seat most likely to make it."

"Don't even."

Marc chuckled. "See you tomorrow, Auttenberg."

Chapter
TWO

*M*arc broke the kiss, breathing hard. Henry's lower lip clung to his for a second, enticing him to lean back in. He needed air, but with Henry so close, the scent and taste of him right there, there was no contest. Wrapping his hand around the back of Henry's neck, Marc tugged him forward. Between them, they crushed another kiss, the connection desperate and hungry. Henry groaned into his mouth. Marc caressed the back of his neck, abstractly aware of the warmth of Henry's skin and the prickle of his short haircut.

He pulled away again, breathing harshly into the sliver of space between them. "You taste so good. Feel so good."

Henry smiled, as he always seemed to in moments like these. He didn't gush sentiment. Neither expressed desperation nor frustration. He leaned in to every kiss, though, and he'd forged the current connection between their thighs.

Rocking his hips forward, Marc murmured, "How much did you miss me?"

Henry gripped the back of Marc's hip, grinding them together. "What do you think?"

The pressure against his half-erect cock made Marc groan. "I think we have about ten minutes until someone needs to use the copy room."

"How do you figure that?"

"I might have charted it."

Henry's laugh reflected in his eyes, brightening the gray. The transformation always enlivened him, the affability he held in check behind his quiet and sometimes serious demeanor a secret he only shared with a select few. "When's the peak copy period start?"

"There are three. We've missed the first."

"Crap, crap, crap"—a bump of Henry's hips punctuated each word—"I need ten copies of this file before my first meeting."

Stifling a moan, Marc leaned in to kiss Henry's full lips before continuing. "Second peak is right before lunch."

"Third is right after lunch."

"Mm-hmm."

"You didn't actually chart this, did you?"

Marc snorted. "Considering I've spent the bulk of the past few months everywhere but here, I resorted to a predictive model based on observations made throughout my career at Beck and Meyer."

"Sexy."

"Yeah?"

"Talk numbers at me," Henry whispered, leaning in for another kiss.

Time ticked past, measured only by the shift of lips, slide of tongues, and changing grip of Marc's hands. Henry's hands, squeezing his ass. Henry's thighs brushing against his. The surge of joy toward his groin. Wondering if he could command his erection to stand down if the door behind Henry were to open.

Marc was just reaching for the zipper of Henry's pants when the door did open, nudging Henry forward. Marc hissed at the delicious pressure. One more bump, maybe a quick slide, and he could come. He was that close, shocked expression of Lara Brown notwithstanding.

"Uh, hi," Lara said, glancing back and forth between Marc and Henry.

"Hey." Studiously not reaching down to adjust himself, Marc took a step back. Henry moved with him, creating an awkward huddle as the three of them negotiated the limited space of the copy room. Which might smell like sex. Pre-sex.

Marc sucked in air and wondered if his cheeks were burning. His face felt hot. All of his skin felt hot and tight. Unease did not constrict his breath, though. He wasn't afraid. Not this time. He'd had a couple of months to get used to the idea of being gay and in a relationship with a man. Plus, dammit, he'd been away long enough to need Henry more than sense right now.

Lara finally managed to close her mouth just in time to open it again. "I heard a rumor about you guys."

"All true," Marc said.

Henry simply shrugged, but he did smile.

"So...." Lara's gaze continued to bounce all over the room.

"Did you need to use the copier?" Henry asked.

"Uh, yeah. Sorry."

"No problem. We'll get out of your way." Henry began edging toward the door.

Marc moved to follow and paused halfway through. "Ah...."

"I saw nothing," Lara said with a wink.

Closing the door behind him, Marc turned to Henry. "What was up with the wink? Was she flirting with us?"

Henry's eyebrows drew together. "Seriously, you're asking me? I had to get trapped in a car with a guy before I got anywhere with him."

"You do suck at flirting."

"Thank you."

"I should have just cornered you in the copy room one day."

Henry's eyebrows shot upward, more in alarm than surprise. Marc turned. Oh shit. Shelly Flores was heading their way.

A soft and rhythmic whisper started up beside him. "One, seven, eleven, seventeen, twenty-three, thirty-one—"

"Are you listing primes?" Marc hissed.

"For God's sake, put your hands in your pockets."

Marc shoved his hands in his pockets just as Shelly drew to a halt in front of them.

"Gentlemen." She didn't look down, but Marc knew she knew. "Can I see you in my office?"

"Sure. Now, or—"

"Now."

B and M was not a democracy, even among the partners. They were finance people. Whoever held the biggest wad got the largest vote. Currently, that person was senior partner Shelly Flores. Marc and Henry followed her to her office.

Shelly moved behind her desk and nodded toward the chairs in front of the dark glass rectangle before sitting down.

Marc sat. Henry perched carefully beside him, lips moving slightly. Was he still counting?

Do not look at his crotch.

Just—

Shelly pushed a slim folder across the glass. "Hiddenger."

Marc picked it up. "I thought this deal fell through." Both he and Henry had been studying the Hiddenger case files right before Christmas. He'd been quite disappointed when the deal hadn't happened.

"It's been resurrected, and you two have the most background with it. You leave tonight."

"Tonight?" The dizzy swirl of thought competing for sense inside Marc's head could have been due to a number of things: the lack of blood in his brain; the sharp snap of his head as he glanced up from the file; the quiet whisper of Henry's presence next to him; the fact his plans for the evening had just been dashed; and finally, a niggle of worry that right now, at this very moment, he was thinking about everything but the file in his hand.

When had work started to take a back seat to life?

Shaking his head, Marc flipped open the file. To his relief, facts and figures immediately surged to the forefront of his brain, obliterating everything else. He leafed through the first three sheets and extracted the fourth to hand to Henry. "Is this still current?"

Henry took the page and scanned it. "I haven't closed out my files yet. I can generate a fresh synopsis before lunch."

Shelly made a small noise. Marc looked up.

She was smiling.

He shouldn't shudder. Shuddering would be impolite.

Her smile narrowed. "Can you two work together on this without ducking into copy rooms across the District?"

Marc cleared his throat.

Shelly held up a hand. "This isn't a sexuality thing. We do, however, work in a conservative industry, and regardless of gender, visits to dark corners of client sites are not acceptable. Save it for the hotel room, boys."

Closing the file, Marc accepted Shelly's terms with a careful nod. She hadn't asked a question; therefore she required no answer. He had a question, however. "What about Gernicky and Sons?"

"We can talk about that when you get back." A favor for a favor?

"Will we have access to the client offices over the weekend?" Henry asked.

"Yes. There is a forensics team onsite. You'll have three days to incorporate new data and put together a new proposal." Shelly folded her hands. "I want this deal signed, sealed, and delivered by Monday, close of business."

A rush of adrenaline unfurled within Marc. He lived for such challenges and, barring surprise, had no doubt he and Henry could deliver on this one. Personally and professionally, which meant swallowing his only other question—

Hotel room, singular?

Chapter
THREE

*T*here was something subversively soothing about traveling by train. The pressure of Marc's thigh against his definitely wasn't soothing, but the gentle rock of a car inspired thoughts of longer trains and longer journeys—winding through the Alps, across the graceful arch of rail bridges, whistling through tunnels. The regular pattern of humanity unfolding along the side of the tracks: the blank expanse of trees at night, dotted lights of houses, the brighter spread of towns, more houses, more trees and… signposts.

Henry had been counting the signposts and signals, and the growing tallies formed happy and reliable bubbles in his thoughts. Add in the man next to him, thigh shifting against his in a measurable rhythm, and Henry couldn't remember the last time he'd felt so relaxed, even while optimistic butterflies fluttered through his middle. Traveling with Marc. Working with Marc. Being with Marc.

God, stop, you're twenty-four, not twelve.

Still, he felt giddy and happy and maybe just a little bit anxious—about the work part, and the being with Marc part while doing the work part. *Stop.* He needed to be more like Marc. Not shy, not overly cautious. Instead he should be planning out how they were going to make this work.

We are going to make this work. All of it.

Better. Much better.

He still felt giddy, though.

Snorting, Marc jerked awake, his thigh pushing more insistently into the tenuous embrace with Henry's before shifting away as he sat up and scrubbed at his eyes.

"How long was I asleep?" he asked.

"We just passed New York."

"God, so over two hours. Sorry." Marc stretched and slumped, leaning companionably against Henry's side. "I tried to sleep on the plane last night but probably didn't do more than doze." He checked his watch and frowned. "Yep, that was still last night. Or very early this morning. Something." He muttered unintelligibly before stretching again. "Anyway."

"You're kind of cute when you're all frowsy."

"Frowsy? What's that?"

"Sleep-deprived."

"All in the name of a glass rectangle."

"A what?"

"One day I'm going to be sitting on the other side of Shelly's desk, pushing folders at hapless young up-and-comers like me."

"And me."

"We'll sleep then." A lascivious grin took over Marc's mouth. "Or maybe not."

The giddy feeling returned. He always forgot how "on" Marc could be. Being the center of all Marc's attention could be as unnerving as it was amazing.

All of this was for him?

Marc put a hand on Henry's thigh. "Everything okay over there?"

"This is going to be the most amount of time we've spent together."

Henry hadn't actually meant to say that out loud, but as the words passed his lips, he realized that's where his thoughts had been headed. The next five days constituted a test on two fronts: their ability to work together and keep it professional, and their ability to work together in a more personal sense.

"Are you worried?"

"I'm always worried," Henry admitted.

Marc frowned, but he didn't move his hand. Instead he squeezed Henry's thigh. "Count something."

"I am. There have been three hundred and forty signal posts since—"

Leaning in suddenly, Marc cut him off with a kiss, his lips demanding and sweet at the same time. He pulled away just far enough to whisper, "Still counting?"

"No." Henry lifted his lips to Marc's, offering up his surrender. Really, he'd rather not think.

Marc's tongue swept into his mouth, and the tallies inside Henry's head melted into unrecognizable blips, then into nothing at all as he fell into that space where he knew the man kissing him, knew his lips, his scent, his taste, but not well enough for it not to be thrilling, for the tang of Marc's sweat to be different and exciting. For that remembered feeling of not being alone in his fantasy to roll through him, zapping nerve endings, waking him from sexual slumber. He was alive and with Marc.

When they broke apart for air, Henry's jeans were tight across his crotch. Marc was practically sitting in his lap. On a train. In a public place. A moment of concern flashed through him, making his fingers and toes ache, until he remembered they were nearly alone at the back of the train car, their only audience all facing forward and away.

Henry drew in a ragged breath, one that tasted of Marc, and shifted, trying to adjust his pants. Marc did the same, his leg moving over Henry's enticingly. Henry glanced up, caught Marc's gaze, and was on the verge of leaning in again when the train rocked sideways, causing them to collide in a less sensual manner.

Marc grabbed for the seat back in front of them. Heart hammering, Henry glanced at the dark expanse of window. It was so dark outside that he could barely see an approaching signal tower through his distorted reflection. The darkness unsettled him, delivering a further sense of vertigo. If this were a movie, now would be when he had that last wistful thought about how everything was about to work out for them. Then the train would lift off the tracks, tip, and roll down an embankment, throwing them together and apart in a tangle of broken limbs and glass.

Henry sought something to hold on to, his hands scrabbling along the small ledge at the bottom of the window. Marc grabbed his arm and held tight.

"Breathe."

Shaking his head, Henry continued not breathing while he entertained the weird hope the train might still be about to derail. Surely that'd be easier to deal with than the fact he'd nearly had a panic attack in front of Marc. Lord, why? Or why now? Was it the kiss? The glimpse of everything he wanted tipping toward some invisible ledge?

"What do we do if the train derails?" Marc asked.

You're asking me this now? Of course he was, and not because the train was about to fall into the dark oblivion of night.

Embarrassment stinging his cheeks, Henry forced a smile. "Pretty sure we just switched tracks. Didn't you get to that chapter of the book yet?"

"I'd rather hear it from you. It's all part of your charm."

Henry turned back toward the window and resisted the urge to press his cheek to the cool glass. "I thought you thought it was weird."

Marc touched his thigh. Gently, reassuringly. "Not weird." He leaned closer and lowered his voice. "Knowing that your brain is constantly working, turning over facts, figures, and scenarios makes me hard." Marc moved his hand higher, to the strained denim at Henry's crotch. "This for me or the signposts?"

Stifling a groan, Henry put his hand on Marc's. He breathed in and out and gave up trying to sort the confusion of thoughts in his head. "Whatever it was, you just scrambled it."

"Perfect."

Marc squeezed Henry's erection, making him gasp.

"I wish we were alone right now," Henry said.

"Tell me about it. Sexting with you is fun. Can't wait to get into bed with you, though."

There it was again, the push-pull of *Oh my God this is real* and *Is this all for me?*

"I can hear you thinking," Marc murmured.

Henry leaned away, gulping at cooler air. He met and held Marc's gaze again and resisted drowning in the deep, dark brown. "I've been looking forward to this," he managed. He took Marc's hand in his, releasing the pressure on his crotch, and pushed his reservations away. "Working with you. Spending more than one day or one night with you."

Smiling, Marc took his statement for what it was. He squeezed Henry's fingers. "Me too. We've got this one, Auttenberg."

Union Station was subdued at 11:00 p.m. The somber mood matched the tightening in Marc's gut, the growing unease that had pinched a little harder the closer they drew to DC. He'd been born less than ten miles from this spot. Had grown up in the shadow of Capitol Hill and the Monument and hundreds of other landmarks of greatness.

His father's offices were a fifteen-minute walk away.

February waited for them outside—cold and dark and barely tamed by the more southern latitude. Henry corralled the bags while Marc hailed a cab. Teamwork 101. They didn't talk on the short ride to their hotel, but Marc could practically hear Henry thinking again. He wasn't muttering—or counting things. He sat perfectly still. The distant look in his eyes gave him away.

Before getting to know Henry properly, Marc would not have suspected a dreamer lurked behind the serious exterior. Now he knew better. Not all of Henry's drifts were fantastic in nature, though. He was also a worrier. He needed a set of those beads, the wooden ones on a string. Something he could count over and over.

A visit to the front desk of their hotel revealed the reason behind Henry's current funk: Henry had booked them into separate rooms.

"One room with two beds would have sufficed," Marc murmured as Henry pushed his credit card across the counter.

Henry shook his head, and Marc shut his mouth. They could talk about it later.

They'd definitely be talking about it later.

Marc waited until the elevator doors closed before turning toward Henry—who was ready with an explanation.

"It's nearly midnight," he said, "and we've got a really full schedule tomorrow."

"I think I could have managed to stay in my assigned bed."

"Maybe I didn't think I could," Henry returned.

Marc felt his eyebrows rise.

Henry took a deep breath, signaling an incoming speech. "This assignment is important. It's not a new client. It's a ball someone else dropped. I know it wasn't someone in B and M, but that doesn't matter. These are the sorts of wins that really count. I need this one, Marc. That being said, I—"

"I get it, okay. I do. Separate rooms. It makes sense. We won't always be traveling, right? We were both in the office for three months third quarter. Mostly."

Henry exhaled, his shoulders dropping half an inch. "Okay, cool."

"For the record, though"—Marc smirked as Henry's shoulders rose again—"if we're going to make this work, being able to share a room should be a perk. A benefit. Something…."

Something partners could do.

Rather than show he'd faltered, Marc simply sighed. Now wasn't the time. It was late, and Henry was right. They had a full schedule tomorrow. The elevator doors opened, and he followed Henry down the carpeted hall. Accepted a tired smile as his good night.

Their rooms were adjoining. Inside his, Marc looked at the connecting door. Mischief poked him in the gut, or maybe it was anticipation or something else entirely. His feelings for Henry. Intense like and respect, desire, a dash of disappointment over the current situation, and something that felt a lot like hope.

A short while later, undressed and tucked into his large, lonely bed, Marc reached for his phone and tapped out a quick message: *You asleep?*

The phone buzzed in response. *Yes.*

Dreaming of me?

@@

Did you just roll your eyes at me?

;D

Is that a smirk?

It's me sleeping with one eye open.

Coz you think I'm gonna sneak through that door?

You checked the lock, didn't you?

Nope. Are you naked in that bed?

I'm not sexting with you next door. Too weird.

You know you want to.

I know I want to sleep.

Are you wearing flannel pjs, just like home?

…. Are you?

Nope. Marc flattened a hand over his abdomen and stroked down toward the fold of sheet covering his hips.

Imagine me whining.

Marc grinned. *Done. Imagine me kissing you until the whine changes to a moan.*

Marc….

It's a goodnight kiss.

He inched his hand lower, teasing himself without touching anything important. Henry wasn't going to play tonight. He knew that. But having his hand so close to his dick felt good, especially knowing Henry lay just a few yards away, probably contemplating the same thing.

With one hand occupied, he had to text by swiping his thumb across the little keyboard, a skill he'd gotten very good at over the past few weeks. *Are we still kissing?*

Mm-hmm.

Want to touch you.

Maaaarc. A second later his phone buzzed again. *Marc with the extended a is now in my dictionary.*

Chuckling, Marc tapped out another text. *Have dinner with me tomorrow night.*

What do you mean?

Like a date.

Is this your way of getting around the two-rooms thing?

Marc pulled his hand away from his thigh. This text was going to need more than a swipe of his thumb. *Maybe. Mostly I just want to spend some time with you that isn't work. We have to eat, right? So let's eat together. Somewhere nice and quiet. We won't talk about the job. Just do the Friday night thing together for a while.*

Henry didn't reply right away. Marc sat staring at the dancing dots until his screen went dark. Was Henry composing an essay on mixing business with pleasure?

Henry's actual answer was short and sweet: *We could do that.*

Awesome. It's a date.

:) *Can I go to sleep now?*

Sure. xoxo

xoxo

Marc put the phone aside with a smile. Fatigue rolled across him in a pleasant wave, tempered only by the continued tingle of anticipation in his chest. That bubble of hope that meant all things Henry.

His phone buzzed on the nightstand. He picked it up.

If we're going to call dinner a "date," we should probably come up with an emergency plan. No restaurants with huge front windows, or we just don't sit in the window, or near the kitchen. No restaurants with crime syndicate connections.

Dots bounced under the message. Henry was still typing. *No sushi. No raw anything.*

More dots. *No basements.*

Grinning, Marc tapped out a reply. *We could just get room service. Not call it a date.*

I want to call it a date.

Marc's grin widened to stupid proportions. Thank Christ no one could see it. *A date it is.*

Chapter
FOUR

*T*he reason no one else wanted the Hiddenger job quickly became apparent. Shelly hadn't sent them down here to resurrect a deal. She'd sent them to exhume a corpse, solve the murder, and then somehow breathe life back into something that had already started to rot.

Henry could think of a few more analogies—like the fact the body hadn't been embalmed properly or that someone had chosen a cheap casket—but he didn't have time to verbalize them.

"Either this really is a test, or she's just fucking with us," Marc muttered.

Henry moved the cursor to mark his place on the display and glanced over at Marc. "Who?"

"Shelly." Marc looked up. "She did this on purpose."

"To be fair, with the exception of her, we are the most prepared. We did all the prelims. We both wanted this client, and being able to do this on site is a gift."

Marc grunted. "Unwrapped, dropped, dented, and regifted."

Another hour passed as they compared notes on the findings of the forensic accountants. Hiddenger and Associates was a litigation firm. They wanted to acquire a smaller firm. They had backed out of the deal upon the discovery of an undeclared "partner" on the smaller side of the equation.

The deal still benefited both parties, but the offer had to be restructured—and both firms wanted a new statement of business, including all assets, partners, affiliations, clients. The sticking point that would keep their noses pressed to monitors for most of the weekend was quantifying the value of the unofficial partnership between the smaller firm and the third party. Setting a figure to it bordered on virtual math. Numbers pulled up at random would probably look better on paper than any estimate he and Marc could come up with, even with a three-feet-high stack of printouts from the accounting side of Beck and Meyer.

Henry leaned away from the table and stretched his arms over his head. Things popped in his shoulders. Bending his elbows, he pulled each arm down behind his neck, enjoying the tug against stiff muscles and sore tendons.

"Okay, I think I've figured a way to count the reports without actually having to read through all of them," Marc said.

"Great." He didn't have to ask how. Any shortcut Marc came up with would be solid.

Marc demonstrated his trick, and they got back to work. The next time Henry pushed back from the table, his lower back screamed in protest. He'd been sitting for too long, neck craned at a stupid angle.

But he'd at least glanced at every folder on the table. Set a bookmark in every online document. He had a handle on the scope, and a good feeling spread outward and down. They had this one. The grunt work was going to suck—uncounted hours to distill the right information from all sources and present a restructured deal— but they could do it.

He and Marc could to it.

Marc glanced up, a faint smile playing across his mouth. "We've got this."

"I was just thinking the same thing."

"Let's grab some lunch."

Henry glanced at his watch. It was after two. "Can we head outside, walk somewhere? I can't feel my legs."

"Sounds like a plan."

Marc pulled their coats from the back of one of the chairs and handed Henry's over. "We can grab a sandwich and walk with it if you want."

Henry smiled.

"What? Why are you smiling?"

"You're a lot easier to work with than I figured you'd be."

"How's that?"

"Remember the job in Chicago? You barely spoke to me. Didn't eat with me. Once you held out your hand for a report without looking in my direction."

Marc winced. "Okay, in my defense, I was actively trying not to look at you."

A snippet of conversation floated across Henry's memory. Something Marc had let slip when they'd been stranded by a blizzard on the way home. He'd spent three days trying not to look at Henry's mouth.

Henry's smile widened.

"Yeah, that's right." Marc grinned. "Besides, I knew you had everything ready. That I could just stick my hand out and you'd pass me exactly what I wanted. We make a good team, Auttenberg."

"Good enough to lift the cone of silence?"

"The what?"

"Never mind, let's go get lunch."

"If you'll remember, I wanted you on my team for six months before I took you to Chicago. I knew we'd work well together."

Marc pushed open the door to the small conference room set aside for them, stepped out into the hall, and stopped. Suddenly. Henry smacked into the back of him. Grunting softly, he backed away, rubbing at his nose. Marc didn't move for a few seconds—

but he shifted. His shoulders drew back and up, changing the hang of his coat. Tension rippled through his frame. His neck stiffened. He leaned backward, just slightly, before rocking forward.

Confused, Henry followed. What—

Then he saw what had stopped Marc. The wall he'd just run into, causing him to pause and calculate whether this one would be over, under, around, or through.

A man stood next to senior partner Charles Hiddenger, deep in conversation. A tall man with dark, wavy hair, a sharp nose, severe cheekbones, and impenetrable eyes. It was Marc in thirty years. Still trim, still fit. Dressed in an impeccably tailored suit.

"Is that...."

"Terrence Marcus Hamish Scottling Winnamore." Marc strode forward.

"Okay." Henry took a moment to digest the list of names along with the man they belonged to. Marc's father.

Terrence Marcus Hamish Scottling Winnamore glanced up and watched his son approach. He did not smile or nod. Not even an eyebrow twitched. Recognition showed in his eyes, though, along with the sense he'd known Marc was there all along and had been waiting for him to appear.

"Marcus." Still no smile. No nod.

"Sir," Marc replied, and the single word damn near broke Henry's heart.

He'd called his own father sir out of respect and affection. To let him know he was listening and understood. He would never greet his father that way.

Charles Hiddenger was looking from Winnamore Sr. to Jr. with an oily smile. "I knew with a Winnamore on the job I'd be in good hands."

Bristling, Henry swallowed a rush of invective—and a polite explanation of why his and Marc's hands were probably the only ones who *would* touch this acquisition, given the mess it was.

Winnamore Sr. leaned slightly sideways, his dark gaze brushing over Henry.

Marc turned. "Henry. May I introduce"—*may I introduce?*—"Terrence Winnamore. Sir, this is Henry Auttenberg, my partner."

Hope flared and died in Henry's chest at Marc's use of the word "partner," crushed by the formality of the introduction and the cold way Marc's father regarded him. This man wouldn't consider anyone equal to his son. He operated on too different a scale. Regardless, Henry stepped forward, one hand extended. "A pleasure."

For a second, he thought Winnamore Sr. might refuse to shake his hand—but he did, briefly, the touch fleeting and vaguely reptilian. Then he turned his attention back to his stiffly postured son and inclined his head in a brief nod. "I will assume the fact you did not call was an oversight."

"I'm only here a few days, and my client takes priority," Marc said.

"Of course, but I'm sure you can spare an hour for lunch tomorrow. Your mother would like to see you."

Marc's awkwardness and anger radiated through his rigid back. Perhaps more fascinating than his colleague's legendary control, however, was the expression on Charles Hiddenger's face. He looked on with bored amusement, as though he also had a disappointing child—or understood how one dealt with such matters.

"I might not have time," Marc said. "Henry and I have a lot of work to do."

"Sunday, then."

"No…." Impossibly, Marc stiffened further. "Tomorrow would be better."

"We'll expect you at one o'clock." Another nod to Hiddenger and Terrence Marcus Hamish Scottling Winnamore left the building, apparently taking most of the oxygen with him.

∞

Had he admired Henry's reserve before? Commented on it, surely. Mentally and out loud. That afternoon, Henry elevated the ability to remain quiet and unobtrusive to an art form. Marc barely noticed he was there. Hardly felt the unasked questions between them. Was ever grateful for the fact Henry seemed to understand now wasn't the time.

There would never be a good time to talk about his father.

Not the casual "He's a prick, and guess what, so's dear old Mom" conversation. Could you call a woman a prick? Prickess. Her Prickness. Whatever. And definitely not the deeper conversation about why his parents were the way they were and why Marc was the way he was. He and Henry had a deal to save and a senior partner to impress.

He pulled another file forward and flipped it open, found the relevant figures, and added them to his spreadsheet.

The next time he looked up, night had absconded with the day, leaving the city outside the conference room windows lit up like a demure Christmas tree. Marc eased back in his chair and stretched his arms over his head. After working through a series of alarming cracks and pops, he flipped the lid of his laptop closed.

He'd done enough work for one day.

Speaking of which, where was Henry?

The door opened, and Henry walked in carrying a thick sheaf of paper. Smiling, he dropped it onto the table. "Good, you're done. Grab your coat."

"Huh?" Marc croaked.

"Don't worry. You'll get your voice back after the first beer."

"Huh?"

"I know it's hard to come back from figure-land, but after today, I think we deserve something more than an overpriced sandwich and hotel cable. C'mon. You owe me a date."

Blinking, Marc stood and collected his coat. "So long as we don't talk—"

"About your father. Got it."

He should have expected this. He should have known that visiting DC would summon the devil—by name, no less. Shaking off a shiver that pinched nerves numbed by hours of leaning over a laptop, Marc followed Henry outside. The evening chill refreshed him. He tipped his head back and breathed deeply, heedless of the cold burn in his sinuses.

Henry turned in to a sports bar halfway between the offices and their hotel. He held the door open for Marc and ushered him into the almost too loud confusion of light and sound with a patient expression.

"I'm not sure if—"

"C'mon, you're letting all the heat out. One beer and we can reassess."

Marc moved into the crowded bar. The place smelled like wet wool and desperation. A damp coat hung over the back of every chair, and everywhere he looked, ties were loosened and buttons were undone as men and women laughed together, eager to put the workweek behind them. After finding them somewhere to lean, Henry melted into the throng. He reappeared moments later holding two tall glasses of effervescent amber liquid.

Marc nearly snatched his. "God, I have never been so happy to see a glass of beer in all my life."

Henry grinned. "I figured." He lifted his glass. "Cheers."

After draining nearly half his drink in one extended swallow, Marc found a smile. "Thank you. I needed that."

"I know."

"Three more and I might actually start to feel human again."

"Go ahead, you earned it."

"We've got a deal to construct."

"Marc, you did more work this afternoon than we might have

done together in two days. You were a machine. We're good. We have enough information to start structuring a new deal, meaning we can take some downtime."

Thinking about lunch tomorrow, Marc scowled. "That isn't exactly good news."

"I could break your leg for you."

"You think a broken leg would excuse me?"

"Ah...."

Marc tried to drain the rest of his glass but swallowed awkwardly, catching a large bubble in his throat. Wincing, he forced it down. The tears at the corners of his eyes felt ironic.

"You could just not go," Henry said. The words were barely audible over the buzz of conversation around the bar, but Marc caught them.

"Not how it works. He expects me not to show up."

"I don't get it."

"Never mind." Marc tipped his head toward the bar. "Get you another?"

"Sure."

He elbowed his way through the crowd and ordered another round, this time choosing a darker ale. Henry had emptied his first by the time Marc got back and toasted him with the fresh glass. "We've got this, Winnamore."

Smiling, Marc set about killing his second drink. Somewhere around the middle of the glass, he slowed down. The beer was tasty, and his anger had faded. The bar was cozy, the atmosphere more cheery and less desperate than a beer ago... and the afternoon had been too long. Add in the fact his ire had been replaced by a practiced burn, and he really couldn't convince himself to spend any more of his free time on it.

When the after-work crowd thinned, they found a table and ordered burgers.

Henry made a game out of sorting the sugar packets by color, volume, and ingredients. "Did you know there are about eighteen thousand grains of sugar in a single packet?" he asked.

"I do now. Please tell me you haven't counted them."

"No. I tried once. I crapped out at about seven hundred."

"Seriously?"

Henry chuckled. "No. I got to thirty before my mother swept the sugar off the table and told me to stop counting things."

Marc laughed. "I can so picture it. Did you use to get up in the night and count the silverware?"

"Of course not. I always knew how many books and comics and Legos and things I had, though."

"You're certifiable."

"All the best minds are."

Their burgers arrived and the casual conversation continued, warmed by juicy sirloin and another round of beer.

"This is exactly what I needed," Marc said, leaning back to pat his pleasantly full belly.

"No, what you need is still to come."

He brightened. "Sex?"

Henry tipped his head back and laughed. "Okay, yeah. Sex is good. I was talking about this, though." He tapped the upright placard at the end of the table.

Marc leaned forward to read it. "Kara—no."

"Aw, c'mon. You know you want to. I've heard stories. You rock at karaoke."

"I really, really don't."

"Everyone at B and M has heard you sing but me."

"That's because you don't come to Mulligan's on Thursdays."

"Yeah, well, I would have if either of us had been in town at the same time, on a Thursday, over the past couple months."

"Heh."

"So tonight's the night. I want to hear you sing."

Marc cocked his head with a soft "Hmm," letting beer-and-beef-softened thoughts slip slowly across his brain. "I'll do it if you do."

"What? No."

"You know you want to."

"That was my line."

"It's a good one. I'm borrowing it. You should be flattered. Now…." He held up a hand to ask for a second to make his case. "I'm going to offer a one-time deal."

"Deal?"

"If you're too chicken to stand up there on your own, we can pick a song to sing together."

Henry's mouth dropped open. Sound might have escaped, but Marc heard nothing but his own laughter.

Chapter

FIVE

*M*arc had to know that standing up in front of a pub full of strangers—and singing—was not on Henry's comfort list. Not that he had an actual list. That would be weird. Henry recognized a challenge when he saw one, though, and he could also see the stress of the afternoon melting away as Marc laughed. The lines of tension across his brow eased, and the sparkle returned to his eyes.

Henry couldn't say no to such an expression of happiness, so he quit gaping and set his only condition. "I get to pick the song."

Grinning, Marc slapped the table. "You're on." He glanced at the placard. "When does this thing start? Do we have time for another drink?"

"No more beer."

"Did you lose your nuts on the way over here or what?"

"Did I—"

"It's Friday night, Auttenberg. We're out on a date and disaster has yet to befall us, or whatever disaster does. We're having another beer, and then we're going to find the organizer of this shindig and pick a song. We should practice before we get up there."

Shindig? Also, they had to practice?

Wait, of course they had to practice. Marc never did anything half-assed.

Marc flagged down a server and presented her with his most charming smile. "Another round, and can you tell us who is organizing the karaoke?"

Soon they had more beer and an iPad containing a mind-boggling catalog of songs. Scrolling through, Henry wavered between outbursts of hilarity and cowardice. Marc really expected him to sing? Like, on stage?

This was a terrible idea.

"What sort of music do you like?" he asked.

"Choose something you like and are familiar with," Marc said. "Those are the easiest songs to sing, when you already have a sense of the words."

"Okay." Henry found a menu labeled "popular" and opened a new list. Bon Jovi, Elvis Presley, Whitney Houston—*God, take me now*. Brittney Spears. Henry glanced up. Would Marc judge him if he chose…. No, forget Marc, the entire bar would judge him. He kept scrolling. Queen. Now that would be fun. But probably not the choice for tonight.

"Okay, I've narrowed it down."

"What's our poison?"

"Uh-uh, not that simple. We've got two choices. Pick a letter. B or D."

Marc frowned. "B…. No, D. I pick D."

Henry grinned. "Def Leppard it is!"

To his surprise, Marc pumped his fist in the air. "All right!" He lowered his arm. "What was B?"

"Garth Brooks."

"Dude."

"I think I've figured out this isn't a matter of singing your favorite song. Some things should remain sacred."

Laughing, Marc tapped about on his phone until he found the lyrics to "Pour Some Sugar on Me." He forwarded the link, and they practiced reading and singing under their breath.

Behind them, karaoke night started with a surprising display of talent, which only made Henry's heart beat faster and his palms sweat. He gulped his remaining beer and resisted the urge to order another.

Three songs later, their turn came up. Henry followed Marc to the stage, clenching and unclenching his hands. Once up there, he calmed. The crowd felt drunk and amiable. He had the feeling even a Brittney Spears song would get a good reception. It was Friday night, after all. These men and women had worked hard all week and were only looking for one thing: fun.

He glanced at Marc, who handed him a microphone. "Ready?"

"No."

He didn't know he was supposed to dance, but once the music started, Marc was in motion. Hips swaying, he strutted around the small stage, pointing toward the audience each time they were expected to make noise—and they did.

Henry followed Marc's lead, sure he looked ridiculous. The lyrics started rolling. He couldn't remember actually opening his mouth or rallying the attention of his vocal cords. All he knew was that sound was required. His audience expected him to sing—poorly or magnificently. Words tumbled from his lips, the sound of his own voice echoing through the bar completely weird. Surely that wasn't him? Beside him, he could hear Marc singing, and the sound of his voice was both familiar and strange. The fact he wasn't amazing settled Henry's nerves. Then again, who needed an amazing voice to sing this song? Everyone knew this song. When Marc pointed his microphone toward the audience in the second chorus, they joined in, their voices crashing noisily against the small stage.

It was fun too. Singing with Marc and the crowd was fun. Marc's happy grin and the return of his carefree swagger and bright, smiling eyes made it fun.

The instrumental interlude pulled them together as though choreographed. Henry found himself facing Marc, dancing with him. Lighting effects that had seemed cheap and cheesy suddenly enclosed them in a private space. Marc's face glowed yellow and red and blue. His features—dark eyes, sharp cheekbones, and arrow-straight nose—seemed more defined. When he smiled, Henry nearly forgot they were not alone. He wanted to press closer—dance hip to hip. Pull Marc against him and grind to the beat.

Not here.

The lyrics started rolling again, and Marc sang to him. Henry sang back. In that moment, they were magnificent. Coordinated. Moving as one. Henry didn't need the monitor. He knew this song, these words—and if he forgot one, he could read it from Marc's lips. Together they turned and sang toward the audience. The crowd sang back, and the bar rocked with them.

God, what a high. Even as the music faded, the roar of it pushed against Henry's ears as Marc wrapped him up in a hot and sweaty hug. Lips pressed to his forehead in a loud smack. The bar cheered as Marc stepped back, punching the air again.

"More!"

"Do another!"

No one was jeering them over the kiss. Not a single person. A whirl of emotion flooded Henry. He rode high on the good feeling surrounding him, but a little tug of fear kept his feet on the ground. Marc had kissed him in front of a bar full of strangers.

"Thank you. Thanks, everyone!" Marc said, responding to their audience. "Maybe after everyone else has had a chance to embarrass themselves." He handed his microphone off to the next participant, collected Henry's arm, and tugged him from the stage.

Henry followed, trying to arrange his face into a single expression of emotion. The point in the middle of his forehead, where Marc had kissed him, tingled and burned.

At their table, Marc slid into Henry's side of the booth before pulling him in after. "How was that?"

Henry turned to face him. "Amazing."

"Right? Now you have to come to Mulligan's on Thursdays. We'll rock that place to rubble."

Henry's thoughts ran in an entirely different direction. "I can't believe you kissed me."

Marc laughed. "Are you kidding? I had no idea you could dance like that. You had fun, didn't you? C'mon, admit it."

Shaking his head, Henry turned a self-conscious smile toward the table. "I did. I... I really did. I'd even do it again. Still can't believe you kissed me in front of everyone."

Marc sobered a little. "It was just on the forehead."

"Sorry. You just caught me by surprise. I... I haven't had someone do something like that before. In public. Show he was with me. Liked me. I know we didn't make out or anything, but dammit. I'm not explaining this well."

"So it was a good surprise?"

"You weren't worried the crowd would take it the wrong way?"

Something sad flitted across Marc's face, there and gone in an instant. "No. I didn't even think about it. I mean.... Well, I guess I did figure kissing you on the mouth might be going a little far, but I think I could have gotten away with it." His eyebrows crooked together. "You weren't afraid when Luke caught us in the basement. Or yesterday, in the copy room."

"We weren't in a bar full of drunk people."

"Is that what this is about?"

"I'm killing the mood, aren't I?" Henry looked for his drink and found only empty coasters.

"No. Maybe. Is it me? Did you not want people to know we're together?"

Henry shook his head, then stopped as the light in Marc's eyes dimmed as though a cloud crossed the sky. "Not you. I... just...." He breathed out. It couldn't be simple fear. Marc had been right about the basement. He'd been embarrassed when Luke found them, but not afraid. Same deal yesterday in the copy room.

Was he still hung up on the idea Marc was conducting one big experiment?

A cold finger of fear traced the line of his spine. Henry scrubbed a palm over the side of his face, the imagined sting of a dislocating punch not magically evaporating under the quick friction. He glanced up at Marc, who was studying him with a worried expression.

Dammit, he'd killed the mood, buried it, and exhumed the rotten corpse for needless study. Hadn't they done enough of that at the office today? "Sorry. I'm just being weird."

"You're just being Henry." Marc put his arm around Henry's shoulders and pulled him close. "You worry too much."

"It was you. Is you," Henry said. "In a good way. You surprised me in a good way. Most of the bar patrons probably think we're just really close friends, but some will know why you kissed me. They'll have seen how close we were to grinding on each other up there on stage and they'll know. And… you're okay with that, aren't you? That's what I'm getting at. Yeah, I'm freaking out over something I should have accepted years ago. I've been gay forever. You've been gay for a couple of months. But you know what I'm just starting to figure out?"

Marc didn't answer, but his expression was less cloudy day and more rapt attention.

"It's kind of humbling to have you go through this and not make a big deal out of it. I didn't think I had either. I came out to my parents and anyone who mattered. There were ups and downs, nothing major. Some slurs, looks. The guy who nearly broke my jaw—"

His face hurt again. One quick flare of pain, there and gone.

"That's not nothing."

"I wasn't bashed and left for dead in an alley." Broken somehow, though. Why was he only just starting to realize that?

With another deep breath, Henry tried to shake it off. "What I'm trying to say is…." He didn't really know. The beer had loosened his tongue, and the dizzy whirl of his thoughts was slowing, leaving him with little idea why he'd even started this conversation. "I admire you."

Marc frowned.

"I wouldn't have had the courage to kiss you on stage, even on the forehead."

Marc smiled. "All those words for that."

Now Henry really wanted another drink. Even a glass of water would do. He needed somewhere to hide his face for a second or two.

"Hey." Marc caught his chin, turned his face upward. "I get it, okay? It's all right. I like the way you do things. I like that you're cautious and reserved. It's why we make a good team." He leaned in. "I know that under your skin, you're anything but reserved. You are freaking hot, and if I'd thought I could get away with kissing your mouth up there, without pushing you up against the nearest wall, I would have. Because I don't think you've had enough of that in your life, Henry. It's not about you being all serious or maybe scared. You've just been picking the wrong men."

Marc kissed him then, sweeping forward so quickly Henry couldn't refuse, even though his brain pinged with warning. But as he fell into the invitation of Marc's insistent kiss, his worries receded. Yes, he'd decided the back corner of their booth was dark enough, and that the crowd seemed amiable enough, and that he'd stop before zips came down—but that was all just sense. Not fear.

To prove it, he wrapped his hand behind Marc's head and pulled him closer. Swept his tongue inside Marc's mouth and groaned in response to a sharp intake of breath. A tremble passed through Marc's shoulders. Henry's hips jerked in response. He knew exactly what Marc was feeling: a need to be closer, to climb inside the skin of the other. To kiss until they melded. He wanted to feel Marc's smooth skin beneath his fingertips. To trace musculature and curves, hard lines, and softer angles.

Sucking in a quick breath, one flavored with Marc and beer and the lingering memory of sugar, Henry pulled back. For a moment, the swish of blood behind his ears and the steady exchange of O_2 for CO_2 between him and Marc obliterated all sound and all thought. Henry swam back to the surface slowly, the loud hum of a busy bar intruding first. Onstage, someone failed to hit a high note. The crowd laughed encouragingly.

If anyone had noticed them all but having sex in the corner, they didn't mention it.

Henry blinked lazily, as though emerging from a deep sleep. "What you do to me."

"No, what I *want* to do to you." Marc leaned in to nip at his lower lip. "Let's go back to the hotel."

Chapter
SIX

*M*arc nearly stumbled as Henry reached past him to push the door open. He found his feet, only to be nudged backward by a very obvious hard-on. Henry must be about ready to poke a hole in his pants. Of course, Marc fared little better. A five-block walk through the February night had done little to cool his ardor.

He let Henry guide him into the hotel room, distracted by the urgent nibbling at his neck and insistent tugs at his coat and belt buckle. Once past the bathroom, he put his hands to Henry's shoulders, meaning to rid him of some clothing, and got lost somehow. Falling under the spell of Henry's lips and the small sounds he made. Grunts, moans, whimpered breaths. The play of Henry's fingers at the back of his neck and the rhythmic rock of hips and thighs bringing them into contact again and again—each moment frozen and important until Henry molded the shape of his erection and cupped his balls, jerking him into motion. It seemed Henry was everywhere, and yet Marc couldn't get enough.

Pulling Henry away from the wall—when had he backed him into the wall?—Marc propelled him toward the bed. Henry's knees caught, and he fell back, laughing.

"Stay right there," Marc commanded as he shrugged out of his coat and dropped it to the floor.

"Can I take my shoes off?"

"Yeah." Marc kicked his shoes off and shed another layer—his suit jacket falling into an undignified huddle on top of the coat. He reached for his belt buckle as he advanced. "Coat too. But leave the rest. I want to undress you."

Henry wrestled out of his coat and tossed it over the side of the bed. Then he stretched his arms up and folded them behind his head. A smile Marc hadn't seen before tugged at his mouth. Maybe it was just the lack of light, but Henry seemed different. Confident, almost arrogant, and it was such a fucking turn-on. The thrill of it zapped beneath Marc's skin, electrifying him. The sensation was more than physical, though. Beneath the stir of his blood, something larger and more important bloomed. Every day he fell harder for Henry. He woke with Henry's name on his lips and fell asleep having typed it out a dozen times.

He was so gone… and so good with that.

Marc finished undressing and stepped up to the bed, barely pausing to enjoy having Henry's undivided attention. He needed to touch Henry's skin. Taste it. Expose the bulge at Henry's crotch. Inhale the scent of his arousal.

He started with the buttons of Henry's shirt, untucking the tails and working from bottom to top, dipping down to lick and kiss the trail of skin as he pushed the shirt away. Dark hair gathered beneath Henry's navel, pointing downward. Marc moved in the opposite direction, kissing shadowed ribs, nosing the small hollow beneath Henry's sternum, flicking his tongue across a nipple.

Henry arched beneath him, uttering a short cry. Marc grabbed the sensitive point between his teeth and pulled. Henry grabbed his head and tugged him closer. He liked having his nipples played with. Check.

Marc kissed his way across to the other and flicked, bit, and sucked. Henry quivered and bucked, his breath warming the side of

Marc's head with soft moans and whimpers. Then Henry was pulling him upward, into another kiss.

When he tried to roll them over, Marc resisted. "Uh-uh. I want you under me."

Henry pushed his hips up, grinding into him. "Get to where you're going, then, because I'm about to come in my shorts."

Getting to his knees, Marc took a moment to savor the need in Henry's expression. Then he got to work on Henry's belt.

Another night he'd spend more time getting to know Henry's legs. Admire the lean musculature of a man who ran regularly. Play with the tickle of fine dark hair against his lips. See if Henry liked the back of his knees kissed. Tonight Henry's cock stole all of his attention.

Really, any night, Henry's cock would take center stage. Good-sized and thick, with a ruddy head poking enticingly from the foreskin. Marc pressed his tongue to the divot at the top, getting his first taste in over a month. He hadn't forgotten the flavor. Nor the feel of Henry's heavy shaft against his tongue. He traced the hood, knowing Henry enjoyed that, and grasped just below the head and pulled back, exposing the part he wanted to suck.

Henry shuddered, moved his fingers up into Marc's hair, and curled them tight. Marc sucked his way down and up, tightening his lips and the grip of his hand. The cock in his mouth pulsed and grew harder. Angled up higher. He reached beneath to fondle Henry's tight balls. Felt the groan pass through Henry as a tremor and vague breath of sound.

Marc opened his mouth and smiled as Henry whimpered at the loss of suction. On hands and knees, Marc crawled upward, dropping kisses to warm skin, smiling at the small twitches and moans. He lined himself up with Henry—chest to chest, hip to hip, dick to dick—and took both of their shafts in hand.

Henry pushed his head back into the quilt, exposing his throat. "Yes."

His hips arched up—once—and that was all it took. Suddenly they were moving together, and it was better than Marc had imagined. The kiss of skin all the way down, slicker as sweat began to gather in secret places. Friction—not just between their cocks, but all over. Thigh to thigh, hair catching and releasing in a delicious tingle. Knees bumping together as they sorted their legs. Ribs and chests.

Henry's scent. The earthy maleness of him.

Marc spat on his hand and reached between them again.

Henry joined a hand to his and paused. "Wait."

"Hmm?"

"Do you have lube?"

"Oh, yeah." Marc crawled back off the side of the bed.

He rummaged through his suitcase until he found what he was looking for and glanced back at the bed, holding up the bottle with a triumphant smile.

Henry shifted his hips, making his erection sway.

Marc dropped the lube onto the quilt and crawled back over Henry, dropping kisses to his chest on the way up. Everything shifted as Henry caught Marc's shoulder and pushed, managing to roll them sideways. Henry leaned in for a deeper kiss, his plump lips driving away all thought until Marc landed on his back.

Henry slid their bodies together, all hard planes and masculine scent. Oh God, he was going to come. Marc squeezed his eyes shut and sought something to count, only to start listing all the ways being with Henry felt good.

"Hold out your hand," Henry whispered.

Marc did so, and a cool dollop landed in his palm. He reached down, fingers colliding with Henry's as he stroked his cock. Another moan escaped him as the lube warmed against his skin and his fingers slid up and down. He squeezed, gave a little twist, and stroked downward again. So, so good. Henry's weight over him only made it better, the push of Henry's erection against the back of his hand. Marc opened his fingers to pull their cocks together. The friction was still there, the heat and hardness. But now there was more glide—the ease that was necessary, even in tight spaces.

He thought about being inside Henry. About Henry being inside him. He thrust and was pushed back down against the bed as Henry moved into him again. Lips grazed his—Henry's. Marc tried for a deeper kiss and fell back, breathless, as their hips aligned and they rocked together, his hand tight about their shafts, thighs rubbing, thrusting, skin kissing and parting. Henry's panting against his cheek, breath hitching and groaning.

This… this was sex. This was moving in time toward a common goal.

Marc's head spun. He'd never been so in tune with another person. That that person was a man had ceased to matter. Hadn't ever really mattered at all. His focus on Henry had changed nearly all of his perceptions. Right now, though, none of it was important. He just wanted to come, wanted to feel Henry shudder in release over him, the hot splash of semen across his fingers and stomach. He wanted to taste it, smell it.

Pushing his head back into the bed, Marc arched up, grabbed a sweaty breath, and yelled. His cock pulsed against his fingers. The rush of his orgasm nearly hurt. He felt another jerk as Henry's climax rocked them, Henry gasping and moaning as jet after jet of come spurted across their hands.

Henry aimed a kiss at his lips and missed. Marc laughed and chased him, catching the edge of his mouth as they continued to rock. He squeezed his dick again and shuddered as sensitivity started to set in, turning each touch from something wonderful into near pain. Even that was good. Not entirely new, but not something he'd shared with someone else.

He'd only ever reached that stage alone.

Henry eased off him and flopped to the side, breathing hard. Body humming, Marc stared at the ceiling until the dance of spots before his eyes calmed. Idly, he swirled his fingers through the cooling puddle on his belly. The edges were getting stickier, ready to pull on the hair below and above his navel. Damn if he could move, though. His legs were numb, dumb lumps of muscle, and he had no idea where his other arm was until Henry shifted.

"Can I...." Marc tugged at the arm pinned beneath his lover.

"Oh, sorry." Henry shifted again.

Marc pulled his arm free. "I can't feel it anyway. Can't feel anything except the buzz."

Henry wore a lazy smile. "Yeah."

"That was...."

"Yep."

Marc shivered as another aftershock traveled through him.

"You okay?" Henry asked.

"Better than. Just going to rest my eyes a minute, then clean up." He felt Henry sit up.

"Where you going?" Marc asked, eyes still closed.

"Getting us a towel."

The mattress dipped again a short while later, and a warm towel landed across his lap. Opening his eyes, Marc reached for the cloth, only to have Henry brush his fingers aside. They hadn't bothered with the lights in the main part of the room. In the half dark, he tried to make out Henry's expression and couldn't, but the moment felt too somber. Too quiet.

Marc couldn't think of anything to say that wouldn't spoil it in some way.

Henry dropped the towel back in the bathroom and paused by the edge of the bed, face still hidden by shadow. Why wasn't he crawling back across the quilt?

"You're not thinking about going back to your room, are you?" Marc asked.

In the time it took him to sit and scoot to the edge of the bed, his heart expanded and constricted in a thousand ways. Henry had never seemed the type to fuck and run, but he'd made such a big deal about getting a separate room. Was this the reason why? So he didn't have to linger?

Was he not as committed to this as Marc?

Surely he didn't *still* think they were experimenting?

Marc reached out and stroked Henry's hip.

Henry moved forward, his face coming out of shadow. His eyes were large in the dim light, darker than their customary gray, but no worry lines marred his forehead. Instead he wore a familiar smile. This was what Henry looked like when he wanted something he didn't think he could have. Ah, his shy and sweet man. His Henry.

Taking Henry's hand in his, Marc tugged, pulling him toward the bed. "Stay," he said softly.

Henry hesitated only a second before climbing back into the bed and slithering down under the sheets. Marc prodded him until he rolled onto his side, allowing Marc to sidle up behind him, forming the larger spoon.

A sense of rightness radiated up and down, warming Marc from head to toe. This was what he'd been waiting for. The sex was outstanding, but this? Forget icing and cherries and all the other things that were supposed to make something better. Holding Henry, feeling him relax, bit by bit, into his arms, was another experience entirely.

Marc didn't want to ruin it with words. Qualify or quantify. But he had to say something. Make it known that he wanted exactly this. Expected it.

Curling his arm around Henry's shoulder, Marc pulled him a little closer. "You forgot that I like to snuggle after I come."

Henry twitched as he chuckled. "How could I forget that?" he whispered.

Marc kissed the back of Henry's neck. "Exactly."

Chapter
SEVEN

*H*enry had expected a plan. A conference over breakfast and a set of instructions. Not a simple request to order a cab. Thinking back, that was the weirdest part. Being asked. Not that Marc made a habit of ordering him around, but he could be very direct in his requests.

So no plan, no list of what he should or shouldn't do. Just an uncomfortably quiet taxi ride to Bethesda, Maryland.

The morning started with sex, as only the best mornings ever did. Lazy and furtive at first. All-consuming as he and Marc delighted in rare full-access passes. Then the invitation: "Come to lunch with me today," asked casually as they leaned against each other in the shower.

Marc did nothing casually.

Tension roiled between them in the back seat, and Henry had no idea how to cut through it. Or even if he should. He took hold of Marc's hand and squeezed.

Marc glanced over.

"Who do you need me to be today?" Henry asked. "Colleague, friend, partner...." Lover?

"All of the above. Be you. I'm done with being someone I'm not, and you shouldn't even think about it."

"I can be circumspect."

"I'm not going to hide my relationship from them."

"Are you going to tell them you're gay?"

"What did I just say?"

The tightening grip around his hand should have underscored the hostility of Marc's tone. Henry read only the anxiety of a man facing a meeting with an uncertain outcome.

He extracted his hand and flexed his fingers. "I'll just follow your lead, okay?"

Marc visibly considered and tossed aside several responses before settling on a short nod. Then he resumed staring holes in the back of the cabbie's head.

Today was just going to be one of those days. They'd get through it somehow and breathe out afterward.

Five minutes later, they were in a wide, tree-lined avenue, and Henry felt as though he'd slipped into a movie set. Neighborhoods like this actually existed? Even swathed in graying and slushy snow, the houses were spectacular, each a model home for the perfect American family. Meticulously trimmed hedges, stately old elm trees, flagpoles, luxury-model cars, and people walking dogs dressed in brightly colored sweaters.

The contrast to Dorchester was extreme—and Henry's parents lived in the nice part. The not so crappy part. No one had died in their part so far this year.

Marc's parents lived in a mansion. White stone, columns up to heaven, porticos, or whatever those round balconies were called. Tall, graceful windows, a circular driveway, elms, hedge, and a flagpole.

"Do you guys have a butler?" Henry asked.

"No. God. Why would you ask that?"

"To make you laugh?" Because admitting he hadn't set foot inside such a large house before wouldn't.

Marc's smile was almost sad as he shook his head.

They did not hold hands on the way to the front door. If Marc had tried, Henry would have stopped to tie his shoe or something. As it was, he had to lengthen his stride to keep up with Marc's determined gait.

The door opened as soon as they stepped up to it, held by a woman who was, without a doubt, Marc's mother.

Mrs. Winnamore could not be considered beautiful. Her face was too sharp. A quick glance would convey an impression of perfect hair and careful makeup. Closer inspection showed an uncomfortably shrewd expression, as though Mrs. Winnamore expected answers to questions she hadn't asked yet. If she smiled, she might become a different woman—softer of face and manner. But then, perhaps no one would recognize her.

"Good, you're on time," she said.

Not: *Hello, dear, or son, or Marc, or*…. No hug. Not even a kiss on the cheek.

She stepped aside, inviting them in.

Marc made introductions, and Mrs. Winnamore turned to study Henry. "Where are your people from?"

People still asked that? "Boston, ma'am."

He hadn't expected her to answer with anything like "Oh, call me Alice," or "Mrs. Winnamore is fine." He didn't even know her first name. Marc's brief introduction had been… brief.

A maid appeared out of nowhere and asked for their coats. She disappeared under the grand curving staircase. He hoped someone would retrieve his coat for him before he left. He could get lost trying to find it for himself.

Inclining her head toward the interior of the house, "Ma'am" led the way through the two-story foyer, her heels meeting the marble floor in precise taps. As he followed, Henry tried not to let everything inside him scramble for cover. Parts of him were dying, though. This house would kill a gentler soul in six seconds flat. How had Marc escaped with any humanity intact?

Mr. Five Different Names Winnamore awaited them in the dining room, at a table set for three. Henry paused in the doorway, sure his face matched the bright crimson napkins folded at each place.

Marc hadn't let his parents know he was bringing a guest. Did that mean Henry was a big "Fuck you," or had he simply forgotten?

Winnamore Sr. stood and extended his hand toward Marc. "Marcus."

"Sir."

The hand pointed in Henry's direction. "Mr. Auttenberg."

Henry managed not to shudder as dry, cool fingers briefly gripped his own. "Sir." He swallowed the natural urge to thank him for the invitation or for seating him at short notice. At this point, if someone asked him to wait in the foyer or the library or some other room regular houses didn't have, he'd be tempted to duck and run.

The same maid appeared with a fourth place setting. Marc beckoned him toward the table and pulled out the chair next to his. Mr. and Mrs. Winnamore claimed their seats and soup happened.

"Thank you," Henry murmured as the maid set a shallow bowl in front of him. She did not respond, and his words echoed like a giggle in church. Sure his blush would be set to permanent for the next however long this lunch would go on, Henry reached for his spoon, only to stop when he noticed no one else had made a move to begin eating.

He put his hand in his lap and waited, ears ringing in the quiet. Winnamore Sr. picked up his spoon and lunch began. So did the small talk.

Or would it be better to describe it as a small lecture? Mrs. Winnamore spoke for five minutes, giving Marc an outline of what she and his father had been doing over the past few months. Not once did she look Henry's way.

Henry tasted his soup but had trouble swallowing even a small mouthful. Never had he felt so uncomfortable or more unwelcome.

Though he thought he understood why Marc wanted him here, anger at his predicament replaced the churning in his gut. He could say some of the anger was on Marc's behalf, that his parents were so unpleasant, but if he was honest with himself, he was more upset with Marc. That he allowed this treatment. That he had subjected Henry to it.

The soup plates were cleared away and larger plates set down.

"Thank you," Henry said, louder this time, despite knowing the maid would not respond. He eyed the arrangement of fish and vegetables with one simple question in mind: Where had the extra serving come from? He glanced over at Marc's plate to confirm they were eating the same thing.

Winnamore Sr. picked up his silverware, and the main course began.

"Will you be recommending the merger between Hiddenger and Dilworth Associates?" Winnamore Sr. asked.

Marc poked at his fish. "You know I can't talk about it, even if you and Charles Hiddenger go back to potty training." He forked up a mouthful.

Across the table, his mother winced. "Marcus."

Marc raised a dark eyebrow in her direction but did not pick up his knife or retract his comment.

Henry tasted his fish.

"Hiddenger and Dilworth have an interesting history," Winnamore Sr. said.

"Your point?" Marc replied.

"Who else is on your team? Are you still partnered with Shelly Flores?"

"Occasionally. Do you have information on her too?"

"Why do you have to be so combative?"

"Why do you have to pretend to be interested in my career?"

Henry couldn't figure out if they were arguing or bantering. No one raised their voices, and the back-and-forth had a tired, practiced quality.

"We are interested." Mrs. Winnamore this time, her cut-glass appearance in direct opposition to her tone.

Why Marc had left home was no longer the question. Why hadn't he crossed the country? An ocean or two?

"Then let me give you a quick rundown of the past fifteen months. I still have a job, I'm still on the partnership track, and I still like my choice of career. If that's too much detail, let me know."

"Marc—"

Marc cut his mother off. "I still live in the wrong neighborhood and will continue to do so until November 2019."

Henry wanted to ask what happened in November 2019 but kept the question to himself. Marc was a stick of dynamite surrounded by too many flames.

"What about your personal life?"

Henry nearly choked on a mouthful of fish. So the previous report was part of a pattern? The Winnamores actually communicated in statements of accomplishment and intent?

Beside him, Marc stiffened. His fork paused halfway between his plate and his mouth. He didn't glance Henry's way, but Henry could feel his attention.

Don't do it.

He'd said he would stand by him if and when Marc came out to his parents, whether they were friends or more. He'd meant it. Then. Now, after witnessing the lack of warmth that was the Winnamore home—no, house; this couldn't be called a home—Henry knew with absolute certainty that any announcement Marc made regarding his sexuality would not be well received.

Not today.

Maybe not ever.

Before Henry could argue with himself, for Marc's rights, for his, for something as simple as equality and confidence in self, Marc dropped his bomb.

"I have a boyfriend."

"I'm sorry, what did you say?" Mrs. Winnamore asked.

Winnamore Sr. was turning an interesting shade of purple.

"I brought him to lunch with me today. Aren't you pleased to meet him?"

"Marc, don't," Henry murmured. He felt like a traitor but could not condone being used as a tool to gouge the veneer of this not-so-perfect household.

Marc didn't look at him. Instead, he put his fork down. "Henry and I have been seeing each other for two months."

"You've barely been in Boston these past few months," Winnamore Sr. said.

"God, how do you know that? Why do you care?" Marc shuffled in his chair and produced his cell phone. "Is my phone tapped too? Have you been reading the texts between me and Henry?" He held the phone out. "Maybe you should. You might learn something about your son you don't actually know."

"That's enough," Winnamore Sr. growled. He directed a steely look in Henry's direction. "I apologize for Marcus's behavior."

Henry swallowed. "Maybe I should go."

"For fuck's sake." Marc tossed his phone down. "Do you really think I'd embarrass a guest like that?"

"Wouldn't be the first time," Winnamore Sr. said.

"But I haven't used this tactic before, have I? Is that why you don't believe me? Do you think Henry is in on the joke? Look at him." Three pairs of dark brown eyes turned in Henry's direction. "He's embarrassed, sure. But he hasn't left yet. Want to know why? Because he's the only goddamn person in this room who knows who I really am."

Henry found his voice. "Marc, don't do this."

"Do what?"

"Let it go."

"I'd listen to your *friend*, Marcus," Winnamore Sr. said.

Marc cast his gaze heavenward. "Henry is my boyfriend. We're lovers. I had his cock in my mouth this morning, and guess what?" He tossed a feral grin into the stunned silence. "I loved it. I was born to it. What do you think of that?"

Dropping his silverware, Henry pushed back from the table. "And that's my ticket out of here. Thank you for lunch."

"Where are you going?" Marc's question was bitter and clipped.

"Somewhere else. I think you and your parents need a moment"—or a year. Henry made a vague gesture—"to talk."

"Your manners are appreciated, Henry," Mrs. Winnamore said. "Can I call you a cab?"

"No, you cannot call him a fucking cab. Isn't anyone listening to what I'm saying?"

Henry rocked on his heels. Should he stay and try to calm Marc down? Was that his job? Jesus, why hadn't Marc outlined a damn plan so he'd know what to do here? *Hey, I'm going to insult my parents and probably use you like a cum rag along the way. Just go with it, okay?*

Yeah, no.

The anger in his gut had climbed toward his throat. Henry swallowed bile and the urge to yell. A small part of him knew leaving now would break something between him and Marc. A greater part knew that staying wouldn't help. Marc needed to finish what he'd started, and it would be easier if the tool of his destruction wasn't there.

Henry backed toward the dining room door. "It's okay. I can take care of myself."

He didn't run. He walked quickly. The sound of his shoes did not echo neatly or precisely as he crossed the foyer. At the stairs, he turned into a short hall, hoping to find an obvious closet where he could grab his coat. The hair at the back of his neck prickled as he approached the first door, and he turned to find the maid behind him, holding the coat out for him to shrug into.

"Thank you," he said.

Again, she didn't respond, and a heavy wad of sadness nestled into his chest. This house was so completely fucked up.

The chill outside air provided a much-needed slap to his cheeks. Henry stood there a moment, swallowing against the burn in his throat while watching his breath make furious clouds. Anger hadn't driven him out of the house, though. Marc had managed to flip a deeper switch.

Henry had decided long ago that being out was important to him. His sexuality was an essential part of his identity, and he didn't want to hide it. No, he didn't make a lot of noise in life, but he had the quiet assertiveness thing down.

Right now he felt ashamed. Of who he was, of what he was… and because he'd left Marc alone. But Marc was the one who had made him feel deviant and dirty, like something that should be hidden away.

Resisting the urge to rub his jaw, Henry pushed off the porch and pulled out his phone.

Chapter
EIGHT

*H*e'd fucked up. His temper had left the bottle like some vengeful genie and wreaked havoc on the best and worst aspects of his life simultaneously. Except he couldn't blame an apparition for his mistakes. A Winnamore didn't hide behind excuses.

Standing on a street corner that was at once familiar and not, Marc had never felt less like a Winnamore. He looked across the road at the strip mall he'd frequented as a teen. His memory of summer—the only time he'd really been home—fit over the dreary February afternoon like a mismatched slide. He almost couldn't picture himself at fifteen, his legs suddenly too long, shoulders wider than the day before. An awkwardness inside and out, only accentuated by his determination to be someone. Misjudging a doorway with his new frame had not stopped him. Every time he needed new clothes, the old set became a skin he'd shed on the way to....

Here, apparently. A miserable Saturday afternoon in February.

The deli across the road was closed. He'd probably ordered and eaten a hundred plain cheese sandwiches from the place. Half a pound of Muenster on rye with a pickle on the side. When Marc closed his eyes, he didn't picture a sandwich. Instead he saw the guy behind the counter. Amal? Amman. He remembered watching

Amman's hands as he folded slice after slice of cheese onto the bread. His eyes, fringed with thick, dark lashes. Soft and doe-like. His smile.

Marc opened his eyes.

Why was he remembering this now?

The world tipped and swayed. Marc reached out blindly, seeking balance, and found a pole next to him. A parking sign. The cold metal bit into his palm. He gripped the pole tighter, breathing in short, sharp gasps.

Winnamores didn't vomit in public.

But why should he care what a Winnamore did? He didn't feel like one anymore, and if he were truly honest with himself, he never had. He'd spent his life trying to fit into a suit that wasn't his. What he'd called determination was fear. His forward momentum? A headlong run in the opposite direction to expectation.

Eyes burning with the threat of tears, Marc pulled his hand from the pole and stuck it in his pocket. He looked back across the road. The office supply place next door to the deli had given way to a tanning studio. The variety store was gone, taking endless dusty rows of useless knickknacks into the ever after. He didn't recognize the rest of the shops. Couldn't remember any beyond the three he'd liked. That one remaining piece, though, closed and shuttered tight, felt like an omen.

Marc turned away from his childhood and started up the sidewalk toward Old Georgetown Road. If memory served—hah!—the Metro station was up that way, on Wisconsin. He'd walked this far; he could stand a few more blocks. Maybe if he walked all the way back to DC, his mind would go numb and he'd stop thinking. Stop hearing the echo of his father's voice as he ordered him to leave.

Not asked; not requested. Ordered.

"You are not welcome in this house."

"As if I ever was," Marc had tossed back.

"This home has always been open to you, Marcus."

"Not to me. Never to me. Only to the boy, the man you wanted me to be."

Marc winced at the memory of his tone. He'd been pleading. Even then, half an hour after Henry's sudden departure, he'd been begging his parents to accept who he was, to invite him to stay. And now, dammit, he was blinking away tears on a public street, where anyone might see him.

"Fuck my life."

He found the Metro station and descended to the platform, grateful for the subterranean gloom. An afternoon crowd, heading into DC for the evening, milled about in small groups, laughing and chatting, the scent of their perfume, cologne, and high spirits harsh against Marc's senses. He wanted to hide from them, and the urge felt unfamiliar. Winnamores didn't hide.

From the shadow of a pillar, he studied one of the groups, two men and two women. Couples, he decided, and each had been together for a while. They had that ease where they liked to stand close but no longer needed to touch each other with every breath. But touch they did, in casual ways. One of the women catching her partner's fingers in a quick squeeze as she laughed. One of the men brushing hair away from his girlfriend or wife's cheek before leaning in to gift her with a quick kiss. Jealousy stabbed him in the heart. Marc reached up to rub the center of his chest and breathed through the pain.

He wanted what they had. Wanted it enough to weaken his knees. He'd almost had it with Henry. They were so close to that stage. If not for their jobs, they might already have been there. The connection he felt to Henry, with him, was that strong. As though he'd been waiting for twenty years for the answer to that one formula he couldn't solve.

Had he ruined what they had?

Marc didn't care if he ever saw his parents again. He knew he'd regret the way things had ended. He'd always wish it could have been different. Henry was another issue entirely. What he'd been building with Henry was the most real thing in his life—and he'd used it like a blunt instrument to beat upon the illusion that was the rest of him.

"I am such an idiot."

The ache in his chest was so bad he almost didn't care if he collapsed in the Metro station. He was foundering. He leaned against the printed map on a pillar, a linear route laid out in block letters beneath his cheek. A map that wouldn't take him where he wanted to go.

"Hey, are you okay?"

One half of one of the happy couples stood in front of him. The guy's brow creased with worry as he touched Marc's arm. "Do you need to sit down?"

"No." Marc cleared his throat. Shook his head. "Sorry. I'm okay."

"Are you sure? Can I call someone for you?"

Henry.

Swallowing a painful lump, Marc shook his head again and made an effort to stand upright. He breathed, wincing at the burn, and steadied himself against the pillar. "Really, I'm okay. I just...." Came out to his parents, introduced them to his boyfriend by telling them he'd sucked his cock, and was subsequently kicked out of the house, all at the tender age of twenty-eight.

Grow up, Winnamore.

Marc stood straighter and battled the urge to tell this stranger his story. So not the time, and what did it matter, really? Whether he flinched away or started in on some speech about how "Love is love, dude, you do it the way you want," none of it mattered. Not to him and the man he wanted to love.

The man who needed to be loved.

God, the hurt and betrayal on Henry's face as he backed away from the dining room.

The stranger was looking at him with expectation.

"I just lost my parents," Marc said. "But I'm okay. I'm...." If he stood any straighter, he'd crack his spine. "Everything is going to be okay."

The man's face creased sympathetically. He gave Marc's arm another squeeze and a pat. "I'm sorry for your loss. You take care, okay?"

"Thank you."

The train arrived and swallowed them. Marc moved to the opposite end of the car and sat down to practice what he was going to say to Henry when he got back to the hotel. He'd start with an apology. Admit he'd been an ass. Ask Henry to forgive him. Not ask for sex. Instead, he'd ask if Henry would simply spend the night with him so they could fall asleep together and wake up together, the way couples did. The way they had last night and this morning.

Then they'd put this damn Hiddenger proposal together, present the hell out of it, and return to Boston to collect their reward.

Forward momentum didn't always have to represent escape.

The rest of the ride passed in a blur of statistics as Marc tried to engage his thoughts with something other than the catastrophe that was his personal life. He didn't feel much better as he covered the short walk to the hotel, but he no longer wanted to crumple up and die. Familiar determination dogged his steps, pushing him forward, relentlessly forward.

He wasn't surprised to find his room dark and empty, Henry's few belongings packed up and probably shifted next door. He paused in the soulless quiet for a moment, gathering his resolve. Then he knocked on the connecting door.

No answer.

Marc checked his watch. Five thirty. Maybe Henry had gone out to get something to eat?

He knocked again. "You in there?"

When nothing but silence answered, Marc tried the handle. It wasn't locked. He pushed the door open and peeked into the adjoining room. Dark and empty, just like his. Marc switched on one of the lamps.

The undisturbed bed blinked like a vacancy sign until Marc remembered Henry had slept with him last night. Also, hotels had housekeepers. He glanced around the room for other signs of residency and breathed out a shaky sigh as he spied Henry's case on a small stand in the corner.

He was still here.

Of course he's still here. Henry doesn't run away from his responsibilities.

He'd just gone out to eat.

Marc considered finding him for all of thirty seconds before pulling out his phone. Let the man eat in peace. They could do what they needed to do later.

He sent a text. *Hey, I'm back at the hotel.*

Half an hour later, he still didn't have a reply.

Marc sent another text. *Really sorry about this afternoon. Can we talk?*

No reply.

He sent another text at eight. *Everything okay?*

At nine: *I get you're probably pissed. I deserve it. Just let me know you're okay.*

At ten: *Worried about you.*

At eleven: *Henry.*

Sometime before midnight, the strain of the day left him in a dizzying rush. Resignation settled across his chest, heavy and immovable. Too done in to even be angry, Marc reached for his phone to send one more text.

Miss you. xoxo

Chapter
NINE

*H*enry glanced up as the door to the conference room cracked open, expecting to see the security guard. She'd seemed unperturbed by the change to her Sunday routine. After a quiet glance at his credentials, she'd added him to her round, presumably to check he didn't wander somewhere he shouldn't.

Marc stood in the doorway, virtual storm clouds gathering across his brow. His eyes snapped with dark lightning, and his mouth was set in a short, hard line. But as Henry watched, his features softened. Fear and relief replaced the anger, and something else. A lot else. Marc was an expressive guy. It hurt to watch him stand there and struggle to find the right mood.

"Have you been here all night?" Marc asked.

Henry shook his head. "I was here last night. I came back this morning." He'd stayed too late and returned too early and hadn't really gotten anything useful done. He was not the guy who would sit in a hotel room waiting for a knock at the door, though.

"Did you get my texts?"

"Yes."

"Why didn't you answer any of them?" Marc stepped inside the conference room and shut the door. "I was worried about you."

"Can we not do this now?"

"Do what?"

Henry breathed in, counted to ten, and breathed out. "I've confirmed our presentation for tomorrow at 9:00 a.m. Do you want to go over the details?"

"No, I do not want to go over the details. I want to talk about lunch yesterday."

"That's not what we're here for."

"So… what, you're going to ignore the fact I just flushed my life down the toilet?"

Henry winced. "No." The small word sounded even smaller in the leaden quiet. "Marc…."

Marc gripped the back of the chair in front of him. "I need to say I'm sorry. I tried to do that last night. But you don't want my apology, do you?"

"It's not that. It's this." Henry tapped the screen of his laptop. "We're here to do a job."

"The job is done, Henry. You know it as well as I do. Whatever you were doing last night and this morning wasn't work."

"We still have to pull everything together."

"Which will take us an hour, maybe two, this afternoon."

Not if they wanted to check it and recheck it. Practice their presentation. Prepare a list of anticipated questions. They could spend all day on this. Should spend all day—

"Henry."

Henry pushed away from the table and stood. "I tried to tell you this would happen. But you don't listen to anyone else, do you? Only yourself."

"What are you talking about?"

"In New York. In the car. I told you this"—he gestured between them—"would interfere with our work."

"That's a shitty excuse and you know it. What are you really afraid of? No, don't answer that. Answer this instead. Where were you yesterday? Because that's something else you told me by the side of the goddamn road in New York. That you'd be there when I told my parents I was gay. Whether as a friend or something more. You said you'd be there."

"I was there, Marc. Right there. Apparently with my cock out, ready for you to suck."

"Not fair."

"You used me!"

Marc let go of the chair. "Right, because that's what I've been doing all along."

Ouch.

Marc pressed his palms to his eyes and moved his fingers back over his scalp, pushing his hair away from his face. He took a backward step toward the door. "You know, I expected what I got from my parents. I knew they would react the way they did. But I really thought you'd be there for me. I was counting on you."

Henry looked down at his hands. They were shaking. When he clasped them together, a fine tremor shot up his arms and landed in the middle of his chest. It hurt to swallow. To breathe. The space behind him, a blank and featureless wall, had given way to vacuum. Standing there, Henry could feel his entire being tilting toward nothingness. He could hear the roar of it.

Oh, it would be so easy to just give in. To fall back and be swallowed—except there was nothing but a blank wall behind him, and if he tipped backward, he'd only fall on the floor.

He picked up his coat instead. Jerked one arm inside an uncooperative sleeve.

"Where are you going?" Marc asked.

"Back to the hotel."

"Why?"

"You said it yourself. We're done here."

Marc grabbed his arm. "You're really going to walk away from this?"

Henry made no answer. He pulled his arm from Marc's grasp

and left the conference room.

Marc called after him. "What are you so afraid of, Auttenberg?"

Henry stopped. Turned. He opened his mouth, ready to tell Marc this had nothing to do with fear, and found he couldn't say the words. Because he'd be lying. He was angry about yesterday, sorry about last night. Ashamed of the way he'd behaved and of the way Marc had made him feel.

And he was afraid, which was stupid considering the fact what he feared most had already happened.

He'd fallen for Marc, fallen hard, and any attempt to halt his downward slide into believing this man could be The One, his partner in all things, had been weak. He'd let this happen. He'd welcomed it. God, that jerk of happy surprise whenever his phone chimed with a text from Marc. His heart danced at the sound of Marc's voice. Every touch rendered him helpless to resist.

So why was he wrecking it? Breaking the one thing he'd always wanted?

Because....

"It's you, Marc. I'm afraid of you."

It didn't click right away. For uncounted moments, Marc stood there trying to figure out how Henry could possibly be afraid of him. Yes, he'd acted like an ass yesterday afternoon. But he often acted like an ass.

It was his thing, wasn't it?

Henry had warned him that coming out would be messy. Some people wouldn't understand, and others simply wouldn't care. No amount of planning could have eased this one confession, though. His parents weren't going to accept it. Or if they had, if they'd had a list of potential partners for their possibly gay son....

Focus, Winnamore.

What had Henry running scared?

"This can't be a work thing," Marc said, grasping for a reason. He gestured toward the abandoned conference room. "We have this. We had this on Friday. Us being together made this happen faster than it might have had we been approaching from different directions."

Henry shook his head, looked as though he might say something, then bit his lower lip.

"What is it? You have to help me out here."

"I don't want to do this," Henry said, his voice soft and scratchy.

"What? What is it you don't want to do?" Marc took a few cautious steps forward. Closer, he could see Henry was shaking. His hands twitched and his shoulders kept tucking in. "Help me understand, please? Are you breaking up with me? Is that what this is?"

Henry seemed to crumple at the suggestion. One minute he stood upright; the next he bent forward, grasping his knees. Before Marc could go to him, a security guard appeared at the corner and rushed forward. "Sir? Mr. Auttenberg, are you okay?" She glanced up at Marc. "Are you—"

"His partner, Marc Winnamore. We're with the same firm." Marc waved at the open conference room door. "We're working on the proposal together."

Henry straightened. "I'm fine."

He looked a long way from fine.

"Out too late last night, in too early this morning," Marc provided, taking Henry's arm. "Let's get you back to the hotel." To the guard, he added, "Can you lock the conference room for us?"

"My laptop." Surprisingly, Henry hadn't pulled away from him. He did lean toward the conference room, though.

"I'll get it." Marc let him go and ducked back inside the room to grab Henry's laptop. He straightened the papers on the desk while it shut down and shoved everything into the open bag on the chair. When he returned to the hallway, Henry was gone.

Dammit!

The guard was still there. "Mr. Auttenberg said he'd wait downstairs for you," she said. "I think he wanted some air."

"Thanks."

Marc ran past the elevator and took the stairs. They were only five floors up. As he bounced from stair to stair, bones and teeth jarring from the pace of his descent, he wondered why he was running. Why he should chase Henry. Obviously the guy wanted out. Even if Marc didn't truly understand what had gone wrong, he got that.

Damn if it was as easy to let him go, though.

He pushed through the door at the bottom of the stairwell and skidded into the lobby of the building, nearly knocking someone down along the way. It was Henry.

Henry caught his arm and held on until they both found their balance.

"Jesus, what are you doing standing right outside the door?" Marc asked.

"Waiting for you."

"Waiting…." Marc's mouth stopped working for a second. "I thought you'd be halfway back to the hotel."

"That was my plan, but by the time I got down here, I realized you'd just follow me."

"Damn straight."

"We need to talk."

Breath gusted out of Marc, leaving him feeling weak and insubstantial. "That's what I've been trying to do."

"I know. I'm sorry. I… I haven't had much sleep."

He looked about as exhausted as Marc felt, and something else. Young. Marc didn't often think about the difference in their ages. Four years wasn't much, and as they grew older, the gap would no doubt shrink. But right then, Henry looked younger than twenty-four. Younger and way more vulnerable.

The security guard at the entrance to the building was giving them the evil eye.

"Can we go back to the hotel and figure this out?" Marc asked.

Henry nodded.

Marc didn't take Henry's hand as they made their way back to the hotel. He hadn't all the other times they'd trekked back and forth, either. There was a time and a place to show his affection. He understood that. As they pushed through the revolving glass doors to the hotel lobby, however, he couldn't help wondering if he'd missed his last chance.

Chapter
TEN

*H*enry eyed the unmade bed in Marc's hotel room with trepidation. Maybe this wasn't the right place to talk, not where a fold in the sheets stirred a hundred small memories and just as many urges. He tried to focus his gaze elsewhere, but he was so damn tired that it kept landing back on the bed.

He slumped into one of the chairs by the window and tipped his head back. "I don't know where to start."

The other chair creaked as Marc also sat. "How about yesterday when you walked out on me?" His tone held mild hurt, but not a lot of accusation.

Still.

Henry lifted his head. "I...." The temptation to run returned. His legs weren't cooperating, though, and neither was his heart. He breathed out, long and deep. "It felt like my fault. Logically, I know it wasn't. That lunch would have been a disaster whether I was there or not, but when panic sets in, logic is the first thing to go."

"You didn't look like you were panicking. You never panic. You're like the calm in the middle of a storm."

Where the hell had Marc gotten that idea?

"I panicked in the basement," Henry said.

"Only because your book doesn't have a basement chapter."

"It does, actually." Henry shook his head. "Listen, it's more than that. You know how close I am to my family. I… I don't know how you've survived not having that. How you ended up so you when your parents are so what they are."

Marc returned a blank look.

"I don't want to be the reason they don't accept you."

A tired sigh gusted out of Marc. "You're not. But even if you were, at least you're something tangible."

"I don't want you to point to me and say 'you're the reason my parents don't speak to me anymore.'"

"You really think I'd do that?"

"I don't know what I think anymore. I…." He shook his head again. His brain felt like mush, his reasoning circular. He squeezed his eyes shut.

Marc gripped his shoulder and spoke gently. "Henry, what is it? I can tell something's going on in your head, but I don't know what it is. Please let me in."

Hadn't he been doing that? Hadn't he been opening himself to this man, bit by bit, for months now? Henry reached for his jaw, the movement habitual, and froze with his fingers resting lightly on his cheek.

Let me in.

"It was my junior year in college," he said.

"I don't follow."

Henry opened his eyes. "The guy who nearly broke my jaw."

Marc's eyebrows twitched together.

"He…." Henry swallowed drily. "He was my best friend growing up. Brian Harkness. We prowled the mean streets of Dorchester together from age twelve to eighteen. Then I went to college and he didn't."

That last summer had been so awkward.

"The summer before college, we drifted apart. He was already working at his dad's garage. I was working at my parents' store, but we didn't hang out as much. I used to think it was my fault, that I was the one who was drawing away. I felt so damn guilty for leaving him behind, even though I'd still be in town." Henry stared at his hands for a moment before continuing. "And the crush I'd had on him since I was about fourteen was making me miserable. He was straight. He knew I wasn't and seemed okay with it. We didn't talk about it much, which I was grateful for, you know? Made it seem like it wasn't such a big deal. But if I...."

The rest of the sentence disappeared behind a shuddering breath. Henry's chest tightened under the strain of trying to figure out how much to share and how much to keep.

He glanced up into Marc's dark eyes and saw expectation. Patience too, but also a quiet belief that Henry would finish his story, the complete version. And why not? Marc had shared so much of his life with him.

"I loved him," Henry admitted with a quiet gasp. "I knew I couldn't tell him, and it hurt, you know? So that summer, I was glad of the space. It was sad, but one of those necessary things."

Marc nodded.

"We started hanging out again my junior year, and it was really good. We were both a little bit older, but the stuff that... that bound us together as kids was still there. It was like I had my best friend back. Then it started feeling like more. He kept asking questions and touching me. More than just a shoulder bump or bro hug kind of thing. I knew he was feeling me out."

Or had he stupidly assumed? He would never be sure.

"So one night I kissed him." Henry locked his fingers together so he wouldn't stroke his jaw, touch the spot that still ached sometimes, even if only in his memory. "You know the rest of the story."

"Shit." Marc clenched his fists and pressed them to his brow before relaxing his fingers and pushing them through his hair. The familiar movement tugged at something in the center of Henry's chest. At his heart. Despite their work schedules, he knew this man intimately. Or felt like he did. He'd studied Marc for months—years—before getting close to him.

That was his pattern, though. Pick a guy he probably couldn't have. Get excited when it seemed he could. Live through the pain of heartbreak when it didn't work out.

"This isn't the same," Marc said.

"I know."

"Do you?"

Henry shook his head and rubbed at his cheek. Played with the top of one ear. Made a dozen small gestures, each supposed to aid him in finding an answer.

Marc touched his knee, his hand warm and steady. "Henry."

"I'm tired."

"You and me both."

"No, I'm tired of this."

Marc's expression shattered. His hand slipped from Henry's knee.

Henry caught it and held tight. "I'm tired of looking for excuses to not fall for you. Because it doesn't work. I've wanted you for so long. It was the stupidest want, but I couldn't help it." The confession hurt, but the pain was liberating in a strange way. He'd now given Marc everything. Almost everything. "Did you know I used to get in early when I knew you'd be back from somewhere just so I could watch you stride into the office with your success smile in place? I'd offer to shake your hand, congratulate you, and you always took a second to smile right at me, like you knew I was there. Not just some random office stiff, but me. It was so dumb."

"I did see you. It was like the only time you'd ever talk to me."

"I wanted you so much it hurt, but I was so used to hiding it that it's hard to let go now."

A glimmer of understanding finally lit Marc's eyes. "Okay."

"I want to. Not let you go, but let me go. I want this. I don't know why I'm making it so hard."

"I can't guarantee I won't ever hurt you, Henry, but I'd never hit you. That's not me." Marc stabbed a finger into his chest. "This is me. The man who has been chasing you down. I may not have handled the whole coming out thing with grace, but I'm not going to punish you for it."

"I'm so sorry I left you alone with your parents yesterday, and ignored you last night, and then compounded it all by trying to walk away from you again this morning. Why are you even still here talking to me?"

"Because I was the ass. Not you." Marc leaned back in his chair and sighed. He looked over at Henry. "I used to look forward to those handshakes too, you know. I didn't know you got in early those days, I just knew you'd be there. This is even before I saw you jogging. I was always aware of you, Henry."

Henry drew in a quick and shaky breath. Was Marc telling the truth, because if he was, then… this really wasn't the same. Not at all. This wasn't another unrequited crush. Marc had never forced himself into Henry's life. He'd never played on something that should have been precious. He'd always just been Marc.

Henry acknowledged that with a nod.

Marc exhaled. "This has been really intense," he said.

"Yep."

"Are we going to move past it?"

Henry opened his mouth. Closed it. Drew his shoulders up and put his heart on the line. "Do you want to?"

"Are you going to believe me if I say yes?"

"What do you mean?"

"This is not an experiment, okay?" Marc said. "What you and I have is the real thing. A thing I want very much."

"Even though—"

"Just say yes, Auttenberg." Marc leaned forward. "But if we're going to do this, I need all of you. Even when I'm being an ass, I need you. You can tell me to stop or drag me somewhere else, but don't ever walk out on me again."

"Don't ever use me as a prop again. Especially not with your parents."

Marc's expression darkened. "I doubt we'll be seeing them anytime soon. But yeah, okay."

"I'm really sorry, Marc."

"I think we've done worn that word out."

A small smile creased Henry's cheeks. "You've been in Boston for eight years, and you still sound like you're south of the Mason-Dixon Line."

"So not from the South. DC is another country entirely."

"Yeah, I'll give you that."

Marc grinned. "So can we get to the kissing and making up now?"

"God, yes."

Chapter
ELEVEN

*M*arc leaned across the gap between them. Henry did the same and stopped, looked down. Following his gaze, Marc saw the arm of the chair had caught him up. They both leaned again, coming within inches of a kiss.

"Most unromantic moment ever," Marc murmured, stretching out as far as he could.

Henry smiled and the moment broke. The tension of the past twenty-four hours shredded like mist in the wind. They'd run a gauntlet of a sort and come out the other side—victorious but wrecked. Henry's laughter was Marc's reward. His gray eyes lightened, and his expression lifted. A sense of peace and warmth rolled through Marc. Now, more than even a minute ago, Henry's confession fresh and sharp, he knew everything was going to be okay.

Lifting his butt out of the chair, Marc leaned out a little more and touched his lips to Henry's in a brief caress before murmuring, "Come here."

Henry left his chair and moved to straddle Marc's legs, settling into his lap. He was heavy. Not ridiculously so, just enough for Marc to have a brief flash of "this is a man." *This is Henry*. Even before

Marc reached for him, Henry was leaning forward, seeking a kiss. He all but fell into Marc, as though worried he'd miss a connection.

And oh, the kiss.

Marc's thoughts scattered before it. Kissing Henry had become a favorite pastime, but this kiss changed everything. Where before he thought he'd had Henry, now he had all of him. The difference couldn't be quantified. Lips, tongue, hitched breath, small sounds. Henry leaning in and hanging on. Clinging to him, moving into him.

Marc felt as desperate. He'd nearly lost this. He didn't want to lose this. He held Henry as fast as Henry held him. Kissed him as fiercely. Beneath their urgency thrummed something new, deeper.

They were in a hurry, but not in a hurry. They had all morning or afternoon or however long to make this right. To take this kiss and use it to describe everything that came after.

Marc's breath hitched and caught. The backs of his eyes burned. This was *it*.

This was everything.

Henry left his mouth and skimmed his lips along Marc's jaw. Breath stirred the air behind his ear as Henry kissed there, his cheek, his brow. Then he was leaning away, his thumb at Marc's lips, his gaze curious, anxious. He moved his thumb to Marc's cheek, swiping gently at what he found there, his eyebrows drawing together in a gentle frown.

"What did I do?" he asked.

Marc shook his head.

Henry nosed his cheek, the movement pushing a waft of air across Marc's skin, cool against the moisture that wasn't sweat. Jesus, he was weeping over a kiss.

"What happened?"

"You," Marc whispered.

"I don't understand."

Marc drew in a deep, shuddering breath. "No one has ever kissed me like that before."

"I'm so sorry."

"No, don't be. I knew there was more, Henry. I knew you were holding back, but this. I...." Marc grasped the back of Henry's head, pulling his face closer so their foreheads could touch. "This is everything I ever wanted."

Henry blinked rapidly, his eyes glinting in the darkness. "Me too."

"Then let's make this work."

Henry pressed a soft kiss to his mouth. "Make love to me, Marc."

"You mean—" Surely he didn't mean....

"Yes."

"I was starting to get the idea you didn't do anal sex."

"I don't, not really. I haven't been with enough guys to make a habit out of it."

Marc smiled. Oh, his sweet, sweet man. His Henry. "I'm going to ruin you for all of them."

Henry returned the smile. "I think you already have."

He slid off Marc's lap and started pulling at his clothes.

Marc stood, meaning to follow, to rid himself of clothing, but his fingers weren't being very helpful. They trembled as he tugged at his coat and totally failed at button duty. His scattered thoughts chose that moment to reconvene and tumble back inside his head with one goal in mind: a freak-out.

So, yeah, he'd wanted to get inside Henry's skin, inside *him*. Now it was going to happen, on top of the emotional overload of that kiss. He'd accepted the fact sex was something more than sticking tab *A* in slot *B*. Sex with Henry was connecting in myriad ways. Touching, caressing, getting each other off. The high of a climax shared with another person. The tastes and smells. Just getting into that groove with someone else.

Still, he'd wanted more. Whether it was because he came from a straight world or he just wanted to know how it felt. But how did he, how would he, what if he....

Henry caught his hands and squeezed his fingers. "You're freaking out, aren't you?"

"Maybe."

"Are you making plans?"

"Plans are on hold. All I can think about is being with you."

Henry kissed his hands. "Then you better get your clothes off."

Right. Clothes off. He could do this.

By the time he was naked, Marc's heart beat so hard he actually looked down to see if it was leaving a mark in the middle of his chest.

Sprawled naked on the bed, Henry grinned and patted the spot beside him. "C'mon, let's do that cuddling thing you're always talking me into, and then we'll get to the sex thing you're always talking about."

Marc crawled forward and settled onto his back next to Henry. "Sounds like I do a lot of talking."

"I haven't counted the words, but—"

Marc elbowed him and rolled onto his side, propping his head up with his hand. He trailed the fingers of his other hand down the middle of Henry's bare chest and smiled as goose bumps appeared around his nipples. "Cold?"

"No, just naked."

"Someone mentioned sex." Marc tweaked a hardening nipple.

Henry covered Marc's fingers and moved his hand down his torso toward his thickening cock. Marc allowed himself to be guided, his own dick jerking in response. Wrapping his fingers around Henry's shaft, he squeezed. Henry moaned and reached for him, pulling him down and into another breath-stealing kiss.

He hadn't taken a lot of time to explore Henry's body on Friday night. Now he did. They weren't just making out. They were making love. Marc paid homage to Henry's face in much the same way Henry had done for him—kissing a nose that was almost too small, but so well suited to his regular and handsome features. He kissed

Henry's mouth again, Henry smiling beneath the soft benediction. His eyes. Marc kissed each one closed. Henry's cheeks, flushed with color. Stupidly perfect ears.

"Tickles," Henry said, squirming.

Marc bit his earlobe, gently, then more firmly as Henry gasped.

He kissed Henry's shoulders, smoothed his hands over neat pecs and gently delineated ribs. Dragged his lips over one nipple, then another. Revisited each with a quick nip.

Henry arched beneath him. "Marc."

His name on hitched breath. So, so good.

Moving lower, he glanced upward. Henry had lifted his head to watch.

"You'll tell me what to do?" Marc asked. He turned his head sideways and kissed the upright shaft of Henry's erection. It jerked against his lips.

Henry breathed out sharply. "Every time I see you near my dick, I feel like I've fallen into an alternate universe."

Marc chuckled. "Right here with you."

He reached down to cup Henry's balls, rolling them gently before squeezing.

Henry moaned again and spread his legs. "Get the lube."

It shouldn't have been possible to get any harder than he was, but Marc's cock tried, and a delicious ache speared him in the groin, clutching at his balls. Breathing in short, shallow gasps, Marc pulled away and grabbed the lube and condom that had mysteriously appeared on the side of the bed.

Lube and a condom.

"What are you grinning about over there?" Henry asked.

"I'm about to have sex. What do you think?"

"You look way too amused for that."

Marc lifted his gaze heavenward and looked back down at the man sprawled out next to him, cock jutting upward, legs spread invitingly. "Can't I just be happy without agenda or plan?"

Henry reached for him. "Yeah."

After another round of worship—both of them apparently competing for number of kisses per square inch of skin—Henry instructed him on prep. Marc had thought touching his own ass, breaching himself with a fingertip regularly over the past couple of months, would prepare him for this. It didn't. Henry was another person, and so obviously not a woman.

"Stop thinking and just touch me," Henry urged.

"I'm not used to being this anxious."

"It's cute."

"So not."

Marc glanced up to find Henry grinning at him. Breathing out, he touched, and it was okay. More than okay if Henry's quiet gasp and shiver were anything to judge by.

"Slowly, open me up," he said.

Another misconception fell away as Marc pushed his finger inside Henry. What they were doing was undeniably sexy. He'd hoped it would be. In good porn, it looked good. Something he wanted to try. In actuality? Watching Henry move against him, accept him, feeling the heat and tightness of him, was pretty much the biggest turn-on Marc could imagine. Another finger and he felt Henry opening beneath him. It was nothing short of amazing.

Then he found that much-vaunted bundle of nerves. Henry's eyes rolled back. He shuddered and arched. Groaned a deeper cadence. Reached down to grasp Marc's wrist, halting his movements. "Stop. God... you need to stop or I'm going to come before we get to the good stuff."

"Looks like that was the good stuff."

Henry regarded him with a heavy-lidded expression. "You have no idea."

"Can't wait to try it."

"You'll get your chance, don't worry. Where's the condom?"

Marc eased his fingers out of Henry, wiped them off on the small towel that had been folded under the lube and condom, and reached for the shiny square. Henry sat up, leaned in for a kiss, and used the pressure of his lips to nudge Marc down toward the bed.

Just before he was rolled onto his back, Marc asked, "What are we doing?"

"Rolling around naked." Henry reached down to squeeze Marc's harder-than-hard cock. "Condom?"

"Here." He handed it up, confused as Henry straddled his thighs. What were they doing? He'd prepped Henry, right? "Shouldn't you be down here?"

"Stop panicking."

"I don't panic."

"Lay back, Marc, and let me take you for a ride."

Seeing Marc this turned on was... sexy, yeah. A moment copied straight from Henry's fantasies. But also tender and personal in a way he couldn't have predicted. He was about to take this man inside himself, thereby sealing a different sort of deal. He wanted to give Marc this, trust him with this, and Marc needed to have it, this piece of him.

Henry ripped open the packet, rolled the thin latex down Marc's bobbing shaft, and reached for the lube. Marc moaned and shuddered beneath him, trying to arch—a difficult proposition with Henry sitting on his thighs.

Henry tried not to laugh. "Don't come yet," he instructed.

Marc's sheathed cock pushed through his fingers as he applied the lube.

Lifting to his knees, Henry leaned forward, supporting himself with one hand. He pressed a soft kiss to Marc's lips. With his other hand, he reached back to apply the last of the slick to his hole. Marc's gaze remained locked with his, but in the dark depths, Henry could see the knowledge of what was happening. Of Henry finishing his prep, of what they were about to do. He reached for Marc's erection, and those dark eyes didn't waver, though his lids did lower a little, showing pleasure at Henry's touch.

He lined them up and closed his own eyes, not able to do the soul-gazing thing as he lowered himself onto Marc's cock. Marc sucked in a quick breath and gripped Henry's braced arm.

"Oh God," he whispered.

Shh, Henry thought, but didn't say. He didn't want to hear how good this was, though he couldn't say why. Maybe because Marc was barely inside him, the intrusion not yet welcome. Henry breathed and counted—backward, not forward. Inwardly and outwardly, he opened. Moved past the pinch and burn. Moved a little more. Settled, opened, settled again. Breathed. Marc was inside him, almost fully, and….

Henry opened his eyes and looked down at Marc, who looked like he'd touched heaven. "Ready?"

"I was born ready."

Marc and his greeting card quotes. Taking in another draught of air, Henry moved, lifting himself up an inch, lowering himself down.

"Oh! Ohh…." Marc's eyelids fluttered. More moans, deep, breathy groans. He tightened his grip on Henry's arm and reached out with his other hand, catching hold of Henry's hip. Henry moved again, and again, increasing his range of motion each time until he found the drop-off point. Up to there, down to…. Oh God.

He hadn't lied. Bottoming wasn't a habit of his. He'd liked it enough the first time to be able to imagine it being better. To understand the why of it. He'd liked it better the second time.

Third time? Still collecting data.

His inexperience didn't feel like a hindrance. Rather, this was truly something he and Marc explored together. It felt good. Really, really good. Physically and mentally.

And… he really needed to stop thinking, examining, counting.

Tipping his head back, Henry let go. Let his body take control of his mind. He became aware of Marc's hands, the one still wrapped around his forearm, the one cruising up and down his torso. Marc's gasps. The scent of them—sweat and arousal. The lingering taste of Marc on his tongue. The space between them and the point of their connection—the latter a glowing ember of all things good, warming, spreading, encompassing.

He put his other hand to the mattress and started moving in earnest. Up and down. Riding, feeling, working toward that point where self ceased and nothing else mattered. Where only Marc's breathless commentary measured time.

"Oh man. Oh God. So good. So close. Fuck…. Oh. Ohhh."

The small words matched their rhythm. Marc's movement beneath him was beautiful. The sudden jerk of tension signaling his impending climax? Perfect.

"Going to come," Marc hissed. "Are you close?"

"Yes." His voice felt tight. He'd been close for what seemed like hours, flirting with adding forward motion to his up and down slide, teasing his prostate.

Unplanting a hand, Henry reached for his cock. He'd jerked himself once when Marc thrust up hard, his yell cut off halfway as he gave himself over to his climax. The pulse inside him was seductive, teasing Henry with the fantasy of his own peak—so close, but not quite there. He clenched his ass, drawing another yell from Marc, and pumped his dick harder, possessed by a need to come soon, to fall into the same happy envelope.

Two strokes became three, then four. It was only as he imagined Marc coming inside him bare, the heat and thrill of them making another sort of commitment, that he pitched over the cliff of his orgasm and fell. Hard.

His dick pulsed in his hand. Henry squeezed and stroked harder. Had he just whimpered? God, he was unraveling from the inside out.

Coming apart. For countless minutes, he existed in a place defined by the seemingly boundless limits of his climax and almost afraid he'd be trapped there forever. That he'd quake and shatter into pieces and simply cease to exist.

Marc brought him back with two warm anchor points—one hand at his hip, the other on the side of his face. "Henry."

Henry dropped forward and felt Marc's dick pull from his ass. Whoops. He flailed one arm in a vague backward direction. "Condom?"

"Still there."

"Cool."

Beneath him, Marc chuckled. "Wow."

"Yeah." He should move. Roll off Marc before they fused together in a puddle of drying come. His bones had melted into rubber, and his skin was numb. Body nonresponsive. "Need to clean up," he slurred more than said.

Marc shifted, lifting one hip enough to roll Henry off to the side, and left the bed. His absence felt like a hole in space-time. Henry patted the empty spot next to him and smiled, aware he probably looked as though he'd been struck on the head. At least he wasn't drooling.

He wasn't drooling, was he?

He'd just finished licking his lips when Marc arrived back with the towel, now warm and damp. Henry cleaned himself up, hissing quietly as his skin proved a long way from numb. He felt sunburned. Had he ever come so hard? So… fully?

"Third time's a charm," he murmured.

"Hmm?"

"Tell you later." Henry handed over the towel.

Marc tossed it over his shoulder and climbed back into bed. "Tell me now."

"Need some Marc-mandated cuddling first."

After an orgasm like that, he needed to be held close. The fear of coming apart still threatened.

Marc willingly complied, dropping flat onto his back and scooping Henry into his side. Henry slid one of his legs over one of Marc's and tucked his hand across Marc's tummy. He settled his head into a firm pec and inhaled. Shivered again. Closed his eyes and let the hum building inside him settle and spread.

This was contentment. This was what sex was supposed to feel like. Or no, this was what making love felt like.

His eyes popped open.

"I felt that," Marc said, his voice mostly a rumble beneath Henry's cheek.

"What?"

"You start thinking."

"Thinking is impossible after sex like that."

"Yeah? Glad you think so."

Smiling, Henry lifted his cheek. "So…."

"So…? I liked it. Yeah. Loved it. Can't wait to do it again. Did you have any doubts?"

"No, but, yeah, okay. I'm just going to stop thinking now."

"Tell me about the third time charm thing first."

Henry breathed in. Sweat and sex and afterglow coated his tongue. He swallowed. "Third time bottoming. I told you it's not a habit or whatever."

"You know there's a rumor about you at B and M, right?"

"That I'm fucking Marc Winnamore?"

Marc laughed, his chest rumbling again. "No, that you're secretly really kinky. Behind the quiet, reserved thing."

"Yeah, I knew about that one."

"I never believed it." Marc's tone was thoughtful. "I mean, I spent way too much time imagining what you did get up to in your off hours, but I didn't get kinky with it until that time we talked about the ties."

Henry swallowed a chuckle, coughed, and let the next one happen. "Me neither. Honestly, as long as we're both into it, I don't care what we do. As long as it's just you."

"What, no threesomes?"

Henry shook his head.

"I'll just be grateful that sex with you is already the best I've ever had, then."

Henry looked up again. "Lay it on a little thicker, Winnamore."

"Hey, I've told you that before. With you, everything is in color. The full spectrum. I wasn't living before. Now I can barely get through the days until I see you again. It's scary and thrilling, and you've changed my mind about so many things I really should have just shut down at some point. But I can't." Marc paused for breath. "I always want more."

Henry's chest ached. "Me too. All of that."

Settled back down, Henry nestled into Marc's chest and closed his eyes. He listened to the steady thump of Marc's heart and let go for the second time that night. It was easier now, to let Marc in. To let Marc be what he so desperately wanted to be. To let himself go there, to just fall. To be in love.

It was too soon to say it, and he didn't want to be the guy who declared his heart after shooting his brains from the end of his dick. But he could let the feeling creep over him, acknowledge that it had been there for a while and that he no longer feared it.

"So," Marc said.

Henry roused himself enough to answer with a grunt.

"We're up to Plan C, just so you know."

"What were Plans A and B?" Henry asked.

"You derailed Plan A on the side of the road in upstate New York. Plan B got turned on its head by a locked basement door."

"You named your plan to kiss me at midnight? Like, formulated it?" Henry didn't know if he was more alarmed or amused.

"Sure I did. Plan C nearly didn't survive contact with the enemy, but I think we just…. Oh man, I was going to say plugged any holes."

Henry laughed. "So, so bad."

"I know."

"Anything else I can think of sounds like a bad cliché."

"Let's just go with Plan C, then. Plan C is good."

Marc's arms closed tighter around him. Henry looked up to find Marc angling his chin down for a kiss. With some shifting and rearranging, Henry managed to turn the cuddle into a slow and languid make-out session and discovered that the easiest way not to think was to kiss Marc. To just be with Marc. He had the feeling that the same proved true for the man he was kissing. Each met a need in the other. Separately, they were good. Together, they were whole.

Chapter
TWELVE

April

Before his phone could buzz more than once, Marc snatched it from the desk and woke the display. He smiled when he saw the text from Henry—the usual simple, single-word greeting that sent his stomach into ridiculous spirals.

Hey.

Marc tapped out his usual simple, double-word response. *Hey you.*

Good time to talk?

Yep. Lemme just save my work.

It's nearly 11. All work and no play makes Marc a cranky boy.

Ignoring the jibe, Marc saved his progress and shut the laptop before picking up the phone and hitting the little phone symbol.

A moment later, Henry answered. "Hey."

"I'm too tired to text tonight. You mind if we chat instead?"

"Of course not. Did you hear back from Lehman?"

"All done and done," he said. "I was just tidying up my presentation."

"So you're still due back tomorrow?"

"Barring freak snowstorms, tsunamis and hurricanes, tornados—"

"Not sure a tsunami could get as far as Chicago."

"You haven't seen the lake when the wind is up."

"True." Henry paused, and the quiet space felt thoughtful. Marc was about to ask what was up when Henry let out a quick, clipped string of words. "Want me to meet you at the airport tomorrow? We could grab something to eat on the way back to your place, or you could stay at mine. Or if you—"

"Yes."

"Yes?"

"All of that. Any of it. Meet me at the airport."

Another pause. "I could just—"

"Henry."

"Yeah?"

"I missed you."

"I missed you too. Five freaking days and I feel like I haven't seen you in a month."

"I know what you mean." They'd texted and talked every night, but it wasn't the same, not anymore. Not after DC. In the weeks since, they'd become closer than ever, especially as their success with the Hiddenger deal encouraged Shelly to team them up more often.

"So I'll come to the airport."

"Will you kiss me when I come through the doors?"

"Do you want me to?"

"Yeah, I do. We can be like a Hallmark moment. A gay one."

Henry laughed. "Sure."

More silence, and it was weird. They never just sat and listened to each other breathe, though the concept of it didn't seem all that strange. The quiet seemed filled with things they both wanted to say. Marc wondered if the words they were holding back were the same.

He heard Henry take a breath and rushed to fill the pause. "Henry, I—"

"Listen, Marc—"

Exhaling, Marc gripped the edge of the desk and pushed back. He could see his head bobbing in the lower left-hand corner of the mirror and the reflection of the bland hotel room behind him. He glanced up so his eyes cut over the frame. "You first," he said.

"I was going to save this for tomorrow, but maybe you want to think about it on the flight and not, like, be confronted with it at the airport or whatever. I did kind of think that asking you there would be, heck, I dunno."

A cold shiver attacked Marc's spine. "Ask me what?"

"I want you to move in with me."

Marc watched his eyes widen in the mirror. "You—"

"It's too soon, isn't it? Look, let's just leave it there. Pick it up in a few months, or a year or—"

"No."

"Or never."

"No, I mean, let's not leave it there. I think it's a great idea. I... your apartment is great. It's bigger and nicer than mine, and even with your mortgage, I'd come out ahead on expenses. I can move up my timeline."

"Your timeline?"

"My loans will be repaid in November 2019. I was going to start looking for my own place sometime around then."

"So this would be a practical move."

"*And* I'd love to wake up next to you every morning." When their schedules allowed.

Could you hear someone smiling over the phone? Marc was sure Henry was smiling.

"I can't believe you've already run the numbers," Henry said.

"Let's call it Plan D."

Henry chuckled. "So, that's a yes?"

"Yeah, it is."

"So what were you going to say?"

"Hmm?"

"I interrupted you."

"Oh, I was… it's stupid now."

"Can I decide that?"

"I'll tell you tomorrow, at the airport. After we finish scandalizing everyone in the arrivals terminal."

"I think everyone will be too busy kissing their loved ones to care."

Marc sucked in a quick breath. "I… yeah. You're probably right."

"You okay?"

No, he wasn't. His heartbeat had gone off track, as though someone had tipped the organ sideways in his chest. "This week has… I've done a lot of thinking."

"Me too, obviously. Hence the whole let's move in together thing."

"I mean, January and February, we kind of had this routine. I liked it. I worked all day, and every night I got to talk to you. Even though we hardly ever saw each other, it was like the closest I'd ever been to being with someone, you know? Then DC happened and we've had a chance to actually be together properly. These past couple months have been amazing. Like every day is better than the last." God, he was rambling. "I can't believe how much I missed you this week. I kept imagining all the things that could happen that would mean I couldn't get back there."

"Why would you do that? It's my job to read survival books and worry about the state of the world."

"Because I love you, Auttenberg." Okay, that would have sounded better with a "Henry" or if he'd just left it at "you."

Silence, deep and hard. Then a breath. A quiet one. "Wow."

"Okay, that's a good reaction. Wow is good." It had sounded like a good wow.

"Sorry. I just… I didn't see this coming."

"Should I take it back?"

"No. Wait, is this Plan E or something?"

The amusement in Henry's tone soothed the burn of near embarrassment. "No," Marc answered. "I've been thinking about it, but…. No. I just needed to tell you."

"I've been thinking about it too. That's why I asked you to move in with me."

Marc grinned. "Good."

Henry took another audible breath and said it. "I love you."

Ignoring the happy dance his body wanted to do—which would probably result in the hotel chair being flung back and him whacking his head on something sharp—Marc said, "We could have saved this for the airport tomorrow."

"Maybe, but now we can just do a lot of stupid grinning when we see each other, instead of being all weird and anxious."

"You know, no matter how much we plan for tomorrow, it's not going to work out the way we want it to."

"I'm not going to find a parking spot."

"My plane is going to be delayed."

"An old lady with a walking frame is going to get right in front of me, and when I try to get around her, there'll be a family with a ton of kids, then one of those airport security carts."

"My bags will probably get lost."

"It's going to be a disaster."

"Maybe we should call the whole thing off."

"No way!" Henry huffed. "I'm going to be there, and we're going to have a stupidly romantic moment."

Marc laughed. He could hear Henry laughing on the other end of the line, and it was nice, laughing together about something so stupid and weird and uniquely theirs. This was togetherness. Being a partner and a lover and a friend.

He found a quick breath. "I really do love you." His heart jumped only a little that time, and he hoped it never stopped moving when he told Henry he loved him. That it always felt this exciting and this good.

"I love you too."

And that Henry's response was always as instant, always as wonderful.

"See you tomorrow?" he asked.

"I'll be there." Henry said.

Chapter
THIRTEEN

May

Henry hoisted the box onto his shoulder and passed it up to the hands reaching down through the hole in the ceiling. "Got it?"

"Yep." Marc pulled the box out of his grasp and disappeared.

Henry bent down to grab the next box. The couple of times he'd been in Marc's apartment, he wouldn't have guessed the guy had so much stuff. "Did you have a storage unit or something?"

Marc's head appeared in the attic hole again. "What?"

"You came with a lot of boxes, man."

"I haven't counted the boxes you've got stashed in your attic, but I think you're winning."

"Pfft."

"Boys?" Henry's mother appeared at the end of the hall. "Heinrich is going to get the pizza now. What sort of soda do you want? Or should he get beer?"

"I've got beer, but soda would be good," Henry said.

"All right. I'm heading down to the laundry. Do you have anything else to go through?"

"No, I'm good." Asking his mother not to do his laundry would be the same as asking her to cut off an arm or a leg, or both, and asking her and his father not to help Marc move in would have been like asking them to go lie in their graves. This was as big a deal for them as it was for him. Their son had picked someone to go on with. Their son was in love.

They could quite possibly be happier than he was.

"Why is he going to get pizza? Don't you get delivery up here?" Marc asked.

"He's going to a different place, over near the market. A friend of his owns it. They grew up together, so they'll need to talk about how well their sons are doing and who their daughters married. He won't be back with pizza for a couple hours, but he'll have enough to feed us for a week."

Marc smiled, but even though his face was half-hidden by attic shadows, Henry could see the sadness in his eyes. They'd talked about what happened with the Winnamores in DC only once before Marc declared the subject closed. Done and done. More than done. He might have also said "beyond done."

"I'm sorry my parents had to be here today," Henry said, even though he wasn't, not really.

"I'm not. I like that they're here. Your dad gave me another fifty bucks, by the way."

Henry laughed. "He'll never ask if you used the last note. He'll just keep giving you new ones, just in case."

"He's a good man."

"He is," Henry agreed. He crouched down to grab the next box. "Ready for another?"

"Yep." Marc extended his arms. "Nice deal, you having the top floor apartment and attic storage."

As Henry hefted the box upward, it tipped a little. He reached to steady it, pulling a flap loose. Something slid from the top, hitting him between the eyes before bounding toward the ground. "Crap."

Marc grabbed the box and lifted it away, leaving Henry free to rub his forehead. He glanced down to see what had hit him. It was a picture. He picked it up.

"Here, pass it up," Marc said.

"Hold on." It was a picture of Marc as a boy. Maybe ten or twelve. He was playing golf with his dad. He had the club behind his shoulder and a determined expression on his face. A very Winnamore expression. That ball was going up, over, around, or through. It was going into the hole if he had to chase it down the green.

It was the lightness of Marc's father's expression that surprised him. The man was smiling. Mr. All the Names Winnamore was smiling, and not in a calculated way. He was simply watching his son play golf and apparently enjoying it.

"Henry." Marc waved his hand through the hole in the ceiling.

"This is a great picture." Henry held it up to show him. "You should leave it out."

"No." Marc swept his arm down and snatched the frame out of Henry's hands.

"Your dad is smiling in it, and you look adorable."

Marc had disappeared into the attic. Henry climbed the stepladder and stuck his head and shoulders through the access to look for Marc. He was at the far end, tucking the picture back into a box.

Without looking up, he said, "Just drop it, Auttenberg."

"We could put it in the bedroom where he'd have to watch us have sex."

Marc's mouth twitched, but he managed to hold a firm line. He shook his head. "Look, I appreciate what you're trying to do, but no."

"Maybe remembering a better time would be...." Henry moved to the top of the ladder and hooked his arms over the edge of the hole. He pulled himself up and slipped, his legs crashing into the ladder, which swayed out from beneath him. "Ah...."

Marc glanced over, saw him struggling, and quickly crawled to help. "Hold on. I've got you. Jesus."

Below them, the aluminum ladder hit the floorboards with an echoing clang. Marc hauled backward and Henry crawled forward until he was inside the attic, then flopped onto his back, breathing hard.

"Shit."

"You okay?" Marc asked.

"Yeah."

"Are we stuck in your attic?"

"Yep."

"I don't fucking believe this. Wait, call out for your mom."

"She's in the laundry."

"Okay, we'll just wait for her to get back."

"She doesn't have a key."

"And your dad is somewhere in Boston exchanging baby pictures with an old friend."

Henry started laughing. Each pitch of his lungs pushed his back into the uneven flooring beneath him, but he couldn't stop, even when he started coughing. Beside him, Marc was moving back and forth, around him, peering down the hole.

"It's not that big of a drop, except the ladder is right there. Goddammit."

Henry laughed harder. Then he started hiccupping.

Marc's face appeared over his. He seemed to be fighting a strong wind, his expression stern, his brow tightly furrowed. His lips twitched once... and again. "You really need to stop laughing."

"I... can't... help it."

"Where's your cell phone?"

"In the bedroom."

"Mine's in the kitchen. This is fucking ridiculous."

Working to control his laughter, Henry reached up to stroke Marc's cheek. "We'll jump down. It'll be fine. You can lower me or something."

Marc's smile won whatever battle played inside his head. He dipped down to kiss Henry on the lips. "This is your fault."

"Probably."

"How long do you think it will be before your mom starts knocking on the door?"

"Depends if she meets anyone else in the laundry or not."

Marc licked Henry's lips, tickling them, and kissed him again. He shifted so he was straddling Henry's hips and sat right below his groin. "So, maybe you can be the one to explain why we made her wait." He rocked forward, applying pressure right *there*.

Moaning softly, Henry reached up to pull Marc into a deeper kiss. "Okay," he mumbled. He swept his tongue inside Marc's mouth and arched beneath him, moaning again as he felt him begin to harden.

Faintly, the sound of someone knocking on the door filtered upward.

"Dammit," Henry said.

Marc kissed his lips closed, then open again, before sitting back and reaching down to cup Henry's half hard-on. "I should make you answer the door like this."

"Oh God."

"Henry?" His mom's voice was far away. She'd be more audible to the occupants of 6B and 6C.

"Lean through the hole and tell her we're coming," Henry said.

Marc grinned as he delivered a squeeze. "Not quite there yet."

Henry groaned.

Taking mercy on him, Marc climbed off and leaned through the hole in the ceiling. "We dropped the ladder," he yelled and pulled back up. "Okay, how do you want to do this?"

Henry sat up. "Will you think about the picture?"

"What?"

"The picture of you and your dad."

"Why is it such a big deal to you?"

"Because it is."

"Are you two okay?" Henry's mom interrupted, her voice faint but insistent.

"Can we do this later?" Marc asked.

Henry sighed. "We don't have to. I just wanted you to have a good memory somewhere, that's all."

Marc's expression softened. He leaned forward and touched his forehead to Henry's. "I have you. I have your family. I'm pretending that's my mom knocking on the door right now."

"She adores you, you know."

"Of course she does."

That was the Marc he knew and loved. Sure of himself and his place in the world. Henry leaned up to kiss him quickly. "Love you."

"Love you too. Now let's get out of this attic and pretend we're rescuing someone else for a change."

Henry glanced over his shoulder one more time, to the box where Marc had put the picture, marking it so he could maybe pull it out again one day. Then he was struck by the thought he might not have to. It was here. Here with Marc. In a box, but here. Marc hadn't thrown it away, even while sorting for this move. He'd kept it. He understood what that picture was, and he'd kept it.

He turned back to Marc and touched his cheek again.

Marc shook his head. "Don't say it."

Henry smiled. "C'mon. Get through the hole. I'll lower you down."

"One more kiss."

Bang. Bang. "Henry? Did something happen?"

"No!" Marc called as Henry lowered him down to the floor, where he did not break his ankle on the fallen ladder.

He lifted it and held it in place for Henry, who managed to climb down without breaking anything either. Henry opened the door to his mother, who looked from one to the other with a knowing smile on her face. "Maybe I should go for a walk?"

"No. No…." Henry pulled her inside. "We're fine. We just thought we were stuck… together."

"But of course you are," she said, eyeing them both again. Smiling. "Stuck together is good."

Henry glanced at Marc, who shrugged and grinned before slinging his arm around Henry's shoulders.

"Yep. Stuck together is very, very good."

Counting
OUT

*T*he story you are about to read is nearly fifty pages of camping fluff. I wrote it for the sheer pleasure of spending more time with Henry and Marc, and the plan was to send them to the woods for a little adventure and romance.

At over 19,000 words, Counting Out is actually longer than Counting Fence Posts, the first novella I wrote for these two. This time, though, instead of getting trapped somewhere, they get lost. And then found. And along the way they find a beautiful waterfall and a not-so-great bear. But because this is romance, everyone lives happily ever after.

I hope you enjoy this extra outing with Henry and Marc!

Chapter
ONE

*M*arcus Winnamore checked his appearance in the dark glass enclosing Shelly's office before knocking and entering. His reflection had been properly serious, but a smile had cornered his mouth as he imagined Henry's reaction to him not waiting to be invited inside. Would Henry's cute little nose wrinkle upward, or would he go with a neat and tidy frown? Maybe he'd try censure instead. Reach out to tug Marc's sleeve as if he could hold him in place.

"Is the smile for me?" Shelly asked.

Marc felt his mouth straighten as he faced his boss across the wide expanse of her executive desk. He liked Shelly's desk. Not so much the woman sitting behind it.

Helping himself to a chair on his side of the coveted desk, Marc aimed for cool, calm, and collected. "That depends. What do you have for me?" A summons to Shelly's office could mean a number of things, most of them requiring a visit to the travel department and a quick coordination of his and Henry's schedules.

To give Shelly her due, she did consider Marc and Henry a team. She recognized their complementary skill sets and usually sent them out together. Marc couldn't help noticing the empty chair beside him this visit, however.

Shelly turned her laptop around and tapped the trackpad a couple of times until the document on the screen enlarged. It was his employee profile. Marc's stomach soured. Ignoring the bitter creep up the back of his throat, he leaned forward and focused on the point of Shelly's lacquered nail.

"You have four years of accumulated leave, minus the weeks absorbed back into the system under our use it or lose it policy." Shelly rapped her nail against the screen, causing the figures to ripple and jump. "I know you've signed off on the lost weeks every year, because I have to sign off on them too."

Your point?

Marc glanced at Shelly to find her studying him with quizzical consideration. "While I admire your dedication, Marcus, Beck and Meyer has a new policy regarding leave. You have to take it."

Jaw loosening, Marc managed an inarticulate, "Wha—?"

"As of Monday, you're on vacation."

"I'm what?"

Shelly pushed out a sigh. "Do I need to put it into numbers for you? Your leave starts in fifty-six hours. You are not expected back at the office until August twenty-seventh."

"That's two weeks."

"The two weeks you would normally sign off on, yes."

Scalp itching, Marc leaned back in his chair and worked his mouth a few times over such questions as: "Why do I have to take leave?" and "What the hell am I going to do for two weeks?"

He went with the latter option, omitting the soft curse. By the sardonic rise of her eyebrows, Shelly heard it anyway. "Take a vacation, Marc."

"But—"

"In fact—" Her finger was at the trackpad again, nail scraping across the dark gray plastic. "Oh, look. Henry Auttenberg is due some leave as well." She smiled at Marc as she tapped a few keys. "There. You're both on vacation. Now get out of my office and don't come back until August twenty-seventh. And I want to see a tan when you return."

Marc half-rose out of his seat. "A tan?"

"And bring me a box of saltwater taffy or something."

"Saltwater—"

"I know you're familiar with the concept of a beach vacation. It's a suggestion, okay? Now get."

Marc got, but instead of returning to his desk, he decided a trip to the men's room was necessary. He needed four walls, a locked door, and five minutes for a mini-crisis. Pulling out his phone, he turned down the wide hall to the breakroom and jerked to a stop as a familiar pair of shoes came into view. Marc looked up from his phone to find Henry standing in front of him, holding his own cellphone up, screen illuminated and displaying an email from HR: Vacation Confirmation.

"Do you know anything about this?" he asked.

Marc gave up scrolling through his own list of emails. "Shelly's making us take a vacation."

Henry's eyebrows jumped upward. "Making us? But what about the Heckworth-Packington merger?"

Marc's phone chimed. Henry's beeped half a second later. Determined to be first to read the bad news, because from this point forward, it could only be bad, Marc scrolled quickly to the top of his inbox and accessed the email. It was from Shelly. In front of him, Henry read it aloud.

"Thanks for the preliminaries on Heckworth-Packington. Jorge can handle this one. I've set alerts on all of your clients and if either of you accesses the system before August twenty-seventh, a note will be added to your file." Henry looked up. "A note?"

Marc's scalp was itching again. He scratched behind his ear and then opened the document attached to the file. It was an article from a prominent financial journal about the effects of employees not taking adequate vacation time.

He scoffed. "I am not suffering from burnout. I'm not sarcastic or rude." He scrolled down a little farther. "I'm very happy in my personal life and my relationship hasn't suffered." At Henry's continued silence, Marc looked up. "What?"

"I didn't say anything." Henry's expression spoke volumes, however.

"You haven't taken a vacation this year, either," Marc pointed out.

Henry shrugged. "I was going to take some time off around Thanksgiving. Two days, maybe. Spend them with my family— same as I did last year."

"Heh." Marc hadn't willingly spent Thanksgiving or any other holiday with his family in over a decade. "Two days isn't much of a vacation."

"Says the guy who has thrown away two weeks a year since he started with Beck and Meyer."

"I travel enough with work. Why would I want to go somewhere for vacation?"

Henry shuffled toward the side of the corridor to let someone pass. "I don't know. Maybe to see somewhere other than the inside of an office or hotel? Do the tourist thing."

Marc tucked his phone into his pocket. "Me. Do the tourist thing."

"Aren't you curious about other cultures?"

"Not—" Marc let his mouth twist and watched with vague amusement as Henry's gaze followed the movement of his lips. When Henry glanced back up to meet his eyes, Marc smiled. "Are we having an argument about this?"

Henry returned the smile. "I don't think so. I'm curious about why Shelly thinks we need a vacation, though."

"Right? It's not as if you two don't get enough personal time in all those hotel rooms you've been sharing."

Coughing, Henry leaned back, only to discover he was already pressed up against the wall. Stifling a laugh at the perplexed (and cute) nose wrinkle that followed, Marc turned to address Carmella from the travel department. "I'm sure our clients approve of the decrease in expense reimbursement."

The pallor of Henry's cheeks disappeared beneath a healthy flush and Marc found himself wondering what Henry would look like with a tan. In a bathing suit. Smiling and eating saltwater taffy. Without allowing a thinking or considering pause, Marc mussed Henry's smoothly combed hair. "Beach or mountain?"

"What?" Henry batted Marc's hand away from his head. "Where?"

"Exactly. Where do you want to go?"

Waving both hands in a semi-panicked flail, Henry said, "I don't know! I need to call my mom."

"And I need to go have a mini-crisis." Marc gave Carmella a pointed look.

"Call me if you need a flight or a rental or something." Carmella grinned. "You're going to have a great time, guys!"

Chapter
TWO

A hand grabbed his shoulder and Henry glanced up just in time to avoid headbutting a window.

"Door is this way, doofus." Marc's laconic voice brushed past his ear, tinged with amusement, and the fingers on his shoulder delivered a short squeeze.

Tucking his phone away, Henry followed Marc to the actual door, which looked just like the glass panel he'd been about to challenge. The door slid away and the scent of leather and pine wafted out around them.

"Whoa." Marc jerked to a halt just inside the entryway, mouth agape.

Henry adopted a similar posture before for about three seconds before tugging Marc's sleeve to indicate they should move away from the flow of traffic.

"We could just wander through here for a week and call it a vacation," Marc said as he stepped to the side.

"Uh huh." Henry was trying not to stare at all the shiny. Fishing and kayaking and biking and… they had running gear, and was that a display of Leatherman multi-tools?

Marc turned a grin on him. "This is like a wet dream for you, isn't it?"

Closing his mouth, Henry surveyed the approximate ten acres of outdoor supplies that made up Cabela's and nodded. "Totally worth the drive."

And the forty minutes on the Metro to get to his father's place to pick up the car they'd be borrowing for their vacation—which would not be taking place inside a camping store. Still, until this moment, Henry hadn't been particularly excited about the prospect of going away. Now... Now he was ridiculously excited and had to acknowledge, with some quick mental reshuffling, that he'd been excited yesterday when he and Marc had finally agreed upon a plan: To visit the Green Mountain National Forest for seven days of camping and hiking. He hadn't actually believed they'd do it until stepping inside the store, though. That Marc wanted to spend a week inside a national forest.

Sensibly, they'd left the second week of their enforced vacation open. Henry hoped they'd spend it back in Boston, doing stupidly mundane things like walk the waterfront, shop the farmer's markets, and maybe meet up with the rest of the team from B&M to sing karaoke on Thursday night. Couple-type things.

But first...

Marc flashed his phone in front of Henry's face, showing him a copy of the list they'd put together last night. "Okay, first stop..." He glanced at Henry and lifted his eyebrows. "Tent?"

"Let's do it." Henry grinned.

Marc returned his grin and they stood there, smiling at each other, hopefully both feeling as light and buoyant and excited as Henry was, until they both obviously realized that grinning at each other just inside the doorway of Cabela's was really weird and stopped.

"So, a tent," Henry murmured.

Marc tapped his phone and showed Henry another screen. "I downloaded the store app. It has a map."

"I love you."

Marc laughed. "I know you do, even though I sort of hate myself for putting the app for a sporting goods store on my phone. Only for you, Henry." He seemed to be thinking about kissing him, then and there, and Henry ducked out of range. He still wasn't super comfortable with PDA. He did brush his fingers over the back of Marc's hand in passing, though.

"This way?" Henry pointed toward an arch, over which stood a massive four-footed creature with impressive antlers. Was it a moose, or just a very big deer? Either way, it was dead and stuffed and really freaking big, and they had to walk underneath it to get to camping supplies.

Marc followed and they walked in open-mouthed silence as they took in the mountains of gear flowing away from every side of them. Not just fishing rods, but bags and reels and lines, tackle boxes, and rows and rows of lures. The shoe department was the size of a supermarket, and there were clothes. Kayaks in every color of the rainbow, all pointing toward the ceiling, popped up everywhere, either to remind shoppers they really needed something extra, or maybe just because they were colorful. Like huge plastic flags. They passed more stuffed and mounted dead things, an aquarium, which appeared to be babysitting several children, and finally, a small city of tents.

"Wow," Marc breathed. "That's a lot of tents."

"Yep. Let's find the two-man variety."

Quickly located through deduction—they were pretty small, but not as claustrophobic as the snake-like hiking tents—the two-man tents formed a single row of muted color. Marc dropped to his hands and knees and crawled inside the first. Henry followed, wincing at the feel of the hard store floor beneath his knees until he crossed the nylon threshold and crawled onto a sleeping bag. Dropping back to his heels, he looked around. The walls were very near. As in, if he knelt in the middle of the tent, he could probably extend both arms and touch either side.

Marc was kneeling in front of him. "Too cramped?"

Henry tilted his head as he considered. Yeah, the tent was small, but the material was thin enough that he could still see outside, albeit in a shadowy sort of way, so it didn't feel super small, putting aside the fact two grown men took up a lot of space.

"I think it'll be okay."

"We should see how small it packs if we're going to lug in any distance," Marc said.

They hoped to do a little hiking between camping spots, see more of the forest than the backside of a hundred RVs.

"Good idea." Henry shuffled on his knees, turning to check all sides of the tent. It was longer than it was wide, to accommodate sleeping mats and bags, which were already in place. Two backpacks rested by the flaps. "Pity we can't just make an offer on the whole setup," he mused.

"And deprive you of the joy of shopping an entire store of survival equipment?"

Henry laughed. "It is kind of huge, though. We really could be in here for an entire week."

"We'll come back before Christmas," Mark replied with a smile.

This time when he leaned in, Henry didn't shy away. The thin screen of blue nylon should provide them with enough privacy for a kiss. He met Marc's lips, eager, even after all these months, for the feel and taste of his lover. His partner. Marc's lips were generous and dexterous. Soft and talented. And, as always, he kissed with intent, as though he'd been waiting all day to taste Henry's mouth and intended to feast there until he was satisfied.

Henry groaned and tangled his hands in Marc's thick, dark hair. Between kisses, he mouthed soft words over Marc's lips and chin. "Can't wait to be alone in the forest with you."

Marc kissed his nose. "Me too."

Henry looked up to meet Marc's nearly black gaze. "Are you sure you want to go camping? We could still do a beach rental."

Marc dipped down to kiss him again, sweetly, then spoke against his lips. "This is our first vacation together. I want it to be memorable. Not bland, not something we'll do when we're fifty. It should be fun for both of us."

Smiling, Henry kissed him again and pulled away with a heated flush when a throat cleared by the tent flap.

He turned to find an amused store clerk, who asked, "Can I help you gentleman find anything?"

An exhausting hour and a half later, they had nearly everything on their list. They'd shop for food on the way back to the apartment and spend the evening packing, repacking, and according to Marc, "breaking in the sleeping bags."

Their path to the checkout led them directly past the hunting section and Henry paused to ogle the Leatherman display. The case held a dozen versions of the tool he already owned, though with upgraded features and scratch-free casing. His attention fell on a curvier tool, and his pulse kicked up as he examined the sleek shape of it.

Marc leaned in beside him. "See something you like?"

Henry pointed it out. "Look at this one. It comes with a pocket clip, and that extra knife has a really nice blade."

"Why don't you pick it up?"

Henry shook his head. "I don't need it. I already have a good multi-tool."

"It's not always about what you need. Sometimes you have to treat yourself."

Thinking back over what they already had in the cart, Henry shook his head again. "I think we've spent enough for today. Maybe when we come back."

Marc took a pause, considering him silently for a long moment before nodding. "Okay. We should get out of here before all those stuffed animals come to life and attack us."

Henry laughed. "If you get any more whimsical, people are going to mistake you for me."

Marc pressed a quick kiss to his temple. "All the better."

Chapter
THREE

*M*arc depressed a button and breathed deeply as the passenger side window slid down, allowing warm, forest-scented air to flow into the car. The tang of bark and mulched leaves stirred memories of summer camp and the few times he'd signed up for overnight hikes, mostly because he'd always liked the idea of sleeping out under the stars. The reality of it rarely lived up to the fantasy, but that was life, wasn't it?

He glanced over at Henry, who was tapping the screen of the phone mounted on the dash with the GPS function active. It was Marc's phone, because Henry's cheap piece of trash didn't even have a touchscreen.

"Debbie giving you trouble?" Marc asked.

Henry flashed him a grin. Ever since their night on the road somewhere between Syracuse and Albany, they'd called every GPS Debbie. "Signal keeps dropping. Route Nine will take us most of the way, but I don't want to miss the turnoff to the campsite."

"I'm sure there'll be a sign."

Henry relaxed back from the dash and put both hands on the wheel. "So we never finished talking about the last time you went camping."

Marc felt his brow furrow. "I went camping with a group from summer camp. That was the story."

Henry clicked his tongue. "But how was it? Where did you go? What was the weather like?"

"It was like fifteen years ago. I don't remember all of that... Actually, I do remember it was really humid and that my sleeping bag stuck to me all night. And I got bitten to death by mosquitos."

"Obviously not to death." Henry gave him a sideways grin.

"It was close. And it was overcast, so I couldn't see the stars."

Henry was smiling.

"What?"

"I like the idea of you looking up and trying to see the stars."

"Wasn't much else to do."

"No campfire stories?"

Marc fiddled with the armrest on his side of the car, clicking the window lock on and off. "No, because the older boys snuck off to the girls' camp, leaving us younger ones to fend for ourselves. As I remember, that was the big draw of the overnight camp. It was near where the girls camped, or if they weren't camping, only a couple of miles from their summer camp."

"You went to an all-boys summer camp?"

"Ah, yeah. It was owned by the school. That way, they could care for castoffs year 'round."

Henry made a sympathetic noise. "So why weren't you over at the girls' camp, then?"

Marc shrugged. "I wasn't that interested in girls until I figured out I was supposed to be." He shot Henry a rueful smile. "Looking back, I sometimes can't understand why I didn't work things out sooner."

Henry met his gaze with a solemn expression. "You had a lot going on."

A sign appeared just up ahead and after a quick scan, Marc pointed it out. "Woodford State Park. That's us, right?"

"Yep!"

Henry made the turn, and in short order, they were bumping through densely packed trees, following signs to the tent area. Check-in consisted of finding their pre-booked site number and parking next to it. Then it was time to unpack and get set up. This late in the season, the campground was crowded, with nearly every site boasting a setup of tents, pavilions, fire circles, piles of musty sneakers, and knots of suspicious looking children. But the grass was green and the forest hemmed the campground on three sides, making the space… somewhat attractive. Then there was the lake, sparkling in the early afternoon sunlight and dotted with colorful watercraft. All in all, it wasn't terrible, even if Marc would have preferred a little more privacy.

He turned back to the open trunk of the hatchback they'd borrowed from Henry's parents, and reached for one of the backpacks.

Henry leaned in close and murmured, "We'll have more privacy on the trail to Grout Pond." The hike would have them camping in the forest overnight, and seeing more of the park.

Marc bumped his shoulder against Henry's. "And miss the opportunity to scandalize all the wholesome families camped around us?"

Henry gave him a half-smile before heaving his backpack out of the back of the car and dumping it on the ground. They both reached for the tent at the same time. Marc grabbed a hold of the straps at the top of the tent bag and hauled it upward, out of Henry's grasp.

"I can carry it over," Henry said.

"I've got it, it's fine." Marc lifted the strap of his backpack over one shoulder. "Why don't you grab the food box and stove?"

Marc rounded the car and surveyed their small site. Springy grass with a smooth patch of packed earth where everyone else had likely set up their tent. It wasn't a bad spot. A large log had been dragged close to the circle of rocks making up their fire pit. But if he set up the tent facing the fire, they'd also be facing the rest of the campground. Marc dropped the tent bag, eased the backpack off his shoulder, and turned around, taking in all the views. Would it be weird to have their tent facing the forest behind them? They wouldn't be able to sit in the doorway and look at the fire if he did that, though.

He crouched to unzip the bag and pulled out the instruction leaflet tucked in on top of the tent. While he was unfolding the instructions, Henry started pulling out the tent.

"What are you doing?" Marc asked.

"Getting the tent out."

Marc waved the leaflet. "You have to do it in order."

"I'm just getting everything out of the bag."

"Okay, well if you can line it all up—"

"It's not that complicated, Marc. We don't need the instructions." Henry leaned forward, hand outstretched as if he planned to swipe the instructions.

Marc pulled the leaflet closer to his chest. "Can we just read them over? I'd have thought this'd be your thing, reading the instructions."

"For something complicated, yeah. This is just a tent. It basically pops up on its own."

"We should have practiced yesterday."

"Where, in our living room?"

"Yeah!"

Frowning, Henry lifted his chin slightly. Marc glanced over his shoulder at the site next door where a husband, wife, and three kids were all sitting in a group, facing them. Watching them argue over a tent.

Marc turned back around and handed Henry the instructions. "Let's just see how we go, okay?"

Rather than take the leaflet, Henry clasped the back of his hand. "You all right?"

"Yeah. Just..." Not sure how to express how he felt, Marc

shrugged. "I'm fine. Hot. I'm going to grab a drink. You want something?"

"Sure."

By the time he'd selected two sodas from their small cooler, Henry had the tent laid out with the door facing the fire pit. He looked up with a somewhat rueful smile. "I thought it'd be nice to sit in the doorway and watch the fire."

Marc smiled.

They got the tent set up without mishap and all their stuff stowed inside. It was on the second trip through the flap that Marc realized the doorway wasn't exactly wide enough for them to sit side by side to watch any fire. Kneeling just inside the doorway, he pointed this out to Henry, who glanced up from whatever he was fussing with and measured the gap with his eyes.

He shrugged. "We'll just have to lie on our sleeping bags and look out, then."

"Like this?" Marc tackled Henry to the ground—their wrestling cushioned by mats, sleeping bags, the odd article of clothing, and at least three shoes. How had they managed to make such a mess already? He covered Henry's body with his and leaned in to kiss him, barely able, as always, to keep the urge to thrust down and meld them together. It'd been eight months and still he wanted Henry every day. To kiss him, hold him, make love, fuck, cuddle, taste, touch, and just be with. Sometimes his obsession felt just beyond healthy. Other times, it was as though he'd been waiting all of his life for this: to love and be loved. To be with the other half of his whole.

Realizing he'd been staring at Henry rather than kissing him, Marc dipped his head. Henry pecked at his lips, then put a little distance between them by touching Marc's cheek. "I love it when you look at me like that. Scares me, but I wouldn't swap it for anything."

Warmth bloomed inside Marc's chest. "I love it when you say things like that."

"Not too mushy?"

"So long as we confine it to the tent." Grinning, Marc kissed Henry gently again.

"You know, I can't see the fire from down here."

"We haven't lit it yet."

"Oh, well, in that case…" Henry lifted his chin and offered up his mouth.

Marc accepted the invitation.

Chapter
FOUR

*A*fter a long and sweaty kiss inside the sweaty tent, Henry suggested they go swimming to cool off. He figured they could both use it, and couldn't think of another way for them to keep their clothes on until it was dark. Of course, Marc in a swimsuit wasn't exactly dressed and all Henry wanted to do while watching Marc strip, then search his backpack for his shorts, was grope. And maybe stroke his thickening shaft. And lick things: Marc's skin, his back, his thighs. Pretty much everything.

A beach rental would have meant they could do all of that. All the time. Why had they chosen to go camping? What had they been thinking?

"Why are you still dressed?"

Marc had apparently utilized the time Henry had spent daydreaming to get into his shorts. They were dark blue and unadorned.

"That's what you're swimming in?"

"Well, I left my union suit at home."

"Your what?"

"Yes, this is what I'm swimming in." Marc plucked at the navy material. "What's wrong with my shorts?"

"Nothing. They're just… so plain. I thought you'd have orange shorts with penguins or something."

Marc stared at him blankly.

Shrugging, Henry pulled out his own shorts, which were navy blue with white piping.

Marc chuckled. "Where are the green shorts with turtles on them?"

"Humph." Henry shucked his clothes, skin heating under Marc's interested gaze, and pulled on his shorts. "Okay, let's go."

They grabbed towels and sunscreen and hats and drinks and then looked at each other and laughed. "How are we going to hike from one campground to the other will all this gear?" Henry asked.

"We'll figure it out tomorrow, or the next day."

"That's not very forward thinking of you."

Marc grinned. "My forward momentum is on vacation, thank you very much." He started off along the path toward the lake.

Henry followed.

The lake was beautiful. Late summer drifted across the water in a palpable haze of heat, humidity, and the scent of fresh water and the surrounding forest. Kayaks floated on the surface, and children called out to each other. Parents lazed on the green grass of the beach and splashed in the shallows with toddlers. Music drifted over it all, from at least four different radios, and the blend of notes became one long song—not exactly of summer, but this day, this hour.

Marc laid out his towel in a precise rectangle and put his sandals at one end, the cooler at the other. Henry did the same and smiled at their setup. "It's like we've been doing this for years."

Marc rolled his eyes. "You probably have. This is what you did every summer with your family, right?"

"Sometimes? We never came here, though. We generally stayed closer to Boston and most summers we visited with family. Either up in Maine or Rhode Island."

"Auttenbergs all over the east coast?"

"My mom's family too. I have, like, thirty-five cousins."

Marc shuddered, but the gesture was obviously faked.

"You'll meet most of them at Christmas this year," Henry said with a grin. Marc's second shudder didn't look manufactured. Henry squeezed his arm. "You'll do great. People love you. My family loves you."

"Uh huh. Let's swim."

Marc demonstrated the fact his forward momentum was decidedly not on vacation by striding into the water and then diving under the surface when he got just over knee-deep. Henry followed a little more slowly, picking his way over the muddy bottom and trying not to wince as it squished up between his toes. The water was cold and he wondered if his heart would stop if he just dove in. He wondered why Marc's heart hadn't stopped.

Marc surfaced with a shake of his head, water spraying everywhere, and splashed to Henry's side. "Water feels great!"

"It's colder than I expected." Henry wrapped his arms around his torso.

Marc caught him up in a cold, wet hug.

Henry swallowed a toddleresque squeak.

Laughing, Marc snuggled closer. "Are you shivering?"

"In fear. My balls are retreating, maybe never to be found again. What did you do with yours?"

Talking about their balls was the exact wrong thing to do. Marc took it as an invitation to press his groin to Henry's and it wasn't sexy. Not at all. Wet fabric adhered to his thighs, Marc's skin a cold press behind. Growling softly, Henry ducked out of Marc's embrace and pushed forward at the same time, toppling Marc back into the water. Marc grabbed him on the way down, pulling him along for the ride, and before Henry could take a breath, the cold lake engulfed him.

He let go of the squeak, which ended in a stream of bubbles as he rolled around under the water with Marc, pushing and tugging until he needed air. Surfacing, Henry coughed, spluttered, and drew in a deep breath. And discovered he hadn't actually died, and that the water wasn't that bad once you were completely wet.

Marc shot to the surface beside him, grinning widely. "Still cold?"

"Ass." Henry flicked water at him and Marc dove forward again.

After another few rounds of barrel rolls, mock drownings, and splash fights, Henry floated on his back, some distance from the shore. Marc was somewhere beside him, his trailing fingers touching Henry's now and again as they paddled gently backward, both staring up at the sky. Overhead, cottony clouds crept across a vast expanse of blue. An occasional bird drifted from left to right, but never back the other way, making counting them easy. Unless they were making a wide circle somewhere out of view. He'd just counted the twelfth pass when Marc's fingers closed around his and gave a soft tug.

Tipping his head to the side, Henry met Marc's deep, dark gaze. He'd spent minutes at a time trying to find where the pupil met the iris and could only usually see the line in bright daylight. Not so today, with that same daylight glaring off the surface of the lake. Marc's eyes were impenetrable. His gaze, not so. He wore a look of contentment and happiness.

Henry worried about Marc's happiness sometimes. He knew his boyfriend was as driven as he was, but feared that without the support of his family, Marc might reach his goals and find that having no one to celebrate with would sour his victory. The old Marc, the one who'd refrained from appending "doofus" to the end of his statements of the obvious, would have pretended he didn't care. This new Marc, the man Henry loved, might still try to pretend—but he wouldn't have to.

Smiling, Henry squeezed the fingers wrapped around his own.

Marc shifted in the water so that his body sank downward, leaving his head bobbing above the surface. He shook water from his face. Henry lifted his ear away from the quiet burble of the lake and did the same before paddling forward so that he could touch his lips to Marc's in a gentle kiss. Marc leaned in to deepen the kiss and Henry tensed. They were in full view of the beach and passing kayaks.

"Relax. No one's looking at us." Marc's fingers tangled with his again, deep beneath the water.

"But everyone can see us."

"So what? Everyone could see that dude and his girlfriend basically having sex on the beach and no one said anything."

"But—"

Marc silenced him with a kiss and Henry forced himself to soften, to let go, even if that act of will came with a tightening of his fingers around Marc's. He closed his eyes, blotting out the world, and concentrated on the man in front of him. His lover, his friend, his partner. And kissed him.

When Marc pulled away, Henry opened his eyes to find Marc smiling at him.

"This was a good idea," Marc said.

Henry managed a half-submerged shrug. "We could have kissed in the water at the beach."

"No, I mean taking a vacation. Shelly was right."

"Shelly was just covering her ass by making us comply with work safety bullshit, or whatever new guideline they put in place to make us take adequate vacation time. She's probably swearing twice for every minute we're away and not doing whatever she needs us to do."

Marc chuckled. "She's got other kids to grumble at."

"Okay, new rule."

Marc's legs collided with his under the water. "We're doing vacation rules now?"

"I refrained from listing out all the things we couldn't do in case of disaster on the drive up."

"You did show remarkable constraint. I was almost disappointed."

Laughing, Henry pressed a wet kiss to Marc's cheek. "I'm making an effort. But this rule has nothing to do with our survival."

"Oh?" Marc trailed his fingers across Henry's ribs, causing him to shiver in the water.

Henry grabbed his hand and grunted softly as Marc drew their clasped fingers lower, to the front of Henry's shorts. "Wait...Ung."

Marc had found his way through the fold at the front and was busily tugging on Henry's cock. "You were talking about rules." Marc gave him another tug.

"Um. No work talk. That's what I wanted to say. I don't want to talk about Shelly while your hand is on my dick."

"Good rule."

"And I want to..." He'd been going to say he wanted to do this in the tent, away from prying eyes, but to heck with it, they were on vacation and no one was watching them, and Marc's cock was within reach, a firm ridge just behind the placket of his own shorts.

Henry reached within the fold and began returning stroke for stroke until he found the coordination of treading water and keeping up too difficult.

"Just hold on," Marc murmured over his ear. "To my cock, yeah. Don't let go. You can do me after I'm done with you."

And so Henry hung in place, one hand on Marc's sun-warm shoulder, the other wrapped around Marc's hard shaft. He dropped his head back, pointing his face toward the sky, and closed his eyes. Let his body go for a ride. His hips rocked forward and back in time with Marc's strokes, and his balls tightened quickly. The threat of exposure—the almost thrill of it—worked with his desire. The slickness of the water and the cool swish around his thighs. Marc's hands on him. His need. Always his need. He came with a jerk and short cry—muffled as he dropped his head forward, his lips finding

Marc's shoulder. Sucking hard, he shuddered through his climax until Marc stopped stroking, then drifted serenely in Marc's arms until a small nip and whisper at his ear told him it was his turn to do the stroking.

Chapter
FIVE

*M*arc had been drifting between sleep and wakefulness for what felt like an eternity when Henry rolled toward him, dropping his arm around Marc's ribs, and snuggled in close. A muffled whisper landed somewhere near Marc's ear. "Hmm."

"Hmm?" Marc returned, adding a questioning note.

"You're awake?"

"Sorta." But not ready to leave the sweaty heap of sleeping bag all scrunched up underneath him. Or Henry's embrace. Henry could be so weird about affection, particularly in public. But he always indulged Marc's need for after sex cuddling, and seemed to like snuggling up in the morning. Which should have been strange. Marc only found it endearing.

Extracting his arm from a tangle of cloth, he slid it beneath Henry's shoulders and pulled him close. "It's really too hot to snuggle."

"I know," Henry said. "Was hot all night. Did you get any sleep?"

"In between worrying about bears and trying to figure out if the frogs were screaming or singing or simply programmed to be annoying, yes. A minute or two."

Henry shook lightly against his side.

"Are you laughing at me?"

"Absolutely not." Henry snuggled in an impossible degree closer. "I'd forgotten how noisy the outdoors could be at night."

"Tell me about it. Give me traffic and sirens, any day."

"Right? The soothing sound of the city."

"And did you hear that mournful bleating at something o'clock?"

"I think that was a deer."

"I had no idea deer even made sounds."

Henry leaned back enough to look up and Marc angled his head so he could look down and meet his gaze. His smile.

"You want to just hang out today," Henry asked. "Do nothing and hike up to Grout Pond tomorrow?"

"No, let's do it today. The walk should wear us out enough not to care about the frogs tonight. And by tomorrow night, we should be used to it."

"Very optimistic of you."

Marc initiated a roll so that Henry ended up beneath him. They wore nothing but boxers and the feel of Henry's skin sticking to his shouldn't have been as sexy as it was. They were sweaty and smelled like lake water, bug spray, and wood smoke. On Henry, it was intoxicating.

"This was such a good idea."

Henry grinned. "You keep saying that."

"Worried I'm going to jinx it?"

Henry's grin narrowed. "You had to go and put that idea in my head, didn't you?"

Marc reached down to find Henry's morning wood. "Let's do something about that then, hmm?"

Heat aside, the hike through the woods was… fun. Yes, fun. Marc hadn't considered hiking a viable form of recreation before now, but decided he liked it. He could even sort of see why Henry liked to run so much. They were going somewhere, even if that somewhere would, eventually, be back where they'd begun.

It's the journey, not the destination.

The humidity wasn't as heavy as the day before, but the weight of the pack on his back made up for it, causing his shirt to cling to him in damp wrinkles. He was pretty sure his shoulders would ache by the end of the day. Maybe Henry would rub them for him.

Reaching up, Marc dropped a hand on Henry's shoulder, then moved his hand to cup the nape of Henry's sweaty neck, kneading with his fingers.

"Mmm. How did you know my neck was sore?"

"I didn't. But mine is. Shoulders too. I wonder how we're doing for time." Marc tugged his phone from his shorts pocket and checked the display. It was just after eleven. A quick glance at the top corner of the screen showed they had no signal—but rather than feel a squeeze of panic, Marc's chest expanded slightly beneath the constraint of his backpack straps. They were out in the woods, away from email and to-do lists. They were on vacation.

"Can we check the GPS?" Henry asked.

Marc opened the navigation app. "When are you going to get yourself a decent phone?"

Henry was the keeper of the paper map and he was smoothing out the laminated folds to the section they should be hiking. Marc angled the phone screen toward him and watched as Henry compared the glowing blue dot indicating their location with the map. Being the survey variety, the paper map showed a lot more detail—elevation, terrain, and all known trails. By comparison, the phone showed only featureless green bisected by blue creeks.

Henry tapped the map and said, "We're about here."

Marc measured the distance they still had to go. "I thought we'd have come further."

"Yeah. It's hard to judge distance when you're hiking. Always feels longer because we're not walking in a straight line, or on a smooth path."

"You're telling me."

The ground hadn't exactly been rocky, but not like any kind of highway, either. And there were a lot of trees in this forest. And the trail wound around all of them. Not terribly efficient.

"Want to take a break?" Henry asked.

"No, let's keep going. Where are we camping tonight?"

Henry indicated the bottom of the large reservoir they'd be hiking around the next day, finally bringing them to the camping area where they planned to spend another couple of days before catching the park shuttle back to their car—a mere fifteen miles away. They'd save the round trip hike for when they'd had more practice hauling the essentials on their backs... and just walking. Walking, and walking.

Marc shifted his feet inside his dusty sneakers, glad Henry had talked him out of buying hiking boots. They hadn't needed anything special for this trail and comfort was more important than looking the part.

Of course, Henry wore the appropriate footwear. Henry owned three specific pairs of hiking shoes. The low-rise, walking pair on his feet now, and two pairs of boots for different weather and terrain. Henry also owned several pairs of running shoes. But only two pairs of dress shoes. Marc had him beat, there. He owned seven, and way more casual boots. Between them, they had managed to fill the narrow shelves circling the bottom of the closet.

"What are you smiling about?" Henry asked.

Marc glanced over. "Shoes."

Henry's eyebrows performed a complicated wrinkle as he looked down at their feet. "These shoes?"

Indicating they could walk and talk at the same time, Marc started along the path winding between the trees. "No, all our shoes, and how we'd probably have to sacrifice a pair if we bought anything new. Those shoe racks you have are full."

"Then we'd buy a new rack."

"And put it where?"

"Hmm." Henry's lips twisted adorably and Marc leaned over to kiss him.

Henry put a hand to the back of Marc's head and held him in place as they kissed properly, mouths fused together, tongues fully involved. When Henry groaned, Marc felt the sound reverberate through his middle. He reached for Henry's fly.

"Not here." Henry nudged his hand away.

Impatience flaring up suddenly—probably because he was kind of hot (in both senses of the word) and his feet were sweaty—Marc set his features to obstinate. "Why not here? There's no one around for miles, Henry. No one is going to see us."

Henry rocked back a little, as if in reaction to Marc's sudden anger. "It's not that. I swear it isn't, and I've been trying. I have. I kissed you in the lake. I let you jerk me—"

"You let me?" An invisible band tightened around Marc's chest.

"No, that's not what I meant!"

"Then what do you mean?" Marc blew out a breath and told himself to calm down. Now so wasn't the time for an argument that really didn't need to happen. It had to be his feet. Or maybe he needed a snack.

Turning away from Henry, he swung his pack off his shoulders and rooted around in a side pocket for the trail mix they'd made. He hadn't been into the idea of trail mix. It felt so very Vermont. But, they were in Vermont, so… Ugh, why was this stuff so dry? And why was he hiking and camping and arguing with Henry?

Henry shuffled in front of him, brow all wrinkled, nose too. His eyes more green than gray with the forest around them, his pale skin flushed with color and contrition. He was holding out the map, folded to a particular square, and pointing at a spot maybe an hour from where they were. His throat moved as he swallowed. "Can I explain, please?"

After taking a swig of water to wash down his mouthful of grit, Marc nodded.

Henry tapped his map again. "There's supposed to be a waterfall about here, along this creek. I read about it on a trail site when I was researching the park. There's a pool at the bottom, and rocks all around, and apparently you can climb behind the waterfall and there's a cave back there." He looked up, cheeks flushing harder. "I was saving it as a surprise. I figured we'd be able to look for it around lunchtime and we could spend a couple of hours there. Not because it's private or hidden, but because I thought it would be… nice. Um." He scratched the side of his head, map fluttering as he did so. "Romantic? So when I asked you to stop, it wasn't because I thought we'd get caught making out on the trail. I'd be embarrassed if that happened, but not because I'm with you, or because we're gay. Just because I'm…"

"Shy," Marc provided.

"I really am trying not to be so reserved when we're out together."

He was, damn it. Now that he'd had a moment to cool down, Marc knew that. Henry had become a regular at Thursday night karaoke, and he sang. He kissed Marc in front of their work colleagues and held his hand as they wandered the streets of Boston together. Surprisingly, he loved to dance and liked to grind close on the rare occasion they visited a club. And he was pretty free with his affection when they were at Henry's parents' place in Dorchester. But not outside the house, because, well, Dorchester.

"Henry…" Marc didn't know what to say besides sorry.

Henry stepped in close and lifted his chin. "Kiss me."

Marc felt a crooked grin pull at his mouth. "What, here? Where all the squirrels can see us?"

"Right here."

Henry puckered up and it was pretty damn cute so Marc kissed him.

Chapter
SIX

The waterfall was a fair way off the trail, nearly forty minutes. Henry tried to track their progress through the endless expanse of green on Marc's phone, but figured if they did get lost, he wouldn't really be able to tell one patch of green from the other without measuring the distance between the blue dot of them and the nearest edge. The creek they were heading toward was marked, though. They could follow that if the need arose. Which it wouldn't, because they had a map and they weren't in the Alaskan Wilderness. This was Vermont.

Catching the faint sound of rushing water, Henry refolded the map, and handed Marc his phone. "We're close!"

Marc smiled and made a let's-keep-moving gesture.

A few minutes later, they were scrambling down the side of a hill. The dense forest hid most of the creek from view, but Henry caught the occasional sparkle through the foliage, and the sound of the waterfall kept growing louder. Henry grabbed for the tree in front of him, swung around the trunk, and skidded across loose gravel until he could grab the next tree. The downward slide was exhilarating in a way—especially if he didn't think about how they were going to go about climbing back up.

He finally slid to a stop where the ground evened out to a rocky shelf and waited for Marc to catch up. The shelf extended a few feet in front of him, forming a cliff, and now that they were out of the trees, he could see the creek shimmering below, the waterfall off to the left, about two hundred yards distant. The falls dropped a long way, maybe fifty feet or more, the rush of water broken up twice by outthrust ledges of rock. According to the directions he'd copied down, the private alcove was behind the middle section, and they could either climb up or down to it.

Marc stopped beside him and looked toward the waterfall. "Wow."

"Right? All this rain we've been having is good for something."

Grinning, Marc nodded. "So where's this cave?"

Henry pointed. "The second ledge. Do we want to try to climb down from the top or up from the bottom?"

Marc hummed softly in thought as he surveyed the waterfall, then turned to peer over the cliff and down at the creek. "I think I'd be more comfortable getting down to the creek from here and then climbing up to the ledge."

"Sounds good."

About halfway along the cliff, Marc pointed out a way down: another scramble, with both of them holding on to rocks and exposed roots as they slid from stop to stop. When Henry finally made it to the bottom, he was hot and tired. And he had dirt in his mouth, crunching between his teeth.

He dropped his pack on a large, flat rock at the edge of the pool. "Want to take a swim first?"

"Yes, please." Marc dropped his pack and then himself, sprawling on his back with his arms and legs spread wide. "In fact, I think we should camp here tonight."

Henry scanned the clear blue sky above them and the ground around the creek. They could maybe pitch a tent down the way a little, away from the water's edge. Or they could just roll out sleeping bags and a mosquito net. The forecast was clear for most of the week. "I don't see why we couldn't," he said. "Means a longer hike tomorrow, though. We've only come about five miles."

"Seriously? Feels more like fifty."

"We'll eat, swim, have sex, get in a nap, and then see how we feel."

Marc rolled his head sideways and grinned. "Sounds good."

Swimming and eating happened at the same time. After changing into his shorts, Henry laid out the sandwiches they'd prepared that morning, took a bite of one to quell the empty twisting of his gut, and slid into the pool while chewing. Cold water lapped up around his calves, soft and sweet, then covered his hips as he sank down to sit on a submerged rock.

"I have died and gone to Heaven." Sighing, he leaned his head back against the shelf behind him and closed his eyes.

Marc splashed into the water beside him. "Open your mouth."

Henry obeyed and bread touched his lips. He took another bite of sandwich and chewed and drifted, listening to the crash of the waterfall and Marc's lips smacking beside him.

"This is perfect." Marc spoke in hushed, reverent tones.

Cracking his eyes open, Henry glanced sideways. "Yep."

"It's a great surprise."

Warmth bubbled up behind Henry's breastbone. He'd forgotten that part. Had all but forgotten their argument back on the trail, even though it had stung at the time, and gazing into Marc's dark brown eyes, he wondered if they'd ever share a more perfect moment than this.

Henry had marked the waterfall as a spot where he might be able to broach the subject of feelings. Marc never seemed to have trouble telling Henry exactly what he was feeling and when, but Henry always needed a... moment. A space cut out of time where he could be sure what he said wouldn't... what?

He'd told Marc he loved him, countless times. Today, he wanted to tell him something more. He wanted any sex they had today to be making love. Afterward, he wanted some of the cuddling he was rapidly getting used to. Marc was a demanding cuddler and Henry found he more than liked being folded into Marc's deeply affectionate embraces.

Apparently done with the long, lingering look they'd been giving each other, Marc flashed a grin and disappeared. Henry blinked himself back to reality, and when Marc returned a moment later with one of their water bottles, Henry watched him drink and swallow. Marc glanced sideways, offered a small smirk, and drank again, apparently fully aware Henry was watching him and admiring him.

Where did he get such self-confidence?

After finishing lunch, it was time to climb the waterfall. Chewing his lip, Henry studied the rocks and slabs of stone arrayed around the pool and leading up to the first ledge. "Do you think we'll need shoes?"

"Let's try without. We can always come back down and get them if we need them."

"Good call. Bring your phone, so we can take some pictures."

Though it was next to useless, Henry pocketed his phone out of habit, picked up his laminated map, and then reached into one of the inner pockets of his backpack for one of the small packets of lube he'd bought for such occasions as wild-and-spontaneous-outdoor-sex.

Or making love.

Lips touched the back of his neck. "Such a boy scout."

Smiling, Henry tucked the packet into his shorts. He hadn't packed any condoms. They'd dispensed with those two months ago.

The climb was fun. The rocks were warm beneath the soles of Henry's feet, and reassuringly sturdy as he picked a route from the edge of the pool to the first ledge. Marc happily followed his lead, apparently more content to enjoy the experience than direct it. After clambering over the last shelf, Henry waited for Marc to scramble up beside him, then stepped back to take in the view. Not wildly impressive, yet. More pretty than anything else. The pool was close enough to be enticing—if he were the type to take an ill-advised jump from the side of a waterfall, and the creek spun away in an every narrowing ribbon of sparkly light.

The sounds of the forest had disappeared beneath the shush of water behind them, and the slight breeze from the falls picked out goosebumps on his skin.

"Onward and upward?" Marc asked.

"As ever."

Henry let Marc take the lead for the next stage, which proved a little more strenuous. Where the ascent to the first ledge had been more of a clamber over large boulders, now they had to climb from ledge to ledge, looking for hand and footholds. And the spray from the waterfall made many of those slippery.

After failing to hold yet another short wedge of stone, Henry called up to Marc, "Should we go back for our shoes? Or maybe some rope?" Gloves wouldn't be a bad idea, either. But neither of them had packed gloves.

"We'll be fine," Marc called back. "I'm nearly at the top. Once I get over, I'll hand you up."

Rather than take offense at the idea he might need help, Henry simply nodded. He'd rather accept a hand up than fall. Tumbling down even a short cliff into a rocky pool wasn't his idea of a romantic interlude.

Marc got to the top and reached down for him. Henry managed to find a perch for his toes that didn't feel too slippery and grabbed Marc's hand. Together, they pushed and pulled until he was over the ledge. Henry pushed to his feet and stood beside Marc.

"Wow." The view was better. Still not like looking from the top of Niagara, but pretty good for a hidden waterfall in the middle of a forest. The creek seemed a long way below them now, and Henry's gut twisted a little at that. He hadn't realized how far they'd climbed. The pool looked smaller. The sound of the waterfall was almost deafening and the splash of water as it crashed into the ledge constant. It was like standing on the edge of a shower. A very big, wet, loud shower.

Marc grabbed Henry's shoulder, his fingers and palm warm against the spray. "Is that the cave? Back there?"

He leaned back a little, so Henry could look past him at a slice of darkness behind the water.

"Let's check it out!"

Chapter
SEVEN

The cave wasn't very big—more a large dent in the rock than anything else. A dent with a slight curve and bend, so that after they passed beneath the waterfall and turned inward, the constant spray no longer reached them. It seemed quieter back here, too. And not too dark with daylight filtering through the falling water.

Marc instantly liked the enclosed feel of the space behind the waterfall. It was cozy and intimate and perfect for their plans, even if he'd be happy having sex beside the pool below. Being up here, behind the water, felt… Not secret. Not even private. But somehow both of those things in a way that felt special. As if they were the only two people in the world.

Beside him, Henry slipped, and Marc reached out to steady him. Water obviously got back here on occasion. The rocks were smooth and patches of moss hung clung to every convenient crevice.

The back of the cave loomed out of the shadows and Marc stopped. He turned and Henry moved right up beside him before turning a short circle. "Cozy, isn't it?"

Marc smiled. "Yeah."

"And not as romantic as I imagined it might be."

Marc smothered a laugh.

"What? What's so funny?"

"You, assessing the romantic possibilities of a cave. It's fine, by the way. Very intimate."

"But it's so…" Henry wrapped his arms around his ribs and looked around again.

Marc leaned in close. "Dark? Dank? Cave-like?"

Henry turned back, conveniently bringing his lips into line with Marc's. Seizing the moment, Marc kissed him and smiled inwardly ad Henry immediately softened.

He loved the way a kiss could gentle Henry in much the same way a soft word could soothe a skittish colt. Henry's awkwardness always seemed to melt away when they kissed—except in certain situations, which so did not apply right now, with gallons of water tumbling in a screen outside the cave, and copious darkness pressing in from every side.

Marc knew it wasn't the implicit privacy of the cave that had appealed to Henry, though. It had been the idea of it. His boyfriend was a dreamer. While Henry had initially been resistant to the idea of them having a relationship outside of their work partnership, once convinced, he'd become a man who enjoyed making gestures. He gave into most of Marc's whims and seemed to like planning romantic encounters of his own. He cooked for Marc. Bought him little gifts. Left notes for him when Marc had to travel alone. Called. Texted. Even when they were in the same city. Henry had blossomed—if one could apply such an analogy to someone who spent his days crunching numbers. He'd become softer, more open. Sweeter, if that was possible. And, thankfully, more essentially Henry.

And Marc loved him more every day.

With his lips still attached devotedly to Henry's, Marc trailed his hands from Henry's shoulders to his hips, then moved them backward, over the wet material clinging to Henry's ass. There, he paused, letting his palms flatten, his fingers stretch out.

"God, your ass."

Because all the miles he ran, Henry was beautifully toned and Marc always liked to appreciate the firm shape of his glutes before groping.

With a sweet murmur, Henry kissed him again, and Marc continued with his posterior worship, gripping Henry's ass and drawing him closer, bumping their hips together. Marc was already hard. The poke of Henry's corresponding hardness against his groin stirred a low groan—and the need to grind.

"You feel so good," he breathed.

Henry nipped Marc's lower lip. "So do you."

How had Marc not known this was what he wanted?

Probably because he'd spent close to ten years with partners who didn't have a dick. He couldn't have known how it felt to have that same hot hardness pressing to this thigh, his stomach, his own cock, between his legs, nudging his balls... inside him, until it had happened. Until Henry had taken him there.

Henry had his hands locked behind Marc's shoulders and it was an easy thing to pick him up and carry him toward the mossy shelf at the back of the shallow cave and sit him there. Marc did that, leaned in as he settled Henry, then pulled back, loosening Henry's grip on the back of his neck.

Marc was so turned on, his voice came out in a rough bark. "Shorts off." He kicked his own down his legs.

"Aye, aye, Cap'n."

Grinning, Henry stripped his shorts off and tossed them onto the pile of cloth at Marc's feet. Marc nudged his toe beneath a fold and kicked it all out of their way. Slipping on their shorts right now was not a part of the plan.

Henry held up the lube packet. "We want to use this?"

Marc settled himself on the shelf beside Henry. It wasn't wide enough for them to lie down. "What do you feel like doing?" He put his hand on Henry's thigh, fingers curling close to the erect shaft of Henry's cock. Shifting his hand slightly, he brushed the back of his knuckles to the warm skin and grinned as Henry's breath caught. With his other hand, Marc fisted his own erection and gave it a lazy stroke.

Clearly having difficulty tearing his gaze away from Marc's cock, Henry looked up with a smile. "I don't really care. We can just jerk off together if you want. Save the lube for tonight."

"Why don't we do that?" Figuring out angles in a cave wouldn't be half as romantic as just getting down to the business of getting off. "But I want to blow you."

Henry's smile widened. "Not going to say no." He opened his thighs.

Marc got to his knees on the smooth stone floor and leaned in, going straight for the gold. He grasped Henry's cock and put his lips to the half-hooded tip, dropping a quick kiss there before wrapping his tongue around the head in a brief caress.

Henry moaned.

He grasped Henry's cock mid-shaft and stroked downward far enough to fully expose the head, which he quickly sucked into his mouth. Henry responded with higher pitched sound and a soft hiss. Marc took him deeper. The timbre of Henry's moan deepened correspondingly.

Marc loved the taste of Henry's arousal—now appropriately spiced by the tannins of the creek—and the warmth and weight of firm flesh against his tongue. Even the full feeling of his mouth, the stretch of his lips. He loved the tight grip Henry had on his own thighs, as if he was trying to keep them apart, but was also just hanging on. As Marc started to take him a little deeper, one of Henry's hands came up to hold the back of his head, fingers sifting through his hair. As always, Marc rewarded the sweet and gentle touch with renewed effort, working to open his throat, to give Henry a blowjob that would have him seeing stars.

He cupped Henry's balls and rolled them. Stroked the smooth skin of his taint. Sucked up and down. Closed his lips tighter at the top, loosened at the bottom. Established a hard and fast rhythm that encouraged Henry to thrust.

With a sudden sharp cry, Henry came, his hips jerking forward on the shelf, his fingers clutching at Marc's head. His thighs trembled with the force of his orgasm, the shudders moving through Marc, almost making him let loose his own climax. But he'd hold on for the feel of Henry's lips and tongue. The sight of Henry where Marc was now, between bent knees, head bobbing up and down as he milked his boyfriend's orgasm, sucking him dry.

Licking his lips, Marc sat back and looked up. Henry's eyes were open and he wore a dopey grin. Henry patted the stone shelf beside him and Marc sat there before leaning into Henry's side to accept the kiss he was offering. Henry explored Marc's mouth with his tongue before murmuring, "Love the taste of myself in your mouth."

It wasn't really dirty talk, but it was something no other lover had ever said to him—regularly or otherwise. More than that, it was Henry saying these things. Henry who always looked neat and pressed and buttoned and so secretly sexy.

Marc kissed him again before pulling back to whisper against his lips. "Want to taste myself on you."

Grinning, Henry dropped from the shelf and settled between Marc's thighs, using his shoulders to push Marc's knees a little farther apart. He put his hands under Marc's legs and said, "Scoot forward a little. I want access to all of you."

Marc complied, shifting forward so his butt was only just clinging to the shelf. Henry quickly got to work, stroking Marc's hard shaft a few times while he spoke to the tip. "Going to make you come so hard."

Then he leaned in and began much as Marc had, wrapped his tongue around the head, and then licked down the underside. Marc had wondered at the similarity of their styles early in their relationship and Henry had explained it as them both unconsciously delivering what they liked for themselves and going from there.

Made sense when he thought about it, which he wasn't going to do now, because Henry had tightened the ring of his lips and was sucking downward, his mouth hot and close and wet and so amazingly fantastic. Already, Marc wanted to buck his hips. Sitting so far forward, he couldn't quite find the balance for it, though... and somehow, that added to the tension already building in his thighs. The fact he couldn't move as he wanted to.

Henry had his hands on the insides of Marc's thighs, stroking toward center as he sucked down, sending all sensation directly to his groin. Marc groaned every time Henry's throat closed around the head of his cock. Not able to thrust as he wanted to, he concentrated on giving over control of his pleasure to Henry, which was pretty much exactly why Henry had him perched like this. He knew, damn it.

When Henry touched his ass—a careful stroke of his buttock— Marc clenched and then breathed out noisily. "Oh, yeah."

Henry sucked him harder. Stroked his thighs. The hand at Marc's ass ventured behind his balls, nudging his sac from behind. A thumb... God, was that a thumb? Yes... the broad pad of Henry's thumb circled his hole, and Marc clenched again, groaning and shuddering. His lower back tingled and his balls tightened.

"Want to come," he all but moaned. His balls nearly hurt with the effort of holding back his orgasm.

Henry didn't answer, he simply continued his assault. Sucking hard, squeezing Marc's thigh, stroking his hole. And Marc fought to stay right where he was, hovering in that space between pleasure and pain, because this moment before climax was the ultimate high. Only one thing was better than this and it was too late to ask for it now. If he got to his knees and turned around, offered up his ass, he wouldn't last beyond that first, halting thrust—and being thoroughly fucked was too good to sacrifice so quickly.

Tonight. He'd ask for that tonight.

"Hngh. Oh God, coming." Marc came, his yell echoing off the

stone walls, barely diminished by the rush of the waterfall and Henry's own nonverbal encouragement.

He came, jerking forward so he could quite possibly be bruising Henry's throat. Henry gripped his thigh and sucked him hard. Pushed his thumb just inside Marc's ass.

Marc came and came and came, feeling like he'd never stop. Until he did, trembling, empty, and so utterly blissed out he couldn't move his legs or his arms.

Slack with delicious lassitude, he melted into the shelf, not minding the rocky protuberances behind him. He was boneless enough to become one with the stone—until Henry sat beside him and gathered him into a sideways hug.

Marc leaned into the warm and staid presence of the man next to him and let the world spin. Finally, he raised his lips for a kiss.

"Hmm." He tasted himself. Continuing to hum with satisfaction, he smiled and laid his head on Henry's shoulder.

"Good enough?" Henry asked quietly.

In the aftermath, the waterfall seemed louder and the cave a little more cramped.

"You know it," Marc murmured. "Always is. You give the most amazing blowjobs. One day—"

Henry cut him off with a kiss and a quiet murmur of, "Practice makes perfect."

Marc laughed. "Are you pretending to be me?"

"I'm giving you the advice you would give me. But you know I don't care if you just want to lick my dick all over, or do whatever. I love your blowjobs because it's Marcus Winnamore kneeling between my thighs, looking up at me. It's you, loving my cock. Loving me. Nothing compares to that."

Marc silently agreed. Henry might be more talented in the blowjob department, but he was right: skill didn't matter as much as attention. Not in this. Not in many areas of their lives. And here, in a cave behind a waterfall in the middle of a forest neither of them had visited before, that thought felt like the ultimate wisdom. Something he'd remember forever.

Chapter
EIGHT

*W*here are our shorts?" On his hands and knees, Henry scoured his hands over the dim floor. Though it wasn't so dark in the cave that he couldn't see the smooth stone and patches of moss, their shorts were nowhere to be found. A few crevices at the back of the cave formed deep, dark holes, but they'd dropped their shorts here, near the entrance.

Marc crouched down beside him and swept his palm over the stone. "We dropped them just here."

Henry crawled toward the back of the cave. "Maybe we kicked them into one of the cracks over here."

Marc's head jerked up. "I did kick our shorts, back when we dropped them. My feet were tangling in them and I didn't want to step on our phones."

A bell of alarm sounded in Henry's head. "Where?"

"Oh no, oh no."

Marc was crawling forward, and although his ass and dangling tackle were super sexy in the half-light of the cave, Henry was more concerned with the direction he was headed: toward the waterfall.

Oh no.

"I can't see anything." Marc was leaning forward, his head practically under the falls. He jerked back suddenly, before rising to his knees. "It's really slippery over here, be careful."

Henry approached with caution. "Do think they might have gotten caught in the waterfall? Fallen out of the cave?"

Marc returned a tight nod. "I'm so sorry."

Carefully, Henry leaned forward to peer through the spray. He couldn't see much beyond the outer edge of the pool below, and the creek meandering away into the forest. If their shorts had been swept into the pool, would they still be there?

"We need to get down there."

Marc responded with another nod.

The climb down—naked—was interesting. The warm sun felt good on his skin, but his dick kept catching on the bare rock during the first part, when they had to use all the hand and foot holds to get to the lower shelf.

"I'm beginning to see why nude rock climbing isn't a thing," Marc said from just above him.

Snorting, Henry said, "Beginning?"

"Okay, if I'd stopped to think about it, I could have figured it out. But who thinks about naked rock climbers?"

Henry shrugged. "If he's good looking enough, I'll think about him naked."

"Tease."

Grinning, Henry lowered himself to the first shelf and waited for Marc to land beside him.

Marc wasn't grinning. "Our phones were in our shorts pockets."

Henry's smile narrowed and fell away. "Crap." The map too, though it was covered in plastic. A couple of the folds had started to flake, though, and he'd formed the habit of worrying a peeling corner. But if he'd opted for stiffer lamination, he wouldn't have been able to fit it into his pocket, and Marc surely would have drawn the line at him carrying a map case along with the slightly bulky survival book he had at the bottom of his pack. A book they might need now, with no phones and no map.

One thing at a time.

Marc gripped Henry's shoulder, his fingers warm. "Breathe, Henry."

"Breathing."

While climbing down a wall had threatened his genitals with the occasional scrape and bounce, clambering over the large boulders forming the lower part of the cliff caused a lot of uncomfortable bouncing. No wonder loin cloths were a thing. Being nude just wasn't practical.

Their shorts weren't on any of the rocks near the base of the waterfall. Henry crouched by the edge of the pool and peered into the brown water... and saw nothing but brown water and his own wavering reflection. Marc appeared next to him, another rippling reflection, and Henry absently noted that Marc's hair looked longer.

Probably because it was wet and hanging around his face, dark strands clinging to his cheeks rather than smoothed into precisely styled waves.

Henry tried to look through their reflections, but really couldn't see anything but brown water. "We're going to have to go in and swim around."

With a nod, Marc slithered off the rock and into the pool. Henry joined him.

The fifteen minutes it took them to find their shorts felt like fifteen hours. Henry was exhausted by the time they climbed out of the water and laid supine on the large, flat rock that had served as picnic table and headrest only one hour earlier.

After catching his breath, Henry rolled over to search the pockets of his swimsuit. Thankfully, his phone and map were still buried deep. The phone wouldn't turn on, though, and the map felt squishy. Water had crept in through the seams. The edges remained unblemished—for now. But the center, including the part where they supposedly were, had become a pasty blur of ink.

Henry looked over at Marc who was pressing every button on his phone in repeated patterns, face screwed into a determined scowl.

Marc met his gaze and sighed. "Tell me we're not hosed."

Unbidden, Henry's lips twitched.

A muscle in Marc's jaw jumped slightly, then his full lips parted over a short laugh. "You know what I mean, and seriously, you trying not to laugh is going to freak me out. You not freaking out is going to freak me out. Why aren't you panicking yet? I'm panicking. Jesus, Henry—"

"Breathe, Marc."

Henry wrapped his fingers around Marc's wrist and squeezed tight. Marc breathed. Then he turned to survey the cliff behind them, and the forest crowding the edge. "We just have to head back that way, right?"

Nodding, Henry delivered another squeeze, not sure if he was reassuring Marc or himself. "Right." Right?

Crap.

They decided to start back toward the trail rather than spend the night at the creek.

"Being lost somewhere close to where we're supposed to be is better than being lost in the middle of nowhere," Marc said as he ducked under another low hanging branch. He glanced over his shoulder. "Are you sure this is the way we came? I don't remember the trees being so bristly."

No, Henry wasn't sure. "Bristly?"

"All these branches poking out." Marc straightened and pointed off to the left. "Did we pass that rock before?"

Following the jut of Marc's finger, Henry studied the rock. It did look familiar. He patted his pockets, absently searching for the map, and bit off a curse. Why had he put the damn map in his pocket to climb up a waterfall? What had he thought he might find up there?

Buried treasure? A doorway into Narnia?

Blowing out a sigh, Henry looked back at Marc. "Maybe?"

Marc started moving toward the rock, his passage marked by the crackle of twigs and crunch of old leaves littering the forest floor. When he got there, he slid his pack off his shoulders and leaned back in a half recline. "Makes a good rest stop, anyway." He patted his pocket and stopped, a flare of annoyance wrinkling his brow.

"I keep doing that too. Reaching for my phone."

"Now is so not the time for a lecture on our modern reliance on technology."

Henry gave a choked laugh. "Yeah, no. Wasn't going there."

"At least you have a good excuse for an upgrade now."

"Heh." Dropping his pack at his feet, Henry shaded his eyes and peered in the direction they'd named west. Where they would supposedly pick up the trail connecting Route Nine with the bottom edge of Somerset Reservoir. From memory, there was a road connecting the two as well, but that was to the east of the creek. Behind them. Maybe they should have gone that way instead?

"How long do you think we've been walking?" Marc asked.

"Since we left the creek? I dunno. Maybe half an hour?"

"We really are useless without our phones, aren't we?"

Henry answered with a sigh. Tugging on the strap of his pack, he heaved it off the ground and over his shoulders. "C'mon. It shouldn't be much farther."

Marc picked up his pack and followed.

Half an hour later, Henry was starting to believe they might be lost. He'd briefly considered the possibility shortly after the big rock slipped out of view behind them. He'd thought about it again when they'd passed through a stand of pine that was vaguely familiar.

Although close study showed one tree was remarkably different from another, there were too many of them to keep separate. Even he couldn't count all the trees in a forest.

Now, though, as Henry turned a short circle in the densely packed trees, he couldn't see anything he recognized. "How could we have gotten so lost between two fixed points?" he asked when he was facing Marc again.

Marc blew out a breath. "Maybe we discovered the Vermont Triangle."

A finger of unease traced a cool path down Henry's spine. "Don't even."

"Are we sure that way is west?" Marc nodded toward the brightest part of the sky.

"Roughly. Maybe I should check it."

"You have a compass on you?"

"No." Why hadn't he packed one?

He dropped his pack and started undoing the flap. "I've got a book—"

"You brought books?"

"Just one. Basic survival. What to eat in the forest. How to build a shelter."

Marc's mouth dropped open. "Tell me you didn't plan this?"

"What? You kicking our shorts into a waterfall?"

Mouth clamping closed, Marc made a dangerous sound.

Henry dug down the side of his pack until his fingers brushed the spine of the book. "I figured it'd be sort of funny, actually. I was going to pull it out while we were sitting in front of a campfire and regale you with stories on how we could survive out in the wild. As a joke."

"You have a warped sense of humor."

"Mm-hmm."

Marc's expression had softened, and as Henry started to flip through the pages, Marc moved to peer over his shoulder. Henry stopped at a chapter on navigation and they both read silently for a few minutes.

They'd already tried using the sun, but the second method of marking a moving shadow seemed like it might be more precise.

Marc surveyed their immediate surroundings. "I don't think we have a large enough patch of sunlight here to do the stick thing."

At least he wasn't mocking the book.

Henry rubbed his thumb across the facing page, vaguely tracing the simple star chart replicated there. "Do you want to make camp and wait for the stars to come out, or just keep heading roughly west?"

"I don't know. My feet are sore and I'm hungry and I'm still trying to think forward." Marc sounded almost resigned, which wasn't like him at all.

Henry turned to face him. "It's different out here."

"What do you mean?"

"We'd know what to do if we were in a city, or even if there was a road. But this is…" He licked his lips.

"Different."

"Yeah." Henry looked into Marc's dark eyes. "Do you think it's possible we just got totally turned around and crossed the creek or something?"

"No. We climbed back up the slope and the waterfall was in the same place as we left it."

Behind them and roughly north.

"So we must not have been paying attention on the way to the creek, then. We've missed something." Henry tried to visualize the map, but his head only returned a swirling jumble of topographical detail and light ache behind his eyes.

Marc pressed his thumb between Henry's eyebrows and smiled. "No need to get all frowny on my account."

Ducking out from beneath Marc's thumb, Henry turned another circle, taking in the close-packed trees and lack of actual trail. He was tired of pushing through branches that swung back to slap him across the face, and stumbling over rocks jutting up from the leaf mulch covering the forest floor.

"Maybe we should find a place to camp before it gets dark."

"It's probably going to be light for at least another five hours."

"Do you want to spend all five of those hours wandering around lost?" Henry gritted his teeth over the slightly exasperated note in his voice and tried again. "Maybe we should?"

"Let's head west for another hour or so and see what we come up with. Then we'll pick a spot and take a break until morning." Marc's smile looked a little forced. "Maybe we'll find the North Star tonight and all will be well."

Except for the fact they'd pretty much been heading west all afternoon—unless the poles had magically reversed while they were behind the waterfall—and so they already knew where north was. And all most definitely was not well.

Chapter
NINE

Marc opened his eyes and blinked a few times, puzzled by the hazy nothingness in front of him. Then he remembered. He was in a tent and lost in the woods—though being lost somewhere in Vermont hardly seemed to make sense. The state wasn't that big. The national forest they were camping in was nearly 400,000 acres of wilderness, though. Squeezing his eyes shut, Marc willed the massive number to shrink. To stop pulsing behind his eyelids like a measure of fate.

Was Henry obsessing over the acreage, or had he chosen something else to count? Hours lost, maybe. Miles walked? Days wasted.

Jesus. They weren't going to be lost here for days, were they? All the trail mix was gone (thank Christ) and they only had two more camping meals apiece in their packs.

Did Henry know how to hunt?

Did the book have a chapter on hunting?

Marc rolled over, planning to study Henry's sleeping profile, hoping that would lull him back to sleep. Henry's eyes were open.

"How long have you been awake?" Marc asked.

Henry's hand covered his mouth, pressing his lips closed. Marc tasted sweat, semen, and bug spray. "Shh." Henry's shush was barely audible. He pulled his hand away.

Marc raised his eyebrows. "Wha—?"

Then he heard it, the noise that had pulled him awake and left him floating on an island of sweaty nylon in the middle of 400,000 acres of national forest: a low, gravely grunt. Snuffling followed. The sound of large nostrils industriously parsing myriad odors. Then there was a beat of silence, the curiously loud absence of sound Marc should have noticed when he first opened his eyes. No chittering, no rustling, nothing stirring.

All other woodland creatures had temporarily vacated this spot because there was a freaking bear outside the tent.

Marc swallowed and the down-up action of his throat was too loud. Henry's eyes widened, becoming very, very round. His fingers, still near Marc's face, pressed into Marc's jaw. Marc edged a hand upward to touch the back of Henry's hand and thought about rolling back over. Sitting up. Tried to remember everything he'd learned about what to do if he met a bear in the woods. Realized he'd either forgotten, or had never been taught, which should be a capital crime because his parents had paid a fortune to send him away to school and summer camp. Surely someone during those twelve formative years had had something to say on the subject?

The snuffling started up again, moving closer to the tent. Marc clenched everything. A grunt sounded right behind him, and the passage of massive paws scuffed twigs and leaves in passing. Marc rolled his eyes toward their feet and the barely secured tent flaps. Their packs were there. Could the bear smell the sealed envelopes of food they had inside them?

Something fell over with a tinny clang. Marc swallowed a gasp. Were there two bears out there or had the one near the tent teleported around to the other side? What had fallen over? His heart banged painfully inside his chest, bruising his ribs. Air suddenly seemed like the most precious commodity, and a mental gif of Leonardo DiCaprio being mauled by a grizzly started up an endless loop.

Oh hell no.

Nope. Not happening. They were not going to die on this vacation, and not because the idea of being some sort of statistic made his stomach swoop and swirl. Winnamores didn't lie down and take what was coming to them. They met life head-on.

Marc sat up.

The grunting shifted direction, coming back toward the tent.

Henry scrabbled at him, pulling at Marc's shoulder, arm, waist. Pulling away, Marc rolled forward onto his knees and threw himself toward the front of the tent. He didn't know he was going to yell until the words tumbled from his lips. "Get out of here! Go on, shoo! Stop sniffing around our camp. Go find someone else to maul to death because I've got stuff to do in the morning." He was through the flaps, now, and pushing to his feet. Arms raised over his head, Marc continued to shout. "Go on, piss off and leave us alone. I am not getting killed on this camping trip. Do you hear me! I am not fucking dying tonight!"

Dropping his arms, Marc turned a slow circle. He was ready to yell again, either in fright or defiance. He didn't care. He wasn't going down without a sound, though. The night was surprisingly bright with moonlight washing across the small clearing. The night was also very quiet. Then something rustled off to his left. Marc jerked in that direction, his heart skipping a beat. A bird called from the other direction. With that cue, the night restored itself. A cloud drifted halfway across the moon, dimming its ghostly radiance. Leaves rustled, and twigs snapped.

And Henry burst out of the tent holding up a shoe. "Is it gone?"

"Are you going to hit it with your shoe if it's not?" Marc was surprised by how calmly sarcastic he sounded. Inside his skin, his organs were all crimping and ballooning. His body felt dangerously close to collapse. He also needed to take a piss.

Lowering his arm, Henry looked around. His shoulders bowed inward as he did so, giving him the appearance of someone collapsing in on themselves. Then he dropped his shoe and wrapped his arms around his torso in a familiar gesture of self-comfort, and Marc found he could only respond one way. He put his arms around Henry and leaned in.

Then he started to shake. "Damn."

"Are you okay?" Henry asked, shifting so he could actually hug back rather than stand there and be held.

Marc shuddered again as Henry's arms circled his ribs. He clutched at Henry and pulled him even closer. "I'm somewhere between weeping, pissing myself, and wanting to dance around a fire screaming. The fire one is what I should do. But we don't have a fire and I really need to take a leak."

Henry chuckled. "I'm with you on that. Holy crap." He shook himself and let go.

Marc stepped back. In the dim night, Henry's features weren't all that clear, but his eyes were still large and round. Marc pressed a kiss to his cheek, needing the contact as much as Henry might, and then turned to take care of business, moving a few feet away from the tent before seeking to relieve the pressure in his bladder. He could hear Henry pissing beside him and the moment struck him as oddly mundane, the lingering buzz of adrenaline aside.

After shaking himself off, Marc returned to the tent, picking his way over the soft ground. The cloud that had briefly covered the moon had drifted past and the clearing was awash in light again. Henry came around the other side of the tent, his skin silvery white in the night, and a finger of absurd humor tickled Marc's belly. He laughed.

Henry's head jerked up. "What?"

Gesturing at himself, fingers fanning downward from his hips, Marc said, "We're naked."

Henry managed an endearing sideways grin. "So we are."

"I can't believe I was going to fight a bear naked."

Eyes widening again, Henry opened and closed his mouth. "You were going to fight the bear?"

"I wasn't going to let it eat me. Or you."

"Jesus." His expression dimmed and his arms came up to wrap his ribs again. "I was just going to lie there and be eaten."

"No, you weren't. You were being cautious. Sensible. If anyone was going to get eaten, it was me."

Henry's lips twitched. "I'd have thought about saving you. That's what I was going to do with the shoe. Hit the bear on the nose."

"While it was savaging me."

"Um, hopefully not? I was going to throw it if all your noise hadn't already frightened it away."

Marc chuckled and the urge to weep poked at him again. Fear was doing strange things to his emotions. The aftermath of it, anyway. He jerked his head in the direction of the tent. "Want to head back inside?"

Nodding, Henry ducked through the flap, his butt wiggling enticingly until it disappeared. Marc bit back a groan as he followed, catching Henry before he could lie down, wrapping one hand around his hips from behind and bringing his groin into contact with that sexy ass. He kissed the back of Henry's neck. Tasted bug spray. Grinned, and then had to clamp down on the urge to shiver, curl inward, and maybe even cry.

"Damn."

Henry turned around so they were on their knees, facing each other. "What?"

"This isn't how it works in the movies. We're supposed to be having explosive sex right now."

Henry's grin was much fainter inside the tent. "Are you okay?"

Marc took stock. His dick was half hard, but his hands were shaking. His heart hadn't decided on a proper rhythm yet and he might have to piss again. "Um…"

"If it's any consolation, my head is spinning in a hundred

different directions and twice I've wondered why I don't carry a Ventolin inhaler."

"You have asthma?"

"No, but I'm having trouble catching my breath."

"Why?"

"Because I thought you were going to get eaten by a bear and the shoe thing was completely stupid and I was going to get eaten too and it's my fault we're lost in the woods and this is the worst vacation ever." Henry looked sharply away, his profile hazy, but somehow managing to communicate regret. It was something in the angle of his neck. How far down he'd tipped his head.

Marc sat back on the mess of mat and sleeping bag and leaned over to grab Henry's pack. He dug deep until he found the book. "Where's the flashlight?"

"Why?"

Marc patted a patch of mat and sleeping bag beside him. "Sit." After grabbing the flashlight, Henry did as he was told, sitting next to Marc. "Light," Marc instructed. Henry obliged, pointing the beam of the flashlight toward the open book in Marc's hands. Marc flipped to the index at the back and scanned the list of tiny words until he found the chapter on bears. He turned to the right page and traced his finger down through the paragraphs until he got to the part detailing what to do if a bear walked into their camp.

"Believe it or not, bears spook really easily," he read aloud. "Most of the time, announcing your presence should be enough to scare them away. Human voices are the number one deterrent for bears, so start by making loud noises." Marc looked up. "Oh my God." His insides did a few melty things, leaving him suddenly exhausted. "Wow. Just... wow. I seriously thought that was going to be the last thing the book said."

Henry glanced up from the page. "What were you hoping to find?"

"Something about a shoe!"

"Why?"

"So you'd know you'd done the right thing."

"That makes no sense," Henry said with something of a whine.

"I also thought maybe reading about bear attacks might make you feel better."

Henry gaped, then started laughing. A hiccupping sort of chuckle escaped first, then a yelping laugh. He clutched his ribs, this time not in comfort, and rolled forward, gales of laughter rolling across his shoulders. After watching him for a few long seconds, Marc felt a tickle. Then an itch, then his lungs convulsed and he was laughing too. He ignored the fact his eyes were tearing up because that had been known to happen when he laughed intensely. He fell onto his back and laughed, loving the way the boom of mirth moved through his chest. Henry landed beside him, hooting.

When he caught his breath, Marc glanced over at him. "All the noise we're making now, any bear within a mile is going to run far, far away."

Henry laughed harder. Marc joined him. Finally, his chuckles died away to small eruptions of giggles, then a random bark, then nothing, leaving him even more exhausted than before. But lighter. As if he was floating on top of his sleeping bag.

Rolling over, he came face to face with Henry once more. "Thank you for coming after me with a shoe."

"Thank you for scaring off the bear." Henry's smile dipped and fell away.

Marc touched his chin. "What?"

After chewing over whatever it was for a short while, Henry looked up. "Does it bother you that I was stuck here frozen while you went after the bear?"

Marc shook his head. "No. Does it bother you that I was prepared to throw my life away on a whim?"

"Not a whim. You were being brave."

"Didn't feel that way. I just didn't want to go quietly."

Henry's smile was a soft and gentle thing, but again it didn't last long. Sadness and recrimination began to creep over his features and Marc got ready to tell him again that nothing was his fault. That they were in this together. That tomorrow they'd find the trail and hike their way out of here. That no damn bears were going to ruin their vacation.

Then Henry's eyes widened. Before Marc could tune into the wildlife frequency, check to see if there were more grunts and snuffles outside the tent, Henry gasped. "I think I know what happened."

"What? When?"

"This afternoon. I… Oh, man. Yes. Fuck!"

Henry didn't curse a lot. Neither of them did, as if by mutual agreement, they saved curses for necessary moments.

Marc wasn't getting the message, though. Why Henry was using one of his carefully hoarded fucks. "What are you talking about?"

"I know where we are!"

"You do?" Something inside Marc's chest perked up. "Where?"

"Well, not where, exactly, but sort of. We crossed the trail, Marc. We crossed the damn trail and kept heading west."

"How? When?"

"Remember the big boulder we stopped at? It was just after that. We were following what looked like a game trail and we went past that clearing, the one with the pine trees, and I thought it looked familiar, but we were at the top end of it, not the bottom and it looked different. And we couldn't see the trail through there because the ground was covered. The needles were like a carpet. We even commented on it!"

Thoughts rolling backward and forward, Marc sought out the memory, and found it and what Henry was saying snapped into focus. "Oh my God, you're right. How did we not know?"

How could they have done something so dumb?

Henry shook his head. "I have no idea, except to say that there are a lot of stands of pine throughout the forest and we don't know any of these trails, or these woods well enough to tell the difference. But it wouldn't have mattered. We would have crossed the Appalachian trail tomorrow morning. We couldn't be that far off it now. Half a mile, maybe. In fact, it'd be easier to find that now, hike it up to Stratton Pond and find a ride down to Grout Pond, if we still want to go there."

Marc didn't have the same visual in his head that Henry obviously did—no representation of a topographical map, no snaking trails and elevation lines—but he did remember noting that the Appalachian trail bisected the western portion of the forest. Breathing out a sigh, he flopped onto his back and pressed his hands together. "Thank you."

Henry shuffled closer, propped up on his elbow. "Are you praying?"

Marc put a hand to the side of Henry's face and pulled Henry down on top of him. "No, I'm thanking you. You found us, Henry. I might have scared off a bear, but you figured out where we were."

Henry looked as if he was going to argue the point, then he just smiled.

Chapter
TEN

Shapes danced in the flames, at once confounding and mesmerizing. Henry thought he saw the figure of a man, then a dolphin, which didn't really fit with the flickering, melting gold. Or maybe it did. His weary mind seemed to think so, anyway.

Marc slipped an arm around his shoulders and Henry leaned against his side before letting his natural shyness or self-consciousness take hold. Instead of grimacing, he forced a smile and relaxed. He could do this. Next to him, Marc's fingers closed around his shoulder in approval. Henry let his smile widen.

Across the fire, a woman named Giselle titled her head and smiled—apparently at the sight of Marc and Henry being sweet and cozy… or maybe because they looked awkward? Then she turned to her companion and continued talking in low tones.

Marc nuzzled the side of Henry's head. "See, we're cute."

Henry scoffed lightly and turned as the log they were sitting on jostled. A large man was sitting beside him on the other side. He dipped his chin in acknowledgment of Henry's notice and said, "So Martin says you two saw a bear?"

Here we go.

Since finding the Appalachian Trail three days ago, they'd been surrounded by people. A group of hikers had caught up to them midmorning of that day and hiked with them to Stratton Pond. Marc had shared the story of the bear. The group that had ridden to Grout Pond with them, asked if they were the "dudes with the bear." Henry had told the story that time, taking uncommon delight in describing Marc's charge from the tent. Marc followed up with Henry's part, not leaving out the shoe, and sage nods had circled the minivan.

"Hit them on the nose. Best bet if you don't have bear spray or a shotgun."

Of which they'd had neither. Henry had wondered if whacking the bear with his survival book might have done the trick, but elected not to say so out loud.

The story had already reached the Grout Pond campground where a ranger wanted to know if the bear had been aggressive. When Marc explained his naked rush from the tent and subsequent complete absence of bears, they all decided that, no, the bear had not been aggressive.

"My canteen wasn't even dented."

The tinny rattling sound. They'd found Marc's canteen a few feet away from the camp the next morning.

Everyone on the minivan ride back to Woodford had heard the story. Henry didn't really get the big deal. They'd heard a bear and had frightened it off. But according to the ranger, the big deal was that they had been able to frighten it off. If they hadn't, there would have to have been a bear hunt. So here he was, on their last night in the national forest, alive, tired, oddly satisfied by their vacation, and preparing to tell the story again.

Henry glanced into the flames, fancied he saw a bear raised up on its hind legs, forepaws spread wide, and laughed. "We didn't even see it. For all I know, it was a raccoon sniffing around outside the tent."

Beside him, Marc shook lightly and the sound of his chuckles tickled Henry's ear. "Yes! Or a squirrel. I ran out there, naked, ready to take on a squirrel."

"A rabid squirrel."

"A chipmunk."

Henry let out a giggle-snort and was immediately embarrassed. Then amused. "Oh my God."

The guy next to him was watching with a half-smile. "So... not a bear?"

Marc sobered enough to answer, "Probably a bear. Ranger seemed to think so. Not aggressive, though."

"Pretty ballsy of you to run after it in the buff," the other guy said.

Marc let out a chuckle. "Wasn't even thinking about it. I just wasn't ready to lie there and get eaten."

"Right on."

Marc still had his arm around Henry's shoulders. He curled his fingers and pulled Henry in and Henry pressed a kiss to Marc's laughing mouth. And no one flinched. Not the guy next to them, not the folks gathered together on the other side of the fire. No one came charging out of the dusk. No one cared.

"My hero," Henry murmured before tucking himself more closely into Marc's side.

"Hey, you came after me with a shoe. We're both the heroes of this story."

"Truth," said the guy on Henry's other side. "I'm going to tell my girlfriend we have to keep our shoes close tonight." With a grin, he saluted and stood up. "Have a good one!"

Marc stood a moment later, leaving Henry's side and back comparatively cool, and held out his hand. "C'mon. Let's take one more walk before we turn in."

Henry unfolded himself and stood up. "Another walk? I thought your feet were sore?" Henry's feet were sore. They'd managed a hike a day in between interviews and shuttle rides to various parks. There had been a lot of trails around Somerset Reservoir, and another falls to visit. Not as private as the first, though, and the trail had been well marked on the way back. There had also been a lot of campfire sitting and sleeping bag snuggling. Sex and Marc mandated cuddling. All things considered, it had been about the best vacation Henry could remember.

Marc led the way to the lake. They were camped pretty close to where they'd been the first night, except this time they had access to the water from the back side of their tent. Another thoughtful someone had dragged a log into place about halfway down the sloping bank, forming a perfect seat from which to view the water, and at night, the stars.

Henry sat next to Marc and circled Marc's ribs with his arm.

Marc leaned against his side and kissed his head. "This is the best vacation I've ever had."

"I was just thinking that."

"Really? I'd have thought you'd have had a lot of fun with your family, going here, there, and everywhere."

"What about you? I seem to remember you've been to Europe and Singapore."

Marc shrugged. "Literally as a baggage handler for my parents. Or another piece of baggage."

Mentally kicking himself for introducing the subject of Marc's parents, Henry said, "I've had some great vacations with my family. But this is different."

Marc lifted his chin, bringing his sharp profile into the light. "Yeah. For all we've traveled together a lot, this is the first time we've really just, I dunno. Not hung out. We've been doing that too."

"It's the first time we've done a lot of nothing together. In between getting lost and bear attacks."

"Not nothing. Vacationing."

Henry pressed his nose to Marc's cheek and inhaled the familiar scent of him. Skin and sweat. Wood smoke and man. "Mmm."

"We should do this again. Every summer."

A flame leaped inside Henry's chest, taking on the shape of his love. Bright and boundless, but still lightly constrained. As it had to be. He couldn't give all of himself to Marc, although he sometimes feared that's what would happen. Marc was so damned seductive. When he wasn't with Marc, he craved his presence. When he was with him, he only wanted to be closer. But Henry was always conscious of keeping a part of himself back. Not because he didn't want to be wholly invested, but because he knew it was important that he remain his own person.

That was the only way he'd survived the fire that was his lover so far.

"Are you so horrified by the idea?" Marc asked.

Startling lightly, Henry thought back to the last thing Marc had said and shook his head. "No, no. I love that idea. I was just… thinking."

Marc chuckled. "My thinker."

Then he jerked and pointed out across the lake. Up at the sky. "Henry, look! A falling star. You see it?"

Following the compass of Marc's finger, Henry peered into the sky and gasped as a star winked once and dipped out of sight. "No!"

"You missed it?"

"No, I saw it. I meant… Wow. I've never seen that happen before."

"Remember when we were stuck in the woods looking for the North Star?"

Despite the frustration attached to that particular memory, Henry smiled. "You mean when you were calling Scorpius the happy whale?"

"Fine, but I stand by the bucking goat. It's a real thing. Look it up."

"Hah! I intend to when we get home."

"So, did you wish on the star?" Marc asked.

Could he share the wish that they'd always be together?

Clearing his throat, Henry offered up a substitute. "I wished for a new Leatherman tool. One of those sexy curved ones I can clip to my belt loop or keychain."

Next to him, Marc started laughing. Then he disentangled himself and stood up. "Wait here."

Henry watched him jog back up the bank and disappear around the side of their tent. After a few moments, he reappeared and trotted back down the slope, sat on the log, and handed across a small box. "Merry Christmas."

Eyeing the box, Henry said, "It's August."

"So you'll get nothing in December."

Henry took the box and pried off the lid. It was a new Leatherman tool. The curved one with the clip in the leg. "Oh my God! How... When?"

"While you were in the bathroom. You nearly caught me."

Henry shook his head. "Thank you."

Marc shrugged. "It's not much. But, hey, wish fulfilled, right?"

"Absolutely." Leaning forward, Henry kissed Marc soundly. A smack of lips that was more forceful than romantic. "Thank you." Then, stupidly, his eyes misted. Blinking, he pried the tool out of the box and held it up to the starlight. He couldn't see much, just enough to make out the shine and shape. "You're the best boyfriend I've ever had."

"I'm the only boyfriend you've ever had."

Laughing, Henry nodded. "Point." He glanced up and looked into Marc's dark eyes and saw something reflected. The shapes from the fire. The outline of his love.

His moment had finally arrived.

Extracting a blade from his new tool, he reached between his feet and cut a few strands of grass that had grown long beneath the shadow of the log. Then he balanced the tool on the log and started braiding his grass.

"What are you doing?" Marc asked.

"Making something." He could see his fingers well enough, but not really the grass. Regardless, Henry continued to braid by feel until he had one long strand. "Hold out your wrist."

Marc did so and Henry looped the braided grass around Marc's knobby, but sexy wrist and tied it off. Then he simply stared at it, feeling stupid. Why had he made Marc a grass bracelet?

Apparently unperturbed, Marc fingered his new decoration, turning it gently so as not to loosen it. "What's this?"

Henry swallowed. "It's a promise."

Marc looked up, met his gaze.

"That we'll do this every summer." Henry gestured toward the lake. "And that I'll always follow you with a shoe. That I…" He licked his lips. "That I welcome every kiss, no matter where we are. That I'm not afraid." He looked back into Marc's dark eyes. "I know who I am with you and it's who I want to be. Always. You terrify me, but I'm learning to love that part too and I don't think I'd ever want to live without it."

Henry stopped there and chewed on his lip, suddenly afraid—in a different sense—that he'd gone too far. Added too much mass to what should have been a relatively weightless moment.

But Marc only reached over him to grab the knife and then he started cutting grass. Minutes later, he was fastening a braided grass bracelet around Henry's wrist. His was neater and more secure, of course. Henry grinned at it as he traced his fingers down the entwined strands. Marc's fingers touched his chin and he looked up.

"Everything you said goes for me too."

"You're never afraid, Marc." Henry winced as he said it, but he forced his shoulders square anyway, sitting up straighter.

Marc smiled into the night. "Why do you think I'm always so determined to push ahead? I've been running for a long, long time, Henry. But for you, I'll wait. Always."

"We're getting pretty deep for grass bracelets," Henry said, feeling suddenly that he might have started something they weren't ready for.

Shrugging, Marc looked down at his bracelet and turned it around his wrist. "We could say it's just grass, or…"

And the look he gave Henry then said everything. In one way, it was the most open expression Henry had ever seen on Marc's face. Henry was reminded of their trip to DC, when he'd almost messed everything up. When Marc had looked at him with such need; when his eyes had clearly communicated one simple fact—Marc wasn't invulnerable as he pretended to be.

Henry worried constantly about Marc hurting him, but rarely about the opposite. About how much he could hurt Marc.

Swallowing over a sudden dryness in his throat, Henry put a hand to either side of Marc's face and drew him in for a kiss. He touched his lips to Marc's gently and sweetly, making his kiss another promise. Then he pulled back just enough to whisper, "I love you so much it hurts. But it's a good pain. I need it, Marc. I need you. I don't know if you believe in forever, but…" The world dipped and turned. Fell away. Unaccountably dizzy, Henry concentrated on where his skin touched Marc's. The scent of his lover. The not quiet night. "This is what I want. Forever."

He nearly choked on the last word, but got it out, then Marc's lips were on his, kissing him not sweetly, not gently, but with hunger. Fervor. Marc pushed him backward and Henry let himself be laid out on the log, Marc over him, owning his mouth, Marc's body warm and hard against his. Henry wrapped his arms around Marc's back and pulled him even closer. Heedless of the knots of wood pushing into his spine, he gave his all to the kiss: his fear, his love, his need, and desire. The certainty that only a life lived with Marc at his side would be worth living.

After a mini forever, one that Henry took as a down payment on the one he'd asked for, Marc pulled away and smiled at him. He nodded, and while his head continued to bob, said, "Yep." He pulled Henry into a sitting position beside him again.

"Yep?" Henry asked, settling back against Marc's side.

"When you kiss me like that, yes. Forever. That's what I want too."

"Fuck."

"Henry!" Marc laughed.

"Sorry. But, wow. We just…"

"Yeah, we did."

Henry jerked his head toward the sky. "This falling star stuff is seriously powerful."

"Useful for tools and love stories."

"What did you wish for?"

"Shelly's desk."

Henry laughed.

"What? It's a really nice desk. That office is going to be mine one day. You know it is."

Grinning, Henry tangled their fingers together and squeezed. "So where do we want to go next year?"

Marc returned the squeeze. "Canada. The woods are wilder and the bears are bigger."

"We had better practice all our survival skills, then."

"Mm-hmm."

"If we get eaten next year, I'm going to say it's your fault."

Marc turned to him and grinned. "As long as we're together, I'm good with that."

"You're a nut."

"I'm happy, Henry."

"Yeah?"

"Deliriously so. Super happy. Like…" Marc's shoulders lifted as he drew in a deep breath, then slowly dropped as he exhaled again. He pressed his forehead to Henry's. "Love you."

Henry angled his chin forward so he could brush a kiss across Marc's lips. "Love you too."

Dear
READER

*T*hank you for reading *The Complete Counting Series*! I hope you enjoyed Marc and Henry's story from beginning to end—not that this is the end, really. In my mind, they're still getting locked away and getting lost. But they're always together. <3

Would you consider leaving a review? Reviews and ratings are the lifeblood of independent authors as they help bring our books to the attention of others, and I appreciate each and every one.

To talk about books, join us in my Facebook reader group, **Kelly's Keepers**.

Not on Facebook? For new release news, sales, exclusive giveaways, and all the extras, subscribe to my newsletter at: http://eepurl.com/czGhYz

About
THE AUTHOR

*I*f aliens ever do land on Earth, Kelly will not be prepared, despite having read over a hundred stories of the apocalypse. Still, she will pack her precious books into a box and carry them with her as she strives to survive. It's what bibliophiles do.

Kelly is the author of twelve novels—including the Chaos Station series, co-written with Jenn Burke—and several novellas and short stories. Some of what she writes is speculative in nature, but mostly it's just about a guy losing his socks and/or burning dinner. Because life isn't all conquering aliens and mountain peaks. Sometimes finding a happy ever after is all the adventure we need.

Connect with Kelly online:
https://kellyjensenwrites.com/

Facebook
https://www.facebook.com/kellyjensenwrites/

Twitter
@kmkjensen

OTHER TITLES
BY KELLY JENSEN

Out in the Blue
Wrong Direction
When Was the Last Time
Best in Show
Block and Strike
To See the Sun

The Let's Connect series
Let's Connect
Let's Go Out

The This Time Forever series
Building Forever
Renewing Forever
Chasing Forever

The Aliens in New York series
Uncommon Ground
Purple Haze

The Counting series
Counting Fence Posts
Counting Down
Counting on You
The Complete Counting Series

The Chaos Station series
(with Jenn Burke)
Chaos Station
Lonely Shore
Skip Trace
Inversion Point
Phase Shift

www.ingramcontent.com/pod-product-compliance
Lightning Source LLC
Chambersburg PA
CBHW030804260626
47169CB00001B/189